Dirty Sneakers and a Rifle

Grace Lahmeyer

Cover Design Art by Firehouse Design
Cover Polaroid Photography by Landon Hunting

ISBN: 979-8-9913903-0-9
LCCN: 2024919991

Table of Contents

Introduction

I first want to explain that this tale started as a short story; no more than ten pages. Then more inspiration struck. Then I knew I had to fulfill it to an endgame. Of all works and novel plots that have floated aimlessly in my brain for years, this was the first that I was able to complete. I'm very proud of it and myself for that.

This book took me just under a year to write. Don't tell my teachers, but I spent more time typing away at this first draft than I worked on their classwork.

I struggled deeply for many nights on how to approach this book. I knew I was dealing with something heavy that required a real glimpse into how someone may cope. In the end, this is my way of commenting on how the individual can comprehend the mess of what I inflicted on this innocent main character.

I want to express now that this was my attempt at diving into the nuances of the human experience. As you may notice, some internal monologue points conflict with what she may do or vocalize. This is something I've observed for myself. Some things in such a trivial world are more complex to explain than "I think this. This is because the world does this to me."

I think it's important to note that this book is a memoir written by Vivienne herself. This was my play on the unreliable narrator. This is how she remembers it after the years, so this is the version she will share. Even with something as integral to the story as exactly how many people are left on Earth… how is Vivienne Hammond supposed to know that? She didn't. That's the beauty of it. These doubts and falsehoods spread by news and word of mouth (while the world was literally and figuratively on fire) I use as a keystone for the uncertainty. She, and those around her, only know what they know. True to our world and ourselves, the truth can only be found in our narrow perspective.

It was intentional to leave out the reason humanity drove itself to the brink. I see this as too complex of a hypothetical to extract it myself. Everyone in the story only has their own theories, their own perspectives. Experiencing the world from Vivienne's limited perspective, we will never know.

Nuances are layered in everything we experience daily and in every complexity that riddles our minds. That's the magic of creating these characters that, I intended to, mirror who we are and what we know.

Interpret this book however you may. You may love it, you may hate it. I just ask that you don't be rude about your feelings towards others who don't agree. Nothing gets achieved through that.

The Beginning

June

i.

I don't like war jokes.

There used to be so many kids at my school who joked about World War 3. Every new international political issue sparked a fresh flurry of jokes that a third atomic bomb would save us from the Algebra test. Those were tolerable. It would never happen. It was like joking about an invasion of Mexican food-addicted aliens who came for Taco Bell's *Doritos Locos Taco* secret recipe.

Then there were genuine threats of a third World War for a while. Most kids I knew used humor to cope with anxieties that their home cities could become a wasteland. I'm a little more okay with those people than the ones who joked about being kidnapped and enslaved by the North Korean president. There were even some pricks that joked about the Holocaust.

I wonder where they are now. I wonder where all my former classmates are now. Probably dead, I know that. But it's nice to be optimistic sometimes.

I went to a small private school. It was the closest, and my parents would rather pay the tuition and fees than let me attend one of the local public schools. Did they both have horrible experiences at public school? I don't know. I regret never asking. It always intrigued me, because that private school never seemed like a step up from anything.

When I grew up, Sansbury Middle and High School was a tiny private school that was just far enough off the beaten track to be a recognizable name. Fairly well funded, yet most activities outside of sports had to run on donations and community goodwill. It was a stepping stone school for new teachers fresh out of graduate school. No one willingly taught at Sansbury longer than five years.

I was supposed to graduate alongside 32 other hormonal teenagers with some form of mommy or daddy issues. We were a good group of kids, I would say. No one got into any horrible crimes that I know of. I'd say we did high school well.

Nothing any of us did in life should've ended us up… where we all ended up. Ninety percent of us are gone now. By my estimations, only one other member of my graduating class remains. And who even knows if they survived the last five months.

How do I know the mortality rate of the end of humanity? For five weeks that was all news stations would broadcast. No more feel-good funny video of the week. No more sports. No more politicians. No more Hollywood stars forever stuck in complicated love triangles.

At first, the news was announced over the 7 o'clock channels by burdened broadcasters. I hated to watch them. Then the satellites and electricity stopped working. After that, we got daily updates by radio. This lasted for another week. We didn't want to risk draining the precious batteries on that crap.

The mortality rate of The Great Global Paranoia War (the unofficial name; no one ever bothered to properly name it between putting out fires to your front lawn) was upped to ninety percent two days before we gave up on the radios.

We went camping in the seventh week. That was when we as a family decided it would be safer in the middle of the woods than in our own neighborhood. At least for a little while. I think it was a Tuesday when we left.

You read me right. It only took us seven weeks to wipe out the entire goddamn human race. *Homo sapien extinctus.*

But we can't be extinct yet. I'm still kicking it… as are roughly 400 million all around the globe. I think. Calling us extinct is easier, though.

I say there are roughly 400 million people left. And that rough estimation is *rough.*

Whoever finds this in the future may be thinking, "Well, author, 400 million is a big number. I can't count that on my fingers and toes. What's there to worry about?" And yes, mystery future person, that is a big number. That's an enormous number! But compared to the human population one year ago it's a drop in the bucket.

Last I checked, there used to be 7.9 billion people walking this planet. I think people underestimate the sheer difference between one million and one billion. One million seconds is twelve days. One billion seconds is thirty-one years. My youngest aunt just barely lived past one billion seconds! Now imagine all those seconds as individual human beings and multiply that by eight. You have the human population at its height.

We managed to wipe all that away by ourselves. No aliens. No natural disaster as I expected we would go out. We killed ourselves, and now the 400 million of us left across the globe have to deal with those consequences for the rest of our lives — however long that may be.

I don't know when my parents died. I guess it's not important to know when they died.

We were camping to get away from the madness of society for a few days. We rented this nice camping trailer on a goodwill trade, not knowing the chances that anyone at the dealership would be around when we returned it.

I left the camper to clear my head for a few minutes. The three of us had been stuck together for nine days. I needed a break. It wasn't anything against them. We weren't fighting. I just needed to breathe. It couldn't have been more than an hour.

When I returned, no one was there. No sign of life inside the camper. They didn't run off to leave me to fend for myself. All of their belongings were still in the camper. The keys were still in the glove box. They *disappeared*. It was as if they were too weak to handle the early summer sun and evaporated into thin air.

For a while, I expected them to come back. I assumed they went out to stretch their legs and got a little lost. We were in the middle of the woods. There were lots of opportunities to get lost or lose track of time. I waited for them to return that night. We had been resilient through the downfall of the entire world. They could make it in the woods for a few hours.

My hopes were shattered the next evening. I remember being in a good mood, too.

I got curious after seeing a fox and followed it away from the trail. He was surprisingly calm and didn't mind my presence. I followed him as far as I could before it slipped under a bramble bush. It wasn't far from a river, so I went to wash my face and hands.

The water was at just the right depth flowing over just the right amount of rocks to make the most lovely sound. I still love the flow and trickling of water over a good bed of weathered smooth rocks. Do you know that sound? It tickles your brain just right. You could fall asleep to that sound in the middle of a war zone.

Sitting by that river was the calmest I'd felt in weeks. Just me and nature all around. No distractions. No news stations shouting at me to check off every possible box on my bucket list, cause who knows how many days we may have left before humanity kills each other straight out of existence.

I sat by that river for a good while before I saw the body. I don't know how I went so long without it catching my eye. It didn't lie more than five meters away from me.

It was cast over the dirt and rocks, limp, and successfully out of commission. I knew it was a human body immediately. We'd seen plenty of those over the last few weeks to be familiar enough with the look of a dead human. They hadn't been dead for so long. There's a distinct smell of death that settles over everything dead. This body didn't have the Death Smell yet. I know it's morbid, but I couldn't take my eyes off it as I approached.

I did not, however, know it was my father. Not until I got close enough to see his haircut.

His body was already bloating. Scrapes littered his arms and hands as if he had been struggling. Dried maroon painted the rocks around his head and shoulders. Once lively and humor-filled eyes stared past my face, dull and lost. My dad was dead.

Turning away was too hard. I vomited on his legs.

Maybe saying "already bloating" is inaccurate. I don't know how quickly bodies decompose. I know the skin loses color almost instantaneously when blood stops flowing. White eyes turn yellow. After that, rigor mortis sets in. I know there are two other "rigor" whatevers. Then somewhere along the line, you start to bloat and release gasses as everything exits your carcass. The rest is a matter of Mother Nature taking over and returning you to the ash you started from.

I never found my mother's body. I never want to find it.

Assuming my parents died at the same time, they could've been dead for an hour or twelve. They could've died looking for me when I took that simple, hour-long break. Sometimes I think that they may still be alive if I didn't walk out. If I didn't get annoyed by such close proximity.

Once you start living in a camping trailer in the middle of the forest with no sign of any other remaining civilization, you start to realize just how little you know about anything. Looking back on it, I'm starting to realize just how stupid and ignorant I used to be. It's astounding how someone can be that stupid.

I don't mean just in the metaphysical sense. I mean the literal sense. I was *stupid*. I nearly got myself killed at least eleven times.

How long would Mom and Dad have lived had I not stepped out?

I didn't spend much time crying over Mom and Dad. I was quiet about it for a few days… as if there was anyone to hear me be loud about it. I had bigger things on my plate than crying over my parents. I think they would understand.

Everything was so quiet. Not the comforting kind of quiet. Dead quiet. Unsettling quiet.

Animals are louder than you would expect. There are so many sounds intermingling and forming one cacophony of nonsense. And yet, it's dreadfully quiet. When I lay down on my little couch to get as many hours of shut-eye as my body will allow me, all noise filters out and leaves an empty silence in its place. I still hate falling asleep. I despise that time in between consciousness and unconsciousness where your mind is just… gray.

It was a difficult change at first. I'd never lived on my own before, much less without electricity or running water.

My parents left the keys to the truck in the glove box. It took me a week, but I finally got to the point of grabbing the keys. After I realized and accepted that I was alone and needed to learn a lot of survival skills quickly, my first move was to get back home. If I was going to die when the food and toilet paper ran out, I wanted to be at home when such happened.

I know how to drive. I'm pretty good at it. I was so close to raising enough money for my own 2009 blue Corolla when people started dropping off like flies. So I made my plan to leave. I packed everything up and made sure the trailer was connected securely just like Dad showed me. We were camped twenty miles from the little neighborhood I grew up in. Thirty miles from Sansbury High. I could've had that entire area to myself…

…if I made it out of the woods.

Even if I did check the gas to see how low it was, there would be no way to fill it. We left in a hurry. Dad didn't have time to fill a spare gas container. The truck had horrible mileage. The next thing I knew the stupid thing conked out on me after ten minutes of going down that stupid dirt road. I knew where I was — about ten miles closer to town. That didn't make me any less stranded, though.

Now you future anthropologists may be thinking, "Well, why not just pack the biggest bag you can find and walk the rest of the ten miles? Get your steps in?" The honest answer: I got scared. I got scared of the unknown and didn't stray from the camper past my trusty little creek for months.

That's where I've been for the last five months. Stuck here in this moderately luxurious camper trailer for God-only-knows how many sleepless nights.

I estimate I've been out here for three months. If I'm right, it should be August. My birthday is in August. I could be eighteen by now. But I could be completely wrong. It could still be June.

We truly were people of the twenty-first century — all three of us. We didn't keep any paper calendars in the trailer. The only paper things we bothered to pack were books. Dad always loved to be up to date with the latest technology. We probably didn't *have* any paper luxuries like calendars or clocks to pack, period. We just relied on our cell phones to start working again after so many days.

I hate my phone now. I still keep it buried in my backpack just in case the grid magically revives one night with a full charge, though.

I miss physical things. A physical map, a physical compass, physical pictures. Oh, what I would give to have a full binder of all my beloved pictures. I can barely hold onto what my one closest friend, Mikey, looked like. I know he had this crazy perfect swoop of blond hair. He grew it out just enough to get a wavy middle part the summer of our freshman year, and it's never looked better since. I nicknamed him Ken Doll.

The age of technology screwed us all over. We thought it would be immortal.

Three people packed for a week. Two of those three disappeared. The single person left had to ratio that for themselves over an amount of time that was impossible to know.

I cut my hair to my chin after weeks to make it more manageable. I didn't need a rat's nest of hair tangling up in a bush while I tried to hunt, leading me to be trapped until I died. Hair is also very flammable. My seven inches gave me a good burning fire to cook dinner.

I still felt uncomfortable bathing in the river, as if the deer and birds were going to come up and judge my body.

I tried not to think about what would happen come winter. Maybe a bear would come along and eat my head off.

You always read survival or dystopian books about the protagonist who makes it through the bombs and alien invasions with little to no trouble. Maybe they get shot here and there. Maybe the trusted sidekick dies a gruesome death in sacrifice to help them along. But they always make it back. They always have someone to return to; a motivation to keep going and make it out of the war territory. There's a promise that needs to be upheld.

I didn't have that. I know Mikey died in the second week when someone detonated a pipe bomb in the bookstore where he worked. On the news, I saw my brother's car swerved off the interstate and he was never heard from again. I know my parents are gone. My dog ran away in the third week. Who's left for me to survive for? What's my motivation to keep going every day?

I'll tell you what my motivation is. Spite. I'm gonna survive this living hell just to spite the entire human race who died and left me in this situation.

Eff you, humanity.

ii.

The camper was cramped even for one. The truck was no better. I have no idea how the three of us survived together in such close quarters for almost two weeks. But I figure it's no worse quality of life than if I were to have made it back to my neighborhood.

The weather was horrible out there. The sun bore on my head and shoulders hour after hour. I was sweating and exhausted by the end of every day, but it was better than the inevitable ice, come winter months.

The temperature was just bearable at night. The shelter of the camper was only good for protection from the elements. I curled into a cocoon of every jacket, blanket, and anything that could be used as a blanket on top of the tiny couch. My parents got the only bed when we started this trip. I could never take it from them.

I ran out of food in the mini-fridge three days after they died. Since then, it was one hunt a day and prayers that I could get the creek water clean enough not to ingest three different species of viral bacteria.

Hunting and gathering got easier. I only broke one knife from the collection we wisely brought along. There was only one incident of eating poisonous fruit. That handful of berries left me emptying my bowels on the base of a tree for hours, clutching my torso through vomit over my feet. Tears carved tracks down my cheeks with every lightning convulsion deep in my abdomen. After emptying both ends of organs, I slept. I slept on that poop and vomit-stained grass from sunrise to sunset. I've since learned my lesson.

My appetite for various animals grew over the months. And it's so much easier than you would think! Squirrels, lizards, and small birds are dumb enough to try socializing. They socialized straight into my waiting knife. The largest I've been able to get was a hare. That hare fed me for two meals.

I hated myself for days after eating that hare. He had black speckles down his back and one missing toe on his back foot. Did his hare wife and ten hare children wait for him to come home that evening?

Sometimes I don't mind the work of hunting. Catching, skinning, cooking. I had nothing better to do with my days. In three months I read the two books I brought with me four times each. I can recite the pop star-centered articles in Mom's tabloids by heart, forward and backward. There's an imprint of my butt in the moss bed around my Sitting Tree.

My Sitting Tree is where I sat and contemplated the chances of survival if I were to get into a fistfight with a cougar just for the sake of a fun story to bring back to my new friends: the mushrooms growing underneath the truck. I was at the point where I was willing to risk testing if the mushrooms were poisonous or hallucinogenic.

The days blurred together. The only thing that let one day stand out among the others was when it rained and I was confined to my portable jail cell for hours. At least rain meant fresh water.

My schedule had no structure. Wake up when some creature comes sniffing on my territory. Complete whatever hygiene routine I can spare water for. Wait around for small animals and make my kill of the day. Spend an hour starting a fire to cook the stupid thing. Bathe in the river. Try not to be killed by water moccasins. Fall asleep when my eyes can no longer handle staying open. I know it's time for bed when I start seeing the Hat Man at the front of the camper.

Can I call the entire forest my territory? I lived out there for what feels like forever and only lived my daily life within the bounds of a one-mile radius. But the entire forest felt like my world. My forest. It doesn't make any difference to the deer and squirrels.

Dear squirrels, if I offended any of you by claiming the entire forest as my land, I offer my sincere apologies.

...I'm going insane.

I don't think I like the taste of snakes. At least, I don't think it's worth the trouble of catching and killing one.

It was a small guy. Don't get the idea that I'm some strong fearless hunter who slays rattlesnakes on the weekends. I stepped on him. His spine cracked under my flimsy shoe heel. I don't know if what I ate was the actual muscle or some otherworldly substance specific only to snakes.

Either way, I don't like it. But I needed it. That's why I ate every last bite. It took me an hour, but I got it done.

The cooking fire refused to stay lively. Even after so much practice, fire is not my strong suit, but I'm always able to keep it going once it grows. This flame was refusing to cooperate, though.

I played with that fire longer than I picked the meat off the slender body of the snake. I restarted it with another technique in my arsenal, managed to cook another sliver of meat, and the flame would die once again.

Over and over and over we had this battle. It was like the element of fire itself was playing a cruel trick on me. Me personally. It was a puzzle, perhaps the most enrichment my brain was getting in the last three months. But for the life of me — literally — I could not riddle the answer.

I was ready to give up. My snake was stripped half bare. Half of what went into my mouth ended up spat back out in the dirt by my feet. I buried my head in my hands, pulling my legs up to my chest. Time to accept my loss. It wouldn't be the first time I had to make it through the day on a measle-full stomach and would not be my last.

The soft dirt at my side was disturbed by the weight of hoof steps. My head jerked up, my eyes making contact with a doe. She stood not three meters away. I could stand up and walk only a few steps to touch her short, beautiful brown fur.

She stared at the fire and me. I stared back. Her black eyes never wavered, never blinked. I didn't know whether to move casually or sit still as a statue. Deer were infamous for their fear of humans. They're not vicious creatures but will run to the opposite end of the Earth if they feel threatened, and humans threatened them all too much.

Not this one. She treated me like any other surrounding. I think she knew I was no threat. I was just like her; pushing through every day for survival, relying on nothing but myself to get the job done.

I named her Molly. Molly leaned her neck down to investigate the ground. I shuffled in place, trying to prompt any reaction from her. Nothing. I was as good as another tree to her.

A silence settled between Molly and me. Her nose gestured to the flames with a downcast huff. Molly seemed to be just as displeased with the pathetic flames as I was. I couldn't help but smile.

With a final comment on my failure as a woodsman, she moved on, clopping silently away to my left.

I knew pets and zoo animals were harmed in the fallout just as any other human. When owners never came home to feed their dogs, those dogs either starved to death or found ways to break out of the house. If they happened to break out, indoor house pets would die on their own soon enough. They didn't know how to hunt or how to find adequate shelter.

Zoo animals either broke free or were let loose and started wandering the cities. Snow leopards were spotted sauntering down the streets of lower Manhattan in one of the last news reports I saw before the electricity died. There were no zoos anywhere near where we lived, so it would be a while before any exotic or endangered species made it to my part of the world. But what about in ten years? What about the Northeast American species? We have whales and bears and puffins. What about them?

My grumbling stomach snapped me out of my thoughts. If I was lucky, maybe there would be a few ripe persimmons left.

Being out here has led me to think a lot about life. About nature. About the entire point of the world.

There were times when I'd be at my Sitting Tree when my senses would otherwise be overloaded by twenty different streams of input, I could find myself only focusing on one thing. Everything sinks away.

Frogs singing. Squirrels scurrying up and down the trunk of a tree. Wind rustling branches. Birds chirping amongst their friends.

For weeks, I jumped and bolted at every snapping branch or falling acorn. When out here, you need to find a middle ground between seeing every inch of the area as a threat and seeing everything around you as peaceful.

Every other living organism on the planet wants to survive just as much as you. Some are better at it than others. The big scary animals are just as afraid of you as you are of them. That took me a while to get into my thick skull.

I'm within the folds of the food web now. I'm another individual link in the chain. Your outlook on life changes when you no longer have the height of power at your fingertips.

We destroyed our ice caps for a few more cars and changed the topography of the rainforests for a few more suburban settlements. For so long, humans could change ecosystems and wipe out species. Then again, so did Mother Nature. She was always a little more powerful than us, wasn't she?

Nighttime is my favorite time of the day. Falling asleep is my least favorite, but nighttime itself is a blessing. Everything is asleep but the tree frogs, the owls, and the foxes I see hiding behind the tree trunks. I almost became nocturnal myself during firefly season.

Late one evening, I was on my back in the wide open, staring into the darkness of outer space. But it was the opposite of dark. The Milky Way is so bright and colorful. You didn't see that before that fateful April. A time traveler from ten years ago would never believe their eyes. It's incredible how brilliant the natural world can be when light pollution has been eradicated.

I watched one of the useless hunks of orbiting metal that is a satellite cross the sky when a thought hit me. It was the type of thought that only comes at the best times of your day to throw your good mood to the ground and stomp it into a pulp.

What if my bold calculations about the human population were so completely wrong? I know they were poor. I was never good at math, and certainly not good without a calculator. The final report of the mortality rate for this fallout was 90%. Ninety percent of people are dead. I'm no Matilda Wormwood, so my estimation of 400 million people remaining on the planet is just that. An estimation. What if there are 100 million fewer? Or 100 million more?

What if the news mortality rate was inaccurate? What if there are so many more or less, we're just more spread out? What if everything continued steadily after we left, and there was nothing left to calculate?

What if I'm the last human being on Earth?

It makes sense that the problem would be more concentrated in big cities. That's where my brother was when his car ran off the interstate. We watched the helicopter footage in week three and picked his 2011 Suburban out from the pileup. How many people lived in New York City? Los Angeles? Tokyo? Shanghai? Does this mean the mortality rate could've been bumped from 90% to 95% for those big cities? Or is it just the same, and they're one of the last remaining places on Earth where you can have a next-door neighbor?

I swore to myself that I would never think about the human population again after firefly season. The release of my firefly friends was symbolic of my releasing all those nasty thoughts. Yet here they were again; knocking down the front door to my brain like police officers with a warrant.

Who am I kidding? These bad thoughts are a whole SWAT team surrounding my brain, ready to break down every conceivable entrance to drive me to insanity.

iii.

I needed to restock supplies. There was no alternative. My fragile twenty-first-century self could not handle this anymore.

My first aid supplies were running dangerously thin. Life-saving materials were dwindling. I had this unquenchable craving for some factory-processed food made to outlast the apocalypse.

I had it all planned out. The distance from the camper to the edge of my neighborhood clearing was roughly ten miles, twelve miles to my house. That's not too much. I could walk that distance in several hours; a few more if I was weighed down by my backpack. If I started at dawn I could be in town, stock up on the necessities, and be back to my home away from home before nightfall. This is all assuming everything goes according to plan and nature doesn't decide to throw me a curve ball. No rain. No spontaneous wild animal attack.

It's fine. Everything will be fine. I can do this.
Get over yourself and go into town.

The truck was stopped in the middle of the dirt road. I became very familiar with this dirt road during my months out there. I knew every turn and every scraggly root leading up to the creek ravine. Past that, I was ignorant. If I stuck to the road, eventually I would find myself back in town. The street signs pointed me in the right direction, and I was confident in my abilities to get back once the dirt road met asphalt.

I would be lying to myself and all of you if I said I wasn't afraid to go back into town.

I knew what I needed. Gasoline. Enough to make it twenty miles at least, and then some. But gasoline is heavy, as is the harsh truth for every other liquid.

How would I find it? What gas stations would be running?

Carjacking is always an option. Their former owners wouldn't mind, I'm sure.

To any future readers, I would not recommend being stranded in the middle of the woods in a camping trailer. *0/5 stars.*

You younger readers probably don't remember 5-star ratings.

Two days after Molly, I set out on the ten-mile hike to my hometown. In my heart, I know not to expect anything good. But if you go into a situation expecting bad things, bad things will come. It was time for a little optimism.

I set off at dawn.

The August heat bore down on my back with a force I didn't believe was possible for the Northeast. My backpack tugged on my shoulders incessantly. With every step, it gained another pound. My one of two remaining pairs of socks hadn't been cleaned properly in a month. I was ready to peel the outer layer of the bottom skin on my feet along with them when I was done with this walk.

The ground was soft and squishy from the previous night's rain. I was sidestepping puddles and boggy spots every ten feet. Only once did I slip. My knee took the brunt of that fall. Within ten seconds, my fate was solidified of having a crusty dirt-caked knee for the rest of the trip.

In a cruelly ironic way, these experiences hardened me against all the problems one builds up in one's mind. If I dared make this trip three months prior when I was afraid to go down a muddy gravel driveway in my white shoes, my sanity wouldn't have made it. I used to be such a freak about the quality of my shoes. Since then, my Chuck Taylors have gotten so dirty and crusty that you would never believe they were once white. You should also see my pair of boots. Yikes.

The dirt road met asphalt in no time. I estimate it had been an hour of walking, and much easier than what I'd procrastinated about for so long. It turns out that even at the end of the world, a professional procrastinator will put off the simplest of tasks in anticipation of it being horrible.

I was walking down Propst East for what seemed like a decent mile with no trouble. It felt so weird to walk straight down the middle of a paved road and know I never had to worry about being hit by a car.

There was nothing better for my mind to do than wander to horrible places. What would I find in my town? In my house? Bodies, wild animals tearing apart couches, fires? How overgrown will it have gotten in the time of five months? Will anything be usable anymore? What if I get to my house and nature has torn apart everything necessary for my survival, leaving me with nothing? Will it all have been a waste?

Then I saw him. Another person. And a rifle.

A person with a rifle.

The man was a good distance ahead of me in the trees. His back was turned, his eyes in deep focus on the treetops. He couldn't see me. He couldn't hear me. If he did, there would be a hole in my chest before I could scream for help from nonexistent saviors.

The first person I've seen in six months… *of course, he has a gun!*

My backpack was suddenly louder than a jet engine as I backstepped. My eyes never left the back of his head as I backed up several meters to the other edge of the road. A pounding in my ears deafened me.

Surely he could hear every tiny movement of mine. Even from a distance, he could hear every beat of my heart and sense every shallow breath that left my body.

His hand moved to the neck of his rifle.

I almost face-planted immediately upon turning around. I caught myself on a tree trunk, the force scraping my palm against the rough bark. Pain shocked down my wrist.

"Hey! Ma'am!" The man's voice hit me like a semi-truck.

My hand stung. My skull was throbbing. My backpack bounced relentlessly, hitting my shoulder and hips with every step.

I took a sharp turn down a hill. My feet skidded down the mud. The force of the abrupt level-out of the ground jammed my knee in on itself. A scream shot from my mouth. With any luck, the hunter would trip and give me another minute to get farther ahead.

"Come back! Miss!"

A weight slammed into my back, sending me face-first into the mud. We went down together, the thud resounding through the trees. I was gifted a nice snack of mud and grass.

"I'm sorry! I'm so sorry, Miss." The man scrambled off my back, hand on my shoulder.

I pushed myself to my knees, swatting his hand away. "Don't touch me!"

"I didn't mean anything by it," he swore, wiping the mud portrait from my face. "I tripped."

"Get the hell away from me!" I threw my foot into his stomach.

He backed away several paces. He displayed his hands in front. "I'm sorry," he muttered, watching me push myself to stand. He slowly brought the rifle down from his shoulder and set it on the ground. "Do you need help?"

"Does it look like I need help?" I shot back, attempting to scrub the mud from my thighs but only smearing it further.

He held a hand out, offering a polite smile. "My name's Tate."

"Good for you." I ignored his offer for a shake. This made Tate clear his throat, sliding his hand into the back pocket of his jeans.

I picked my backpack up and inspected the contents. The dwindling first aid kit, as was the small pouch of mulberries I brought for later, was alright. My knife without a sheath poked a hole through the side of the bag, though. I could patch it up with no problem. Nothing seemed harmed but my clothes and ego.

Tate was not eager to drop the conversation and move on with his hunting. "Do you live out here?"

I slung my backpack over my shoulder, scuffing my shoes on the grass. "No, I'm on vacation."

I know the man named Tate meant well. But I didn't care. Meeting another person was not on the itinerary for the day — especially not one with a gun and a pretty face. That's never a good mix.

He sighed, crossing his arms. "Okay, I just wanna know who you are. Normally that process starts with a name…" Tate ushered me to answer. Tate's Southern accent wasn't missed on my ears. A stranger to the area.

I crossed my arms just like his. "Vivienne."

Tate smiled. It made me want to vomit. "Nice to meet you, Vivienne. What are you doing out here?"

"Nothing. Goodbye."

I spun on a single heel and bid him ado. Tate didn't accept this. He jogged ahead of me, putting one hand on my shoulder. Just one poison-filled glare was enough to let him know his hand was not welcome anywhere in the vicinity of my body.

"You can't catch a hint, can you?" I demanded.

Tate gave me space. "Excuse me for being concerned about the young woman running through the woods alone!"

"I only ran because you have a gun!"

Tate held his hands up by his head, fingers spread wide. "I'm not gonna hurt you, Vivienne. I just want to talk."

"You're doing that already."

"Let me help you home. It's the least I can do," he suggested, offering a kind smile.

I shoved past him. "No, the least you could do is leave me alone."

Tate watched me walk away for several meters. I waited for him to follow me or protest. I waited and waited and waited… nothing. Just as I was ready to pat myself on the back that I'd successfully shaken him off my trail, his shout reached my ears once again.

"Do you even know where you're going?"

My feet stopped in their tracks. Reality crashed down on me. Every tree looked the same. Every small hill looked like all the other small hills.

I slowly turned around, facing him from a distance. He said nothing, only stared back at me. I took a long look at the trees around me. If I'd turned around and gone straight back, I could get back home with no problem. But I didn't do that. I ran in any direction that wasn't Tate. We went so far that I couldn't even see the asphalt road now.

My silence was enough to tell him everything he needed. Tate retrieved his rifle, slung it over his shoulder, and jogged to catch up with me. "Do you need food?"

"I'm alright."

"I don't believe you," Tate stated. I shot him one more poisonous glare, and that was his cue to drop the subject. Didn't stop him from chuckling, though.

I told him that I knew what general direction to go in. West. A little to the southwest, maybe. He assured me that once we went far enough southwest I'd be able to find my trail back. As if he knew the forest like I did.

Tate made sure to keep me within arm's distance at all times. Every time I tried to move away he followed without a word. He reminded me exactly of our old dog. I didn't know whether to take this as waving red flags of a creep, or protection.

I didn't use to be one to judge someone. However, I've found that living in the middle of the forest with your only blossoming friendship being fungus tends to change your view of other people.

"How old are you?" I asked once we found the dirt road again. Most young adults died in raves or mass attacks on universities. If not in big cities, they died in the army.

"Twenty-two. You?"

"Seventeen."

Tate gave me a narrow side-eye. "Do you live with your parents?"

I nodded instantly without thinking. Tate didn't question me. "What were you doing so far away from home?" He continued.

He will not stop talking…, I internally rolled my eyes. "Supplies." I motioned my head in the direction of a fallen tree. "And we get off here for a bit," I directed.

Tate perked up slightly. "You were heading into town? Which one, maybe I live there?"

"I know you don't live anywhere near me. I would've known," I grumbled.

"That small, huh? You know *everyone*?"

"Yes."

Tate lowered his eyes to the ground. "Yeah, you wouldn't know me. I've only been up here for a few weeks now," he admitted.

I didn't respond. I didn't care where he came from or how long he'd been in Maine. And I wished he would shut up and be quiet for five minutes. I was beginning to miss the silence of pure loneliness, and it hadn't been half an hour.

Neither of us spoke for a long while after that. He let me walk further ahead for the remainder of the journey. I was grateful. I was even more grateful when I heard the beautiful flow of my creek in the nearby distance. I ran forward with a wide smile breaking my cheeks.

"This is my creek! I can find my way back from here," I announced. Every ounce of my body resisted the urge to jump with joy. I could have literally jumped.

The splashes of the creek drenched my legs up to the knees, relieving the pain of the heat. A giggle bubbled from my throat; the best feeling imaginable.

Tate watched me kneel by the rocks of the opposite creek bed, after jumping across a thin patch, washing my hands in the chill current. I savored the way the water trickled over my fingers, reveled in the cleaning sting as it touched my open wounds.

"You can find your way back? Where do you live?"

"Just a little down that direction." I pointed to my seven o'clock. I was as familiar with the way to and from the camper and this creek spot as I used to be with my own bedroom.

Tate placed his hands on his hips, staring into the distant trees. "You said you live with your parents?"

I cupped my hands further upstream and brought the fresh drink to my lips. Bacteria be damned. "Yep. Just the three of us," I stated with a much more curt tone than intended.

If Tate didn't believe me at the time, he didn't say anything.

"I can come back if you want," he said.

I set my backpack down, staring at him across the water. "Only if you want to come back," I offered. In my language, that translated to "Please don't."

Tate saluted. "I'll bring food and whatever supplies I can find," he promised.

My eyes shot to the ground, nodding. Here it was at my fingertips: food and necessities without a walk into town. Tate was willing to get it for me.

I just needed to put my trust in him.

Tate bid me goodbye with a kind smile and retreated up the ravine. I watched him climb the rocks and disappear over the side.

He promised to come back. I washed and tucked into bed that night not so sure if Tate was a man to be trusted. He had everything to gain from staying away and keeping his resources to himself, nothing to gain from helping a rude teenage girl in the middle of the woods.

I would be lying if I said I didn't enjoy the conversation with another living human being.

iv.

Tate stayed away for the first day. After twenty-four hours of no return, I gave up hope. I detached myself from any expectation that he would be back. But I was impatient.

When he did come back, he waited for me at the ravine. He returned after two days to check on me, stayed to share a rabbit, and was on his way. I didn't see him again for another three days. He came bearing two well-sized fish. I hadn't had fish in months. They were always too hard to catch. It was a delicacy.

At first, our conversations stayed polite and few. Tate understood after our first interaction that I was accustomed to a life of solitude. He didn't find my silence offensive. If he did, he never said anything.

On the third meeting, he brought two squirrels and a fish for me to bring home. "I just realized yesterday that I never bring food for your parents. Are they alright?" Tate asked, handing the gift over in a gray rucksack.

I stared at the two additional animals. "They get their own dinner every night. I tell them to eat what would be mine when you come around," I explained, begging my facial expression not to betray my excitement at having two more meals without any work.

I know Tate did not believe that one. But he didn't pry for an honest answer.

After that interaction, he came every day. He arrived at different times, never on a reliable schedule. But I couldn't complain. Seeing Tate meant food and bandaids. That was all I needed.

But there were downsides. There was someone else sharing my little slice of the world. And he was noisy. I'd come accustomed to a quaint life and quiet days. Tate disrupted that quiet. Tate spoke with confidence, he killed dinner with confidence. He even breathed with confidence; like he knew he had full control of the world around him, and the forest was blessed to have him in its presence.

Tate aggravated me. My face lit up when I saw him at the ravine. Tate made me want to punch a tree. I looked forward to seeing him again every night as I drifted to sleep.

I never touched my leg hair while on my own. But now there was someone else in my space, looking at my Sasquatch legs in shorts every day.

I only brought sweatpants to sleep in when we packed for June. Those sweatpants became everyday wear around Tate. I didn't even think to pack my razor. I was supposed to just be around my parents for the rest of our lives. Not some Southern pretty boy who was far too nice to make any snide comments about the state of my calves or armpits.

While my natural body hair was the least of our problems, it was a problem for me. It turns out that even during the apocalypse, Western societal beauty standards will remain engraved in your head. For the rest of eternity.

It hit me one night as I stared at the constellations: what if I forgot algebra? What if I forgot how to calculate the slope?

Though, I figure algebra is just another obsolete practice these days.

We were sitting inside the camper one day after the second week. I wasn't happy to let him see my home at first. I was perfectly content meeting at the ravine and staying there. But I couldn't leave him out there to go home alone when water bullets started shooting down from the sky.

Tate didn't say anything about the truck and camper on the road.

He didn't ask much about anything unless I brought it up first. That's what I liked about his company. He kept to his own business once I got comfortable... most of the time.

It was raining for hours. The landscape beyond my dirt-spotted windows only offered a world someone put a filter over. I had to keep glancing around the camper interior to remind my eyes that color existed and we didn't live in a dreary world of twenty thousand grays.

We didn't talk much. The water pellets hammered at my roof, reminiscent of my last *Steak N' Shake* experience. The icy shiver ran down my spine when the armored men broke through the door. They pointed their weapons at the young waitress behind the register. She cried and fumbled for her keys. The line chef yelled at us to get down. I hit my neck on the way to get under the table. Mikey slapped his hands over both our mouths. Somewhere above the table, someone tried to fight the intruders. A man's voice was calling the police in the booth next to us. I knew no one would come. My eardrums were pierced with the resonant bang of bullets. Glass shattered from the decadent barriers above. Two bodies fell.

"Are you okay?" A gentle hand touched my shoulder. I flinched out and hit Tate away. He backed up, holding both hands in the air. "Peace. Are you okay?"

I didn't respond. I faced the wall and clamped my hands over my ears until the room quieted. Tate didn't speak again.

The rain settled after a while. We sat on opposite sides of the camper; me on the couch covered in blankets, him on the floor by the door with a pillow against his back. I chucked a stress ball at the opposite wall.

"What's your accent?" I asked out of the blue.

Tate popped his knuckles, gaze fixated on my crusty Chuck Taylors. "I was born and raised in Mobile, Alabama."

I tilted my head, chucking my stress ball at the window again. "And how did you find yourself up here?" I prodded, catching the circle of rubber and repeating.

"School. I was a sophomore in electrical engineering at NYU," Tate explained, his head following the ball traveling back and forth.

"NYU is like… 500 miles away. How are you here?"

"Four hundred fifty miles," he corrected.

"Whatever." I threw the ball at him.

He chuckled, easily catching it. "Bike. I always wanted to see a few Humpbacks before I die, so… you know, what better time than now?"

"That's oddly rational." It was a stupid reason.

Tate tossed the ball back. It soared over my head, but I was too lazy to retrieve it from three feet away. He apologized.

"Are your parents out there? Can we be expecting them anytime?" Tate asked after another several minutes.

This made me pause. I didn't respond for a moment, considering how to go forward. I can't remember what I ended up saying; if I responded at all. I do know that Tate didn't respond to me.

I'd always assumed that after so long, civilization would return to the Dark Ages. Could we call this the second Dark Age? But even after everything humanity had lost over the months, the one I met remained bountiful with modern privileges. It didn't make sense. Tate had so much ammunition; so many fresh clothes.

What if things weren't as rundown as I expected?

"Can I ask something incredibly morbid?"

We were washing my clothes in the cleaner part of the river — the part that wouldn't leave me cleaning sediment out of my jeans pockets for days afterward. More so, I was washing my clothes, he was watching. I refused to let him touch my dirty underwear.

A slight smirk tugged at the corners of Tate's mouth. "How many people did I know that died? Or how many people have I seen in the last four months?"

"It's been three months."

Tate looked up from the water to stare at me. "Four."

"No. It's August." I stared right back.

"It's September."

My eyes lowered. Tate was the one of us who had access to a calendar. "It's September?"

"September 13."

"Oh…" How could it be September? "I'm eighteen, then."

 Tate smiled. "Happy birthday, Vivienne."

I remember sitting on a rock for a long time, belting to myself popular songs as they came to my head. In hindsight, it wasn't the smartest to be doing that when waiting for someone in the otherwise dead silent forest. I was probably dehydrated and delirious.

When I was done harming the ears of innocent wildlife, peace returned to the ravine. A few tadpoles swam by my bare feet.

A stray domestic cat inspected me from afar. He wore a thick red and brown coat, his whiskers buried in the mess of long fur around his face. I held out my hand to him. The kitty approached close enough to sniff at my fingers, body pressed as close to the ground as possible. I moved my other hand just enough to scratch my ear and the cat ran off, pupils in his pale orange eyes wider than the water bed he splashed into.

All serenity coating my brain was wiped clean at the thought of Mikey. He would've loved to watch that cat with me. Mikey collected pets like Pokemon cards. My older brother, Peter, would name the cat a funky Middle Ages surname.

I left the ravine happy Tate never came. He would try to cheer me up, and sometimes the only way to get through a sour mood was by not being cheered up.

Tate never explicitly mentioned when he called my bluff about my parents. I think he always had a suspicion from the beginning, but that suspicion was confirmed after the third week. When I casually mentioned their deaths in conversation he didn't blink an eye.

We were cooking our dinner one night. Thoughts of the previous day raced through my brain. I peeked up from my meal to watch him stoke the fire, remembering one question he'd hesitated to answer previously. I wanted to poke the bear.

"You never answered my question before. How many people did you meet on the four hundred fifty miles up here?"

Tate sat back on his knees, clearing his throat. "Forty-seven. Including you and my sisters."

My head whipped up. "You have sisters? You never talk about them."

"You never ask." He shrugged.

I sighed, playing with the inedible bits of my meat with a sharp rock. "I haven't seen anyone else since my parents died. That was back in June," I whispered, leaning my head back to stare at the stars.

"You're not missing much."

V.

"Will you go into town if you're not alone?" Tate asked me one Friday afternoon. I know it was a Friday because he told me.

"A fear of being alone isn't what's keeping me from going back there." That was precisely what kept me back.

"Don't you want to see your old house? Bring back a few modern-day luxuries?"

"Yes. But that's not the problem." That was exactly the problem.

I became so attached to my camper and the woods over the last four months that the thought of returning home scared me. It terrified me.

I wasn't always a coward.

"I'll be with you the entire time," he promised.

Tate had this annoying way of making promises that let you know immediately how sincere he was. Every time he opened his mouth you knew the words that tumbled out were coming from a deep place in his heart. Every. Single. Time. It bugged me so much. People don't act like that in modern-day Maine.

A small smirk stretched across my face. "Sounds like a plot to brutally murder me."

He shook his head in that stupid solemn manner of his. "I promise I'm not a psycho killer."

"Sounds like something a psycho killer would say."

This evoked a grin from Tate.

A life of scarcity is more jarring than you would ever be able to imagine. Seriously. You can zone out in the middle of your English teacher's lecture and imagine, "What would I do if I had to make ten Ibuprofen last four months?"

But you'll never know what it feels like until you find yourself rationing to make every ounce of material last until… God only knows when. Tate gave me a bit more to work with. I was a lost cause on my own. I was playing with fire blind.

I was finally down to the last straw. Tate could see that. No amount of breakfast or socks would change that.

We left the following day. My hippie grandmother would be proud of me on one note. I made my remaining modern-day luxuries stretch for two more weeks. I could have died in the middle of the woods, lost and ignorant of any direction. But I didn't. Grandma Siobhan would be proud of me.

Tate suggested catching breakfast on the way. He adhered to the modern ways of hunting: his trusted rifle and a full magazine of bullets. Tate offered to teach me how to use his gun in case he found one to bring back to me. I laughed in his face. I didn't trust myself in the vicinity of his gun in his own hands, much less in my own. I'd gone on several of his hunts by now, and the blasting echo of gunfire still made me jump. Putting that blast right by my face didn't seem like a good way to remedy that.

"How many sisters do you have?" I asked to puncture an uncomfortable silence.

He lowered the rifle, glancing back at me over his shoulder. "Two."

I nodded, my gaze locked on the trigger of his weapon. "I had a brother. He died around the second week," I muttered. Even after so long, I still was not used to that gun.

Tate's grip on the barrel tightened. He cleared his throat with a cough. "I'm sorry. I didn't mean to offend or anything. The three of us were really lucky."

"I wasn't offended." I stepped away from him. "Why would I be offended that your sisters are alive?"

Tate aimed the rifle into the trees, slowly cocking it. "A lot of people were when I mentioned that part."

I watched his movements, anticipating the bullet. "Did your sisters come with you?"

"Mhm. Diana is nineteen and is the most complacent person you could ever meet. Chrissy is fourteen and whined all the way up here. Complete opposites. But they knew better than to split up."

"Bet that didn't get annoying."

"It's better than being alone." He threw a discarded glance my way. "They're fine. They keep me honest."

"And it was your grand decision to go whale watching in your final days?" I crossed my arms when a breeze hit me. September now.

Tate remained still as a statue, the prey trapped in his hunter's gaze. "There were multiple reasons for us to come up here, I'll be honest."

"As opposed to lying previously?"

"That's not what I meant."

"I know. Just giving you crap." I winked. Tate shot a woodpecker from a tree. The bird fell with a disgusting thud. He whistled. I inhaled sharply and watched him retrieve the woodpecker. "What happens when you run out of ammo?"

Tate shoved the bird into his bag, slinging his weapon over his shoulder. "I find more in another house. You'll be surprised how many people stock up on weapons and ammunition at the end of the world," he answered simply.

"And when that runs out?"

"It won't."

"But what if it does?"

Tate shrugged, leaning down ever so slightly to be closer to my eye level. "Cannibalism, I guess."

The fear in my eyes gave him all he needed. A laugh erupted from his throat as he turned away and walked on.

"Did you three meet up somewhere?" I asked. Tate hummed and slightly turned his head to me. He hadn't been paying attention. I kicked a large rock out of my path. "Did the family move to New York with you when you started school? Or were you on spring break and just happened to be home?"

Tate stared at the trees ahead. "I drove home after the first week. Our parents died in May within three days of each other. So we came up here and ran out of gas in the jugs somewhere in the middle of North Carolina. We stole three bikes and got here after a month or so."

"That's a lot of biking."

"It's good for your health."

Since leaving the camper, we'd been together for four hours. I felt like I was overstaying my welcome as his walking partner.

"How long have you been up here? Your journey started in May?" I asked. He nodded. "So you've been here for three months?"

He grabbed my arm and helped me down a mudslide. I thanked him with a smile. "One month. We stayed a little further south for a bit. Moved on when the locals drove us out."

"Locals?"

"A commune of green livers. About thirty of them. They were already out there long before things went to crap," he explained. I wasn't gonna mention how that opened more questions than answered.

I flinched when something fell out of a nearby tree. Probably an acorn — I hoped. "If you're not with your sisters now, where are they?"

"Probably arguing about the phases of the moon. They're back at the house we're borrowing."

He said borrowing as if they weren't using a dead family's house. Were the former owners still in the house when Tate and his sisters arrived? Where were they now? Where did they go? Were they our neighbors?

"You left them?" I demanded.

"Chrissy was thrilled when I mentioned leaving for a hunt the first day. Diana was happy to have my testosterone stench out of the house. I don't think they mind."

Everything made sense. That was why he couldn't stay overnight. If I had the opportunity to live with my parents and brother again, I don't think I'd be able to part with them for a whole day. Knowing what I know now, I would handcuff all of our wrists together. Tate was stronger than me. Or maybe he didn't know to take advantage of them in his life while it lasted.

"Is it at least a nice house?" I asked.

Tate nodded slowly. "It was."

We reached town a little after noon. We came out to see the edge of one of the more urban areas. My neighborhood.

I stood at the edge of the trees, staring into my frozen-in-time hometown. Just from the edge of the woods, I could see weather damage on houses and cars.

Unsteady roofs caved in from rainfall. Windows were blown out from the season of harsh storms back in July. Plant life and the elements took over everything in sight. The previously neatly trimmed lawns and upkeeped asphalt roads overgrew to be unrecognizable. Cookie-cutter suburbanite houses were now detailed with their own tales of time and ruin.

I knew exactly where we were. I saw those houses thrice a week for seventeen years. The chain link fences were no different, despite wear and tear. My house was one mile away, just down the left bend. Every afternoon, for eleven years, at 3:46 the school bus number 4 would go down that exact road and turn at the round-a-bout. I spotted one elementary friend's house. Her name was Alice. I went to her ninth birthday party. A fox circled Alice's garden bed, which was now overrun with weeds and snaking vines.

We could smell the town's reek of death from the trees. It was less prominent than the smell of a town when everything first began. But towns always have a stench. That never goes away, even after years.

It puts into perspective just how liminal our impact on the world is. The pollution remains but will dilute with time and movement. But our structures; our great marvels of the modern day… Mankind nearly disappears in a snap and six months later Mother Nature's taken back everything for herself. With no one to keep things in check, my world looked like something out of a concept art piece.

Landscape: Disappearance of Mankind.

My legs turned to stone. My hands trembled at the straps of my backpack. I don't know what I expected… but it wasn't this.

How many still lived here? What wild animals had broken windows and rotting wood to destroy what fragile histories were left of the house interiors? There were looters and squatters all around when things were lighter. What if there was a stranger living in my house, using my supplies? Tate and his sisters were "borrowing" a house. How was I to know someone wasn't doing the same for mine?

Tate charged forward without me, only noticing my absence until he was meters ahead. He turned and urged me forward. I stared back at him.

He jogged back to the trees. "What's up?"

"This was a bad idea," I whispered. "I can't go back there. You need to do it for me. Please."

"I'm not doing that." Tate placed a hand on my back.

Not good. *Red alert. Red alert!*

My organs shriveled inside. I hit him away, feeling the nerves down the core of my soul. Tate backed away. "I'm sorry. But we need to go. We came all this way."

I threw my bags to the grass. "I can't do it."

"Vivienne. I'm not gonna have this argument with you. You know you need this." He kicked a bag closer to me. "This already looks mild."

"Someone's gonna be in my house!"

"Possibly. Ignore them."

"I despise you."

"Then walk away." Tate stared at me. "Walk away. I dare you."

He has me there. When I didn't move, Tate grabbed my bags and nodded toward the abandoned neighborhood. The abandoned lives. "That's what I thought. Come on. You want to be back home by nightfall."

vi.

Even in rural Maine, there are always clues of the neighbors and their pets. A screaming toddler through a screen door. A lawnmower. A sprinkler watering the garden of unwittingly invasive species because the owners were too busy binging Better Call Saul for the fourth time.

A neighborhood had life. People living together. People trying to coexist without taking a gun to their mother-in-laws.

I've never walked through a neighborhood so quiet. Any noises were of our own footsteps, our own breathing, and wild animals humping lawn flamingos. Gray clouds and the sickly pre-rain smell weighed on us.

To describe it as a ghost town wouldn't be right. Ghost towns have the sense of time passing. You see those in low-budget Wild West movies. This place I grew up in had a population of decent-mannered Maine residents at one time, that was clear. Everyone had livelihoods. Everyone had their own passions; their own careers. But where did they go? Archaeologists of the future would be forever baffled. Another Roanoke.

I kept expecting someone to pop out from behind a dumpster and announce the trick was over. It was all a big setup. Just an elaborate prank to mess with me.

Tate would be in on it. Chrissy and Diana would reveal themselves too, wearing party hats and armed with confetti. The three of them would laugh at my reaction. They would lead me to my house, where my parents and brother would wait for me with an eighteenth birthday cake. Mikey would be with them too, armed with loads of presents. They would all explain that it was all a big ruse. It was difficult to pull off, but they managed to convince the entire neighborhood and the entire planet to play along. My dog would jump on me and lick all over my face, just like nothing had changed.

Tate's voice brought me back to reality. "Watch your step," he held my elbow, dramatically keeping me from face-planting over a fallen tree trunk. "Careful."

One question burned at the back of my mind. I meant to ask him since the beginning of the trip but never had the courage. Now seemed as good a time as any.

"Have you been in many houses where the pets are still there?" I whispered, my gaze fixed on a pothole ahead of us.

Tate glanced my way. "What?"

I avoided his eyes. "Like… dead? You know what I mean."

"Oh. Yeah." Tate cleared his throat. "A few. Some of them managed to get out. Others didn't. Some dogs ate the cats. Cats ate birds. And each other."

The grip on my backpack strap tightened. Tate lowered his head. "Sorry. Some animals got out," he promised. I peered into the windows of a house we passed. I was so afraid of seeing a body… I don't know why I looked for so long. "You said you had a dog?" Tate asked.

I watched a hawk land on a trestle painted abstractly with bird turds. "My brother's thirteenth birthday present. He wanted a dog so bad, he teared up when Dad walked into the living room with it wrapped up in a blanket. His name was Freddie."

"The dog or your brother?"

"The dog." I forced out a chuckle. "My brother's name was Peter."

I knew Freddie wasn't going to be in our house. When we walked out to the camper the day we left for the woods, Freddie bolted out right after us. We tried to catch him, but he was too fast. I watched him run down the paved road and into the horizon. If Peter were with us, he would've chased that dog until his own legs fell off.

"Peter," Tate echoed. "How old was he?"

To this, I didn't respond. What did it matter how old he was or would be? He wasn't anything now.

"It's gonna rain later," Tate observed, his neck craned up at the graphite sky. "We need to be quick. If you're outside too long in a storm, you're as good as dead. Pneumonia is a sure promise."

"Do you think we can make it back?" I mutter, watching the slow, taunting movement of the clouds.

"Maybe."

Tate looked at me for instruction once we came to the end of the street. The road branched off in both directions. I nodded my head to the left, heading to my house without him. He shouted after me to slow down.

I could see it. Mom's dark blue SUV was still in the driveway, parked right by the black mailbox that had been run over countless times in the last decade. We never bothered to replace it.

I stood on the lawn, staring at the empty building. The living room blinds were wide open. I could see the television that had been black for nearly seven months. I could peer into the dining room, where Mom's collection of antique glass nick-nacks still stood proud. And my bedroom window. It faced to the side, directly into our neighbor on the left, Mr. Hengeller's, office window. Mr. Hengeller was on two sexual harassment watch lists. I always kept my curtains shut at all times.

No matter how hard I tried, I couldn't tear my eyes from the window; from the brown leather couch that held my laughter and tears, from the table I'd done my meaningless homework on for almost thirteen years.

All those years studying complex math and all the different ways to structure a sentence… just to end up here. A waste of brain space.

Tate came up by my side. "Now, be prepared to find a few things missing or broken. There was a problem with looters around late June," he warned me. I ignored him and charged forward.

The lock to our front door was broken. Smashed to pieces without the courtesy to kick the broken metal off the pavement. Someone had gotten inside. I let the door swing open. A spiderweb split open at the top of the doorway. After checking for Tate's gun on his back and my single knife in my bag's side pocket, I stepped one foot on the carpet of the front room.

"Vivienne," Tate grabbed my arm. "I don't think there's anyone else like me and my sisters around here, but just in case… You should be careful."

I stared up at him, my posture rigid with fear I'm sure he could smell. "Please get your hand off of me."

Tate obeyed. I flipped the light switch to my left. Dead.

We stepped further into the living room, studying everything in and out of place. The window was in shatters with a broad hole. A rock lay on the floor by the foot of Dad's Lay-Z-Boy. Glass crunched under our shoes, digging deeper into the carpet.

A mouse scurried out from behind the couch. I backed up, knocking Tate back a few inches. "You okay?" He whispered. I nodded, charging on.

Whoever broke in didn't find much value. They left the TV and DVD player. They left most blankets and pillows. I jogged into the kitchen. Everything was kept together. It was the strangest thing. While leaving most treasures, they treated the furniture like playthings. Only a shelf's worth of food was missing.

"Squatters," I muttered, kicking over the remnants of a broken house plant vase. "Like you guys."

"Maybe. But we never did… this," Tate muttered. He righted a discarded dining chair. "You got more bags tucked away in a closet or something?" He threw open the cabinets left and right. I nodded, reaching out my hands pathetically to help. "Great. Use them. Only get necessities and fill up as much space as you can. We can find a wagon or something to handle the weight. I think we have one to spare in our garage. I'll get the food and water. You left out the bowls for this rain before we left, right?"

"They never go anywhere." I nodded.

He grinned with a quick wink. "Good job. You get materials: clothes, blankets, medicine, a spare gun in your parents' closet. Things like such. Understand?" He ordered. I nodded, backing out of the kitchen. Before I got too far, he grabbed me one last time.

"Okay, Vivienne, listen to me. We don't want to come back a second time," Tate leveled with me, putting one hand on my shoulder. "If anyone dangerous is out here and we haven't found them yet, they've found us. They could be watching us right now. Coming back would tip them off that there's something about this house important to you. They'll come back and wait for you. As long as it takes. Get it?"

I wanted to vomit. I almost did. This was never something I considered. "Why don't they come for me now?" I whispered.

Tate considered. "They think you're just another looter. And if they know me, they think I'm helping you."

I watch Tate stuff the bag with sugary cereal and cheese crackers. I know I had no reason to distrust him after so long. He was nothing but good to me. Every day he dutifully came bearing fresh food and a smiling face. If Tate wanted to hurt me by now, he would have. Still, it was hard not to wonder.

"How do you know so much about how these bad people think?"

Tate slowly turned around, staring down at me. "What do you mean?"

Defense was my best weapon, knowing I was poking into unwelcome territory. "You said it yourself that you've only seen like 40 people, and half of them were some hippie cult." I crossed my arms, avoiding his eyes. He thought I didn't trust him. I did. But I didn't.

"Are you suggesting I'm one of them?" He demanded. My reflexes flinched at the raise in his voice, making him hold up a hand. "Sorry, sorry- Vivienne, I've had so many opportunities to hurt you by now. Don't you think if I wanted to I would have?"

I regretted ever bringing it up. But now I needed answers. I needed to *understand* him.

"If they're tracking people who return to the same place, wouldn't they be after your sisters right now? Wouldn't they be watching them, too?" I stared right back at him with all the courage I could muster.

"Who's to say they aren't?" He shot back. My eyes lowered. Tate shook his head. "Who's to say I didn't do something I regret and am now trying to save you from having to do the same? Because *maybe* I care about you too."

I watched a beetle scurry across the floor between our feet. "Oh."

"Don't think that again," Tate muttered curtly. Something flashed in his eyes — hurt. Genuine hurt. He returned to the cabinets with one jerky movement. "Get moving. We don't have time for this crap."

Walking down the hallway and up the narrow stairs was better than the front part of the house. This part was relatively untouched, which worried me more. Everyone knows that a family's largest treasures are hidden in the heart of their homes.

I first went to Mom and Dad's bedroom. They housed all the big travel bags in their walk-in closet. Pushing down the vomit in my throat as I passed their queen bed, I surged into their closet. Their clothes were the worst to touch. The worst to smell. I finally came up with a duffel bag and one large fabric carry-on handbag.

This was the bag she would carry our sunblock, inflatable toys, goggles, and snacks for summer outings to the public pool. We hadn't been to that pool in two, three years.

Endless afternoons I hid in the depths of my mom's side of the closet, whether it be playing Hide and Seek with Peter or escaping from family Thanksgiving dinner.

Eight years old I was, fidgeting with Mommy's high heels on my hands, my chubby fingers relishing in the soft padding and light wear of her fancy shoes. She never had any time to wear those white heels, but I loved to see her in them. She looked so happy and tall when she wore the white heels.

The closet door opened. Yellow bedroom light cut through the edges of shirts and skirts, broken by a moving object. "Vivienne? Are you in here?" My daddy called.

The shoe dropped from my hand as both hands slapped to my face to conceal my mouth and ears. If I can't hear him, maybe he can't hear me, too. My daddy crouched down, his cargo shorts riding up to expose those scarred knees. I didn't know how his knees got so hurt and marked up. He told me he gets it from his job, but I didn't understand how a job could be so injury-prone.

"Do you wanna help Mommy with the brownies?" He spoke to Mommy's bottom row of clothes. *How did he see me?* I shook my head. "She really wants you to help. You can put the caramel on top."

A painful cramp twisted in my calf. That leg jutted out, revealing itself in the open air of the closet. "*Gotcha!*" Daddy exclaimed before grabbing my foot and dragging me from behind the outfits. I screamed and giggled, the rug burning a comforting thrill.

I don't cry often anymore. I didn't let my dad's spirit see me cry, either.

Their bathroom was the first to get a visit. I hit the jackpot for toothpaste, deodorant (not my top priority, but a woman can stink), soap, bandages, and rubbing alcohol. Any pill bottle I set eyes on got swept in, not bothering to read what exactly I was taking. Knowing my parents, it was either for pain, allergies, or a stool softener. The essentials.

It wasn't until I closed the drug cabinet that I got a real shock. Some unrecognizable face stared back at me.

My reflection became a memory when dust and dirt started covering the rearview mirrors of Dad's pickup truck. I had other priorities than wiping it clean every few weeks just to make sure I looked pretty for the squirrels and mosquitos. Now, looking at myself with no filter or obstruction, I wondered where Vivienne went.

Where was that lonely seventeen-year-old — fresh into orphanhood and struggling to make it twenty miles back home? When did I leave her behind and pick up this… thing?

The copper hair was grown out fair past where I'd cut it before. It now hung wimpily inches above my shoulders in a lump of oil and dirt. Choppy and uneven in all sorts of places, my head was a hairdresser's nightmare. A scar had formed on my upper right cheekbone — much too close to my eye for comfort. One poor foot placement… a slip on riverbed rocks sent me flying to the ground and walking home with a bloody face. Rubbing alcohol was my only weapon against infection.

The worst part of the sight was my face. Starvation over a long period can ruin a good facial structure. Your cheeks become hollow, yet swollen by fluids trapped in the tissues. Your skin loses its perfect Instagram complexion. Chapped lips. Acne. The whites of my eyes were lined with more red than ever.

Whoever was in the mirror was not me.

How did Tate look last year, I wondered. *How would Peter and Mikey look by now?*

I kept my eyes trained on the floor for the walk out of the bathroom. It was disgusting to think how long it had been since they laid to sleep in that bed. Their comforter used to be so ugly to me, but now I wanted nothing more than to be a small child climbing into that bed after a bad dream.

The next victim of the raid was the hallway closet. After many minutes of stuffing in spare blankets and washcloths, flashlights, and spare batteries, I nearly emptied the closet of all it's worth.

Pete's and my bathroom was next. In went Peter's "secret" stash of pain relievers and Melatonin. My eyes landed on the travel toothbrushes and toothpaste, and I almost reached Nirvana. *Months* I'd gone without toothpaste. Now to feel the fresh cleanse of the mint paste... I almost forgot the roll of gauze.

A guilty nerve tugged at my conscience as I smashed the boxes of pads and tampons in. The plastic trash had nowhere to go. But I doubted the monthly blood sacrifice would be much of a problem. I stopped menstruating in July. Just dried up. But a few trickles of maroon dotted my pants a few days ago, so you could never be too sure.

I returned to the open hallway at the sound of Tate's footsteps on the stairs. Our eyes met. He was still upset with me. "Where's your pantry?" He asked.

"A bit down the hall from the kitchen. Double brown doors-"

He was back downstairs before I could finish.

I stopped dead at the sight of a closed door. My bedroom. No one touched my bedroom.

I don't know why I was so surprised to see all my belongings in the exact place they were when we left, as if some magical teenage dream dust would settle over the room and make all my posters disappear.

What did I expect when coming back to my childhood bedroom? Did I expect to see myself in a third-person perspective, watching myself in some horrible coming-of-age movie? Was soft, dramatic music supposed to settle over the scene as I inspected my treasures, souvenirs and art projects?

I set the bag on my bed. I didn't make the bed before we left. I didn't clean up, either. There wasn't a point. My comforter and pillows remained discarded just as I left them after a fretful, cold night of little sleep. My last night in the house.

My attention moved to the foldable desk at the far end of my room. My laptop was still untouched, along with two nearly empty notebooks and a collection of assorted pens. I used to imagine myself as an astute businesswoman at her office desk. I would pretend my assistant came in every few minutes with coffee, messages, and later bother me with our needy clients. Those fantasies made me feel better about my 3.3 grade-point average.

Into the smaller bag went more clothes. Pants, sweatshirts, and many underwear articles. I managed to fit one more pair of durable shoes in the duffel bag. Anything in preparation for the oncoming winter months.

I rushed to the bookshelf where I kept an entire section dedicated to scented candles. Before everything, there were few possessions I prized more than my candle collection. Two large and three smaller candles made it into the bag, along with two different types of lighters. I may starve and freeze to death in that camper come winter, but at least my space will be smelling like *Cinnamon Moon* and *Wonder Berry*.

My eyes landed on two picture frames. I picked them up with each hand, studying the colors and smiling faces. Mikey and I on the Fourth of July of freshman year. Peter and I in front of the Washington Monument last year, which just looked like a sad slab of gray bricks from the perspective.

To this day, I remember both of those pictures vividly. Mikey took the picture with his phone. It wasn't until August that he finally sent it to me. We both adorned glow stick bracelets and patriotic-colored tie-dye. The neon of Peter's crazy knee-high socks proudly showed through the shadow of the Washington Monument.

I slid the two picture frames in as well, Tate's rules be damned The glass protection may serve as a weapon against vicious chipmunks.

For just a moment, I felt like things could be alright. It seemed as if everything would be okay from here on out. I would go home after all this and be back in my little corner of the world. My own safe, secure slice of Earth.

That illusion was shattered when I peeked outside. Raindrops decorated the pavement and asphalt below. The world around us was tinted smokey. It hadn't been half an hour, maybe. Tate's voice hit me from another room in the form of a very loud, very obscene swear.

"Is everything okay in there?" I shouted, peering into the hallway.

Tate jogged into the room. Two black trash bags hung off his shoulder, filled with a collection of nonperishables. Two milk jugs full of water hung from his fingers.

"Are you ready?" He demanded.

I stared out the window. The pavement was already painted darker with raindrops. "Can we make it back?"

"No. You don't want to be caught in the woods for so many miles in this-" Tate waved his arm angrily at the window. "I'm sorry. Sorry. This isn't at you. I thought we had more time," he promised. He tightened the grip on his bags. "Did your dad have a wheelbarrow or something?"

I let my head drop. Not one we can use. He let his sister's boyfriend borrow it last year and we've never seen it since."

"Dammit… *okay*. Alright. We can make something work," Tate muttered. I tripped into the hallway with him on my tail.

Getting everything out of the house was torture. Just going down the stairs, the straps turned abusive digging into my palms. The plastic food bags kept slipping through Tate's fingers. I squealed every time the heavy-duty plastic stretched. The fabric ones were so dense and heavy, I had to set them down immediately. Tate finally closed the door behind us and stared into the wet, gray world.

"What are you thinking?" I let the water drip down my hair and into every imaginable crevice of my face. In another world, I would tip my head back and let the water fill my mouth. I would let myself fill, sit on the porch step, and let the freshwater overflow from my mouth until I became a perfect stone fountain; the last testament to our family.

Tate slapped his hands on his hips. "I don't know. I thought I would come up with something on the way down here," he admitted.

I rolled my eyes, shaking a few droplets off my bangs. "We can't just stand here!" I shouted, hugging my arms close to my body. My shirt had turned near transparent, clinging to my bones in a sad heap of cotton and seeping me cold to the core. Grandma Siobhan would say I was melting away.

"I know!" Tate groaned, throwing his head down. "*Okay!* Okay. Come with me. Be quiet and keep your head down," he ordered. I must've been too stunned to move. He ushered me along impatiently. "*Come on.* Take all of this!"

It was a mad dash through the rain. Water dripped into my eyes. Hair stuck to my neck like flypaper. My fingers and shoulders begged for mercy. The handbags obstructed my knees with every jog. Three straps rubbed against my shoulders and neck, sure to leave marks for days.

We came out to the back of a red-bricked house. A single white door stood on the ground level, with a wooden staircase leading up to a door on the second level. The extended roof only allowed us six inches of shelter from the rain.

Tate set the water jugs down and banged on the door three times. No immediate response. I tried to spy through the dust and cobweb-covered basement windows. All I could see was inky blackness. A minute passed before a body formed in the door's fogged glass. It opened to reveal a girl of early high school age.

vii.

"Hi, Chris-" Tate stepped into the house, but she blocked the doorway with her arm. He sighed, peering down at his sister. "Chrissy. Let us in. It's freezing."

"No. Who is this?" Chrissy demanded, eying me. Her sandy hair was pulled back in two tiny pigtails. A grumpy scowl seemed to be permanently embedded in her cheeks. She reminded me of a stereotypical cartoonish tomboy; the one that would beat you up for squashing ants on the school playground.

"This is Vivienne. The one I've been helping for the past few weeks. Can we come in?"

"Please?" I added for good measure.

Chrissy moved to the side, gaze never tearing from my bags. "I thought you stopped bringing her food," she whispered very loudly to her brother.

"We didn't talk about this. You talked. I listened. But I never said I would stop helping her," Tate remarked, helping me pull the bags into the house before slamming the door behind me. The thud my bags made hitting the floor urged me to drop to my knees and fitfully check. Chrissy sent me a peeved glare.

"Hey!" Tate physically turned her head to look at him. "She deserves it just as much as we do."

I wanted to interject that I appreciated him opening their home to me and that I was happy to be out the minute the storm stopped. Tate sent one quick look, telling me to stay quiet and let him handle it. Another sign that he was psychic.

"Bring everything in here," he led us down the basement's narrow hall and into an even smaller closet. It took me a moment to gather it all up again. Chrissy helped me with a bag — the lightest one. Tate slid his packages to the floor, directing me to do the same. Our bounty formed one large pile on the cement floor of the closet.

Chrissy pulled Tate to the side. "Why did you bring her here?"

"Because in case you haven't noticed, it's cold and wet and she lives ten miles away! And I am not gonna let her sleep alone out here!" He exclaimed. I sunk to the back of the hallway. "I don't know why we're still having this conversation."

Footsteps clambered down the set of hidden stairs. The girl who could only be Diana appeared, rushing forward to separate Chrissy from taking a sure swing at her brother. "Hey! What are we doing?" She demanded, putting a single hand on her sister's arm. Chrissy didn't respond; only stared up at Tate with a cross of betrayal and confusion.

Diana's gaze softened as she pointed one bandaged finger in my direction. "Who is this?"

"Vivienne," Tate responded, his reappearing from thin air. "She'll be staying with us for the night because, as you can see, it's raining. Hard. Miss Vivienne has a very long walk home and it would be a shame if she tripped and died. I'm doing her a kindness, as I expect the rest of us to as well." His words were aimed at the young one.

"*Oh!* Oh my gosh, it's so nice to meet you, Vivienne!" Diana exclaimed. She rushed forward with a hug. I stiffened up, too shocked to hug her back.

Never before had I ever met such two polar sisters.

"Tate's told us so much about you. Do you really live alone in the woods? In a truck?" Diana launched an investigation. "How did you get out there?"

Her hands never left my body; roaming up and down my arms, up to my face. Diana reminded me of a nervous pediatrician inspecting a small child for maladies.

Diana stood out from her siblings. Her skin was the sweetest dark brown, sweeps of black hair bunched in a baby pink claw clip at the base of her neck. She was tall, taller than I envisioned, with shoulder blades that had yet to poke from the remaining weight. Patches of lighter skin dotted her wrist, mapping an archipelago up her forearms. Her deep eyes widened impossibly at the cuts on my hands. The brown coffee of her irises was so rich that it blended with the pupils.

Diana was, quite frankly, beautiful.

I nodded to her questions. She squealed. "Oh, my God! How long has it been?"

"Let her breathe, Dee," Tate muttered.

Diana looked back at him, looked at my startled face, and then to the floor. "Oh. Sorry." She obediently backed away.

Chrissy stared at her brother. "This is our house. Our food. She can't stay here."

He didn't look down at her. "Yes, she can. And she will."

"Why?" She shouted. Diana and I flinched at the sudden outburst. "Why does she deserve it when we've worked our asses off just to find this house, let alone the food, the supplies. *No, seriously!* Why can she suck us dry and leave us with-"

"CHRISTINE!" Tate roared. The young girl's head snapped down, either in shame or embarrassment. "Enough! Vivienne is a human being. That's why she deserves it." Tate allowed himself a deep breath before daring to speak again. His head snapped in our direction. "Is there enough food for her for the night?" He demanded Diana. She nodded.

I timidly spoke up, taking a single step forward. "I can have my own stuff. Don't go into any trouble. We spent all that time getting my own food-"

"No. You're our guest." Tate dismissed me. He turned to his youngest sister one more time after allowing himself to settle down. "Vivienne is not going anywhere. That's final. Stop acting like a child."

Chrissy had nothing to counter with. A thick, tense atmosphere settled in the basement. I felt horrible that my existence caused the family to be in such a fight... but also didn't feel so bad that the little brat was getting her head chewed off.

"I can make soup," Diana stated, breaking the tension. She looked directly at me with a warm smile, "If you want it."

Chicken and rice soup for dinner, courtesy of Diana. Warmed in a flowered pot hung precariously in the fireplace, it was my first meal from a can in three months. I think I cried a little when I used up the last of my canned food.

We all sat around the 6-seater dinner table. Tate at the head, Diana and Chrissy on one side, me facing them on the other. I positioned my chair to face the space between Diana and Chrissy. Close enough to Tate for protection should I need it, and close enough to Chrissy to prove I wasn't a biter. She seemed like one, though. Who do you think I needed Tate's protection from?

I immediately fell in love with the creaky wooden chairs. My butt grew accustomed to dirt floors and cheap plastic seats of the camper. This chunky, polished chair was a blessing on its own. It even came with a red cushion!

The conversation went left and right and up and down. I tried to stay out of it as much as possible; minimize my intrusion on their family dinner as much as possible. The family did a fine job of respecting that until Tate opened his mouth on my behalf.

"I think we need to explain some things to Vivienne," he began.

I stared into my broth, feeling two pairs of eyes boring into my skull. "Like what?" Diana prompted. I shrugged with as much nonchalance as I could muster.

"Vivienne hasn't been anywhere but her camper for four months," Tate explained, stirring his soup absently. The girls gaped. He then looked at me, pointing the spoon in my direction and letting broth fly everywhere. "What all do you know?"

Both girls' eyes honed in on me. No one put me on the spot like that since March. It was a horrid flashback to English class Socratic seminars. "Oh. Well… I know they ran low on people to run power plants by the beginning of May..."

"*Of course*, she doesn't know anything!" Chrissy threw a hand up.

"Chris."

The girl scoffed. "Tate, look at her! She's a wimp. She can't even make a supply run without you for protection!"

I sat there, frozen and shocked. It all came so quickly I couldn't compose my thoughts enough to defend myself. Though as if telepathically reading my mind, Diana and Tate came to my aid.

"We don't know that, do we? She's barely told us anything, and if you keep acting like this, I doubt she'll open up anymore," Diana insisted, putting a hand on her sister's arm. Chrissy smacked the touch away.

"You're being a child." Tate sighed.

"*What?* Cause I don't think she's telling us everything? You're smarter than this, Tate! I knew it was a mistake the first night you came home talking about a girl who-"

"Can you stop?" Diana's spoon clanged down.

I flinched at her sudden raised voice. It was so long since I'd been the bystander of a fight like this. My mom and dad used to fight like this at the dinner table about the dumbest of things as if Peter and I weren't sitting two feet away. I forgot what I used to do to tune them out...

While Tate and Diana struggled to reign in the girl, I couldn't help but wonder if she was right. Was I catastrophizing? What if Chrissy was right? I was already so ignorant about the criminals and their horrendous behavior. What if I truly knew nothing about the world anymore? How out of touch was I?

Diana lowered her voice, trying to rationalize. "You don't know what she's been through. Could you imagine living in a trailer for half a year all on your own?"

"Yes. I could. And it would be great!" Chrissy regarded me with a cold look. "Can't be any worse than living off of rats and rainwater under a single blanket every night!"

The grip on Tate's fork tightened. "You just described Vivienne's exact situation," he stated. One forehead vein bulged across his hairline. "When I found her, she was living on one meal a day and smelled rancid. She was helpless and barely surviving every twenty-four hours. Completely unequipped for the outdoors. Now look at her. Do you think that came from nowhere? That's because of me, because of us. Look me in the eyes and tell me you wish I didn't help her."

Chrissy's mouth slowly shut, lost for words. Tate inhaled deeply before opening his mouth again. "I'm going to repeat this once more and once more only. Vivienne is just as worthy of our help as anyone else. If I hear you make one more remark against her livelihood I will throw you out in the rain and lock the door, so help me, Christine."

A blind threat on his behalf, I knew. But I appreciated the gesture, and it shut Chrissy up.

No one else dared to speak for a minute. It seemed that the next person who opened their mouth would get a soup spoon thrown at their head.

"Why don't you move back to your own house?" Diana eventually asked me. I barely looked up. "I don't mean anything against your camper — I'm sure it's a lovely little setup you have out there. But why not come back? Why not make it easier on yourself?"

I cleared my throat, taking a small sip of soup. The broth lit up my tastebuds, almost distracting. "I got scared for a long time. I was scared of returning without my parents — who are *in fact* dead. I know. I checked. I'd already survived so long out there it just… didn't seem necessary," I admitted. "And now it's kinda more comfortable. Especially… after coming out here today…"

Diana nodded, smiling her beautiful smile. If not for my better judgment, I could've melted on the spot. "Well, you're here now. That's all that matters."

Tate cleared his own throat, grabbing the attention of all of us. "Now that we have *all that* out of our systems, let's fill Vivienne in on what we know. There's no reason she has to stay dumb — no offense."

"None taken."

He sent a quick wink my way, empty of any humor or good nature. I recognized that look on his face only once before. He was tired. Tired and ready to abandon all responsibilities of adulthood.

"So, what do you know?" Diana clasped her hands on the table. I stared at her dumbly.

"She means, what did the news sites tell you?" Tate clarified. "Did you get your information from 24-hour broadcasting or firsthand accounts? They told two completely different stories."

I scanned my memory for anything meaningful I remembered from TV or the radio. Most of it was conspiracy or desperate politics.

"Oh… I guess… nothing," I muttered.

Tate shook his head. "Don't feel bad about that. It makes sense," he assured me. "It took us a while to sift through the lies and propaganda. Anyone with money did anything in their power to cover up their tracks." Tate warily sighed, letting his utensil splash into the last dregs of soup. "And the stories didn't coincide, either! Every one of those politicians and superstars and CEOS spouted nonsense from their own asses, never bothering to corroborate."

Chrissy propped her calf on the edge of the table. "Then people believed the first things they heard and spread that. But someone who heard something completely different got mad and started a fight. It was so stupid."

"And there was the deliria," Diana chimed. Chrissy and Tate scoffed. "There was an outbreak of malaria and E. coli in South America for a little bit. And you know how you can have psychotic episodes? People were making up these crazy scenarios. And all they had to do was shout it from the right rooftop and someone picked it up and spread it!"

"And the rich ones didn't help. Not until the stock market crashed." Chrissy snapped her fingers.

"The stock market crashed?"

She nodded curtly. "But no one cared. No one with their heads out of their asses."

I blinked, completely clueless as to where they were going. "Huh now?"

"When it all started getting rough, celebrities and all those important people went into hiding," Diana continued. "They hid together in their million-dollar bunkers meant to outlive the nuclear apocalypse. But little did they know, they had moles."

When everything originally happened, I was silly enough to think that "important people" were going down with us.

"You remember the different factions that targeted privileged groups in the very beginning? Third-generation rich families, big company CEOs, nepotism babies, et cetera?" Tate asked, waving his spoon. A couple of droplets of broth flew across the table. I nodded.

"Well, they had an opportunity to take it all down from the inside."

Words escaped me. "Like- like *V for Vendetta*?"

"Sure, like *V for Vendetta*."

"What's that?" Chrissy whispered. Diana shook her head.

Tate picked a lump of lint off his jacket. "Essentially, it was an underground, wider-scale civil rights movement. However, they targeted the entire system of organized, hierarchal societies rather than one core factor. I don't think that's what they meant to do. But it got out of hand. It was a war of moles and double agents. No one could trust anyone."

The news we watched at the beginning stressed wartime and terrorism. They called the Middle East villains, or the communist autocracies were putting psychotic chemicals in the water supply. But that was regular. That's been a constant of mankind since we put a microphone in his hand.

I didn't think much about it at the time because it just... happened. No one called it World War 3 because there was no "war". There were no allied powers. Borders dissolved and social groups disbanded. People went rogue and radical all around. The entire incident just... *was*. And no one could tell the bad guys from the good.

"So it's safe to assume Rihanna is-?" I made a slicing motion over my neck. Chrissy shot a glance my way as if it were a personal offense to her that I opened my mouth. My hand dropped. "Dang. I was holding out for her."

Diana pushed her empty bowl away. "After that, everyone lost faith in everyone. Anyone you turn to has an ostracizing opinion about some social group or another. You know how it is. But some stuff you didn't see if you lived in a small town like this-" She jabbed one thumb at the window. "After, no one knew who was next. Anyone in a big city was running around with imaginary targets on their backs."

Chrissy shook her head at the memory. "No more neighborly comradery or compassion. As far as anyone knew, your landlord who baked brownies every Christmas could be one of them."

"One of them?" I repeated.

"The ones that took it too far. But to them, we're the bad guys. They're the bad guys to us because they threatened our ways of life. To them, it was the exact opposite. You see the problem?" Tate pointed to himself. "You thought I was bad the first day we met. You ran and fought. You couldn't have known any better and were scared. It's the exact same, but running from all directions."

"And it isn't getting any better. Not where we've been, at least," Chrissy grumbled.

Diana held a hand up. "That's not entirely true. It depends. Some people are just trying to survive through the day. Others are still trying to lead a revolt of their own-"

"Yeah, and it still sucks!" Chrissy cut her sister off.

"HEY!" Tate shut their bickering down. The girls lowered their heads, both ashamed to get so caught up.

I watched the yellow broth stir and flow with the motion of my spoon. "But how did it start? Did enough guys just one day say, 'Hey, let's bomb this bad place'?"

"It's always more complicated than that. But I don't know." Tate shrugged.

I let my eyes unfocus out the alcove dining room windows. Violent winds pushed a deflated basketball across the driveway.

War is bad, kids. Don't fight.

"Didn't you say you guys met forty-something people before coming here? And were none of them civil?" I looked up at Tate.

He nodded shortly. "Some were. Others weren't. As she said, it's a toss of the dice."

"Everyone is still nervous about meeting new people," Diana explained, taking one final sip of soup. She wasn't halfway done; privileged with her soup supply. "There are little neighborhoods — if you can call them that. But everyone stays to themselves and fights over food. We're back to the dark ages."

Chrissy scoffed. "Literally."

Diana slid her bowl towards Chrissy, who'd been eying it since the discussion began. "People are scared. They don't know whether new people in town will try to kill them or give them clean water."

"Like you." I dared to smile at Chrissy. Her cheeks reddened, though not angrily. Progress.

We were a disaster of our own making. We dwindled ourselves down to such a minuscule population. Not natural disasters. Not cosmic invaders from the next galaxy over. Ourselves.

Simply put, mankind went cuckoo.

The most ironic part of all they were saying was that the "bad guys" could've easily been such a small percentage of the world. Maybe it wasn't "mankind", but every crazy Uncle Joe lumped together and told to have fun. And they succeeded.

Or maybe that wasn't the case. After all, these three were speculating based on what enough people told them that lined up. Maybe the truth was the complete opposite.

It's safe to assume that the four hundred million of us left simply didn't know enough people to be caught so far in the crossfire.

The rain stopped shortly after dinner ended. Tate sent the girls to bed before midnight. Diana gave us both goodnight hugs. The smile it drew from me was enough to balance out the withering stare Chrissy bore into the back of my skull.

I sat on the couch before the fireplace, legs crossed on the cool leather. The flames warmed the front of my body; a mother's embrace for a scraped knee. Tate approached from behind, armed with two lukewarm beers. He tapped my shoulder with one. My head jerked up, staring at the dark glass.

"Are those my dad's?" I questioned, slowly taking it from his hand. He'd done me the courtesy of taking the cap off. "You took beer on our lifesaving supply run?"

He took a quick swig, staring into the firelight. "Necessary tools of survival, my friend."

I glanced back, slowly setting the bottle down. Maybe a year ago

I'd have jumped at the opportunity to drink my dad's booze underage. Now it was the last thing on my mind. After he revealed criminals in town, I couldn't shake the feeling of my mind needing to be at its sharpest.

"Chrissy isn't a fan of me," I chuckle, watching him take a seat on the floor not several feet away.

Tate shook his head, barely grinning. "Don't take it personally. Chrissy's not a fan of anyone. She's fifteen. They come prepackaged like that."

"What are you gonna do when that battery runs out?" I asked, pointing to the watch on his wrist. The flames barely illuminated little hands that read 11:43.

"What?"

He was still mad at me.

"Like, what if it dies in the middle of the night and you can't know what time to turn it to when you replace the batteries?"

He shrugged. "Guess."

I stared at him, begging the old smile I remembered to come back. Never before had I seen him so weighted. The man who once served as the sunshine on my dark, hungry days now frowned into the crackling flames before us.

Was it all a facade? I thought acting was a practice of the past now that no one had time for theater. Tate was good at it, though.

My eyes moved to focus on my shoes. It was my fault. He had yet to look at me the same since our argument in my house. His anger was understandable. I wouldn't forgive me either.

"Tate?" I whispered. My eyes stayed trained on my shoes. "How many people have you killed?"

A shadow partially covered his face. He cleared his throat, sucking in a deep, shuddering breath. "Six."

This was wrong. One part of me wished it to be a misunderstanding; a prank to test what I could handle. The other part expected a number he stopped counting long ago.

Six was too high a number, regardless. Too high for any twenty-two-year-old.

Tate tossed a wood splinter across the room. "The first one was in New York. We were mugged. One of them tried to take advantage of Diana." My throat was starched dry. "I just... blacked out, you know? I couldn't think of anything but him and the gun in my hand."

I shook my head, finally looking up at his grim expression. "I'm sorry- you don't have to talk about it if you-"

"No, it's okay. I need to get it off my chest," Tate admitted with a morbid chuckle.

Silence settled over the room. A cockroach ran over the floorboards.

"It gets easier over time," he promised. I closed my eyes, sickened at the thought. "You kinda... numb yourself to the conscious knowledge of what you're doing. You learn to look away from their eyes. You learn the right time to let go of their neck so you don't have to feel *it*."

"You suffocated them?" My voice came out with a crack I was sure shook the whole house.

"Twice."

I should consider myself lucky for how long I kept myself away from other people. And especially lucky for my first interaction to be with someone as gracious as Tate. A lot of people weren't so lucky.

He shook his head, waving a hand wildly. "I'm sorry. This is bad. You don't need to hear this." Tate dismissed himself.

"It's okay. It's therapeutic to talk about this stuff. I don't mind it that much," I assure him, managing a small smile.

He breathed deeply, calming himself. "Thanks, Viv."

A second uncomfortable silence settled. The orange and red flames died down. Flickering, licking away at the timber.

Flames licked at the old tire shop. Rubber fumes permeated the air, stinking nostrils and sending black plumes to the sky. *Paul's Tires* had been running since 1976, opened and owned for thirty years by Paul Benford. He retired and passed the business on to his youngest son, Christian, shortly after the turn of the century — only because his other son was a dedicated man of the Navy. Christian Benford was a man of many scandals in town; marrying two women within eight years and decorated with a rumor that he spent his Thursday evenings sleeping with a third-grade teacher. A common visitor of the Lutheran church, Christian Benford brought in more profit than his father and blew it all at the casino. But Paul's Tires maintained its reputation as the most trusted place in town for tires of every size and pressure.

Paul made it a staple of the business never to sell to a larger organization. But there were rumors, chatters among the airwaves, that Christian was planning to sell the business name to *O'Reilly Auto Parts* if the automobile economy stayed on the high trajectory. An O'Reilly van was spotted in the back parking lot of *Paul's Tires* on a Monday afternoon. Three days later, the four walls went up in flames.

Christian wasn't at the office when the smoke began flooding from the storage closet. His wife was. Delia Benford's body was found the next day trapped under the front desk, whose metal structure acted as an oven around her.

My dad and I walked past the ruins of *Paul's Tires* after the second day. Christian, Paul, Mrs. Benford, and the five-year-old child searched the rubble. The five-year-old girl played with a stretchy toy, incessantly complaining about her feet hurting. My dad asked if they needed any help. We spent the next two hours sorting through the burnt carnage. Paul offered to buy us lunch. My dad turned him down, which made Mrs. Benford sob more.

Back in the living room, I grabbed the bottle by my knee and brought it to my lips. It tasted horrible and did nothing to lift my mood.

"I'm sorry I didn't warn you about the gangs and looters earlier," Tate finally spoke up. There it was again; the sickeningly sincere voice. "It's a sick world we're living in. You shouldn't be going in headfirst oblivious."

I scooted closer to him, gauging his reaction if it was okay. "Did something happen up here? Is that why you're so nervous?" I dared to ask. Tate looked over at me, studying my face.

"They prey on girls. Not women, girls. It's the way it's always been… and I guess it's the way it'll stay," was all he said.

My eyes lowered. The vulnerable man sitting next to me was not the man I saw in the woods that first day with a rifle in hand. This was nothing more than a man wanting to protect his sisters and a sad, ignorant girl he found living in a camper.

"I'm sorry for doubting you earlier. It just struck me odd that you understood so much. But I do trust you."

"Already forgiven." Tate lightly punched my arm.

I smiled into the firelight. Feeling brave, I picked up my beer bottle. After a moment of mental preparation, I let the amber liquid fall into my mouth a second time. It was worse knowing what was coming. I coughed into the fireplace. Ash got in my mouth, making my eyes prickle with tiny tears. Tate laughed out loud, taking the alcohol from me.

viii.

I never thought I would feel so out of place sleeping in a regular home, on a regular couch, than I did that night.

The rest of the night after our conversation was a blur. I remember drinking, but not much. Tate's face flickered in and out of my brain, clouded by fireplace smoke and the wooden wall paneling.

Tate left me in the living room shortly after one. I quickly wished he hadn't, but didn't dare to leave my place on the couch and ask for company. Neither did I have the willpower to move my legs more than an inch a minute.

We moved the couch to be closer to the fireplace, but it did nothing. The tip of my nose was frigid. My teeth still chattered if I let my jaw relax for too long. The three blankets were more smothering than comforting.

The leather couch almost made my worries seep away. Never had I felt such cushioning. Such light stuffing. A leather-covered cloud. My muscles relaxed, releasing all the tension and letting my spine decompress. It was comforting to know I could freeze to death among the leather just inches too far from the fire's heat.

I imagined I kept sinking. Sinking further and further and further and further down. Until the couch ate me.

Sleep was an even worse story. I was trapped in the gray area between consciousness and deep dreams. That torturous gray area where you don't know if you're alive or dead, lost in the unpredictable wasteland that is a memory-filled dream. A nightmare. My muscles were useless to toss and turn. My words were powerless to fight the monsters creeping into the edges of my brain from all sides.

What felt like days later, Diana shook me awake. Tate was already packing my bags into a wheelbarrow he found in the neighbor's shed. Diana said I had more than enough time to make it home before dark, but there was no harm in getting an early start.

Easy enough for her to say. Every muscle in my body ached. My neck was the worst of it, having been pressed against the armrest for the century-long night. My eyes begged to stay closed. The front of my skull was ready to crack open. Somewhere in the mess of sitting up I kicked over the glass beer bottle. It rolled away into the abyss beyond the couch.

I was a mess. I could barely stand without needing to throw up. There was a lot of whining. A lot of whimpering and falling back on the couch: my safe place. Diana babysat me while Tate was outside. She forced water down my throat, banged pots over my head until I fully woke. She had to *literally* smack the sense into me (which was quickly apologized for).

"I cannot believe he's letting you go home like this," Diana muttered, dragging me down to the basement where Tate was waiting with my luggage.

I caught a glance of the open doorway to Chrissy's room. She was still asleep, oblivious to my departure. "I must've told him to last night." I shrugged.

Diana shook her head, sighing deeply. "Still. At least let you rest from the hangover before such a trip."

"I'm not hungover," I mumbled. I could feel her suspicious glare. Before we reached the door where Tate waited, I turned to her. "Be honest with me. Are you okay with all this?"

"All what?"

I flicked my head toward the basement door's frosted glass. Tate's silhouette was dark on the other side. "Him helping me. Bringing me food and supplies. Letting me sleep here. Letting me eat your food."

Diana brought a hand to my bicep. She had the remarkable skill of drawing you to meet her eyes without a single word. "Tate has good judgment. Better than any of us." She smiled.

"Do you trust me?"

"I trust him, and he trusts you."

My eyes lowered. "I feel like I should be roughing it out there on my own. Like I should have this figured out by now," I admitted. If I maintained eye contact too long, I was afraid I would see something I feared in her too. Fear of the unknown.

Without warning, she grabbed my wrist. I let it happen. "Hey, that's totally normal. Don't judge your own survival instincts off of Tate. That boy was climbing trees and shooting birds from across a field before I was even born." This made her giggle. "Point is: you stayed alive as long as you did without him. That's all that matters."

I shrugged with forced nonchalance. "How old are you, anyway?"

"Nineteen. Twenty in February."

"Nice… I'm eighteen. Didn't know I was eighteen until last week."

And suddenly, I didn't want to leave anymore.

"If you're worried about Chrissy, don't be. Her bitterness with the world is nothing targeted at you. She needs something to be mad at. Doesn't make it right, but that's the way she is. We need to let her figure things out on her own," Diana assured me, rubbing the back of my hand. "You know about the five stages of grief?" I grunted. I could see where the lecture was going from a mile away. "Chrissy's stuck in the anger stage. Ever since we left Alabama, she's been stuck in it. She'll deny it if you tell her. She thinks she's accepted the world as it is-"

"But if she did, she would accept that there are other people on the planet who need food and shelter," I muttered. My eyes tossed back on their own accord, immediate regret making me wish Diana didn't see.

Diana nodded slowly. "I'm sorry."

"It's not your fault she-"

The door swung open, displaying a mildly annoyed Tate leaning in the doorframe.

"I want both of you to know that I've been hearing all of this-" he motioned with the free hand between us "-and it's frankly disgusting. You; stop flirting with my sister." He pointed one finger at me, then at Diana. "You; just… *don't*. Okay? Gross. This is gross."

My lower jaw unhinged from the top. Diana stared at her brother with eyes wide as saucers.

"Are we done?" Tate waved me forward. "Say your goodbyes. Try not to miss each other too much."

Diana held a rigid hand out to me. "Hope you get home well," she whispered, the friendly tone in her voice evaporating.

I slowly accepted her hand. "Thank you. You too."

Why did you just say that? Why, why, why?

I was outside with Tate, the door closed and separating me from Diana, before I could mentally berate myself any further.

He didn't say anything. He didn't do anything, other than stare at the rocks between our feet. I waited until I saw his sister's silhouette retreat upstairs before speaking.

"Who pissed in your cereal this morning?" The words barely escaped my gritted teeth.

"No one."

"Did I do something?" I brought a hand to my chest. Tate closed his eyes. "Seriously, though. I don't remember the majority of last night. I'm tired and nothing is happening up here." I jabbed a finger at my head. "So if I said or did something, I don't know."

Tate shook his head, waving me away. "No. It wasn't you. I get short when nervous," he admitted. "That was uncalled for. I don't care if or how you talk to her. It's none of my business."

"What are you nervous about?"

"Probably the same thing you are."

"Fair." I stepped up to the wheelbarrow, admiring his work of piling everything in with a master's planning. "And I wasn't flirting with Diana. In case you secretly do care," I waited a moment before retorting.

Tate scoffed. "Sure you weren't," he chuckled, peering down at me with a cracked grin. The bad mood was slowly lifting. I could see it in his eyes. "You definitely still have some in your system."

I turned my back, hiding the heat rising to my cheeks. "I did *not* get drunk!"

"Yes, my friend, you did." Tate clapped me on the shoulder, a habit he still had yet to break around me. As always, I shoved his hand off. "You have enough Ibuprofen in there to last you for a while, but if you dare use it all up today, Vivienne, I swear-"

"I won't! I promise."

Faithful to yesterday, two trash bags, two canvas bags, and one duffel bag. He couldn't find ropes or latches to fix everything down. They would be precarious to keep contained when we reached divots and tree roots.

Perhaps it was the hangover. A dark fog hung over the backyard. A stiff air suffocated me. I was on the other end of Deja vu. That very moment was to be the moment some future Me would swear she'd experienced before, but never did. It was all a dream. A fake.

Tate cleared his throat when we'd waited long enough for the grass to grow. He held out a handgun, saying nothing. I backed into the wheelbarrow, furiously shaking my head. "*Nope!* No, thank you!" I shouted, pushing his arm away.

"Just hear me out-"

"No! Where were you even keeping that!" He pointed the barrel of the pistol to his rifle propped up on the side of the house. "I… just… *no*. I don't trust myself with a gun, Tate."

He sighed, holding it down. "Viv, you need actual protection. If you and I could cross paths, someone a lot less kind could come along too."

"Why now? I've managed fine enough so far."

He tilted his head, unamused with me. "Have you? Have you *really*?"

"I don't want it!"

"At least consider it. I'll teach you how to use it; how to make good work of it."

"I've made good use of my steak knives. They haven't let me down yet."

"No, but what do you think they'll do against a stronger man?" Tate countered, sharp and unwavering. His abruptness silenced me. "You never had to worry about shit like this before 'cause you never came here! You never risked being seen by a gang or rogue. But I let you risk all that without telling you. That's my fault! And I'm not letting you go back out there without proper protection."

My eyes fell to the ground. I wanted to tell him it wasn't his fault. Whatever happened to me was not his fault. It was at the tip of my tongue for so long — an eternity. But the words never left my mouth.

"I'm not letting you leave without it," Tate insisted. I shook my head slower, eyeing the black metal in his hand. "Either take it willingly or I hide it in all that. Your choice." He motioned in circles to the trash bags behind me with the barrel of the gun.

"I can throw it out once I leave."

Tate nodded slowly, leaning his back against the brick wall. "You can do that. But you won't."

He's right. I won't.

Tate took my silence as submission. "It's on safety now. Make sure you turn it off if you try shooting something," he instructed, showing me how to turn safety on and off.

I held my hand out. The weight he placed in my palm equaled a thousand elephants. My fingers closed around the handle. The grip rubbed deep into my calloused fingers.

It didn't feel right. Didn't feel real.

"If you won't take it for protection, at least take it for hunting. Imagine how easy your squirrels and rabbits could be if you could just…" He mimed the gun going off with two fingers.

I didn't respond, only able to stare at the weapon in my hand. Tate motioned for me to put it in the wheelbarrow. I made an effort to cover it with my backpack.

I don't use guns. I don't have them, I don't touch them, I don't use them.

"-to take care of before I can visit again. But you should be set for a few weeks on your own," Tate's voice filtered back into my mind.

I looked back. "Huh?"

"Are you ready to go?" He repeated, over-enunciating his words. "You'll be fine on your own. Right?"

"Oh! Oh yeah. I'll be okay." I rubbed a growing knot in my shoulder.

"Really? 'Cause we don't have to leave immediately. It just may be better to take advantage of as much sunlight as possible. But if you're too tired-"

I cleared my throat, stepping between the two wheelbarrow handles. "No, let's not do that. I've overstayed my welcome."

"No, you haven't-"

"Tate. Let's go." With a struggle, I dislodged the wheel from its braking spot between two rocks. I slowly pulled several feet away from the house before glancing back at him. "You coming?"

I heard him approach from behind with a loud sigh. "Want me to help with that?" He offered, already grasping one hand around a handle.

I smacked his hand. "No!"

We made it ten minutes down the road, barely into the trees, before I asked him to take over. He happily obliged.

ix.

Tate never said anything as we unpacked my things. He never commented on my collection of personal keepsakes or the pills that would only be suitable for a 50-year-old diabetic. I figured they could come to some use eventually. One way or another.

He made sure the gun stayed with me. Of the twenty words he said to me before leaving, three of them were, "Don't lose that." I later hid it from myself in the truck's glove compartment.

Tate left that evening. That was the last I saw of him for weeks.

We made a deal. Tate agreed never to come back unless it was an emergency. He had his own priorities to take care of. I agreed not to kill myself, but also to go back once winter hit. That was Tate's one term. The instant I found the winter weather uncomfortable, I had to go back and share their proper shelter.

Desperation begged me to go back. Self-doubt pleaded with me to cut my losses and admit that I could never make it on my own. But something in my gut said it wouldn't be much different in that house than it would be in my camper. My pride was tired of relying on someone else for my survival.

So I stayed. I stuck it out, desperate to cling to the one piece of driftwood connecting me to my old life: the camper.

I kept track of everything he taught me over the past month. He taught me how to properly wield my knives and the quickest, cleanest ways to kill prey. During the few rainy days when we were stuck in the camper, he taught me how to recognize poisonous plants and how to properly sterilize drinking water. Now was my opportunity to put these newfound skills to the test.

With Tate always around, I knew it would be forty-eight hours at best before he came back and I would be saved. It didn't matter how I messed up or how injured I got, Tate was sure to come back the next day and fix everything. Now he was gone.

I never deserved Tate. So I made a promise to myself to start deserving him.

I could feel the weather cooling. The first frost was bound to creep up without warning.

Tate told me to go back to the house. He made me promise to go back the instant the first snowflake fell. Unfortunately, keeping promises was a skill I learned later in life.

My nights were filled with paranoia. Wincing, screaming, jumping at every sound. What forest creatures used to bring me peace and serenity now made my hair stand up. Made my hand grip tighter on the end of my steak knife.

What if we were followed? What if they were waiting for him to go back, and upon realizing he would not, would they make their strike?

Tate talked about these bad people as if they were a cult. A doomsday society like I read about in old books. Whoever they were, Tate had to kill one, or multiple, to protect his family. That was all I needed to draw my own conclusions.

There was no way to know I wasn't being irrational. That's what got me. While my theories were unlikely, they were not impossible. For all I knew, they could be hunting me down as I lit the candles every night.

Second only to winter, that became my biggest fear. Discovery. Discovery by someone who was not as kind as Tate.

It wasn't until the fourth day I took the gun out of the truck. If anyone was going to find me in my home, they were going to find a bullet to the face as well.

My first biggest mistake came from water. Day five.

I already knew how to boil bacteria out of water; Tate taught me to do it better. He taught me how to know when it was safe, not just a wild game of guesswork. I guess I didn't do such a good job.

It was on the morning of the fifth day when I felt a twist in my gut. I had to curl up on the moss to calm the cramps in my abdomen. My first assumption was a period. That was a negative. Pathetic whimpers escaped my lips as I pulled myself back to the trailer.

My next poop came out loose. Then the nausea and vomiting came.

The waterborne poisoning plagued me for two days. During those two days, I only dragged myself out of bed to use the natural loo and stab a small animal. Shivers made practical use of the knives dangerous. What urine I managed to trickle out was foggy and tainted brown. Once, I swear I caught a drop of red spread through the discharge. The fever racking through my body led me to dizzy spurts and sweating my clothes moist. At the end of the second day, I hurled in the fire pit. My "lawn" smelled of dehydrated vomit the next time I cooked dinner.

I had to hide the gun from myself again, just for a few hours, during a particularly rough episode. I was disgusted with my water and with myself. The thing that was supposed to keep my body going was cutting me down bit by bit, making me want to melt away and be absorbed by my blankets forever.

Ironically, the best way to cleanse your body of bacteria is with water. Nature can be brutal like that.

A twig snapped early one morning and snapped me awake so fast that my leg got caught in the blankets trying to fight my way out of bed. My face planted directly onto the disgusting floor. A sharp bang reverberated through the side of my skull, which would end up bruising for the rest of the week.

Stomping outside. Grunts and heavy breathing. They were right next to me; up and down, inside, all around me.

I remained frozen as the sounds persisted on the other side of the wall. My ear pressed against the aluminum wall, ignoring the thump of my own beating heart, trying to distinguish the intruder's movements.

It wasn't a person. It couldn't be. No one on their way to murder me would make so much noise. Unless they knew I would think this and would let my guard down…

During the night, my gun had fallen to the floor. When I fell, a foot pushed it far from the safety of my hand. Honing my ears on the window, I gradually slid myself across the musty floor. Searching blindly on the floor and refusing to tear my eyes from the curtain, my fingers eventually closed over the cool metal. An ache stretched over my upper back in the effort to pull myself up while making impossibly little noise. I brought it up to my face just enough to check the safety. Off.

A single finger stroked the neck of the gun. I could feel my heart in my throat. Every other muscle in my body was too weak to function.

My eyes peeked through the one inch I allowed the curtain to reveal. A large brown creature blocked the majority of the landscape, its broad antlers reaching to the treetops. He wasn't interested in the camper trailer or the truck.

Moving the curtain back a few more inches, I set the weapon down. The moose made no notice of me. Could he even see me through the glass? Had the camper been in the exact spot for so long, the wildlife population accepted it as a part of their home?

Feeling confident to expose myself entirely, I pulled the curtain back halfway — to reveal a second moose. This one was slightly smaller and donned much less impressive antlers.

A sly grin crept across my cheeks. I had never seen wild moose, much less this close. Less than twenty feet from the side of the trailer they stood, inspecting my fire pit and beaten track from pacing relentlessly through troubled thoughts. They didn't seem too curious about the road, which was beginning to overgrow so much you wouldn't know its former purpose.

Still, I dared not to make a sound. Something told me they could sense my heartbeat through the trailer wall. They chose not to acknowledge me only because they knew we were on the same team.

As I watched them, I allowed myself to reflect on the world. On what the last year left behind for the remaining people of Earth.

I hope a newborn future society reads this and doesn't remember or understand anything I'm about to explain. I hope we do better.

Over the years and years since Western society decided all land was our land, animals learned to fear us. They learned to fear man-made objects and anyone in their territory they deemed a threat. Which, thanks to hunting and disrespectful tourists, was everyone.

It wasn't just the West. It was any placeholder of economic power. We wanted more property and more buildings for our ever-growing population. But the Earth only has so much space, and humans kept wanting more. We destroyed habitats and entire ecosystems for wood and corn products to make our precious, cheap plastic goods. It was essential to support such an astronomical population.

Almost eight billion people! We were meeting our carrying capacity. And each person needed so much *stuff*. Humans became so addicted to their things.

I was guilty of it too. Still am. We never wanted to let it go. That's why so many people blew off their lottery winnings and became destitute in less than a decade. We cannot simply take a little. It's too hard. It goes against everything society taught us.

A first-world country was determined by how industrialized they were. How technologically advanced, how many urban areas, the gross domestic product, how educated the general population was. First-world countries took up space. They used resources, renewable and not. I heard an estimation in a science class that if we stayed at our current rate of consumption and production, it would require seven Earths for every country to become fully industrialized. Seven Earths! We don't have seven Earths, only the one.

Materialism. Unsustainability. Miles of trash line the coastlines. Fast fashion created to be worn once and discarded for the sake of a cute video. Oil spills and fast food wrappers thrown out the truck window. Poaching the last member of a critically endangered species to sell on the black market. Thousands of sea creatures dead every day, suffocating on our garbage that has nowhere to go.

We were the farthest developed species on the planet with powers no mortal man deserved. Left and right we watched countless other species drop off as a product of our own doing, and so few cared. We as the mighty humans had our problems to deal with. We had taxes and civil rights to bother us, much less care about rhinoceroses and tigers.

How dare a moose or a bear stand on land that is rightfully the property of a multibillionaire relaxing in his fourth tropical island mansion?

How dare they have the audacity to eat from the trees that could support the entire city of Milwaukee for a week? The Milwaukeeans need that!

We even did this with fellow humans! Indigenous tribes were thrown aside and abused for centuries because they dared to occupy land someone else had a "right" to.

They had something we wanted. We took it. Survival of the richest.

It was a horrible system that countless refused. I do believe that people are good at heart, but it is so easy to be selfish. It's fun. Anyone with the power to do such doesn't see greed as anything out of the ordinary.

After all these things, the two moose didn't fear me. That made sense. But they didn't fear me. Me or my human tools.

I had a feeling after an hour of watching them that I could walk right to the foot of my door, sit on the bottom step, and they would only be mildly startled. The enormous creatures could stomp me to a bloody pulp if they so felt like it. But they wouldn't. I was just another moving object in their world.

This changed the entire dynamic. The food chain didn't disappear overnight. Creatures still wanted to survive, just like humans. We were equal in that dynamic. One part of that equation just happened to be more successful.

I would be lying if I said the moose didn't scare me. If you've never seen a moose, whether it be a picture or in real life, they are gigatons. Pictures could never do them justice. They're not big in the way an elephant is big or the way a blue whale is big. It makes sense why those animals are so big. And their proportions make sense. But a moose is an entirely different story.

You can never fully understand how insignificant you are as a tiny little human compared to the brute might of a fully grown moose. Especially with a full set of antlers. Elephants are acceptably large. Polar bears are acceptably large. A moose seems like it was once a good size, then it mutated after years of ingesting steroids in the water and supersized.

It's even worse after winter and they've shed their old pair of antlers. Seeing a moose walking around with a bare head is so humorous it almost seems bad to laugh. The moose might notice and break your ribs for making fun of him.

I would also be lying if I said endless nights without sleep were doing good things to my mental state. Now that it was solidified that there was really something ready to attack in the woods, every sound had me looking over my shoulder.

I was bathing myself in the deeper part of the river the next morning when I realized one thing: I'd been living in the same spot in the woods for six months and never once did I see a wolf. I knew they were in Maine. I knew they lived in the woods.

What if I didn't see them, but they saw me?

I swatted at a bug on my thigh as it tried to dig into my skin. Its little bug guts made a clear slime on the palm of my hand.

An unexpected struggle of camp life is finding a perfect angle to hold my dinner cooking stick. Back in June, I spent several hours scraping the bark off a two-foot-long thin branch. It was now beautifully smooth and my greatest tool for dinner time. Holding it steady got too tedious and impossible. Multiple times the stick and my dinner would slide right through my grip and headfirst into the flames. There is hardly anything sadder than watching your hard-worked-for dinner burn to an unrecognizable crisp before your feet.

The fire offered a familiar, soothing warmth to combat the cooling outside air. The sun was setting earlier every night. That, or I was waking up later in the morning. Probably both.

The pistol rested only a foot from my thigh. I didn't let it wander off anymore. The farthest it ever got in the last three days was during the river bath — on the beach, just ten feet away from the safety of my hand.

My robin was almost done when something barked in the near distance. A clear dog bark. My head snapped up. The hand that was inspecting the bird meat dropped it to the ground.

Do wolves bark? Do they just howl?

Of course, they don't bark. Stupid question.

…But do they?

A series of long, dramatic barks and yowls hit me from the trees ahead. My hand went to the weapon at my side. My fire was the only source to cast light over the increasingly dark evening landscape.

Slowly, my eyes dared to part from the tree line to check the safety. Off.

Something was running towards me. I could hear its paws hit the ground.

My entire body convulsed, leaping up without my permission. I nearly fell straight back, my elbows breaking my fall. The impact shattered my chest, sending shooting pain into my shoulders and rib cage. Air struggled to come as I pushed myself back and back until the cool metal of the trailer wall hit my back.

What little breath returned to my lungs picked up. The hand that held the gun shivered in the dead, cold nerves.

So many noises. So much closing in from all sides.

Wind whipping the branches. Wolves. Bugs crawling around and on me. Unknown feet bounding towards me. Panic bubbling in my stomach. Wolves. Bird audiences in the trees. A creature drawing closer, its heat radiating closer with every second. My own hammering heartbeat in my ears. Wolves.

Something animalistic panted nearby. Right in front. In my face.

My eyes jammed shut. My arm threw itself out at an odd angle. Acting on its own, my finger closed around the trigger and pulled.

Cannon fire. Deafened ears. Ringing.

Silence.

I know my wrist flew back with the kick, but all I could register was the impact of the bullet on flesh. A shrill bark. A body falling to the ground.

The bang still resonating in my eardrums, I threw the firearm down and rushed to the animal. It had fallen to its side, staring distantly at the ground. A domestic dog — wild only after months of living as such. At least Tate didn't lie; some pets did make it out.

My single bullet hit his neck. Maroon blood dribbled from the open wound, down his dark fur, onto the dirt below. His torso rising and falling was slow and laborious. All remaining energy was spent trying to hold his head up; only a few inches off the dirt. A low, pitiful sound escaped his mouth.

A hand slapped my mouth. His dark, solemn eyes caught mine. He knew he was dying.

I ran a hand gently down his back, scratching behind his ears with my other hand. It was the one thing I could do. Comfort him. Let him know he wasn't alone anymore. I moved my hand under his head, hoping to take the weight and allow him to relax. He sighed.

He still wore a collar. The dark green fabric was battered and bruised from months of efforts to get it off. I couldn't read the name tag from that angle without removing a hand, which I refused to do.

As a last-ditch effort to communicate with him, I began singing. My voice low and gentle as a breeze, I begged him to understand. I always believed animals could understand us, especially pets.

One last desperate whimper hit before he gave up. The weight of his head fell entirely into my hand. The blood soon stopped, as did his heart.

I let his head down as gently as possible. My muscles wanted to give out. My entire body begged to collapse and fail just like his. But I couldn't. If I killed an innocent creature and did nothing... I don't know what I would be. What I would do with myself. That was what I told the angel and demon on my shoulders as I removed the collar and wiped the grime off the tag. Fresh blood got on my skin when I was careless to avoid it. Warm, sticky.

Gizmo. His name was Gizmo. He lived at 2358 Cherry Creek. That was in Point Whallsburge — at least 40 miles from my town.

Giving him one last pat on the stomach, I rose to my feet.

X.

Fifteen days passed. That makes twenty-four days of regaining trust in myself.

Berries became more challenging to find in bushes. Animals would soon go into hiding. I started greeting my mornings with a runny nose and numb fingers. One night I brought the fire up to the side of the truck and slept in the backseat with the door open. Half the animal kingdom joined me in the truck that night.

The first week back on my own was a disaster. A dumpster fire, if you will (if you don't remember/know what a dumpster is, imagine a box where everything nasty and decrepit about the world goes to die. Now imagine that on fire). It took me until the twelfth day without Tate to settle back into a rhythm.

Wake up whenever my body chooses. Indulge in a breakfast of half a can of peaches. Greet the early morning with my best effort for optimism. Forage past the river for anything that could go in my stomach. Start a fire on the roadside. Inevitably fall asleep next to the lifesaving heat. Wake back up. Cry. Eat a dinner of fresh squirrel or flavorless green plants. Inevitably vomit up those plants, because nothing quells dehydration like dry leaves. Wash it down with water. Curl up on the couch and wonder how I ever thought I could make it through the winter months alone. Realize that autumn is only just beginning, suck it up, and prepare for the next day.

I never truly got scared of the weather until the first frost. Day nineteen. It finalized what was no longer a threat but a promise: snow.

Never once did I see Tate until the twenty-fourth day. Early November.

His boots splashed through the river like trumpets. He alerted every fish and bird within ten miles.

I stumbled out of the camper ready for a fight. Armed with the clothes on his body — and barely staying upright — was Tate. He barreled towards me filled with terror, confusion, and bewilderment all wrapped up in one messy cacophony.

"*What the hell?*" I screamed, dropping my gun. He nearly collapsed at my feet. "Are you okay? What happened?"

"Your... brother... dead..." Tate sucked in a sharp inhale, barely able to rise to his full height. "I need... sit." A pitiful wheeze squeezed out of his lungs. I helped him lean back onto the nearest tree.

I crouched before him, feeling the pulse in his neck. "Did you run all the way?"

He loosely nodded, spitting on the dirt. "It couldn't wait- you need... *oh, crap.*" Tate leaned his head back against the tree trunk. Small locks of hair clung to his sweat-drenched forehead. "This is a bitch."

"You need water-" I rushed back to the camper. His low groan faded behind me.

Before I could return with a gallon of clean water, Tate was already passed out on the ground.

He woke with a dripping face and a soaked shirt, my half-emptied water jug on the ground. His eyes searched desperately for where he was. It wasn't until he saw me did he calm down.

"What about my brother?" I wasted no time before interrogating him.

Tate furiously rubbed the water from his eyes. Dirt and dry leaf scraps stuck to his face. "You're very hospitable."

I kicked his leg hard enough to make him flinch. A warning. "Talk!"

"Not when you're kicking me-" He slowly pushed himself to stand up. He still leaned heavily on the tree.

"I won't kick you if you talk."

Tate stared down at me with mild annoyance. "Did you lose all your manners in four weeks?"

"Tate! *Please!*" I threw my hands up. A strangled cat had replaced my vocal cords. "How would you react if I ran up after a month of no contact and mumbled incoherent nonsense of 'Diana' and 'dead'? 'Chrissy, dead'? How would you feel?"

"I know, I know-"

"And not to mention passing out. What if I said something so… so… *catastrophic* like that and then passed out on you? You would be pretty pissed, too, wouldn't you?"

A heavy sigh escaped his lips. "Viv, I just ran ten miles-"

"I never asked you to do that. That's your own damn fault!"

"Would you rather I took my sweet time getting over here? Half a day?" His southern accent came through stronger when aggravated. It was something I noticed but never cared about before that moment.

"If it meant we could have an immediate conversation, yes."

Tate rubbed his forehead with a low, drawn-out groan. "I ran all the way because you need to know now. But now that I think-"

I poked him in the chest. It hurt my finger more than anything. "So you *admit* there's something urgent?"

"Shit, Vivienne- *your brother is alive!*" Tate shouted, righting himself to full height. I stepped back, glowering up. Tate immediately shook his head, pinching his eyes shut. "I think. I think he is. Don't take my word for it. I'm probably wrong."

My face fell — more in disappointment than shock. Disappointment that he could take me as such a fool. That he thought he could trick me in such a cruel way and have the audacity to go back on it immediately. Like he knew he was fooling around and regretted being so horrible the moment the sick words left his mouth.

Tate never lied before. He would never in such a twisted way. I had to believe so.

"Don't take your word for it? How- you- *WHAT?*"

Tate wasn't paying attention anymore. Willfully. "How long was I out?"

"What are you talking about?"

"Can we go inside?"

I slapped him. "NO! We are going to stay *right here* until you tell me *exactly* what you mean!" I willed myself to breathe. Tate's eyes fixated on my feet. "Please. You can't just say that."

Tate nodded, glancing between my eyes and the hand that had just hit him. Regret painted his face. "I know. I know I can't. It isn't right of me." He began a slow walk to my camper without another word. I had no choice but to follow, my slightly lighter jug of water in hand.

"You have a good slap," he confessed as we climbed the narrow stairs.

We weaved through discarded paraphernalia and kicked aside garbage. Embarrassment slithered down my spine. I had no way to dispose of food packaging short of throwing it into the forest, which I refused to do. Over the weeks I got so lazy I stopped going the extra mile to put the metal cans and plastic packages into the trash bags. The floor became my trash bag. One month ago, I would've been mortified if he saw me living in such conditions.

"You're living like this?" He questioned, tossing an empty can of tomato soup away to join the tin can collection under my parents' bed.

I shot him a dirty look — dirtier than the bacteria colony living in the truck's backseat. "I'm doing just fine, thank you very much. I wasn't expecting company."

A slight wheeze escaped his lungs when we settled on the couch. His chest rose with great effort and fell instantly. Like gravity was tugging his chest down. It took all his strength to fight back. A cloud of guilt formed over me for being so brash with him outside.

"You okay?" I handed him the gallon bottle. He accepted it with a discarded wave, not bothering to use it. The water rested on the cushion between us.

"I was always asthmatic as a kid, but it settled down a little as I grew older. I got more in shape. Took steroid treatments. All that fun stuff," Tate explained. He fully allowed himself to melt into the couch cushions. "This is just a flare-up. It happens when the weather changes. I'll be fine in a few days."

I would've never pictured him as asthmatic. "Do you have any medicine left?"

Tate loosely nodded. "Back home. I'm saving it for something bad."

"This looks like something bad."

He tossed up a hand. "I'll be fine. This is my fault. Stupid of me." He waved my concerns away. I opened my mouth to object, but he turned his head to fully face me. "Okay… where do I start?"

"The beginning is usually a good place," I mumbled. The poison on his face was enough to make me scoot back. "Sorry."

Tate pushed himself up, pinching the bridge of his nose. "Your brother's name is Peter?"

I nodded. He asked for a picture. I shot across the space to rifle through my bag of personal treasures. One moment of digging, and I resurfaced with the one photo left of him. Us in Washington D.C.

Tate muttered a string of swears after studying the photograph. "And roughly how old was he? Last you saw him, I mean?"

"Twenty. He was just about to turn twenty-one," my voice barely rose above a whisper. "He was around eighteen in this picture. If that matters."

A sadistic chuckle escaped Tate's lips. He leaned his head back, staring at the gray ceiling. "Damn."

He held the picture directly above his face, not moving his head from the craning position. "This is uncanny…" Tate handed the frame back to me. "Well, this is just sucky, innit? I could've brought him with me."

"What?"

He didn't respond, contemplating the question himself. "Or maybe not. Probably not. He didn't seem up to a long walk… but if he was sincere… wouldn't he be excited? Wouldn't he… well no-sorry, I'm just thinking out loud here." Tate waved himself off, ignoring my growing agitation.

I flew to the couch. "Tate, what do you mean you could've *brought him with you?*" I spoke slowly, enunciating every word with impatience.

His head barely moved. "It's a long story. And, again, I don't know for sure."

"I have time."

Tate repositioned himself. The red was finally settling down from his cheeks. He took a minute to gather his words as if *he* were the one grasping blindly into the void for answers.

"I was on my way home from a hunt — Chrissy found some beans yesterday, so we thought about making something nice," Tate began explaining. I could tell he was stalling and kicked his foot under the couch. He kicked me back. "Stop it — I was on my way back and I got pulled into an alley. This guy had a covered face and had, like, no skin showing anywhere. He covered my mouth and hit a leg pressure point and I went down, and- remind me, I need to teach you pressure points. I immediately thought it was a thug. So I went for my gun, and the guy took off his mask and was begging me not to move. Not to move or say anything. And he looked desperate."

I brought a hand to my mouth, "You think it was Peter?"

"Maybe. Let me finish." He cleared his throat. I didn't fail to notice how his left hand gripped the back of the couch. "He goes on this rant about needing help and that he saw me with you all that time ago. He told me your name and how he knew you. I didn't believe him at first. Even him saying his name was Peter didn't mean anything. Peter is a very common name. It would've been so easy if he heard me say your name even once. But he knew who you were and information he never could've learned from watching. He knew you personally."

A part of it made sense. There was never a confirmation of his death. The traffic pileup made it to the news. I *saw his car* in the wreckage. The body count was high. We assumed he was among that number when he never came home.

But to think Peter was here the whole time? Why wasn't he home? Why did he never come back? If he saw Tate and I together, why didn't he meet me himself?

"He was talking so fast. It was hard to understand the guy. But he really seemed to be in trouble. You should've seen his face. The kid was scared for his life," Tate continued. Every next word made the vomit rise up and up in my throat. I grabbed the nearest trash bag. "He looked exactly like that picture. But older. And with a few scars. A few... he's been *injured*. And minus the smile," he finished, careful of my reaction.

In my head spun countless possibilities to rationalize everything. Some were rational. Some were desperate pleas for mental comfort.

You hear about "stranger twins": people unrelated and with zero genetic connection that have the same face and body. You only ever hear about them living across the world from each other, but there is no reason why two people wouldn't live in the same state. Even so, if Tate and his sisters were able to travel from Alabama to Maine, so could anyone else. This man could've come from Washington State for all we knew! He just happened to have the same face and age as Peter.

But if it was Peter, if he was with dangerous people, that was his cry for help. We needed to save him.

As per his telepathic abilities, Tate spoke up immediately. "It would be dangerous to find him again. I can't fathom any other reason he would be so afraid to find me. I think he's with the bad ones I warned you about. There are too many chances to take. It'll be near impossible to get him alone now," he warned me. I buried my face in my hands. This was real, and I needed to cry. A good sob. Tate rubbed my shoulder. "Or not. I could be entirely wrong. But I don't think I am."

I leaped to my feet. "I don't care! We have to get him!" Before I could move to grab a bag or any weapon, Tate's hand was on my arm.

"I know you're excited, and I know you want to save him. But these guys are dangerous, Vivienne. More than dangerous," Tate repeated. His touch was the only thing grounding me to the earth. With every other word that left his lips, I could feel myself growing lighter and lighter. I could have floated away.

"I killed two of their own! If you walk in there with me, they'll put bullets in our skulls before we even shut the door."

"Then I won't walk in with you."

Tate was on his feet in an instant. "To Hell, you won't!"

I backed up into the tiny plastic table my candles were stored on. They tinked like fairy laughter. "If it's the only way to get Peter, yes I will!"

"We need to think this through."

"Even if it's not Peter, it's *someone* in trouble. He needs our help. You can't spend resources and time on me, but then reject saving someone else. That's not how it works," I argued.

"I'm not saying we won't help him, may it be Peter or not. We'll figure something out. I promise. We just need time." Tate grabbed both of my shoulders, holding me firm. I did everything to avoid his eyes. "I promise you, we'll get him out. But we can't run in headfirst. We need a plan. We need a backup. We need to be prepared in case someone saw him talking to me and is waiting for us."

That horrible lump crept into my throat. Horrible thoughts of anything my brother could've been going through terrorized my mind. "What if they're not as bad as you say? What if there's some ethical code, like rules they have to follow?"

"Viv…" Tate's eyes softened.

My head shook so hard, hair whipped across both of our faces. "No! I'm serious. What if you're overestimating how bad these guys are? What if they're not so much of a murder gang, but more of a… motorcycle gang. Yeah! I always heard they were the nicest guys ever." A panged chuckle escaped me. Tate rubbed my arm. "I mean it. You never know. We could go in there guns blazing and they're in the middle of feeding their pet kittens or something." My voice trailed off pathetically.

"Viv," Tate repeated. I didn't look up at him. He kept repeating my name until I did. "We can't go in there with guns blazing. We can't risk it. But we will find a way to get Peter out. And after we do, we pack everything and we leave. All of us."

A flutter burst my heart open. "Are you serious?"

He nodded, letting the space between us grow as he slowly stepped back. "The three of us have never stayed in any one place longer than a month before coming up here. I figure it's time to move on, and you're coming with us. You and Peter," he drew out. I stared out the window. A chipmunk fell from a tree. "If you want to come, of course. We can't make you. But it would be for the best."

"*Why* would it be best?" I demanded, my voice snapping more than intended. Tate sighed. "Tell me why it would be best if I uproot everything and leave!"

This was too much. Too much happening too fast.

"Uproot what, Vivienne?" Tate countered. My mouth snapped shut. "What do you have here? What is keeping you stuck in this dingy camper living off of beef sticks and pistachios for the rest of your life? What about Peter? Do you expect to live in here with him?"

My eyes never left the floor. He was right. The only reason I never bit my pride and moved back into my old house was because I was afraid to let go of my parents. But they were behind me long ago. I never wanted to face it.

Tate took my silence as submission. "Exactly. Nothing." I said nothing as he lumbered to the door and pushed it open. "We'll get Peter out of there. Then Diana, Chrissy, and I are leaving. You can come with us if you want to or not."

"Would it be safe to travel during winter? Where would you go?"

He shrugged, taking one step down the tiny stairs. "We have to stick together. As for where we would go... wherever our guts take us. That's never done us bad before." He forced open the door with his shoulder. "I'll be back when I have more information. Don't do anything dumb until then."

With that, he left my camper and began the journey back to what was left of our broken civilization.

xi.

The girl sat at the plastic retractable table farthest to the left on the gym floor. One hand absently picked at the midnight blue tablecloth. The other hand twirled her plastic fork through the air, imagining it was ready to launch at a teacher chaperone.

March 4. Exactly one month before the first mass suicide in a small European country, which would unintentionally spark a wave of four others across the globe.

Vivienne had no date to prom. Only one of her friends did. They were on the dance floor, lost within the mad sea of girls in too-tight glitter dresses and identically dressed boys getting too close to their date's backsides.

The booming music shrouded her one remaining friend's voice. Vivienne was too lost in her thoughts to pay attention, even if she could hear anything above the beating in her chest. Mikey had to shake her shoulders before she noticed.

"I'm getting another cupcake. Do you want anything?" Mikey shouted. It took a moment for the question to register in Vivienne's head. The crappy reverbed remix of a famous rapper drowned out any comprehensible thoughts. She nodded slowly, returning her attention to the dance floor. Mikey was gone, leaving her alone at the table with one sophomore boy who'd been so silent and still the entire night, you would think him to be a statue. His head peeked just a few degrees to the right, peering at her through the side of his glasses.

Vivienne's gaze dropped to her lap; to her light blue skirt and white painted nails. They found the dress in Mikey's girlfriend's closet only two weeks before. She had a lovely yellow dress for herself, bought a year in advance. It would have been perfect, had they ever gotten it back from the seamstress. No one ever saw it after leaving the appointment.

The only reason Mikey wasn't on that gym floor with his girlfriend, Paige, was because she'd been suspended the week prior. Vivienne didn't know the full story. Mikey texted her in the middle of work the previous Tuesday, furious. Paige protested the school's dress code in a way the principal found criminally offensive. Rumors filled the school as always. Some said she hit on the younger chemistry teacher. Others said she stole band equipment and stuffed her bra in the tuba horn. Mikey couldn't tell Vivienne the truth.

Song change. A cult-classic pop hit. More students flocked to the floor. She realized Mikey was back with the treats. She threw the cupcakes on the dirty tablecloth and dragged him to the dance floor.

Arms lifted me from the ground. My head lolled back. Consciousness slipped in and out, weaving through my brain like a drunk iguana. My left arm fell out of the cage of arms, flopping uselessly in the air with every step of my captor.

A weak groan poured from my lips. A voice hit me from somewhere above. "Hang on, Viv. I'm almost there."

My eyes could barely peel open. What little I could see was obstructed by a head. Sun peeked through sandy hair. The head turned down at me, opening his mouth to speak a second time. Blackness took me over again before his words could hit my ears.

Gray plagued the front, sides, and back of the car. Nothing but gray and constant white flashes of lightning coated the world.

Two days after the fourth of July, the summer before she turned fifteen, Vivienne was invited on vacation with Mikey's family. The five of them and Vivienne piled into the minivan for the seven-hour drive to New York. Five hours into the seven, electric bolts began lighting up the early night sky. Ten minutes later, the first raindrops hit. Those few droplets became a wall of water, soon obscuring any vision beyond five feet in front of them.

The high beams illuminated the gray mess in front and nothing else. Road signs were a mystery to them until the very last millisecond. It was only sheer luck and Holy good grace that they didn't have anywhere to turn off for another hour.

A car passed every few minutes, rushing by at a dangerous speed that left Vivienne's heart racing. A wave doused the minivan from the left. It was only then that Mikey's oldest brother Leo, the best driver in the family, could see anything in front. The new car's tail lights acted as guides, letting Leo know that he was staying on a paved surface. But soon enough, those cars would surrender to the weather and pull over to wait it out. The minivan would pass them, and they would be on their own again. It was a never-ending routine.

Vivienne clutched Mikey's hand in the darkness. Thunderstorms were fine with her… when seated in the comfort and safety of her home. Between walls and under a roof. Driving was another story.

Mikey's mom vaguely suggested pulling over a few times. Vivienne wanted to scream at him. She wanted to crawl up from the back and yank the wheel herself. But she would probably steer everyone into the ditch. They would flip. Lightning would strike their exact spot. Everyone would die.

A semi-truck passed. A fresh tsunami surged, slamming into the windshield with a violent slap. Light flashed to their side, briefly illuminating everyone's tense faces. The car slid and swerved into the left lane for a moment. Was it the left lane? They couldn't see the lines. Leo regained control, but not before Vivienne screamed and pulled Mikey's arm to her body.

"Sorry!" Leo called back to them.

Little pellets of ice hit the car roof. For a minute, all the five passengers could hear was the pinging of hail and the van forcing its way through the road river. Vivienne buried her face in Mikey's shoulder. He rubbed her knee with his other hand.

"Baby, can we slow down?" His mom urged.

"I'm going 45!" He argued, fists tight around the wheel.

"Maybe just slow down a little more."

"If I slow down anymore, we'll be stopped."

"Good."

Leo glanced back at everyone. The consensus looked the same: surrender to the elements. "Guys, we only have another two hours. We can make it to the hotel by eleven. I think we can do it."

"The hotel will still be there at midnight. Or one in the morning. Or two!" The middle child of the three, Joey, shouted.

"We have to get off the road!" Their father insisted, who had been so quiet and motionless that Vivienne assumed him to be asleep.

Leo slowed when the car in front — their guide — disappeared over a hill. "I really think we'll be okay. It even looks to be lightening up a bit!"

It was, in fact, not lightening up.

Their mother closed her eyes tight and shook her head. "Leonard Andrew Pullman, you can get out and walk the rest of the way if you love this so much," *she clenched back harsher words in front of the present company.*

So Leo pulled to the side. The car was put in park, and the six of them prepared to relax and wait out the storm.

Vivienne couldn't relax or wait. She wished with everything in her that she was in her own bed, in her own house. Away from the water, the lightning, the wind.

Why did she ever agree to this trip?

My head fell off the side of the bed. My neck jerked straight back up, eyes snapping open with the sharp pain.

A sheer pounding at the back of my skull.

I could see only part of the room. Navy blue painted walls surrounded me, dark gray blankets covered my body.

Maybe I was dead and this was my personal afterlife: neck and head aching, ice-cold fingertips, mouth caked in dried saliva.

Straight ahead of the bed, my eyes settled on a young man. He stood at the vanity, admiring collections of jewels and useless keepsakes. My shoulder banged into the headboard, which I swear was not there thirty seconds ago.

The man turned. His battered face struck my eyes.

A scream escaped my throat, tearing at the phlegm blockage. My hands searched the sheets uselessly for any defense tool. All I found was cotton cloth.

I had to be hallucinating. I had to be dreaming. Some horrible, twisted dream.

The young man rushed to the side of the bed, grabbing my arm. My mind fluttered back to unconsciousness.

Peter.

The Zombie

November

xii.

My mind woke before my eyes opened.

I couldn't find the energy to open my eyes. The darkness behind my eyelids offered an odd sense of comfort. I wasn't ready to acknowledge the mystery room or the growing throb in the base of my skull.

My eyelids peeled open finally when a cushion spring squeaked to my left. I wasn't alone.

"Wondered if I was gonna have to wake you up myself," an all-too-familiar voice chimed in on my left. I let my head fall to the side to see Tate admiring me from the armchair. "Good morning."

"What am I doing here?" My voice came out as a strangled croak.

Tate tossed a metal water bottle my way. "You don't remember? You spent the night here."

The bottle landed on my legs. I ignored it, only bothering to stare up at the off-white ceiling. "Here?"

"Don't act like this isn't an upgrade from your couch."

I closed my eyes, biting back the urge to throw the metal bottle at his head. "Am I hungover again?"

Tate let out a dry chuckle. "You didn't break into my stash yourself, did you?" He teased. No response from me. "No. You're not hungover."

A sharp knife jetted up to my skull. One fist tightened in the sheets. A pathetic moan escaped my lips as I tried to push myself up.

My gaze finally landed on the wooden vanity and dresser at the foot of the bed...

Tate rushed forward, helping me to sit. "Are you okay? Do you need anything?"

I clutched his arm, eyes searching the bedroom in desperation. Sympathy filled Tate's face. The mattress by my legs sank with his weight.

"Do you remember anything from the last few days?" He asked softly. The pounding in my chest steadily slowed. "You have to remember something. What's the last thing that happened?"

Peter.

No. It was a dream. A mad vision. It couldn't be true.

I slowly got to my feet, feeling every joint crack and pop. My back arched and my arms stretched to the ceiling. Feeling my petrified muscles pull and loosen was an unparalleled experience. I cried out in relief.

"Need me to pop your back?" Tate observed, holding out one hand like an offering. There was a clean gauze bandage on his forearm. A fresh, pink cut peeked out from the edge.

"What happened?" I demanded, immediately bending down to examine the wound.

Tate hid the arm, waving my concern away. "Don't worry about me," he assured me. "This is fine. Tell me how you're feeling."

"Where are we?" I leaned against the empty armchair. I had to be melting into the leather fabric through sheer sweat.

"The house."

I stared at him. My lungs pushed to escape my ribcage. "There's been a nice bed the entire time, and I was on the couch?"

"This is my bed." Tate stared back. "This is the nicest bed in the house. Because you're injured. I'm nice like that."

My gaze slowly traveled back to the vanity dresser. Bad idea. My eyes squeezed tight together, shutting out all bad things. "Can you leave? Please?"

"I can get Diana."

A stinging ball formed in my throat. "I need to be alone."

"We just need to make sure you're alright. You hit your head pretty hard and you've been out-"

"I don't care! I just need space."

I shook my head, willing the tears and pain and fear into the deepest, darkest part of my soul. I was losing it. Couldn't hold back... hold back...

"Viv, I need-"

"Please just *get out*," I cried, jumping up. Bad mistake. Swirls danced inside my skull. Tate leaped to my comfort, but I backed far from his touch. Closer to the dresser. Closer to the mirage.

Tate stepped closer, holding out his hands. "Listen to me for one second. You need to sit down. You're upset and disoriented."

Couldn't hold back.

"Tell me why I saw my brother!" I screamed. My throat burned and begged for mercy. I ignored it, pointing furiously to the dresser. "He stood right there! And he looked at me, and I *saw* him."

Someone moved in the front of the house. I heard two feet stomp toward the open hall before an abrupt stop. Whispering voices floated in and out through the walls before losing themselves. Ghost whispers in the air.

"Vivienne, you hit your head on a rock. You had a concussion for days! Tell me how you're feeling," Tate commanded.

"Don't try to tell me I made him up," I commanded firmly. One finger jabbed in his face. "I know what I saw. He was *right here!*"

Tate nodded, stepping up to me. "You didn't make him up. I know he was here. That was the plan. But we didn't think you would faint from seeing him!" He held a hand out like he was trying to calm a wild lion. "But I need to know how you're feeling right now."

My hand lowered, and in turn, a fist involuntarily clenched. "Are you crazy? You can't tell me- you- you can't…" I began shouting before catching myself, lowering my eyes to his feet. Shouting would get me nowhere, and Tate wasn't reacting. He was letting me simmer myself out. Like a toddler.

I tried to channel Diana. Her calm, her constant outward peace. Unsuccessful.

"Tate. Where is he?"

"In the living room." Tate nodded toward the open door. "Take your time. He's safe."

I slowly stepped up to the doorway, inspecting the empty hall as if a monster were to leap out and attack. Clear. I looked at Tate for one last shred of encouragement. Direction. Permission. His chest and shoulders rose and fell with a hefty breath, but he would not face me.

Simply thinking about moving isn't enough to actually do the trick. You have to physically move your muscles. That was the tricky part. I stood in the middle of the hallway for an eternity. I must've undergone years and years of age standing in that exact spot. Slowly, foreign feet carried me to the living room.

There was no mistaking it this time. We stood face to face. My vision was clear as day.

Peter stood with Diana by the dining table. I didn't miss Diana's eying me as if I may crumble to dust in the blink of an eye.

The tufts of his hair barely hung past his cartoonish ears. His hair, which was always two shades darker than mine, now glistened in the midday sunlight after months of sunlight bleaching. Circles decorated his under eyes. It wouldn't be so disconcerting if not for his arm.

His right arm was cut off not six inches below the elbow, jagged and scarred with a past infection.

One more thing was missing. His smile.

"Hi." He waved weakly.

The oxygen in my chest disappeared. My jaw hung uselessly from my skull as I stared at Peter, then Diana, him, then back to Diana. I raised a finger to point at him, but it struggled to stay up. My hand weighed a hundred pounds.

"How long has he been here?" My voice came out shrill and on the edge of screaming.

"Just a few days," Diana assured me. Tate and Chrissy watched us from the kitchen doorway. "You suffered a serious concussion running after getting him out. You fell on a rock mound outside of 1125."

I whipped my head back to look at our audience. Chrissy wore a slightly smaller sneer than usual. Tate was impossible to read. "Tate brought you both back here. You've been out since then, yeah?" Diana smiled, mimicking deep breaths to guide me out of near hyperventilation. "Now you're okay. He's okay. Everything is okay."

My feet finally moved me closer to Peter. Up close, I could see the wear of time on his face. Several tiny scars. Many old bruises now faded to yellow. Skin damage, deepened orange freckles, and a well tan from endless untreated sunburns. His eyes were filled with the youth of a twenty-year-old boy and the ageless wisdom of a well-worn senior. The fear. The infinite shock of fear.

And his arm. One edge jutted down slightly lower than the rest. It was not a professional surgical amputation. Loud imaginations rampaged through my mind of how it possibly could have happened. Violent accidents, concentrated bullet wounds, cruel torture or punishment.

One hand slowly moved to observe the nub before retracting itself. Only he could hear my whisper. "What happened to you?"

"It's a long story," Peter muttered, beginning to inspect me himself. He tousled with my greasy hair and horrific split ends. "You look like death."

"Thanks."

Peter laughed, casually leaning against the dining table as if he'd lived there his entire life. "You haven't killed yourself yet."

"Mhm."

That struck a nerve. I don't know why, but the sentence festered a boil in me.

How could he say anything, even as a joke, about my life out there when he's been missing from it?

And about him — why was he here? He never came back. Why was he talking to me as if no time had passed? As if I didn't believe him to be dead for six months? He survived the I-95 carnage spanning miles, and never bothered to come home? He never came back. Why didn't he come back? Maybe my parents and I never would've left home if we knew we had someone to wait for.

He never came back.

I punched him.

Peter barely stumbled as he brought a few fingers to his chin. My fist was instantly overcome with a blazing pain. I ignored it.

Diana shouted and launched herself to my side. "What's the matter with you?" She demanded. "Stop!"

Tate and Chrissy joined the tableside. The two of us were boxed in by the three siblings, each fighting with me to breathe and pulling

Peter away. I launched myself at my brother again, thrashing my arms like a madwoman.

"Girl, you need breakfast. Your blood sugar is *crazy*," Chrissy called, throwing herself between Peter and I. She caught my wrist mid-air.

I yanked my arm away and shoved her out of my space. "Back off!"

Tate was the one to finally separate me, pinning my arms to my side. "Stop! What is *wrong* with you?" Tate shouted.

"He's fine!" I snapped.

Peter massaged his jaw, pressing himself as close to the table as possible. "Ow."

"Vivienne! You need to calm down." Tate's hand gripped my shoulder. Diana pulled Peter far from me. "You're angry. I get it."

My arm flung back, smacking him in the face. "Stop. I'm fine."

"No! Settle down," Tate commanded. I took a deep breath, looking anywhere that wasn't my brother. The anger simmered down, unlike my headache, which returned throbbing. He loosened his grip on my shoulder, letting me move away. "Can we all coexist in peace?"

This was nonsense. What was I doing? How would a fight cure anything?

I held up both hands. "I'm calm."

"Are you sure?"

I wasn't sure. The spark of anger passed and I was crashing back down to Earth. Guilt started to bloom in the back of my mind — guilt and embarrassment.

Chrissy ushered Peter into another room. He said nothing as they passed Tate and I. Wordlessly, Tate guided me to follow them into the hallway.

Diana watched us pass, sighing helplessly. "Do you want water? Or soup?"

xiii.

"I want to talk to him," I insisted for the fourth time.

"I'm sure you do. No."

I was imprisoned in the master bedroom for what must have been hours. Diana brought us dinner shortly after the fiasco.

Peter and I were quarantined to opposite ends of the house. Chrissy was supervising him. Six-month-decayed Peter and Chrissy did not seem like a good pair to keep in a room together.

There wasn't much to do in my cell. The rawest form of entertainment was staring out the dirty window at the barren emptiness of the neighborhood below. No matter how often I saw it, the landscape never failed to startle me anew.

I took to rearranging things. Sorting the numerous jewelry by color or shape or size or estimating how much pieces were worth. Fluffing the pillows and beating the devil out of useless decorative throws. Sorting the women's clothes in the closet and judging which ones I would wear.

Tate tried to strike conversation now and then. Each attempt was met with poisonous silence from my end.

The only redeeming quality of my cell was the attached bathroom. It'd been so long since I used a proper bathroom, just the act of sitting on the white toilet calmed me for a minute. The plumbing was ineffective, of course, but that didn't stop me. Running water wasn't necessary for my mild trickle of mustard urine.

"Is that frost?"

That was the only thing I said to him while staring out the window at the cement and sad excuse of a lawn below. Tate joined me at the window. "Yes. We can't wait much longer."

I walked away and didn't speak again. I was so upset that I…

I don't know what I was thinking. The opposite of whatever Tate wanted.

I removed the bedding and remade it for the second time when Diana knocked on the door. "He's ready if you are," she announced before Tate opened the door fully.

I threw the comforter to the floor and bolted for the hallway. Tate and Diana chased after me. "Where is he?"

"The basement. He said it was too noisy up here for him to think." Diana came up quickly behind me.

"Don't be so harsh on him, Viv!" Tate reminded me in the background.

I paid neither of them attention. My hand found itself clasped over the top of the wooden staircase to the basement. My feet began the thunderous descent beyond my control.

Peter was pacing the back wall of the basement. I peeked over one of the beams and watched him recite lines through silently moving lips.

The thick layer of dirt on the bare concrete crunched under the thin soles of my shoes. Peter whipped around. My entire body flinched at his movement.

"Sorry! I'm sorry!" Peter held his one hand out defensively. I, unwittingly, stared at his nub.

"It's okay. I'm just... uh-" I shook my head, exhaling through my mouth. Dust danced around my face.

"I get it."

Cobwebs laced the basement every other foot. Rat droppings and decaying carcasses of small mammals who'd long since given up on the prospect of life littered the edges of the perimeter. It wasn't that nasty when Tate first brought me there.

The couch looked like it carried five exotic diseases. A dark mold ecosystem was festering on the left armrest. I took a seat, ushering for him to do the same. Peter stared at the cushion by my thigh for an eternity before finally sitting.

Neither of us spoke for a long time. Who should make the first move? Who should grovel at the other's feet first? As I became increasingly aware that one piece of my history could be reclaimed, I couldn't help but lean away from him.

This darker, unfamiliar version of Peter unsettled me. I could feel it in my gut. This wa not the Peter that kissed my boo-boos when I scraped my knee. This was not the Peter who picked me up from the Winter Ball of eighth grade three hours early because none of my friends showed up and I couldn't bear being alone by the chaperone's table.

This was… someone else. Not him.

Why do I never trust my gut?

"So… where to begin?" I prompted.

"I don't know where the beginning is," he admitted glumly.

"When you left school. When you got on the road that day."

He shook his head. "You don't want to hear about that."

"Try me."

He was right; I did not want to hear the story. But I was desperate. I was pleading in the most composed way to know what led us here.

What could explain how he survived? How did he make it out of the last news story we were burdened with watching before the district's electricity failed?

Why did he never come back?

"I was on my way home. There was a bomb about five cars ahead of me. Maybe six, seven cars, maybe. It went off and everyone… People were swerving and flying into the ditch, too full of adrenaline or shock to process and ramming into each other…" He slowly recalled, only meeting my eyes once. "The entire line of cars went up in flames."

A horrified breath shuddered out. "Wow. We didn't see that on the news."

"The news wasn't live. No way they got there in time. I was already long down the road with the guys before we heard the first drone overhead," bitterness tinged his voice.

"The guys?" I whispered. Peter disregarded me.

"People ran off and surrendered themselves to the elements. I know the lady in the Buick next to me committed suicide once she realized no one was coming to rescue us."

"What a horrible way to go out…"

"Eh. I've seen worse."

A disgusted gag hit my throat at how nonplussed he said that. "Good for you."

"I tried to come home, but what I wanted didn't matter. We had places to go. Supplies to find."

"Supplies to steal, you mean."

Peter side-eyed me. "Don't act like you haven't, you little hypocrite. What were the store owners gonna do about it?"

"At least say it as it is, dick wad."

We never spoke to each other like this before. We never did a lot of things before.

"I made it back here a few months ago. We've been sleeping in the Dollar General. That's kind of the base. You saw our setup."

"No, I didn't."

He cocked an eyebrow. "That's where I was. I know the sign is a little broken-"

"No, I don't *remember*. That concussion knocked a few brain cells out of place." I spat on a dirt pile I'd been forming with the toe of my shoe. "It's fine, I guess. It just hurts. I still remember how to walk."

"Nothing we can do about it." Peter dismissed me and continued. Rude.

"I checked the house before you ransacked it. No one was there. I assumed you guys moved or joined a band of sex-craved hippies," he admitted. The faintest of chuckles escaped my lips. "But now I hear you were in the woods? In the camper? What's that about?"

I shrugged, staring out the tiny dirty basement windows. Gray early November light fought its way through the dust and cobwebs. "We moved away from people after you died."

"Why?"

"We didn't have any other plan. Either throw yourself into exile or wait for a neighbor to shoot an arrow through your bedroom window."

Peter's knee shook. That was a new habit. "I assume Mom and Dad bit it?"

"No, they're sipping margaritas on the beach."

"Hey."

"Sorry." I stomped the dirt pile to smithereens. "My only human interactions have been with these guys. I lost my manners."

"Hey, I got so bad I was about to make a period comment," he chuckled.

I scoffed. "You should see how Chrissy talks to people."

"I have."

"You get it!" I threw my hands up with a giggle I couldn't contain. A sly grin spread across Peter's lips. "Why is she like that?"

He leaned back into the sunken couch. "I think she's a twelve-year-old girl who had a long series of unfortunate events happen to her within eight months."

"She's fifteen."

"Same difference."

My nose scrunched with the effort not to laugh. I imagined Chrissy sitting on the living room couch, pouting like a wimpy dog after its owner left out of the house for ten minutes. It was mean of me, I knew. But the first dinner nagged at the back of my memory.

"How did they manage to stay together all this way? I know there are recruitment camps left and right in the south," Peter asked.

I felt my eyebrows narrowing. "Recruitment camps? No one ever told me about those."

"Oh. Well then it must've started after they got out."

I shifted in place, facing him with my entire body. "What do they do? How do you know about them?"

Peter's eyes shifted from me to the dust bunny zoo. "It's different with every group, you know. Some of them are human traffickers. Some are rebuilding slavery. Some just want to rebuild societies, and children are the most gullible and easy to abduct."

The thought of it horrified me then. Now, I just frown.

Such atrocities as human trafficking, slavery, and kidnapping are still horrors in the world. They still hit a nerve any time you hear a new story about another spineless creep getting their way. As long as bad people exist, someone will always find a way to commit the worst. But you get desensitized after so many years. You learn to be.

I cleared my throat, feeling a strange lump float in my throat. The recognizable lump of vomit. "How do you know?"

"What do you mean?"

"I mean how do you know?" I could feel his eyes boring a hole into the top of my skull as mine trained on the edge of the couch. "Did they teach you things in that gang? What did you do?"

Peter huffed. It was then that I could hear the flip switch in his head. I could hear it plain as I could hear footsteps directly above. I could see it just as I could see the veins in my wrist.

"It isn't a gang. It's a business."

"Oh. My bad," I shot. "How do you know about these crimes down south? What did you do in this *business*?"

"Not this again-" Peter pushed himself up. My eyes finally peeled from the safety of ignorance.

I held out my hand, peering up at him with a silent plea. "Again? There was never a first!"

"I don't know what you want to hear."

"All of it. Is that not a reasonable thing to ask?"

"I don't... You-" Peter paused himself, shaking his head like a disappointed father reprimanding his children for drawing on the wall. "You don't want to know what we did. It's nothing atrocious, but you wouldn't like it. So I won't tell you."

I shot to my feet before falling back down. Still too dizzy. "Hey! No. I deserve to know."

"I refuse to tell you." Peter put his hand on his hip.

"Is it because they did that to you?" I demanded, my finger jabbing accusingly at his half-nub of an arm.

Peter lowered his hand, popping each knuckle with his thumb fervently. "They saved my life, Vivienne."

"They didn't seem very life-saving from what Tate told me. Or how much effort it took to get you out." I was pulling stuff out of my butt at this point.

"Tate doesn't know anything," Peter shot with an angry force that could've sent me flying back.

"I trust him more than anyone else on this earth."

I didn't mistake the hurt expression on Peter's face. "I don't think I could've survived without them." He held his nub out to me. "This happened on the highway. I would've bled out had they not found me and amputated what was left in time."

I stared at the stub of the remaining arm. "There just happened to be a trained amputation doctor person?"

"It's not too hard when you have drugs and a bone saw on hand."

My foot whacked his leg. "You let them drug you? They had *bone saws?*" I screamed.

Peter yelped and shoved my leg far away. "It's a weapon!"

"For sociopaths who remove your parts in the bathtub to sell on the dark web!"

"It was all I had, Vivienne!" He shouted. "Either trust them or trust myself not to die on the way home. *Two states away*, should I remind you!"

I threw my hands up. "You don't let strangers carrying bone saws operate on you! That's, like, the most basic survival skill."

"They kept me alive."

"For what quality of life?" I demanded. He lowered his eyes. "Look what they did to you! What they did to Tate!"

Peter shook his overgrown head, defeated. "You don't know they were the same people."

"Tate knows."

"Respectfully, I don't trust him like you do."

I pulled my feet up, relishing in the stretch of my calves. "And? You could've left at any point," I mumbled.

"It's not that simple."

"How is it not that simple?"

"It just isn't." Peter stared at his former arm, letting out a sharp exhale. "I don't want to argue. I'm here now. That's what matters."

I let myself fall silent. I didn't have the energy to deal anymore.

"So you managed to convince them to settle down here? Of all places?" I prompted.

"We've been floating through New England bit by bit. We stayed in New York for a few weeks, then took over an old bar and strip joint in Vermont for a few months. Boss moved us when the crowd got too rambunctious. His words. We'd been up here for a bit when I first saw you come out of the woods with that man."

"Tate. His name is Tate," I corrected, biting back the sour tinge to my voice. "And don't say 'we'. You are not one of them."

"Maybe I am."

"I refuse to believe that." My eyes bore holes into Peter's skull.

He threw himself onto the couch beside me. "Would it be bad? They kept me alive when I was one good kick to the balls away from death. Bad people don't do that."

"They do if they want something from you."

"How would you know that?"

"Common sense."

I wasn't going to confess how I knew Peter was lying. His tells never changed from the facial and finger mannerisms I memorized over years of Poker in our grandparents' basement, betting over hand sanitizers and vinyl stickers.

Peter sighed, pinching the bridge of his nose between his fingers. "I don't know what Tate told you about them. They have their numbers, and they're strict about who comes and goes. That's why it was such trouble to get me out," he explained through a strained tone. I scoffed. "That operation is run like a business. They claim a plot of Earth as their own and act like any chipmunk strolling the soil needs to pay up. But it doesn't make them villains." Peter wiped his hand on the pants of his jeans. The sweat left a stain. "You have no idea how hard it was to get away just to talk to Tate. There is an eye on your back every minute of every day," he muttered.

They kept a roof over his head. They saved him from horrible infection and imminent death. I had to remind myself of these things over and over as a dense silence passed between us.

Peter was alive.

They assaulted the girls.

No one hurt him.

Tate would never kill a man if not absolutely necessary.

"Who was the boss?"

"I called him Cal. I know a few other guys called him Lee or Alec. He wanted me to call him Cal."

"So if they get caught, no one knows the leader's real name. No real connections," I nodded. "It's smart."

Peter agreed. "Everything this man and his inner circle did was calculated. No one was ever given the full plan. No one but Cal. The men and women treated him like a god. Like he was the second coming, but something malfunctioned along the way and no one was ascending. I'm not joking; there were seriously a few that believed it."

"They treated him like God? Were you in a doomsday cult?" A lot of those sprung up before the news went out.

"May as well have been. Cal is the closest thing to God half of those guys have." Peter chuckled. How is one supposed to answer something like that? "But that's not the point. His actions meant more than anything. Every step Cal took was predetermined with two backup plans, days in advance. Every step he took, every shot he tipped back, every piss he took. Everything had a plan."

"Seems a little paranoid."

"Maybe. Or he wasn't ready to risk anything." Peter shrugged. "It worked for him."

I hugged one knee to my chest, letting my heel sink far into the aged leather cushion. His story made sense. But I wasn't ready to move on. I wasn't ready for the conversation to be over. I wasn't ready to let go of the past. Not yet.

"So that's it? They save your life and that's it?" I whispered.

Peter let his head fall loosely to the edge of the couch. "What would you have done in my situation?"

"I would've said thank you and walked myself away the moment I was fully healed."

"You don't understand." He sighed exasperatedly. "It was three months before this was fully healed," he pointed one finger at the nub, "completely disregarding malnutrition. All that fun stuff."

"Oh. Yeah."

Now the conversation was over.

I don't know what I expected after months. Months and months of believing him to be gone from the world. I can't say what I imagined our first encounter would be. There was no reason to imagine it.

Even at the good times, Peter was the more secretive of our duo. I just never expected him to be so... *unsympathetic.*

Or was I the unsympathetic one?

"Do you think dinner is ready up there?" I prompted after a minute of silence. We were over. I needed it to be over.

I barely made it to the stairtop before Diana appeared in my face. She held up one pair of mildly worn orange tennis shoes by the laces.

"I found these in a box in the garage. I thought one of you would want them." She forced them into my hands.

The grin that spread across my cheeks warmed my gushed face. "Thank you."

"Of course. Those old things are bound to fall apart the next time you breathe wrong." Diana nodded down at my faithful Converse high tops. The laces were frayed to near uselessness. The lip was torn in several places. The soles were worn down so my toes almost peeked out the tips. The rubber top was my only saving grace.

"What are you saying? They're in tip-top shape!" I giggled. Diana's eyes lit up, pinching her bottom lip between her teeth.

"So we're actually leaving?" Chrissy's voice floated from the doorway of the girls' bedroom. She stared at us, her sandy hair blocking most of her pout. "It's dumb. We're gonna leave right before winter? Surrender the *roof over our heads?*"

"We'll find another house!" Diana assured her. "Don't worry about that. We have it all covered."

"No you don't," Chrissy muttered pitifully before slamming the door in our faces.

xiv.

We formulated a plan together. When we would leave, how long we would try to walk each day, who kept the weapons. Two bags per person.

It only took an hour for the Dawsons — Peter asked for their surnames, which I never before knew because it didn't matter — to pack their worldly belongings. None of it was really theirs. Each of them only brought a backpack on the bike ride up from Alabama. Most of everything they were taking now was stolen from the previous owners of the house. I'm sure the owners didn't mind.

It wasn't hard for them to leave. It was a cruel reality to grasp that sentimentality was a deadlier killer than a bullet.

I helped Diana pack the food and water. Their once overflowing pantry had been reduced to several cans, a few cellophane packages, an armful of plastic water bottles, and one MRE. I never asked where the MRE came from.

A gnawing monster furrowed at the edge of my conscience. Tate helped me hunt and brought me food, yes. But that didn't feel like enough. The monster told me they were pity offerings, not genuine help.

He brought you back to town when you were too cowardly to do it yourself, I had to remind myself several times as we filled the duffel bag with goods. *He introduced you to people, whereas else you would have gone insane.*

The next step was finding my trailer and loading my things. My beloved camper trailer... I missed her. I never thought I would. She melded into an extension of my soul. I still can't remember the unknown days before leaving her forever; a forever cruel reality.

We left as soon as possible. No one bothered to close the door behind us.

Peter led the way. He was the only one who knew where the lookouts were stationed. Peter assured us that he wasn't important enough for Cal and his inner circle to worry about him taking powerful secrets. But he was leaving. That fact itself was a red flag.

I tried to convince him that we walked through the neighborhood several times in broad daylight and never encountered a problem. No alerting shouts in the background. No missed bullets that should have landed in our heads. To this, Peter responded, "Of course not. They wouldn't have missed."

Between the five of us, there were six bags. Soon to be ten. Ten bags that would steadily dwindle; nonrenewable resources of our old lives.

Chrissy asked the strangest thing once we let the decrepit neighborhood disappear behind our backs. She asked me directly, even making the effort to move to my side and lower her voice.

"Do you ever worry about finding your parents' bodies out here?"

"No." I didn't consider for very long before the word leapt from my mouth. "Well, I guess so. But you would think their bodies would be decomposed by now."

I could tell Chrissy resisted the urge to roll her eyes at that comment. "Well yeah. Duh."

"Right."

"But what about skeletons? Those take years and years to break down." One side glance from the girl let me know she was trying to be sincere with her questions. She wanted to know if we would find bodies in the trees. What a morbid little child.

I stared at the leaves and twigs in front of my feet. "It would be pretty easy to miss two skeletons."

"Still. It's creepy," she mumbled.

We didn't speak for a minute. No one did. I know everyone was eavesdropping, anticipating when the claws would come out.

"I don't even know if my mom did die. She may have run away and found safety in some refugee camp in the Appalachians," I admitted. Chrissy gave me a dead look. I held up my hands. "I'm just saying, there may only be one skeleton we have to look out for."

"You should never have kids."

I tried to chuckle, but it escaped like a strangled bark. "What does that have to do with anything?"

"I'm not an idiot, Vivienne." Chrissy stomped back to the safety of Tate's side.

We reached the camper in much more time than I ever remember taking before. It was the extra weight bogging three of us down. Or the clueless people who didn't have the geography of the land memorized by heart tripping over every scraggly root and large rock.

A hare was investigating the truck when we arrived. I could see him sniffing at the tailpipe before we began the descent down the ravine. Tate held a fist up: stop. The hare's ears turned towards the abrupt clatter of their jostling bags. When nothing else moved, the hare returned to his business. Slowly, Tate unstrapped the rifle from his bag.

"Good idea," Chrissy whispered.

"Shsh."

Every breath paused in their throats as Tate cocked the bullet. The hare stared back at us. I could feel his black eyes from the top of the hill. The bang resonated in my bones faithfully, a feeling I didn't miss. The hare lay immobile under the truck.

"Who was last to eat?" Tate demanded, strolling up to his game.

"Um, *you*, I think." Diana followed. Our bag clatter resumed.

Tate beat the bugs out of the hare's fur. "Really?"

"I think. You, or Vivienne. She was too upset."

I shook my head and threw the trailer door open. "I'm not hungry."

"I don't care. You need food whether or not you think you're hungry," Tate shouted after me. I pretended not to hear him from inside.

Dust covered every conceivable surface. A tenacious spiderweb met my face when I crossed the threshold. Bugs staked their residency on my little table and in my candle collection. A strange smell came from under the couch that I wish I never checked.

"Everything okay in there?" Peter called after I screamed.

A hand raced to my chest, the other clutched the back of the single wooden chair. "Yeah. I'm okay…"

Tate stomped up to the steps. "I'm gonna go out, and if you don't fry up that rabbit by the time I'm back, you will do so with whatever else I bring."

"Why don't *you* eat it?" I shot.

"Because," Tate threw the hare's carcass on the floor of the trailer, "you're smaller."

The flappy ear of the animal hit my shin on the way down. A gag clenched at my esophagus.

"Don't argue with him, Vivienne," Diana appeared on the threshold, too. "He's stubborn when he gets tired."

"I do not!" Tate whipped around to her. Diana threw one look at me before stumbling down the steps.

Peter replaced her immediately. "If you wanna start a fire, I'll help pack up in here."

Tate made himself scarce, but not before tripping over a magazine. I had to take that magazine with me. It was my mom's. I had to take my mom with me, and he stepped on it. Peter investigated every detail of my home: the knife block, the pile of never-to-be-clean-again blankets, the stained and holey socks and underwear beyond hygienic use.

This wasn't the plan. This wasn't right. I didn't prepare for anyone to see my space. For anyone except Tate to see the state I lived in for half a year. For anyone to *touch my stuff.*

I couldn't respond fast enough. He grabbed the canvas bag off from the dirt-plagued floor. A single hand of mine reached out, locking itself around his bicep. "Don't touch my things!"

I didn't mean to shout. But I did.

"Why not?" He smiled uneasily. "We can get two things done at once."

"But don't touch my things."

We had the most uncomfortable staring contest. After enough time to worry the outsiders that we died, I'm sure, Peter surrendered and backed away. "Okay. What do you want me to do?"

I backed deeper into the space where Dad once kept his shoes. "Get out of my house. Please. I need my space," I whispered.

Peter's arms made a wide sweep across the couch. "I want to help."

"Cook the damn rabbit!" I kicked it his way. The carcass' fat squished against my toe. My teeth gritted into my skull.

"Don't yell at me!" Peter yelled back. "This place is a shithole. You need help."

"I don't want your help! I just want to be in here and pack my things. I managed fine enough without you."

Peter said nothing before retreating out of the trailer, leaving me alone in a pile of dirt and animal feces.

We were back on the dirt road in no time. We had far less food and water than I envisioned. Tate said we would be okay for a while. I didn't believe him.

I managed to distribute my remaining resources between Peter and me with no help. It was calming. Serene. One last factor I could control before we embarked on the journey of indefinite endings.

I spent my last time in the trailer ignoring their stares through the cloudy windows. I could feel their silent judgment with every growing minute. Or maybe it wasn't silent. I couldn't hear anything outside after I slammed the double doors shut. Tate returned with his game bag half full of precious lunch as I was finishing. I did not eat that hare. I think it was given to Chrissy.

I didn't say goodbye to the trailer. If anything could make me feel better, it wasn't that.

I lost track of how long we walked after we passed a lightning-struck tree. The once-magnificent structure was split down the near middle. The interior was fried, all signs of former life crisped beyond repair. One half was discarded to the dirt, the other half still stuck broad as daylight.

We threw our stuff over the top of the broad split, helping each other over one by one. Chrissy's legs were too short to step over at all, rather opting to crawl over it sideways like a drunk bear. Diana scraped her palm along the way. I almost stepped on a leopard slug minding his own business. My stolen tennis shoe heel missed him by mere centimeters. The debacle almost made me ugly cry.

The cool air chilled my breath clouds, as proper for the time of year, but my sweat coating raised my internal heat tenfold. An aggressive and incessant throbbing beat at my temple. I needed to collapse. But my pride refused to give in and be the first to fall.

"Why can't we follow the highways?" Chrissy asked when Tate steered us over a paved asphalt road and on.

"A lot of people died on the highways."

Peter spoke up from the back of the group. "If you were scared about skeletons in the woods, that's nothing compared to decaying carcasses left on the roads. Cars travel in packs. We'll be able to smell them from a mile away," he spared no details. Chrissy gagged.

Tate looked over his shoulder. I caught the scowl he sent to Peter. *"Thanks, man."*

We walked more.

My shoulders begged to give out. My nose ran too fast for me to catch up. I gave up trying to wipe it clean after so long. I no longer cared about looking pretty for anyone in the family. If they saw me as a sweaty, puffy, wheezy, snot-covered forest monster then so be it.

I didn't pay attention to anyone until Peter walked up to Tate. He intentionally approached him and went out of his way to willingly start a conversation. So, of course, I had to eavesdrop.

"How long have you known Vivienne?" Peter demanded, not bothering to whisper.

Tate paused and motioned for the rest of us to go on. "A few months," his voice was now behind me, which was a negative for my eavesdropping efforts.

"And she trusts you?"

"We've helped each other. She's with us now. I don't see why not."

Diana peeked over her shoulder at me. I mouthed, "Help." She fully turned around and began walking backward. Her doe eyes conveyed more sympathy than most are able with words, during which time I paid no attention to the boys.

"She went crazy," I heard Peter finally whisper once I chimed back in. I was still close enough to hear. Diana shook her head ruefully.

"I don't think so," Tate muttered.

Peter scoffed. He was the only one who would scoff like that. "The shock of everything is making her lose it!"

"I think she's doing just fine."

"I'm her brother. I know how to read her better."

"Excuse me?" I called out, stopping in my tracks.

Tate's eyes shot directly at me. He exhaled sharply and sidestepped far from Peter as I let the two of them draw up to me. Chrissy and Diana kept steady forward, but I knew their ears were peeled back to us.

"Please repeat what you just said." I glared into the dark pits where my brother's eyes used to be. Another moment when I didn't recognize him.

He shook his head, surging forward with the rest of them before I grabbed his arm. He yanked it from my grasp. "*Chill out.* That was a conversation between Tate and I."

"Am I supposed to believe you two are friends now?" I demanded, casting a weary glance at the Dawsons. They were fleeing farther and farther away. "I just want to know why you were talking about me. Because you were."

"How would you know?"

I surrendered to walking when we lost sight of the others beyond the crest of the hill. "Because this is a silent forest, you weren't bothering to whisper, and I'm not an idiot."

Peter tipped his head so far back his neck could have broken. "Ok, *yeah*, we were talking about the shit at the trailer. Happy?"

"Why?"

"Because you were acting weird. And it ticked me off." He looked down at me with a bitter grimace. "I was trying to help, and you sent me out like that?"

We never used to have arguments. We never hit each other, stole, or stabbed each other with forks. He stayed to his side of the house and I had my priorities over complaining that he got a larger burger patty at the Easter barbecue. We decided early on to settle any squabble with a fair game of rock-paper-scissors. Any complaints beyond there had to be taken up with a parent. There were no parents to solve our problems for us now.

"If that's it... dude, I'm sorry! I freaked." I shook my head, forcing the horrible thoughts and nasty impulses off and away. But they clung to my hair like mites.

"The camper was my last piece of *before*. You never experienced it like I did. At all." I don't know why I cared so much to explain myself to him. He wasn't listening. "I knew it was my last time there, and I was sacrificing my old life. My new old life. I didn't think it would cause such a big... such a... *I don't know!*"

Peter did not express that he heard me for a long time. With every continuing step, I begged him to speak through my mind. Reached into his thoughts and forced him to acknowledge me. I didn't understand the point of the argument. He was being incredibly immature. We caught back up with the other three by the time he finally opened his mouth.

"Fine," was all he finally said.

I could not believe we were handling this like such children. That should have stayed behind when our old worlds went to the grave.

"Next time, talk to *me* about it like an adult," I muttered. A mistake.

Peter marched forward, jogging ahead the group like he was our leader. Tate shouted at him to slow down, but he kept walking. He disappeared over another hill within minutes.

"Don't try to catch up," I called to Tate when he tried to follow him. "He's being a brat. If he wants to get lost and die by a gang of raccoons, let him."

"What was he talking about?" The other man asked. I ignored him.

Peter did not know what the trailer meant to me; how I was

forced to uproot my connection to my land with no warning.

He didn't know. He wasn't there.

Peter was a stranger. I can't even say "a stranger in his body". He didn't have his own body anymore. He was just a stranger.

"There's something over there…" Chrissy announced. Dusk was approaching, as were the nocturnal creatures.

She faced the edge of a clearing. I could see overgrown wild grasses and small trees freshly growing through the gaps between the steadily thinning trunks. I stumbled to her side.

Before us was a lot decorated with destroyed paraphernalia. Not just vehicles littered the area. Someone dumped a busted-up ATM off at the edge — not the little machine kind, the kind bank employees could stand in. Someone must have run into it and instead of replacing it, the insurance told them to screw off.

It must've been two miles wide of metal garbage and unwanted automobile parts that nature was slowly claiming back as her own.

"It's a car junkyard!" I shouted over my shoulder.

"Okay?"

Chrissy turned on her heels, digging a shallow circle in the dirt. "It's *shelter.*"

"Yes, I'm sure half-rusted cars would be perfect shelter," Peter grumbled.

I bit my tongue from what I truly wanted to say. "Would you rather sleep under a bush?" My words shot out. I could imagine them hitting him like a metal dart, piercing and sinking deep into flesh.

Peter said nothing.

"We can check it out," Tate promised, climbing up the hill.

We descended into the land of lost car parts; dreams in their little car minds to be salvaged gone forever.

XV.

I'd never seen a proper junkyard before. The sheer expanse of it unsettled me. Was there nothing more to do with these broken vehicles than trash them in an empty field? Tate later told me that people in Alabama didn't need much of a reason to junk their cars. It was like a game to them.

These metal parts may rust and break apart after some time, but the frames would remain forever; a memorial to the monument they used to hold in our world. Gasoline cars are null, reduced to nothing more than skeletons of the past. The electric cars' lithium batteries are decaying and seeping into the earth through each crack.

Aliens may come down in a couple of centuries — decades maybe — and see junkyards and think, "What were these odd-shaped beings? How did their skeletons defy decomposition?" They may think we worshiped such beings, seeing as there are *so many of them.*

Trees and various grasses grew in the cracks and rusted spots of every single automobile. Dents and carvings decorated the exteriors of the majority of them. Tires were deflated. Windshields and mirrors were cracked if not entirely shattered. I watched a fox scurry out of a blue '12 Jeep when we approached.

The most interesting was the crude or vulgar graffiti some bore. Some detailed particular male/female anatomies, while others warned future readers of inescapable truths. *The end is near. Save yourselves. Don't trust them.*

Pfft. As if we didn't know.

As we navigated through the poorly kept paths between vehicles, a knot filled my stomach. Walking through the overgrown and decrepit junkyard, a sadness settled over me. The useless structures reminded me of humanity. We were the cars. And even though we were the few remaining left to run, you can stick us in a crowd of other creatures forced by Mother Nature to destroy itself and we blend in.

"Spread out. Find somewhere safe and covered," Tate ordered.

"Are we sure this is safe?" I asked, inspecting the brown interior of a minivan with needles spread through the back.

"Sure it is." Tate peered into my van. "Just not that one."

"Can I sleep in the ATM?" Chrissy shouted. The girl teleported herself beside the structure.

Tate buried himself inside a white pickup truck with a double-wide bed. I think I saw LED lights under the carriage. I've never understood the purpose of multicolored lights *under* the car. "If you can make yourself comfortable in there, then by all means, sure."

Peter stepped up behind me. I didn't sense him until he spoke. My soul briefly left my body. I remember watching it float away before gravity pulled it back to Earth. "When are you going to stop being mad at me?" He muttered. There was no hint of remorse in his voice; only annoyance.

As I waited for my heart to settle down, I glared back at him. "When you stop being a dick."

"I'm not the one being a dick."

"Okay."

I pushed aside him, investigating a black SUV with only the hood smashed in. I climbed in, only to listen and wait for Peter to leave. I didn't move the entire time he lurked outside the car. Until I heard the gravel crunch under his feet I only moved my eyes. It was as if I made no noise inside the SUV, he would go blind to me and turn around. He would forget I existed and go back to the neighborhood. Back to Cal and the "business".

I never regretted saving him from Cal. That would be outrageously selfish of me. He was afraid. He was desperate for any way out. To regret saving him — however we did — would be outlandish. Horrible of me.

But I did.

I only had him back for three days, and already it was glaring how he changed. So did I. It was wrong of me to hold him to a higher standard when he was surely just as shocked to see me change.

So why did I want to see him gone again?

We experienced that last spring in two different ways. Two different perspectives of how people could twist things. It was only logical that we approached the new age differently.

Peter was at college, doing his best to be a good civil justice attorney for whatever future we thought we had. Things were bad at the universities; high concentrations of young adults at the most influential time of their lives away from their parents' protection. I was at home, watching my high school and neighborhood deteriorate day by day, never straying too far from my dog.

We were two different people than we left behind. It was time to adapt.

But I didn't want to look at him.

The SUV was safe; minus the glass shards decorating the entire front passenger's seat and the rock on the floor beneath it.

Diana knocked on the side of the wide-open door. I welcomed her into my humble abode. We climbed to the back like school girls ready to gossip about boys. "Are you really okay with this? This doesn't seem weird to you?" She immediately questioned.

"Where else is there to sleep? I see a roof over our heads right now." I shrugged, searching for Tate through the tinted back windows. The late dusk lighting made that nearly impossible.

"That's not what I mean." Diana sighed. I leaned my head against one of the headrests. "We waited so long to leave, but now we're running faster than our feet can carry. I think someone isn't telling us everything. Does it make you uncomfortable? Am I talking crazy?"

"No. Maybe. I'm lost," I confessed.

"Nevermind. I'm probably going crazy."

"Peter is an unreliable historian. But Tate is going with it." I picked at the lint clumps on my pants and threw them at the back of the seat. "As long as I stay alive, I'll go wherever you guys go. That's where I am right now."

Sometimes, that's all you can ask for.

We all joined in the clearest space of the yard for dinner. We had to shout at Peter for him to emerge from his Dodge shelter. There was enough in our food supply for a few days. After that, our modern treats from the neighborhood would be dry. Back to foraging berries and skinning small mammals.

I had a glamorous meal of four apple slices, a chewy granola bar, and one package of peanut butter crackers. I forgot how delicious peanut butter is. The texture and crunch of the white crackers offered diversity to my palette where I had become adjusted to dry-as-a-camel's-foot meat. Don't even get me started about the apple slices! I ate those last. The sugary crunch, sticky juices leaking down my chin… Heaven on Earth.

When dinner was over, there was no keeping Peter around. He took quick note of us finishing the meal and jumped straight to his feet. No one bothered to protest.

We didn't stick outside much longer. As the sun set, the air fell just above freezing. We all herded inside my SUV. It was the largest of all the shelter-worthy cars.

I stopped to admire the sunset. That evening cast a stunning array of oranges and purples across the evening sky.

Pastels turned to navy night. I could see Venus and Saturn shining back. I like to imagine the other planets know about us just as we know of them. They study us. They have their own names for us, and none of them understand why we keep shooting metal junk into the void of space only for it to stay up there for the rest of eternity.

The other planets can't be much different than us. They're cognitive and beautiful, just like Earth. At times like these, I imagine the planets admired me as well. Venus and Saturn are proud of me for making it.

The other three pulled me back to my home planet and burst my cosmic bubble.

"This is cozy," Tate commented when we all piled into the back of my treasured minivan. Legs were thrown over legs. Arms were pinned under butts with many murmured "sorry"s. One of us stepped on Diana's hair and pulled out a clump. Peter probably heard her scream from the other end of the junkyard.

I pulled my leg over the top of the backseat, finding refuge in the high-roofed trunk. "I like to think of it as homely."

Chrissy joined me back there. "I would be okay just staying here for a while. It's shelter and protection from the… *all of that*," she confessed, stretching out in the wide space next to me.

"Chris, someone left their crack bags in the passenger seat of the first one I checked," Diana stated.

"And?"

"I don't want to sleep in crack cars. Think of how many others have drugs or weapons!"

"Not this one!"

"Why do you want to sleep in a junkyard for the rest of your life?" Tate narrowed his eyes. I could feel the humor radiating off of him.

Chrissy shrugged, defeated by her proposition. "I would rather have one crappy place to sleep every night than risk sleeping against trees without protection from… bears or something, I dunno…" she trailed. She played with a few leaves and dead insect carcasses on the floor. "Remember that time after NYC when we slept in a subway? That was cool. I could've happily lived in a subway for the rest of my life. Better than the woods."

"That subway will be flooded by springtime," Diana gently corrected her.

"Then we move to another subway."

"Melting glaciers don't care who's living underground!" I exclaimed. "Out here you only have to worry about flood season if you live by a river."

"That's not how that works." Chrissy rolled her eyes.

I leaned forward. "Oh yeah? Try me."

"I won't, that would just be wasting my time!"

"Girls!" Tate held both hands out to us. "Is arguing about flood season going to help us?"

Chrissy huffed. I shook my head.

Diana rubbed her eyes, crawling out of the backseat before any of us could open our mouths again. "I'm tired. Goodnight," she announced. We all muttered goodnight, sweet dreams, the bug thing, all the works. She was gone.

The remaining three of us didn't speak for a long time. The darkness consumed us, leaving our eyes fighting to function. No one dared to light a candle in fear of alcohol residue being present on the seats. When my vision finally came to, Tate's silhouette outlined against the driver's headrest. He stared into the distance with a lost gaze of those unexplainable emotions I was never able to decipher in him. Chrissy played with the insect carcasses, but that didn't hide the troubling thoughts spinning around her head. *She* was plain as day next to me.

"I'm sorry you guys had to leave," I finally spoke into the darkness. "You guys found a great house. We could've kept ransacking the neighborhood until it all ran out. I feel bad for being involved in why you had to leave that behind and start fresh again."

"Don't be sorry. It's not your fault," Tate whispered.

"It's not my fault. But I'm sorry. I didn't want to leave either."

Chrissy chucked a grasshopper's body over the backseat. "It was bound to happen. It's not a problem," even she assured me.

But *why* was it bound to happen soon? They had a perfect house. A steady stream of resources. While I could tell it was a sore subject for Tate, I was itching for the full truth. Tate never told me the full story of why we had to leave with Peter. Why Peter's boss, Cal, was so dangerous.

I jumped over the back seat to address Tate personally. "Can I ask what your other reason to come all the way up to Maine was?"

"What?"

"When we first met I asked why you came up here from Alabama. You said sight-seeing. But you also said there was more to it, and you've never elaborated since."

Tate and Chrissy exchanged looks. She shrugged. I quickly held up a hand. "If it's personal business, then by all means, you don't have to tell me! I'm just curious," I reiterated solemnly.

"No, no, it's fine. It's stupid, anyway." Tate shook his head. "But you can't think we're crazy, alright?"

"Of course not."

Tate sighed, throwing both hands up. "Someone in Mobile told us we could find sanctuary in Maine. They convinced us the governor of Maine managed to keep his state secure and kept the mad disease of the mob under control. And it made sense! You guys are so self-sufficient up here. We hoped there would be a chance the almighty people of Maine could help us."

I sent Chrissy a side glance. She nodded.

I resisted a maniacal fit of laughter. Our governor died within the first two weeks. We were one of the first reported state governments to give up control. The only reason our numbers didn't dwindle so much faster was thanks to how spread out the general Maine population was.

Tate noticed my expression contorted with the failing attempts to hold back my humor. "We were desperate! We had no other plan, and honestly, we just needed an excuse to get out of Alabama."

"I get it, I get it…" I held one finger up as I had to manually hold my mouth shut to contain the erupting giggle.

"You can laugh," Chrissy said.

And I did. I laughed my butt off. I was soon clutching my gut with every continuous pulse of laughter. I couldn't help it. From my truth, that reason was as silly as the people screaming about the president being replaced by an android. Chrissy laughed at me when I began hiccuping.

"Ha ha." Tate turned his back to me.

I swallowed my giggles the best I could. "Oh, come on! It's *funny*. You have to admit! It's funny."

Chrissy covered her own mouth. "Dude, it kind of is."

He never admitted that I was right. But I saw him grin. I heard the faint, ever-so-short chuckle escape his lips.

"I have a somewhat deep question for you guys," I stated out of the blue. "In ten or fifteen years, do you think anyone is going to consider the states anymore? Or the countries? Will it just be *Earth*?"

Tate considered this; and erupted the *Tate Thinking Face*.

"Governments are void. Ours is. I would assume the same goes for every other sovereign body out there. We go by our means now," he thought out loud, turning back to face me slightly. "In a few years, there are going to be kids born who have never heard of the fifty states. Or any other country in the world. It won't matter. I don't see any reason why any of it would go on."

I nodded slowly. "I get that. But then what if we make a lot of babies in the next year and the population bounces back in three decades. Then they all form another country and name the new territories off of the old ones. And then we're right back where we started."

"That's not gonna happen."

"Why not?"

"Who the hell would want to birth a baby into this new world?" Tate asked. And he had me stumped there.

"What do you think?" I asked the other one.

We both looked at Chrissy. She was fast asleep against the left wall of the trunk. I could hear the soft, long-gone snoozes escape her lips with every exhale.

"I'll take that as my cue to leave," Tate whispered, scooting out through the backseats. I smiled, jumping back down into the trunk.

I curled in on myself at the other side of the trunk, pulling my cardigan as tight around my body as possible. My first night without a pillow, ever. It was more comforting than I ever could have imagined.

xvi.

We departed the junkyard by sunrise. Tate swore we could make it out of Maine by the end of the day. I don't know how he knew where we were or what direction, but I had no better choice than to trust him.

Chrissy and I climbed out of the SUV with cricks in our necks and tender knees. Diana had a cherry red, overflowing nose. Tate didn't bother calming his untamed bedhead. We had to hunt Peter down. For a minute I worried he got lost on his way running from us and got trapped under a carbon monoxide-leaking truck. No, he was calmly dozed off inside a Chevy with a rodent crawling over his foot.

Saying goodbye to the junkyard was another type of bittersweet. It meant we were moving on and continuing this chaotic, unreliable chapter of our lives. It also meant that, in a way, we were leaving behind a certain part of our human nature. Something poetic like that.

The junkyard represented the banged-up, garbage nature we turned ourselves into. Just like a car, there is nothing inherently bad about humans. We treated ourselves wrong, just as the cars were treated wrong. The junkyard was only there because people refused to do something about their problems and threw it on someone else to deal with. Is that not what everyone who died did to us?

Or maybe I overthink everything. Maybe it was just a regular, boring junkyard.

We didn't take a break for the first hour. We made good progress, no matter how painful. I could hear Tate's asthmatic wheeze from several feet away and commended he take a break for himself.

Twenty minutes later, we were back on the road.

Peter stuck to the back of the group, sometimes even going as far as to get lost over a hill. He spent so much of the morning avoiding me before I finally heard his boots crunch on the leaves behind me.

"Hi," he said.

"Yo."

"We should talk."

My eyes fixed ahead, watching Chrissy's sandy ponytail bob with every step. "You're very observant."

He rubbed the bridge of his nose so hard I envisioned him rubbing it right off his face. "I'm being serious. I don't like being in a fight," he sighed.

"We're not in a fight. You're just being an asshole," I jabbed. Diana shot a look back at us, noticed who we were, and turned right back around.

Peter shook his head. "That's what I mean. I think you're being the asshole."

I exhaled icily. "You can think that. It's not true, but you can think that."

"That's my point! I don't want there to be anything weird between us. I don't want things to be awkward, or for you to feel like you can't talk to me, you know?" Peter explained. I could see the breath puff from his mouth with every harsh consonant.

"I can't imagine why things would be awkward." I stared.

Peter stopped in his tracks. "You know what I mean. I'm here now. Everything is how it should be."

Hearing him speak was still enough of a shock to make me cringe. Every moment more I spent around him felt like a horrid fever dream; a curse to keep me rooted in the world which perfectly dead people like him left behind for me.

If he was here and asking me not to feel weird about him, then where was Mikey? Why wasn't Mikey asking the same thing of me? Maybe Mikey had escaped his work in time and could crawl all the way home! *We need to go back for him*, I wanted to scream at someone. If I was supposed to treat Peter the same, why would we walk away from Mikey? He should be back home. In our town. Waiting for me.

"You were *dead*, Pete," I stated, my eyes falling to the crinkled leaves.

"I'm sorry that happened to you."

"There's no need for sorry." I bit my cheek and forced myself to look back at him.

Grainy news footage. Drone-height video over the highway. Over his car. That's all I saw when his eyes met mine. "You were dead. I mourned you with Mom and Dad, then I did the same for them two weeks later. I don't care that you're alive now. *You died.*"

His solid gaze softened ever so slightly. I could see it flash before his time-hardened gaze. "Mom and Dad?"

"Yes. Where did you think they were? Sipping margaritas on the beach?" I let my snap crescendo. It felt good to yell at something.

"I don't know… I thought… I just didn't really think about it…" He shook his head. The light behind his eyes solidified once again. "Never mind them. It doesn't matter."

My eyes narrowed. A sharp atmosphere settled between us as I gave him time to reconsider his words. "*Never mind them?*"

Peter disregarded me and continued walking. We were grossly falling behind the other three. "That was a long time ago. We lost everyone. Don't you feel like they blend into the crowd? They're just two more numbers, aren't they?"

"No. They're my parents. *Your* parents." I jogged to catch him, never tearing my eyes from the back of his ratty head. "Until thirty seconds ago you thought they were still alive, you ignorant twat! And now you say *never mind?*"

"It was months ago. Move on."

I caught my feet so abruptly that my body kept going forward. My face almost met the dirt. Peter stared at me.

"It took you three years to get over one ex, but I can't mourn my fucking parents for months?"

"I didn't say that. Come on," he waved the discussion away and urged me forward. I was already losing his patience.

"*No!* No. We're gonna stand right here." I planted my feet steady. "Are we picking and choosing who we're gonna be sad for, now?"

"You're putting words in my mouth."

"Then tell me I'm wrong."

Peter took a deep breath, throwing his hand up. "*Okay.* You find out your dead brother is alive, and your first instinct is to hit him. You hear his story and go out of your way to point out every time he was wrong. Instead of being excited and — I don't know — grateful that I'm back, you insist on being fixated on the past. The dead and the gone. Do you know how that makes me feel?"

Truth be told, I had no legitimate argument against that. Not one that I could construct on the dime. But we weren't done. I refused to be done.

"You could have come home immediately once people started going crazy. But you didn't. You stayed there at school and took your time coming back to us. Did you even think that we would worry? That when you stopped answering our calls, it may bother us a bit? Come to find out your mother and father are dead. Your only sibling was left to fend for herself in the woods for months! And you say.... *Never mind?* You think none of it matters?"

"That's not what I mean and you know it."

"I don't know! I think it is."

"Then maybe it is. They can't argue on their own behalf anymore, can they?" He shot. I had to look away, lest I cry. The worst way to lose an argument is by crying. "The past is the past and *none* of it matters now. They're dead. But we aren't. Can't you accept that?"

"We may as well be dead. Look at us!" I threw my hands out between the two of us. "We both look ready to drop at any moment. Malnourished, dehydrated, and sleeping in crack cars. This is a shit life! Am I supposed to be grateful?"

"Then why haven't you killed yourself by now?"

An exasperated scoff hit the cold air in a warm puff. He never talked like that. "I don't know! My body refuses to die," I grumbled.

"Why aren't you happy to have something back? Life as you knew it was destroyed, and a tiny piece comes back. And you insist on being stuck in the past," Peter stated, glancing behind him at where the other three had long since abandoned us. We would never find them by now.

"Geez, I wonder why!" The unintentional grinding of my teeth in my skull made me want to crawl inside my ribcage and lock myself in. Or lock everything out. "I have a right to be mad. I mourned you. I cried and lost sleep over you. That doesn't go away overnight."

I had to shift my focus. Force myself to look at the dreadfully gray sky. This was impossible. This was not Peter Hammond.

"You can't tell me how to process my grief. Not when you stand there pretending none of it bothers you. I can't believe… You don't…" Peter stared at me like a blank puppet as I caught my breath, the emotions rising in my chest like bubbling magma. "The image of our dad on the river bed rocks is still branded in my brain like… like…" Something red and evil blinded my coherence. "Are you telling me you didn't feel some sort of upset when you first saw me at the house? You felt nothing?"

Peter remained horribly calm. So calm it was violent. "I never convinced myself you were dead. I know you're smart and you would find a way to keep yourself going. It wasn't the shock of the century."

"People were dropping dead left and right." I stepped back, pinching my lips together. "It was one of the last stories we saw. It was drone footage. We saw your smoldering car in the rubble. We saw bodies tossed all over the road. My bad for making the *bold* assumption."

An odd pain rose in my chest. It was the most unfamiliar pain. "And now… now I… *dammit*, I find out the person who I thought would understand the most is telling me to never mind?"

"Pull yourself together, Vivienne," Peter rolled his eyes. "You aren't the only orphan. Stop pretending like you're some forsaken martyr that the entire universe is against." He shortened the distance between us, and any ability to form words melted from me. "You are alive. I'm alive. I'd say that's a hell of a better deal than the rest of the world got!"

I murmured something, but it was too sad and pathetic. He ignored me.

"And all this hypocrisy about death… Every life in the world matters…" Peter pinched his nose as if I were an ignorant child who refused to comprehend the simple lesson. His footsteps crunched below to close the last foot between us. "You really don't remember one bit of how you got me out, do you?"

"No."

"Nothing at all? Not even a whisper?"

"Nothing. I swear."

A sadistic chuckle leaked from Peter's lips. That was the instant I knew my brother died in that fiery crash on the interstate. The man in Peter's place leaned down to my ears. His hot breath hit the side of my face like a poisonous fog.

"You killed two men to get to me," he whispered. "Now you tell me every life in the world matters. You fucking hypocrite."

We saw the first snow on our way across a highway river bridge. It had fallen before we arrived, sparing us the encounter. Icy fluff covered the grass and shrubbery lining the edge of the road before it connected to the bridge. Diana slipped on a patch of rivet ice. Tate didn't say anything, but he understood: it was time to settle down. Winter was here.

I counted seventeen cars stalled along the expanse of the bridge. Only two of them had crashed into each other. I could perfectly picture the former drivers getting tired of the world, stopping right where they were, and walking away.

Whatever town this was was nothing more than a dollop of New England with a population of three-hundred-nine. They weren't entirely done for, though. There was a stray set of human footprints on the earth by the population sign. Bare feet in the soft mud; three of them.

I was surprised my teeth weren't ground to the nerves by the time we made it to Carmel Drive.

We had a wide variety of houses to choose from once we found a small neighborhood tucked away in the protection of the trees. They were cute homes, much cuter and more quaint than houses in our little town. Unbothered white covered the overgrown lawns. Icicles hung from the facets. Bare trees were topped on every branch with white sleeves, threatening to fall and cave in every innocent roof. In other circumstances, it would have been a marvelous sight.

We made it to New Hampshire. The license plates told us so.

We had no way to tell where in New Hampshire we were. They didn't have any convenient "You are here" signs with a star posted anywhere. But New Hampshire, nonetheless. Progress.

I officially walked from southern Maine to New Hampshire. Yay me.

We agreed on 4315. It had slightly better siding than 4317 and more bathrooms than 4313.

We spent the next few days ransacking whatever we could from the neighboring houses. These places were astounding. The world was put on pause and the former owners of the house were plucked straight from space and time. We were able to triple our stocks and extend our livelihood by months, roughly estimated.

4315 was a good house. The space was perfect for the five of us. The amenities were decent. We were proud to commandeer it for the winter months.

It was on the fourth day that I became ill.

xvii.

We thought it was a common cold. It was an expected product of spending so much time in the cold weather. Of course, the frigid lake we bathed in would harm our bodies.

Then it never went away.

By the third week I was running a fever of God only knows how high. I had an everything-ache. I evolved into a mouth-breathing phlegm-filled creature. An anvil dug into my chest with every dramatic breath. Water never satisfied my throat. Meals never stayed down. Any quick movement sent me down an incurable spiral of stars across my vision.

They kept me isolated in the third bedroom after I coughed enough to have me wincing with every breath.

Peter started offering me his portions of food. I refused every time. Not out of selflessness, but because I knew it would come right back up.

There was one closet in the house that emanated a suspiciously rotting smell from behind the locked door. The smell never got better no matter how many times the decaying particles entered your nose.

Tate checked it out on the second day. He broke the lock, peeked inside, and promptly slammed the door. No one else has dared to look inside after him.

I suspect someone committed suicide in there.

I read a lot while in quarantine. There was a bookshelf of generic classics in the isolation room. I read all of them in my bedridden time.

That was all I could manage to move: back and forth to the bookshelf, back and forth to the hallway restroom, which did not work. We peed and pooped in a bucket that was later tossed out the window.

I read until I fell asleep with it half open on my arm and woke up with drool on the paper. I read until I wanted to gouge my eyes out. There was nothing better to do in my room.

Some were amazing. Some were horrible. Some I read more than once. Some I wanted to throw in the home's hearth to provide some actual use to us.

I missed books.

Days passed me by like landscapes down the highway. After the day I slept through an entire sunrise to the next sunrise, I gave up keeping track of the days. It didn't matter. I was ready to die, no matter what day it was.

The second snow hit sometime during all of that. Heating the house became immensely harder. The windows had to stay clamped shut. What little heat we were able to give off settled, but did nothing meaningful. The air became stagnant.

Tate still went out every day. We told him not to. He snuck out early the next morning while everyone was tucked in and peaceful. He didn't return that day until past dark.

Chrissy caught what I had after a month. We were henceforth sentenced to sharing the isolation room. We had a lot of time to bond about stuffy noses and pounding lungs.

As it turns out, she can be very agreeable when reduced to a snuffle of a girl.

We huddled together in the coldest of nights. The small girl seemed to fit into me like a puzzle piece. Being able to hold a solid, warm person was of more use to heat me up than any number of blankets. I never once heard a whisper of complaint from her.

There was one perk to being bedridden next to a window. No one ripped you away from the blinding serenity of the snowscape. No one told you to get up and work; to waste your life in front of a cash register or a ten-square-foot cubicle. Just you, your four blankets, and the snow. I can think of no better life.

That's a joke.

Chrissy got better and was out of quarantine soon. I didn't.

There were several times during my period of Immense Sick when I thought I would be okay with falling asleep and never waking up.

I only told Tate these feelings once. He swore never to tell anyone. I believed him. Then Diana started walking on eggshells for the next few days. I stopped talking to either of them until it stopped.

I would've died in that camper. One way or another.

Peter only checked on me once a week.

It wasn't like I was a prisoner in solitary confinement. Anyone could talk to me whenever they wanted, as long as they stood in the doorway and I stayed in bed. Diana visited every hour on the hour. Tate stopped by every evening with dinner. When Chrissy was sick, we read together. After she got better, I kept her updated on any drama in the books.

But hardly Peter. Why would he visit me while I felt on the brink of death? That's asking too much.

I'm not bitter.

I only got better once the snow started thawing. The aches and constant feeling of incoming vomit didn't cease, though.

Peter told me two months had passed since I'd been isolated in the third bedroom. That didn't make sense to me. Much too short.

I had to force down the sour sting of bitterness in the back of my throat. I welcomed that feeling like an old comrade.

Was that anger at the world? Or was that my breakfast?

…Oh yeah. It was my breakfast.

xviii.

The day we left the house was the second day after the snow completely melted. I still wasn't well, but we had to move.

As I was washing up in the freezing hose water, I heard Tate speaking from the room right above. The day was warmer and mushy. Almost every window was open, lest the stagnant air poison us.

I heard him tell someone he planned to get back to New York by the end of winter. Their voices drifted in and out, but I caught enough to piece together the puzzle. Tate estimated we were in the middle of January, and we were close to Massachusetts. If we moved fast and sustainably, we could make it before the season ended.

Diana's voice chimed in. I recognized the pitch in her increasingly frustrated tone when I shut off the water and leaned closer to the wall. "It's not that we're *waiting*. We're letting a sick person... freezing temperatures."

I ran back and forth away from the brick wall to get a good ratio of visual and audio spying.

Tate was pacing. His back came back to the glass every few seconds, each time his arms waving a little more erratically. "It's getting warmer. She's improving... Two of us... another bag off... doesn't have to carry... I'll give her one of my jackets. We'll work it..."

"I don't think she's ready to travel again, Tate!" Diana urged. I imagine myself as a giraffe, as if that'll help me peep. "She's healing, but... back down. What would you do if it were Chrissy?"

"It almost was! But she's back on her feet, and so will Vivienne. It'll take time."

Diana didn't say anything for a minute. The air pressure seemed to drop as the worry crept down my spine that I'd been discovered. "I don't think you're thinking this through," she finally confessed.

I never told them I overheard their argument, and they never suggested they knew I was eavesdropping.

Peter stayed in the living room all day, staring out the grand windows. That was his favorite pastime in the house. No conversation, no stimulation. Just him, the moth-devoured armchair, and the melted winter scenery of gray and brown. I tried to spark conversation with him, even if just to prove to someone that I was healthy and fully functional. I gave up after ten minutes.

Restocking our supplies was the biggest priority.

The biggest raid of the house was our wardrobe. Through the months, all of our clothes went through mudslides after thunderstorms. Sweat and dirt. Shoes got the worst of it. Diana's hiking boots were worn thin and left her with a limp every time she walked more than thirty feet.

Rest in peace, my old Converse. May you be eternally remembered.

Each of us got a new pair of shoes and several socks. It was clear no teenagers lived there, though, so it was hard for Chrissy to find something that fit. I offered to hand her down my good light jeans. They were too loose around the hips. She pouted and abandoned them on the floor of the kitchen.

I was about to embark on the rest of our journey wearing orange and white tennis shoes, gray ankle socks, men's black athletic pants, a middle-aged woman's cardigan, and my trusted black beanie. My outfit elicited laughs from the others, particularly Chrissy. I let her have it. At least I had new pants.

I double and triple-checked before leaving that I stashed my three favorite books in my bag. Both were hardbacks and the most precious gifts of the winter.

We left right after dawn the next morning. As I passed the laundry room for the final time, I bid it — and whoever remained inside — ado.

To say the walk to leave New Hampshire was "less than fun" would be an understatement.

No amount of protein or clean water could dampen the sensory hell in my body. I was left trembling again within an hour. Just one too-quick turn left me in whiplash. Coughs racked my body every other minute. Phlegm bubbled from the depths of my throat.

We took more breaks. Every time we stopped for a breather, no matter how short of a time, it left me begging for more. I laid back on the hard Earth every time and let my spine decompress. My muscles relaxed bit by bit. The cosmos behind my eyelids settled down as my breath slowly regained itself. By the tenth break, I struggled so hard to bring myself back to my feet that Peter had to lift me himself.

We walked. And we walked. And we walked. I know we only walked less than twelve hours, but if someone told me that we were going for weeks, I would not be surprised.

We made it to a small clearing of bare trees. The same bare trees we passed a minute prior. And the same trees from an hour ago. And from the beginning of the day. And yesterday, and the day before, and the month before.

I thought it would never end. Then the hairs on the back of my neck prickled. Survivor's instinct.

Peter held a fist up. Tate and Diana paused in their tracks; a movie's freeze frame.

For all of you that don't remember or understand the concept of a movie; they were the best invention for human entertainment since… ever. A way to encapsulate people from another space and time (video), but the people you see on screen are not who they claim to be. Professional pretenders.

Peter's head swiveled. He urged me to be careful with not one word. The caution in his face, the slight fear in the set line of his mouth. I could read it perfectly. He had the same exchange with Tate. Tate nodded.

No one knew where to hold their eyes. On Peter, on the trees, on the sky above…

"We're being watched," he announced.

The click of a cocked round sounded to my left. The breath caught in my throat. A wave of energy seeped through my ears, escaped my brain. Left me weaker.

One by one, seven people revealed themselves from the evergreen bushes. Each was adorned with military gear and ski masks, pulled close only to reveal slivers of eyes and edges of their noses. All but one man was armed with a rifle or handgun. One was directed at each of us; one more at Peter.

"Stay calm," Tate muttered to Chrissy, who looked ready to hit the person aiming at her. "They're guarding."

"Or a cartel!" Diana seethed sharply.

"Guards."

"State your names and intentions!" The vaguely male figure beside Tate ordered.

Tate raised both hands, acknowledging for us to do the same. My handbag fell to the ground with a deafening thud. "The Dawsons and Hammonds. We seek sanctuary," he explained, making direct eye contact with his match. "We are travelers. We mean no harm to your people or your cause."

"Where do you come from?"

"Southeastern Maine. I don't know the town's name."

"A town? Deserters?"

"It wasn't much of a town," Tate admitted.

The woman directed at Chrissy whispered something in the leader's ear. "We need to search your bags," he stated. Tate nodded, urging us to drop everything. I had to yank Peter's bags off myself to make him comply.

The woman at his side motioned for the extra soldier to take the nearest bag. Diana's chest sucked in deeply as they rifled through her bag and emptied the majority of her treasures into the dirt. Once satisfied, he took care to fix the contents how he found them. The process repeated. When the soldier came to me, I let him know with as much venom in my gaze as possible that his hands were not welcome in my bags. I could only glare; the fear of opening my mouth paralyzed me.

Something in the back of my mind told me that if they noticed the slightest hint of my sick stature, they would raise a red flag. Shout an alarm. Gift me a lead bullet to my cloudy head.

My armed guard stared at me. I stared at him. The stabbing pain in my side pierced the tension between us.

"They're all clear!" They announced.

The leader gave the signal for his people to lower their weapons. Tate's and Peter's hands lowered with them. I suddenly became too aware of the dryness in my throat, of the mucus and inflammation clogging my airways.

Dramatically, the leader yanked off his ski mask. He yanked the scarf down from his chin, revealing a gray beard to match his disgruntled salt-and-pepper head. Rosy cheeks and snubbed nose made him the envisionment of an exotic Santa Clause. If Santa had a few more scars and carried a gun. One gold tooth glistened when his mouth opened.

"I am Tveit." The leader masked his vague accent, which we would later learn was of Mediterranean origin. Tate gave each of our names. "How long do you expect to stay?" Tveit asked, steadily pacing around the circle of us.

"As long as you'll keep us. Until spring, preferably," Peter spoke up.

"I was not speaking to you."

"Well, I answered."

The man slowed, daring him to open his mouth again. Peter dared. "We've been traveling for weeks. We were forced to leave at the beginning of winter." Tveit was nothing but a statue, eyeing down Peter with a blank face. "My sister is sick. We need hospitality and any medical resources you can spare."

I closed my eyes, preparing to hear a bullet hit his flesh. Instead, the leader seemed humored. Flattered, even.

"Anita, do we have space for five more?" Tveit shouted beyond his shoulder.

The woman behind him shouldered her gun. "The Gatwes are leaving in days. After that, yes."

"The Gatwes?"

"Nadia and Rami. With their children."

"Oh… *right!* Right. The farmers." Tveit turned back to Peter and

Tate. "We will take you, if you will agree to the Community's terms."

"Yes! Anything!" Tate stepped forward. "Whatever you ask."

Tveit's shoulders set as rocks. Any semblance of emotion was wiped clean from his face. "We ask you to sacrifice a virgin maiden under the first red moon and smear the blood of another woman's menstruation on your heads to fortify the rite," Tveit announced. His eyes searched the three of us girls. His stoney gaze landed on Chrissy with finality. "She may do."

Diana threw her arm out before Chrissy. "No!"

"You can't be serious," Tate muttered, gesturing for me to move behind Peter.

A blade slowly revealed itself from the folds of Anita's uniform. Three guards took several steps towards us, pulling the circle in. Peter's hand went to the gun at my hip. Inch by inch, the strangers closed in on us.

Tveit marched right up to Tate's face. His hot breath steamed in the air, mixing with Tate's.

Silence settled among the trees…

A Zeus-like laugh boomed from Tveit. Tate fell back, disgust painted on his face. I watched Tveit double over and let a long wheeze escape his thick throat.

"You actually… oh dear… *oh!*" He clutched at his side, stumbling into Anita. She grinned childishly. "They… they *actually*… oh no! *AAA!*"

"*What?*" Diana screamed.

"He's pulling your leg," Anita assured, propping all of Tveit's elephant mass with one arm.

The soldiers around us gave us space and put away their weapons. A soldier at my side giggled. I sent them a rude sign. "You people are horrible."

Tveit straightened himself instantly. "Careful. Or I will feed you to my dogs," his voice hit me like a roll of thunder. Tate reached for me before Tveit had to break character again with a glee-filled chortle. "I joke, I joke! They are useless good-for-nothings."

"Ha ha." Tate grabbed Chrissy's shoulder. A cry bubbled from my throat, leaning my forehead against Peter's bicep.

"Oh, come on! It's a joke!" Tveit exclaimed, outstretching his arms playfully. His accent finally flowed fully through his jovial tone. "Of course, you are welcome in the Community. Of course, of course."

Anita pulled down her mask. The others followed, revealing five perfectly human faces with perfectly human eyes. Not monsters. Not gruesome mutants escaped from a military testing plant. People.

"What are your names?" Anita finally asked. Her mouse hair was cropped just below her ears, the muscles in her neck flexing with every small movement.

"Peter and Vivienne Hammond," my brother answered, pointing between the both of us. I nodded and forced a smile.

"Chrissy," the girl shot. "That's Diana. And Tate."

"You are two families?" Anita cocked her head like an amused peacock. A peacock's soul trapped in a bear's body. "And no parents?"

Tate wiped his sweat-glistening hands on his pants. "No parents. Just us. And these are all our earthly possessions."

"Who are you people?" Diana demanded.

"We are the People By The Sea." Tveit stuck out a large hand riddled with callouses. "The Community welcomes you."

Tate shook the hand warily. "Thank you. We're beyond grateful."

"I know. You are sure to die without help. I know." Tveit turned himself around and made a strange sign to his soldiers. Not any American Sign Language I knew.

Anita tailed Tveit as the man began a swift exit. One by one, we were each herded into a uniform line.

"We're not gonna sacrifice me?" Chrissy whispered. Diana rubbed her sister's hair as they merged into the train of us. The last two guards picked up the rear.

The Community

January

xix.

With every step, my two legs gained ten pounds. As the minutes ticked by I regretted not taking so much breakfast. Tate finally wore me down and I surrendered myself to a piggyback ride. Two of his bags went to a courteous guard. The smallest bag went on my back. Together, we formed one very tall, arcane creature.

Tate checked on me every few minutes. I didn't respond. It was far easier to drift into the terrifying, meaningless space between consciousness than to speak.

The trees started thinning out. I commanded Tate to let me down once the gray sky revealed itself.

The atmosphere was brushed wide with an ashen haze, stretching as far into the horizon as one could see. A wild party of birds flocked overhead, crying out to each other. To the sky. To the universe. Avian darlings swooping in and amongst the folds of the sky. Free.

"The planet's bird population bounced back over the mating season," Tveit explained, pointing his beard to the horizon. "Just... poop raining from the skies. But good for us."

"You hunt your own food?" Chrissy kicked the dirt piles at our feet.

"No, they get bi-weekly shipments from their local *Whole Foods*," I shot.

Chrissy lowered her head and voice. "It's just a question."

"We have hunters, supply foragers, and gardeners working every day to fulfill the Community's hunger. We try to give everyone a rounded diet," Anita answered, putting an end to the brewing argument between Chrissy and me.

"How many people do you have?" Diana asked. "Can you support all of us?"

"Don't worry about that," Anita said.

Tveit lumbered over to Diana to give her an enveloping side hug.

Diana's arms retracted into her side. "Of course! We are a population of over 40! We did not get here by turning people away," his merry voice ricocheted off a few birds.

Five of the soldiers dropped off once we reached the sharp cut-off of trees. Before us lay a field of dead grass, merging into sand, into the ocean.

I could hear it. I could hear the waves and smell the rocky beach. The salt air cured the weakness in my body.

Tents and cement buildings decorated the coast. People busied dirt trails and makeshift roads. As we approached, the vague blobs and lines gradually formed humans of every shape, color, and age.

What was this slice of land before?

I imagined a beachfront kids camp that used to house a summer population of two hundred. The camp owners were a newlywed middle-aged couple who lived on-site and hosted a new group of college-age counselors and tween campers every month. The cement buildings were the dormitories and dining halls. The tents housed stations for the volunteer counselors to teach crafts and basic science projects while every else played flag football on the sand. Whatever the setting truly was, it couldn't be cooler than that.

"Vivienne needs to check in with Cillian first," I heard Anita whisper to Tveit. I flocked a little closer to Tate's side.

We reached the first pole-and-canvas tent when Diana appeared at my side. "You okay?" She whispered. I barely nodded. Diana's hand crept down to mine. "You look green."

I didn't have time to respond before our walking party was bombarded by tiny children. They weaved themselves through our legs, dodging knees and flying feet left and right.

They were skinny things. Young creatures who looked young enough not to remember a time before the downfall. At least, not enough to be of any use for them. The Community could be all most of them knew. Trauma can cause memory loss. Or one thing they knew, their parents moved them out of town and suddenly they hadn't used a light switch in ten months.

A very pregnant woman called for Tveit. He had mercy on her

pitiful wattle, parting from us to meet her halfway. That left us with just Anita and one more guard, whom she promptly ordered back to the trees with their unique sign language.

We were left standing around while the children were herded back to what I assumed to be the daycare. A younger adult woman — visibly tired beyond her years — called for the children to leave us alone. I also heard a threat to take away swim time. One by one, the kids dropped off and returned to their caretaker. Diana waved them goodbye, blowing a small kiss to a girl who was enraptured by the two of us.

"What do you notice about these people?" Peter muttered to me.

All I could see were the smiling faces of children and hard-working adults walking back and forth with large boxes or sacks. Polite greetings and assistance. No signs of pity or slave labor.

"They don't look miserable?" I guessed.

"Not that. They're sheep."

I craned my neck to look at him, dumbfounded. "Because they cooperate in a society? They follow the rules?"

Peter didn't answer.

A man materialized next to Anita; slipped out of the folds in space and time. His dark bronze hair peeked out from a low-hanging hat, shielding his eyes from the world. The rest of his face hid under a thick cloth mask with vague symbols painted in white. Every inch of his body was covered in black and gray gaudy clothing.

He fit into the hidden apocalyptic scenery.

How much food did these people have? How much clean water? Heat? What were they keeping from the rest of the world that stranded loners like me needed more?

"Everyone, meet Dmitri. Dmitri, everyone." Anita waved her hand between the man and our group. "Dmitri is my right hand in patrol. Get used to seeing him."

Anita whispered many nothings to Dmitri. He dutifully clasped his hands behind his back and watched us when their low conversation finished. He reminded me of something out of a science fiction thriller.

His gaze fixated on me and Peter. I couldn't see it. I could feel it.

"Dmitri is going to give you four a tour of the Community. Vivienne needs to stay behind," Anita announced.

Peter clenched his fist. "Absolutely not."

"*Peter*," I groaned.

Anita's posture grew only more rigid. "Sir, your sister is actively struggling to stand on her own. She is dehydrated and malnourished to a dangerously lethal level. We will inspect all of you, but I consider her condition more imperative. Were you not the first to request help for her?"

"We're not separating," he insisted through a clenched jaw. I could feel his teeth gritting as if they were my own.

"We have the resources to help Vivienne as soon as possible. Us merely having this conversation is prolonging her pain."

"Exactly. So let's stop and get her treated!" Peter stomped forward threateningly. Dmitri stepped to Anita's defense.

My head weighed fifty pounds. "I'm okay."

"No, you're not," Diana shot sternly. "I told you to eat more!"

"I highly suggest you take my advice, Vivienne," Anita said. "I think you're fighting off a virus. Or pneumonia, perhaps. We won't know unless Cillian, our head of medical, takes a look at you..." Anita trailed off as a smaller girl walked up. She ignored us for the child.

"This is such bullshit," Peter muttered, shaking his eyes.

Tate stared at him from the other end of the semicircle. I could feel the energy building up in his fist, ready to launch itself at Peter's face.

Anita returned her attention to us. "We're thinking it will be more time efficient to examine her first while we give the rest of you the tour, then examine you four while she's getting the tour. Don't you agree?"

"No. I don't agree. What time are we saving? We have all the time in the world!" Peter shouted, grabbing my arm with his calloused hand.

"I understand your concern, Mr. Hammond. But this way we can put less on our medic's shoulders at one time."

Peter scoffed bitterly. "Wow, *one* less. So gracious of you."

"Stop being rude," I smacked his arm.

Wind smacked our sides. The stars flurried in my nerves. Diana grabbed my shoulder.

"Mr. Hammond, I insist that you leave her with us. She is in good hands."

Peter looked down at me. I looked at Diana. A low huff escaped him. I wanted to shove him away. If I could find the energy. "Fine. But I stay with her. No negotiations," he conceded.

"Peter-" I sighed.

"We can compromise if that will make you happy." Anita clasped her hands in front of her waist. "Cillian will see you both."

"I would rather Tate stay with me."

I don't know why the words left my mouth. I had no control over them.

Peter's head slowly moved in my direction. Chrissy's eyes widened so big they lept out of her skull. I wanted to curl inside myself. I wanted to implode. I wanted to become invisible to the betrayed gaze of my brother.

"*Why?*"

"I don't think that matters," Tate spoke up for the first time. "I'll stay with her."

"Great! Then that's settled." Anita stepped onto the first path, cutting any further debate off.

Dmitri waved the remaining three forward. Peter sent me one more glance as the three of them followed Dmitri into town, soon enveloped in the thin crowd of People By The Sea. Anita smiled and led us into the first tent without another word.

"I'm proud of you for standing up to him," Tate said, clapping me on the back.

"I shouldn't have to stand up to him."

Tate held the canvas flap open for me. "But you do have to. And that's sad, but the truth."

"He's gone through a lot."

"Doesn't give him a right to be a douche."

Lined along the far wall were four plastic cots and one Lay-Z-Boy — their effort for a reclining bed. Shelves and shelves of vials and tins decorated the semi-solid walls. Boxes and bags filled the floor space, leaving only a few trails for one to walk. Windchimes and mobiles hung from the ceiling, for which use I had no clue.

"Lay down over there," Anita's phantom voice instructed, already deep within the maze of the medical tent. I heard metal clanging behind a thick plastic curtain and a thin trickle of water running.

Running water. Plumbing? Or a well?

We made our way to the cots. Tate had to help me lower myself to the finger-thin mattress before crouching at my bedside.

"You guys have running water?" Tate shouted at the plastic curtain.

Anita didn't answer immediately. The clanging continued before she emerged out the back end of the plastic curtain, donning two commercial plastic cups. "Sometimes we have tap. Sometimes our gardeners have to find fresh water and bring back loads by bucket."

"How does it only sometimes work?"

Anita closed a stray drawer with her hip. Her lengthy skirt swayed at her calves. "No one knows. It's a game of guesswork." Anita smiled, handing us our cups.

The water was unfiltered and donned floating mystery fragments. I tried to hold it on my own before spilling the precious liquid down my wrist. Without a word, Tate tipped my chin up and gently poured the lukewarm water down my throat. The desert of my throat relaxed; relishing, crying for more. Every cell resurrected, blooming like ferns unfurling to full potential. One more drink — I was ready to sit up.

"Cillian will be with you two soon." Anita took her jacket sleeve to my wet wrist. "Cillian is good at his job. I promise."

"Thank you." Tate smiled, setting our cups on the floor. Anita nodded humbly, backing away from our cots.

"If Cillian isn't back soon, don't hesitate to find me or Tveit. We'll both be floating around for the day," Anita told us. Tate nodded. Maybe I nodded too, maybe I didn't. Anita left; and trusted us not to steal their precious resources.

Every sense peeled to investigate each shelf and box from afar. What lay within arm's reach… what we've been missing for so long… The drugs. The bandages. The antibiotics. The soothing creams and ointments. Menthal gel to block the *smell*.

How much safer could we be had the People By The Sea not hogged everything left in the region?

"They seem like good people," Tate commented after a minute, flashing a small smile. It failed to raise my spirits.

Vague sounds fluttered in and out through the canvas tent. Children giggling. Adults scolding them. Something fell to the dirt ground. A tough cloth ripped. Someone screamed a curse. The world continued around us while we waited and aged into oblivion.

"Where *is* he?" I asked after an hour.

"It's only been a few minutes. They probably only have one doctor for the entire place."

"Then they should remedy that flaw."

Tate rubbed my arm. "It'll be okay. Just be patient."

This was one of the times I appreciated his accent. It wasn't too thick to distract, but heavy enough to lure you to sleep. You know he would tell the best bedtime stories to a child.

My serenity was rudely interrupted by a man stumbling through the tent flap. A doctor's jacket that had long since stopped being white hung off his limp shoulders.

"Vivienne?" He called, scrambling papers left and right on his three-legged desk.

I nodded. Cillian couldn't see me. "Yes. And I'm Tate," he stood and approached the doctor with a hand outstretched for a shake. Cillian stared at him blankly before walking back to our cots.

Cillian: towering inches over Tate, matched with his gangly limbs and pencil-straight nose, he reminded me of a personified walking stick. Wired spectacles perched on the middle of his nose, dangerously precarious of falling. I could barely see his irises between the thick, light brown bangs hanging over his forehead.

"What have you been eating recently?" He asked me.

"That's funny," I exhaled.

"Vivienne…" Tate shook his head. Cillian looked at him like a lost puppy. "We've been low on food, but anything we get is split equally among the five of us. Leaves, winter berries, mice, fish if we can manage it."

"And water?"

"Scarce."

Cillian stuck a gloved finger in my mouth and pressed on my tongue. I didn't want to fathom how many times that glove was stuck in someone else's mouth. "When she got sick, why did you not give her more water?"

I looked at Tate. Tate's eyes lowered in shame.

Cillian's fingers searched all over my face and throat. "I need to perform some tests?" That was the question. I nodded. "Breathe in… May I press on your stomach?"

"You're not gonna feel anything in there." I giggled at the memory of endless pediatric nurses feeling my abdomen. There used to be something for them to squish. Cillian was not amused. I underwent the rest of his tests with a mouth clamped shut.

When it was over, Cillian scooted himself over the dirt floor and began rustling through the overflowing shelves. He had a way of listening that made you think your words flew right through one ear and out the other. But it helped.

"She'll heal with good rest and nutrients. I have a composition we've been saving for the winter months… if I… hang on…" His head disappeared into a deep shelf. He reappeared with a small syringe and a vial of a cloudy yellow liquid. "Aha! Here!"

"Where did you get that?" I demanded, pushing as far away from the needle as possible. Tate grabbed my arm.

Cillian gently stuck the needle point into the covering and drew the precious immunization out. "I was a nurse for a decade. I was able to get a stash for myself before the hospital went down. This in here is essentially a cocktail of all your essential vitamins; what your body's been lacking since the season began."

"Is that how you got everything in here?" Tate asked.

Cillian shrugged sheepishly. "More or less. Stockpiling, stashing, permanently borrowing…" He observed the syringe, testing the squirt. "I've only needed to use this one once so far."

I reached out blindly for Tate's hand. "Did you sterilize that?"

"Of course. As sterile as it can be."

That made me feel worse. "What will you do when you run out?" I whispered. Tate squeezed my hand.

"Go back to the old methods, I guess. Pre-Industrial Revolution." Cillian crouched next to my cot. I stiffened. My parents never cared much about getting my annual vaccinations. They took me to get the required ones for each age, and maybe three influenza vaccines in elementary school.

He swiped my bicep with a damp rag. Every nerve ending in my body seized.

"You need to relax. It'll hurt more if you don't."

"I am relaxed."

Cillian gently pinched around my bicep. "No, you aren't."

"This is as relaxed as I'm gonna get."

"I'm right here," Tate whispered, giving my hand one more squeeze as Cillian brought the syringe to my right arm.

"I really suggest you relax yourself," Cillian urged. "You'll be sore for days."

"*Stop!* Stop! Why do I need it?" I demanded, my eyes refusing to tear away from the needle.

"You have a severe viral infection. And I assume you battled near hypothermia. We had a lot of hypothermia here. You are deprived of essential vitamins your body was not prepared to operate without. You'll still need to eat better, drink more, and rest. The fever won't come down if not. This is the best solution I have right now."

Tate chuckled, rubbing my arm. "Doctors say that a lot. I guess that doesn't change in the End Times."

Cillian bristled. "Don't joke about the End Times," he muttered, lowering the syringe from my arm. "If you don't want it, Vivienne, I can't make you. But I would highly highly recommend it. Winter isn't over. There are wild bacteria and fungi that our pampered bodies are not used to. It's our biggest kryptonite."

"I've never heard of that," I insisted, studying his glass-covered eyes for any sign of a lie. I could find none.

"Sure you have."

Tate fully sat on the floor by my side. "You should take it."

"As your doctor, I agree. But we can't make you." To prove his point, Cillian set the syringe on the cot by my legs. I pulled my knees to my chest. Cillian held both hands up to show he held nothing against me. No more threats.

I had one more last-ditch effort of procrastination in my arsenal. "Where did you study?"

"Graduated from Northwest Missouri State," he stated proudly. I never heard of that school.

I ended up taking it. If Cillian killed me, Tate would be my witness. I tried to relax as much as possible. My arm was sore for days afterward, just as promised.

XX.

I spent two days on that cot. Two days I spent staring at the canvas ceiling, watching the tent flap in the January wind.

Cillian checked in whenever he could, but the majority of his schedule was spent pushing his little metal cart all around the Community, attending to any scraped knee or broken bone he may stumble across. He had in-office patients, too. There was a young girl who stopped in with a bloody nose. She stared at me, slack-jawed and empty-eyed from the front of the tent, blatantly ignoring Cillian's orders not to be rude.

When Cillian couldn't check my healing or give me another pill to manage the fever, his assistant was happily on call.

Eugene was no older than me. He was the freshest of the adults in the Community, having just started when fall hit. It was clear he respected his boss and his work. Eugene liked to ramble, too. He liked to tell me every portion of his day and every detail he encountered on the way from Point A to the tent. I didn't mind. It was either listening to him and throwing out a "nice" or a "cool" every thirty seconds or sitting in the silence that was the empty medical tent.

Three times a day a woman came with fresh water and a small plate of warm food. Her name was Nina. She introduced herself as the head of childcare and education. Nina often volunteered to visit Cillian's patients during nap time. She was sweet but did speak to me like a toddler. I didn't fault her for it. Her only interactions were with children no older than ten, all day every day.

My healing was not linear. Some hours felt better. I could get up and walk around, observing all of Cillian's gadgets and natural healing potions. Eugene even let me stand outside the tent for a breath of fresh air and sunlight... before I vomited on the beige grass.

Peter and Diana checked in whenever they could. Everyone had already been fitted for jobs around the Community. The People By

The Sea were open and welcome to bring them into their society, so long as they contributed their share. Lest they become useless.

Tate was training to be a patrolman; the same armed people who picked us up in the woods. Peter was in the butcher shop, hunting if need be. Diana was training with Nina. Chrissy was underage, so she did odd jobs in the kitchens between tutoring.

The People By The Sea formed shortly after the downfall began. Almost everyone was a refugee ravaged by greed and insanity. Everyone gathered at this spot on this sliver of New Hampshire coast. Whatever purpose it served before had already been evacuated.

There was always something to do, always some way to help. Unless you were stuck under doctor's orders in the medical tent.

Everyone was welcoming to my people. But naturally, there was an understanding that they were newcomers. They weren't the first asked to help. During meals the four sat at their spot away from others, accompanied only by the dust and tracked-in gray sludge.

We were welcome, but not home.

Cillian discharged me on the third day. I passed all his examinations and wasn't peeing liquid bronze anymore. Anita was supposed to pick me up at noon to begin my tour. Dmitri met me instead.

Today he was dressed in less black, but just as much coverage. He and Eugene exchanged a man's handshake — the obnoxious slapping and clapping and masculine hugging so they could disguise that they crave human touch — before the younger boy retreated into the canvas.

Dmitri said nothing as we walked from the medical tent. Tate took my bags to their sleeping situation after my first appointment. I felt naked walking without them. I was too light; too unburdened.

People watched as I passed with every step. They made a wide berth around Dmitri… or me. My eyes lowered to the backs of his feet after we passed the childcare tent and a small boy pointed at me. Nina scolded him.

"We don't have an official way to assign jobs," was the first thing Dmitri said to me. We entered one of the three stone buildings. "Just show up wherever you want and mentor with the leader for a few days. Test the waters. Then if you want the job just… keep showing up."

I took in the freshly painted entrance hall that branched off into two separate corridors. Armchairs and small cushions lined the floor perimeter as if a game of The Floor is Lava just ended. Divots had been smashed into the wall to hold candles. The destruction revealed perfect gray cement under the fresh layer of blue and sage green color.

"Where did you get this paint?"

"Wasn't ours. These are the dormitories. This is something of a social space…" Dmitri motioned around himself in a wide arc. "No one sleeps in here unless they snore too loud."

"The married people stay in that one-" he motioned at another building through the wall. He moved like a bored toddler who wanted to sit down. "We let them have their own spaces for their married duties. Everyone else stays in here. The kids and their parents are in that room," he pointed right, "and teenagers and unmarried adults are down there," pointed to the left. "The other identical building is the mess hall, kitchen, and butcher house."

"What about unmarried couples that want to do married duties?" I asked, resisting a giggle.

"Then they can have beach sex or do it in front of everyone else."

That did make me giggle. I'm immature, I know.

Dmitri gave me a side eye before straightening. "Your friends put your stuff in the back. We're not gonna have room for all of you yet, but the floor is comfy."

Each bed was empty — obviously, it was the middle of the day. The building trapped heat, but not well enough that you would dare mistake the air conditioning for working. Below, the remnants of a box system lay deceased on the floor.

Only fifteen beds lined the walls of this room. Mismatched bags of personal belongings perched along the sides of each. At the very end, though, were our bags — including Chrissy's over-the-shoulder NASA pack.

In front of our luggage pile was a king-size comforter and three pillows spread out on the floor. Anita mentioned something about a family leaving soon. *Soon.* What did *soon* mean to them?

I emerged from the room. Dmitri was leaning against the nearby wall, studying his dirty fingernails with stubbornly crossed arms. "There aren't enough beds for us yet?"

"The five of you are taking turns on the one cot we could spare. Once the Gatwes leave you'll have more than enough space," Dmitri explained, uncrossing his arms with one swift motion.

"Why would that matter if the families sleep in another room?"

"Only the small kids are over there. The teenagers are in *there*, which the Gatwes have three of. Then we have a pregnant woman due soon. She'll give birth and move out. We'll have space for the five of you in no time."

"But how much time?"

"A month, give or take."

"And what if another group like us comes in? Do you have to turn them away?"

"Of course, not. At that point, we would find more beds. Line the wall out here for them."

"Why can't we sleep out here?"

"Anita says so."

"*Why* does she say so?"

Dmitri scoffed, chuckling like my concern was a game to him. "We'll work something out for everyone."

"I just want to make sure we're on the same page. How do you know so much?" I asked as he led me back into the fresh air with a wide hoist of the door. "This time I ask out of curiosity."

Dmitri peered at me from the side. "We have a small population. And wouldn't you want your #4 to know everything?"

"Number 4?"

Dmitri led me toward the mess hall. "We have a line of succession. Tveit, who I'm sure you've met or *heard*, is number one. Anita is his right hand. Cillian is next. And I am number 4. Anita's right hand, as she so graciously put it."

"You didn't like that?" I watched an elderly woman pass us on the dirt road. Despite the pronounced limp and hunched-back, she smiled at me. Her neon plastic sun visor fell sideways over her eyebrows.

He paused to readjust the woman's visor. "I'm no one's right-hand man. I'm just a man."

I tripped over a hidden sand dip in the dry grasses. Dmitri's hand was frigid as he hoisted me back up. "So it's like the Vice President taking over the country if the President dies?" He agreed. "What if *you* die?"

"Leadership goes to number 5."

"And it just keeps going?"

"Until there's no one left."

I studied Dmitri harder. His eyes missed the age and wisdom of Tveit or Anita. Even Cillian bore a glint of seniority in his eyes. His hair was still full and youthfully healthy under the cap. He couldn't have been much older than Tate. I gave it a year or two, maximum.

"You're so young. They trust you with everyone?"

"We don't judge youth with iron shades," he muttered in a slick tone. I don't know what that meant.

Dmitri opened the door to a second cement building. Three others flooded out. It was as if they had been leaning against the door for hours, waiting for someone to let them tumble out like floodwater. Dmitri pushed me through and let the door slam behind us.

The mess hall had the same layout as the dorms. Three long, hastily thrown-together wooden tables were arranged on the floor. I could see the kitchens through the open doorway to the right room; nothing more than a stove and insulated bins. The door to the left was decorated with a plastic flap and blood splatter stains.

Several people were finishing up their lunches and watched us from the front of the hall. Dmitri pointed for me to sit. He signaled to one of the cooks meandering around the perimeter of the room. She retreated to the kitchen. "The four of you adults are tacked onto the end of the succession by age. That younger one does not qualify. Eugene was final by age. But we also judge by longevity and contribution. Eugene has been with the People since the beginning."

My head snapped in his direction. "How do you know our ages?"

"Tate told me."

Fair. Through all my efforts to find a flaw in their system or any hint that they could have ulterior motives, I was starkly failing. Still, I refused to trust them. I refused to trust Dmitri.

At lightning speed, the cook returned with two bowls. She set them in front of us with a small bow.

"Thank you!" I inspected the stew.

Foreign meat and vegetables swam around in the dark liquid. Warm saliva flooded my mouth. A warm aroma floated to my nose. Senses playing off one another, I savored the anticipation before bringing the metal spoon to my mouth. A gargled moan escaped me. I didn't recognize the spices or type of broth. The game was unfamiliar and so wonderfully cooked. The carrots and broccoli squished under my teeth, releasing flavors with every eager jaw movement.

Maybe it wasn't so bad to stick around the Community…

Dmitri didn't touch his. "We don't include children in the line of succession. Most of them are too young to understand what we do. Do you understand?"

"I guess." I wasn't paying attention. The broth scorched my throat as I swallowed all at once. It was heavenly.

I finished my stew in silence. I was nothing short of impressed at how well-constructed their society was. How well orchestrated every detail of their slice of the world was. Dmitri seemed to have every point lined out, every possibility prepared for. Such a relief to see in a new world of such chaos.

The others in the mess hall left, leaving us in complete silence. Dmitri slurped down two spoonfuls of his stew before pushing it towards me. "You need to eat more. Cillian's orders."

"No thank you."

"Fine. But I can't promise you any dinner," he admitted. I stared at him, the bowl, then back at him. "Resources will be a little tight until the Gatwes leave. Patrol, pregnant mothers, and children take priority for meals. Your choice."

Pretending I didn't care, I accepted. His bowl was cold, which only meant I could chug it all the faster. The burst of the spices had calmed without the accentuating kick of fresh heat.

That was the first meal to leave me full in… a long time.

"Thank you. I appreciate it."

Dmitri nodded. "Any other questions? Any interests in jobs?"

I cleared my throat, clasping my hands together. "I don't know. What's available?"

"For you, I would suggest medicine. Or gardening."

"That's presumptuous of you."

"You can ask a lot of questions in those jobs." He winked.

I wasn't going to admit to him that I loved gardening. I managed our garden at home with pride and so much enjoyment. There was nothing that could beat digging in the healthy soil and treating young plants. It was an amazing routine. Good for mental and physical health.

But I didn't need to prove Dmitri correct. He was too smug.

My thoughts were distracted by the bang of the doors. A young man with a black mess of curls burst through, holding the door open with his back. He dragged a metal cart through the doorway, jostling it up the slight hitch. He hummed without a care in the world, pulling the cart all the way through and letting the doors slam behind him.

"Good afternoon, Anthony," Dmitri called out. He stood up and motioned for me to do the same.

The newcomer looked up towards his voice, peering into the dim lighting of the hall. "Hi, Dmitri. How goes ya?"

Dmitri ignored him and guided me forward. "This is Vivienne Hammond."

"Hello, Vivienne Hammond."

I waved. Dmitri shook his head. "He can't see you," he whispered. "*Speak* to Anthony."

"No, I cannot see you. But I'm not deaf," the words shot from Anthony like a cannonball.

"Oh… I'm sorry!" I exclaimed, stepping up to the cleaning cart. The cart was filled halfway with sanitation chemicals and rags. That was all the People could scrape together. "I'm sure he didn't mean to offend."

Anthony's face lowered into a grimace. "Yeah, well, you did," he mumbled. Dmitri rolled his eyes.

"Don't be so *rude!*" I had the nerve to scold the #4.

"He's fucking with you."

"You know, a lot of people don't understand how demeaning it can be-" Anthony sniffled, backing away from us. One gloved hand moved to his face, rubbing his nose like a child.

"Cut it out, Anthony. She's gullible."

Anthony's hand dropped. His head snapped up. The dark curls flopped with the sudden jerk. "My bad. I can't help it." A small giggle bubbled from him. He held a hand out to me.

"Anthony Lillard, at your service," he announced, bowing deep and dramatically.

"Our local clown," Dmitri grumbled.

"It's a curated craft." He turned completely to me with a soft smile. "It's nice to meet you. I've heard a lot about your family."

I watched Dmitri watch us with a blank stare. I jabbed my tongue at him. "They're not all my biological family. Just my brother. The other three are good friends."

"I don't believe in biological families. We live in a world where blood doesn't have to have any meaning," Anthony shrugged. That made me smile too. His grew with mine.

From that moment, any doubt that the People By The Sea were anything but normal people was squashed.

xxi.

Dmitri wasn't lying when he said he couldn't promise me dinner. The three cooks had to improvise for everyone to have a serving. Seconds were a figment of your imagination. But for the first time in months, my stomach did not rumble with the setting sun.

There was a bonfire on the beach that night. There was a bonfire every night. Attendance wasn't mandatory, but there was nothing better to do.

They called the bonfire the Flame. It was a hollow pit carved from the sand with a log pyramid set perfectly in the center. The goal was to go out every night, light it at midnight, and it would symbolize each day passing in a lovely blaze. As we watch the fire die, it proves that we outlast each dying day.

The People By The Sea began with that practice. After so long timing it exactly for midnight is impossible since most functional watches are a memory. But the symbol stands.

I never told anyone how much of a doomsday cult practice the entire ordeal sounded. Maybe they knew. Maybe the Flame was there for the irony.

Diana, Tate, and I sat on the edge of the grass and reeds. Chrissy mingled with the other teenagers. Peter was in the dorms, being a grouch.

The waves crashed before us. Moonlight bathed us in a serene glow combated with the Flame's light.

Kids ran and screamed around the base of the pit. Parents watched from afar, occasionally shouting at them to be kind or to stay away from the fire. Others swam and waded in knee-high water. Teenagers competed in heated rock skipping contests. You could hear Tveit's chortle from the other end of the beach. His two dogs — a pitbull and a beagle named Barbosa and Fox — ran between legs and drowned themselves in the sea foam.

I could stay there all my life. No work, no responsibilities. Just the moon, the waves, and the fire.

Chrissy and I drew straws of who would get the cot that night. She won.

In the adult dorms, people walked left and right, up and down. You had to get over any body issues quickly, lest you spend days in the same clothes in fear of someone seeing you strip.

There was a spit outside with lukewarm running water. We took turns washing our faces and trying to clean our teeth. But after so long the spit wasn't reliable. It took longer to bring up water, or what came up would be dirty and defeat the purpose of a wash.

I had better sleep in the camper surrounded by moose than my first night with the People. Diana and I practically slept on top of each other. We switched whose limbs cascaded over the other once one of our legs started to go numb. It took another century to drift back unconscious once we repositioned.

Someone close snored too loud. Snot and phlegm froze inside my sinuses. Someone else was mumbling a name in their sleep. Fox and Barbosa partied outside the window.

When I couldn't sleep, I watched the others. People with one arm draped over their face. People subconsciously scratching their butts. People sleeping with all four limbs cascaded off the mattress. A mosquito made itself comfortable by my ears.

The sun was back before I knew it. Work didn't start at dawn, but if you wanted breakfast, you woke with the sun.

Good thing I already was.

After breakfast, I tracked down and found the oldest woman, the one who smiled at me on the tour, and followed her out of the mess hall. The woman led me to the farthest edge of the Community. Dmitri didn't take me out there on the tour.

A metal archway labeled "Izzy's" in gothic font marked a dirt path to the gardens, an area I imagined was once full of color and life. At this time of year, though, it seemed lucky to be sprouting the minimal plants from dinner. A large wooden structure with mono-color vines and leaves spindling off stapled the garden: the root bed, partnered with a ten-by-ten space of messily tilled soil. The hunched-over back of an older man peeked from within the folds of the vegetation.

"Are you interested in the gardens?" The elderly woman spoke up once I stepped through the archway. She slowly turned to peek over her shoulder at me. I didn't mistake the mischievous smirk across her wrinkles.

"How long have you known I was behind you?"

She led me to a large plastic crate without a response. She had trouble unlatching and hoisting off the lid. I assisted and revealed a menagerie of hand-held garden tools and gloves. "My name is Eden," she finally introduced.

I grinned so wide that the bridge of my nose crinkled. "I'm Vivienne."

Eden smiled, holding her feeble hand out to me. A feeble hand wielded by a strong person. Eden held herself as if her hunchback were a figment of my imagination. As another girl walked into the area, Eden handed me a pair of working gloves.

"Do you lead the gardens?" I asked, pulling the cloth gloves over my wrist. They hadn't been washed. Ever.

Eden shook her head. Her snow white hair was frozen in place with fifty pins and decorative needles. I could imagine those as her only connection to the old world. Sorrow struck me for the style and grace she lost.

"Hank leads us. He sleeps in the plants most nights," she answered, loosely throwing a hand out to the other man. Her allure was nothing short of captivating. Her eyes held so much hidden charm and excitement, as if she still remembered her glory days in Hollywood — a staple alongside Audrey Hepburn and John Wayne.

"Is there anything I can do?" I ask, leading myself to the soil-filled box. A younger boy stared at me from the other side through a collection of stems.

"We don't have anything to harvest today." Eden studied the

leaves of a cabbage plant. "There will be work tomorrow. You should know that we take pride in harvesting at the peak of growth. It's all we owe the People."

I never realized how amazing working for a good cause could make someone feel.

"Before you start, you should know that we're disregarded in the Community," Eden explained. I frowned, my eyebrows drawing closer to themselves. "We don't have the drama of patrol, or fantastical stories of hunting. We don't take care of the young, or save lives like Cillian. We stand on the sidelines. People push us to the side. We don't stand out. If it'll ruin your reputation, you don't have to work with-"

I grabbed Eden's delicate, gloved hands with my own. "I love it already," I assured her.

I never before considered the elderly who survived. It seemed like such a needless concept to entertain that someone with such low odds of survival on regular terms could make it through the first three months. But there Eden was, standing in front of me pruning the small winter bushes like it was her solemn life's duty.

I left the gardens after my first day early. Eden directed me to a few other stations that could use my help. The Gatwes chose that time to make their grand departure.

Everyone lined up on both sides of the road out of town. Unwillingly, I was herded to the very middle of the group, squashed between a burly buzz-cut man and the pregnant chef. The couple and their *many* children pass down the center. People were praying over them. Wishing them good luck. Sending positive affirmations their way.

The wife, Nadia, cried all the way down. Her husband held their youngest child's hand to keep him from running to his little girlfriend in the audience.

When the family approached the end of the line, Tveit was waiting for them. He presented them with a red wagon filled halfway with clean socks, two more jackets, several canisters of water, and wrapped food.

"Please take these. It's the last we can offer." Tveit held the handle out to the father. He rejected it before leading his family into the woods.

We watched their backs disappear into the bare brush. The Community was seven people lighter. I knew none of them, but can admit that watching those strangers leave everything behind made me tear up.

I learned from Tate that the family left to move further south. They did a good job of hiding it, but the Community had been hit badly by winter. The Gatwes weren't the first to leave. Every dormitory used to be overflowing.

As the mob dispersed my mind couldn't help but stray to anger. Horrible, cursing thoughts.

The Dawsons and I were doing just fine before Peter came and cried to Tate that fateful afternoon. I was doing fine completely on my own! I didn't starve to death. I never slid over the edge into delirium. By my standards, that's perfect.

Before I convinced myself to fall into a deeper, inescapable pit of an ugly, fear-ridden emotion, I forced the horrid thoughts into a deep corner of my brain. I pushed it deeper and deeper until the void that used to contain Geometry swallowed it whole.

Cheer needed to be found somewhere. Anywhere. Not work, not friends who could read through me to oblivion.

Answers. Answers would calm me.

First step: find Dmitri. I knew Tveit and Anita were out of the question. Cillian would never have the time of day to entertain my pondering. Find Dmitri; find secrets about the People By The Sea.

I found Dmitri outside the childcare tent. He was speaking with Nina. I stepped up to the side of the nearest tent. There is nothing inherently conspicuous about a conversation between two people, but I couldn't risk tearing my eyes away from him. One look away, and he may slip through the cracks to never be seen again.

As the dark-clothed man started retreating from her, my shoulders set in determination. My attack had to be planned. It was then that I realized I didn't have an actual plan.

"Hi, whoever you are," someone said behind me.

I flung myself around, excuses and explanations flying rampantly through my head and missing my mouth. My eyes finally landed on a heap of black hair on a boy's head. Anthony stood at the other end of the tent with his sanitation cart.

I froze. My gaze latched onto him, eyeing his every curious movement. I didn't make that much noise whipping around; hadn't hit anything, hadn't smacked a hand on anything. If I stayed quiet long enough, maybe he would leave…

"I can see you a bit, you know?" Anthony quipped. I let my shoulders relax and surrendered. A deep scowl was carved on his face. "I'm not 100% blind, asshole."

I whipped back to find Dmitri again. He was already missing. Perturbed and my heart still racing, I turned back to Anthony.

"What the crap, man?"

"Hi, Vivienne."

"Did you seriously call me an asshole just now?"

Anthony paused. The emotions dropped off his face instantaneously. He stared at me with no sign of life behind those enigmatic eyes for what felt like a year.

"Can you please just say if you hate me now so I can apologize and we can move on? Are you actually upset?" I demanded.

"….No." He smiled.

"Good. I have to go." I sidestepped, throwing a wave his way. He didn't return it. I didn't care.

"What were you doing?" He asked. I ignored him. "You're not the first newbie to go snooping," he called out before I was out of range.

I stopped in my tracks, slowly turning back to him. He faced my direction with an amused grin. "*Okay?*"

Anthony shrugged. "Just so you don't feel so bad. Little bit of advice, though, if you really want to snoop tell the patrol you want to apprentice with them for a few days."

"Are you serious?"

"No, I'm Anthony."

"I hate you." I stepped forward. "Please stop messing around. No way that would actually work."

Anthony stepped forward to match me, abandoning his cart. "No, you don't hate me. You don't know me. And yes, it does work. It has. They tell apprentices everything, and only apprentices. And no one ever asks questions if you "decide against" a job, and you can move on happily with new information. Works like a charm."

"I don't believe you."

"You don't have to. But it works. It's your loss. Not mine." Anthony stepped back to his cart, shoving it over a stubborn patch of dead grass.

I huffed out my mouth like a child. "Right. How do I know you're not bullshitting to get me in trouble?"

"Why would I do that?"

"I don't know. For laughs?"

"I promise that wouldn't be very funny." Anthony pushed his cart right up to me. A bottle of chemicals fell over the side. I still haven't asked where the sanitation crew got their chemicals. "You have to trust me, Miss Vivienne. Cheerio."

xxii.

Each of us was blessed with a bed within the next week. We were scattered throughout the dormitory. I never felt so cluttered and surrounded, yet so abandoned.

Nighttime was for thinking. It was for thinking and daydreaming. Day-dreaming at night.

I liked imagining the backstories of the people sleeping around me. I imagined their past lives: their homes, their families, their friends, their favorite foods.

I considered taking Anthony's advice. The only downside to his proposal was Tate. Tate was an apprentice for patrol. He would call my bluff immediately.

That idea was shot down for good in a heartbeat when I saw the patrol team in the dining hall for lunch one day. Three of Anita's subordinates had thighs and biceps bigger than my head. Each carried some kind of firearm tucked in a jacket or strapped by a belt. None looked to have a sense of humor.

I believe what Anthony told me. My hunt for answers was not over, but some things need time. Sometimes, people giving you the key to their secrets is the most trustworthy thing they can do.

The days passed in the garden, melting into comforting clockwork. We gardeners talked and talked throughout the day. We talked about our old lives, jokes, and new gossip through the grapevine of the Community.

It wasn't hard to connect with the gardeners. There were only five of us. Hank, who was never involved in those deep discussions. Eden, who I walked with from breakfast every morning. Me, who relished the time to be *calm*. Lillian, a fourteen-year-old with a fairy voice and permanent resting B-face. And Elliott, a ten-year-old who never used his head.

I learned that Eden was Cillian's mother. She didn't want to leave her home when things went haywire. She would have stayed, too, if someone didn't steal half of her belongings late in the night and set fire to her home. Her husband, Cillian's stepfather, died that night.

There wasn't much to do at this time of year. The only things there were to grow were cabbage, carrots, radish, and peas. That was all the winter vegetation they scavenged sprouts for. But this problem was soon to be remedied in the warmer seasons. The hunters discovered early on that ransackers and ruthless thieves didn't care for seeds and sprouts. That left everything for our taking.

Hank accepted his responsibility of mentoring me after the third day. It was during the third lesson with Hank that I discovered his occasional spur of excitement: mushrooms. *Shrooms*, as more commonly referred to. Everyone in the gardens knew about the stash he kept bountiful among the other plants. Everyone was also under the agreement not to let it slip to anyone outside.

He kept them in his many cargo pockets. Carried them everywhere. Any time Tveit laughed just too loudly for his migraine, Hank fried up a shroom or two at the bonfire. Woke up with an insatiable headache no amount of Cillian's dried leaves could temper; Hank turned to the shrooms. The crushing memory of his former life suffocated him at the wrong time — shrooms.

Lily told me how she stole one and shared it with Elliott. It tasted the worst of her life, but the hallucinogenic effects lasted forever. She swore she still sees purple auras around the trees.

Learning about the mushrooms was the garden worker's form of initiation. I started sitting with Eden and Lily at meals. Elliott sat with me at the nightly bonfire. Hank acknowledged me in town with more than a grunt — sincerity in his language.

I was one of them.

None of us had much time to hang out. Peter avoided me; I told myself that was because he was always covered in blood from the butcher room. It soon became that the only time I ever saw Tate or

Diana was tucking into bed.

We were beginning completely different lives. I didn't know anything about them. Shockingly, I spent most of my time outside of the gardens with Chrissy. She wasn't as intolerable to hang around once you learned to decipher her language.

"Where were you today?" I asked as we undressed on the ninth night.

"Shannon had me bussing the tables."

"Really? I didn't see you." I moved around for Chrissy to hide behind me. We got into the habit of shielding each other from the peering side-eye of an older roommate.

"I purposely avoid you." This was a joke. Chrissy never changed her tone between jokes and seriousness. I learned this the hard way.

I heard her sweatpants shuffle up her legs. She muttered a clear. I moved out of the way.

"Did you do any good plant growing today?" Chrissy asked as she moved the same way for me.

I whipped the sweater over my head. Chrissy took the sweater and exchanged it with my ratty sleep shirt in one swift move. "I'm kinda just watching the others. I grab the tools and pick a leaf sometimes."

"Sounds exciting."

"I know."

This was our nightly routine.

The bonfire was my solace every day. The night I was properly inducted into the gardens, Lily and I pranced around the bonfire pit hand-in-hand. We tripped and stumbled and giggled at ourselves. Our knees bumped and bruised. The fireflight flickered on our bodies. The light gleamed through our flowing hair.

Alice and Grace joined in when our giggling magic rose over the tip of the flames. The four of us gathered hands and pranced around the pit, embracing our virgin maiden ancestors.

We would have kept going forever and ever until Alice bumped into Teddy: one of Anita's boys. He fell towards the pit and missed having a pant leg caught on fire by mere centimeters. Teddy screamed. Every head snapped in our direction. We dispersed faster than a sneeze in the wind.

I stumbled back to my regular spot on the edge of the sand, drunk on the thrill of life. I threw myself down. The high of youthful joy settled, leaving me in an empty headspace with nothing left to occupy myself. Peace.

Not a minute later, Anthony walked up and asked to sit with me. He needed help finding his way down to not sit directly on top of me. We made it together. Teamwork is dreamwork.

"How was patrol? Learn anything new?" Anthony asked. This was the first time I saw him stare off into space without focus.

I drew in the sand between my crossed legs. "No," I muttered glumly.

"Did you take my advice at all?"

"No."

He chuckled under his breath. "Good. I didn't think you would."

My head snapped up. "Then why tell me?" I shot.

"I wanted to see if you really don't trust us to keep you safe," he stated. I watched his shoulders bounce as if it were the most simple explanation in the world. "But you didn't go further with your little investigation, which shows you do trust us. A little bit."

I glared at him, unsatisfied after realizing he couldn't see the tinge of my glare. His torso jerked back with my shove. My sand art was ruined. "So it wasn't true? You were tricking me?"

The curls whipped back and forth on his head. "Oh no, it *is* true! I told the same thing to Tate. That's what he was doing when he joined patrol," Anthony explained, gesturing in a vague direction that Tate was not in. "Tate did the same as you. But he got genuinely sucked into the work."

I watched Tate play with the kids on the waterline. He picked them up and swung them back and forth while they giggled maniacally. The waves splashed over his knees, spraying the little ones in the face with salt water.

"Tate was investigating, too?" I whispered.

I don't know why it surprised me. Any good self-proclaimed leader should be wary of who you're letting feed and shelter your tribe. But Tate was one of the most trusting people I knew. He trusted Peter more than I did.

And he hadn't dragged us off that beach yet. They were doing something right.

It did rub me wrong that I wasn't delusional. I wasn't the only one who had concerns about the Community.

"Oh yeah. Definitely. The first day he would not shut up. Asking about our protocols, our safety measures, the succession… everything under the sun." Anthony took a quick swig of water, offered it to me, then took another when I rejected. "Dmitri didn't get tired of answering his questions, but Misha got tired of hearing. It was kind of funny, actually. So I swooped in to save the day."

I pinched my lips, peering at him through narrow eyes. "Then what was the point of all this?"

"Knowledge? The mystery? Adding a little spice to your life?" He nudged my leg. "Admit it. You liked the intrigue. Everyone does."

I shook my head, exhaling hard through my mouth. "All of you people are insane," I mutter.

"Maybe we're the sane ones and you've gotten so used to the voices in your head telling you they're supposed to be there."

Work in the gardens was slow the next morning. Hank was nursing a recovery with Cillian. Eden's arthritis was acting up. The five of us made a unanimous decision to take the day off.

The hunters came back early that morning with enough venison and turkey to feed all forty-seven of us a full dinner. One major downside of the Community's lack of resources was the lack of salt. What we brought in that day had to be eaten quickly lest it rot and be a waste. Which meant there was no time to cook up vegetables.

I wasn't complaining. More time to sit in my thoughts.

Diana found a sweet wildflower patch along the back end of the Community. When I needed to escape and relax my mind, I snuck out to the wildflowers. I made art with the Columbines and Coreopsis. My favorites were the Asters. The flower field quickly became my favorite place in the Community.

Diana taught me how to make flower crowns. We sat among the sage green grasses, interweaving delicate stems to become precious crowns of beauty. In the distance, the songs of nature serenaded us. The wild chorus of the birds. The rolling melody of the waves on the shore. We girls lay in the most splendid patch of the replenishing world.

It was all over when Hank shouted at me to come back, or when the children got so rowdy Diana had to surrender. We helped ourselves up, proudly wearing our crowns back home.

Eight days in the gardens. Eleven days with the People.

None of the others wanted to leave, and for the first time, I understood why.

XXIII.

The next week passed in a natural routine. Wake up when the dogs yowled. Eat breakfast. Head to the gardens. Do whatever Hank or Eden instructed. Lunch. Back to the gardens. Dinner if we could make it — which was rare. Bonfire. Back to sleep late at night. Repeat.

We all found our niche in the Community. There was a place for everyone.

Anthony and I sat together at the bonfires more frequently. He can be very nice to have a conversation with. I soon learned how difficult it was for him to last ten minutes without cracking a joke, no matter how morbid or distasteful it need be, or else he would spontaneously combust (his own words.)

"If you don't mind me asking, how do you find your way around this place?" I asked one evening. I never wanted to ask until he made one too many jokes about himself. He didn't even use a cane unless tromping along the unreliable treeline.

He blew out his mouth with a huff. His lowest hanging curls bounced on the wind. "A lot of practice. *A lot.*"

I watched a dragonfly flit among the few cattails. "What about when people move things? Like what if you visited the gardens and someone laid a hoe on the ground?"

"Then I would trip, fall, and impale myself."

"You're a horrible person."

He winked. "But you keep talking to me, so not horrible enough."

"Is that a threat?" I leaned away, swallowing a giggle.

"If you want it to be."

During these late evening chats, I learned that Anthony, too, lost family before finding the Community. He was an only child who lived with his mother and grandparents. His mom was a hoarder. That's how he learned to keep track of his surroundings so well.

There was a fifteen-year age gap between him and his mother. His dad skipped out on them before he was born — committed a hit-and-run, as Anthony put it. Anthony had a suspicion about who his father was, given stories and what his grandma told him about who his mom dated in high school.

"I'm ninety percent sure she screwed one of the lacrosse players," Anthony explained while we snacked on slices of toasted bread he stole from the kitchens. "My mom told him on his seventeenth birthday, and he never acknowledged her again. Never responded to another call or email, never even made eye contact in school. When she called him out and threatened to tell his parents, he threatened to tell his friends how mediocre she was in bed."

"That's terrible!"

Anthony scoffed, shoving the rest of his bread between his teeth. "I know, right? She was a virgin. Did he expect her to be some... some... *skilled prostitute?*" His voice was muffled by the full mouth. "So she gave had and raised me with her parents. She never moved out of their house, and after a while, she kind of... went off the deep end, in the politest of terms."

His grandmother was paralyzed in one arm but baked an exemplary brownie. His grandfather only called him Tony. Anthony hates that name.

Anthony moved out of home at nineteen. He lived on his own just three miles away for a year; straight from private high school to working at a local motel. Sanitation was always the easiest work for him. It didn't require much knowledge of the landscape so long as your trusty broom could be a guide. Quote, he "could feel mold like nobody's business."

Then that fateful April came and went. He moved back home when the United States government gave up trying. His mom died in a Laundromat in mid-May. His grandmother had a stroke in June. His grandfather died of heartbreak the next week.

Anthony found the People By The Sea two months later. He went out in search of fresh water and got lost in the trees. He explained in great detail how he wandered straight in one direction before a troop of patrolmen found him on the border.

They weren't so willing to take him in at first, considering his disability. It was narrow-minded, to Tveit's mistake. But Anthony was able to prove to them his usefulness. Since then, he's worked himself to be the leader of sanitation and higher in succession than Eugene, who'd been there since the beginning.

I didn't have the confidence to ask about the specifics of his disability until the end of the second week. I asked if he knew what specific type of blindness he had, or if he knew where it came from.

"Don't feel weird asking. No one ever does. *Ask*, I mean. They do get all weird. That's why they never ask." Anthony rambled into dismissing himself. "It's called diabetic retinopathy. It can be genetic, and *probably* my nana's fault. It's… essentially… blurred and darkened evil blobs in my vision. I can see little spots. But not enough to classify as 'seeing'."

"I didn't know diabetic symptoms could pass through genes. I knew you could be more susceptible to it, but not predetermined to suffer through all that."

"It's not suffering. Only mildly annoying."

"That's not what I meant."

"I know."

I moved to sit right in front of him. "Can you see much of me now?" I asked.

"The clear spots are to my left side."

I moved to the right. His head precariously followed me. "There we go." A sly grin split his face. "Kinda. I know your race and hair color. A little of the face if I get at this angle. But not enough to distinguish your definite facial features, or height, or… all the things."

"What more do you need to see about someone?"

He tilted his head, staring at the waves. "Sometimes you just want to see a full face."

The next day was the most clear-minded I saw Hank in all my time I've known him. He was pin-straight, dedicated, and tolerated no crap. Unfortunate for us, though. He kept Lily, Elliott, and me busy with pruning and weeding for hours until our knuckles grew sore and our lower backs cried for mercy. Nothing was to Hank's approval. Elliott had to redo the cabbages three times before Hank let him off.

This was another side of Hank. An alien Hank.

I just started pruning the peppers when the infamous drill sergeant of the Community ran up to the iron arch.

"Meeting! Community Meeting in the mess hall!" Misha shouted at the edge of the garden territory. He didn't give us time to respond before his booming voice retreated back to town.

"*What?*" My eyes shot to Hank.

"Drop everything. Everyone to the mess hall!" Hank corralled us down the path. Elliott tripped over his tool and cried out. Hank picked him up by the armpits, shutting the boy up when he was set down at the other side of the gate.

The journey to the mess hall was chaotic. Dangerous. No one walked at a moderated pace. No one cared or regarded others as they plunged forward to reach the building first. There had to be a better way to do this. There were fifty of us and plenty of wide open space. But there was no way to escape myself and let my body breathe.

I found Anthony and Eugene. Eugene was guiding Anthony through the flowing mob by the elbow. I gently touched Anthony on the other side. His head whipped to me, shocked rigid until I introduced myself.

"*I hate people*," Anthony whispered. An older adult animalistically shoved past us.

I pulled him from the worst of it, stepping on a few toes and smacking a few arms. "I know."

Eugene was lost from us. The doors opened, and each person tackled the other through. Anthony and I waited at the side of the door for the worst to settle before dipping through the double doors.

The crowd. The impatient rush to be the first. Fear coursing through each spine.

When we had to evacuate the school, the students mimicked blood flow. Each cell travels in its own regard, waging war against any obstruction to reach the target.

The workshop classrooms were the first to smell the gas. Both teachers called the office, reporting something noxious. Students covered their mouths and noses with their shirts to little avail. They tried turning on the fan and opening the room, which only circulated the odor to every corner of the hall. The janitor didn't make it down before the teachers made the executive call to let their students outside through the workshop doors. The janitor ran back to the central office to announce a gas leak.

I was in Accounting. The classroom was right by the cafeteria, but not on the side closest to the student parking lot doors. We were reviewing auditing for the fourth time when the alarm blared. It was the alarm for intruders because there was no established alarm or protocol for gas leaks. The principal on the intercom confirmed the emergency. Teachers were ordered to line their students up and calmly exit the building. We were to walk out to the track or soccer field until emergency personnel came.

So, naturally, the students ignored this.

Teachers' pleas to calm us were lost among the terrified student faces. Shouts and screams echoed back and forth, up and down, inside and out. Something heavy fell; everyone assumed guns were going off too. Shoes were uprooted and abandoned behind the owners. Accessories on backpacks snagged and fell.

It was now that we began smelling it in the upper hallways. The musty, wet, rotten scent; sure to ignite on the smallest spark. I was shoved to the floor outside of the gymnasium, my hair trampled into oblivion by the root. My cry alerted Alliona, who pulled me up and dragged me outside by the elbow. The glass door smacked us on the way out.

The student parking lot was worse.

Cars pulled out and zoomed away with no regard for pedestrians. Horns honked from every direction. Those who couldn't make it through the narrow one-way escape floored it through the grass. A right side-view mirror went flying to the asphalt.

The alarm rang high through the mid-morning air; against pained ears, atop trees and baseball stands. The last students and faculty ran through the side doors, coughing through shirts wrapped around their heads. Several passed out on the lawn. No one bothered to pick them up.

I had to find Mikey. We rode together the last week. I couldn't leave without him.

Someone honked at me. I ran from their bumper into another. My shoulder hit the asphalt, igniting in pain.

"Get up! Get up!" A teacher shouted, yanking at my arms. Mr. Leeson. "Do you have a car?"

The echoing walls magnified the roar. Everyone short of Nina, the children, and the morning patrol team was present. Meetings were only arranged for the most important topics; conversations that no one would want their young ones engaged in. Elliott slipped his way in, though.

I couldn't find Chrissy or Tate. Anthony and I squeezed to stand with Diana, who was sitting cross-legged on the stone floor. We sat with her, observing everyone else by their ankles. This was easier than being seen and being a target.

No more than thirty people gathered in the mess hall, which somehow felt more crowded now than ever during a meal. No one talked. No one joked. We collectively waited for Tveit and Anita to make their way through the bushel to the front. When they climbed onto the front table, chaos resumed. The screams now fought to get the first word.

Anita's whistle sliced every one of our eardrums. Silence.

"Two of our hunters have suggested a new method to find food," Tveit announced. He nodded at two men who sat at the head of the room. "Seamus and Eli suggest we take advantage of the waters."

Murmurs filled the room; a low rumble of dissension rose. Those I recognized as hunters, butchers, and cooks were the most apprehensive. The three of us huddled closer, compacting ourselves within our box of protection.

"We recognize we have no boats! We have no nets. Seamus knows where to find boats. We can weave nets ourselves," Tveit continued, settling the roar with one broad sweep on his hand.

"This will be a Community-wide effort!" Anita added, eyeing the younger members. "Everyone will be held responsible for their assigned positions, which will be directly related to their daily positions."

"Are we doing it? Is it official?" A man shouted from the back.

"Nothing is official. That's why we're discussing it now. As we said, we'll need all hands on board to make the nets sturdy and useful. We'll need several people out at once to haul back the boats," Anita explained between sighs.

Tveit picked a spare piece of food from his beard. "Seamus and Eli gave a rough timeline until we'll send a group of fishermen out: two weeks. One to harvest supplies for nets and to find boats. One for construction and training."

Anita inhaled, clasping her hands tight in front of herself. "The vote must be twenty out of thirty."

"We're doing just damn fine," a man to my right murmured to his friend.

"But if more big families keep coming..." the friend commented before noticing us on the floor. I waved at him. His lips pinned shut.

"We now welcome Seamus and Eli." Tveit climbed off of the table, surrendering for the two men to take his place. Anita did not move. She planted her feet when Eli shuffled between her and Seamus. He cleared his throat and nudged Seamus to the side with his shoulder.

Seamus looked to be in his mid-forties. Eli was a bit younger. You could see their familiarity and good-natured chemistry. But would they be able to charm the public...

"I've lived in the area my whole life. Many marine dealerships in the area will have an untouched supply of sailboats and cruisers," Seamus began. His voice came out shaky, showing his passion above nerves. "They'll be heavy. It'll be a lot of work for a lot of people. But no one will be out for longer than two days."

"And whoever isn't bringing in boats will be working on nets," Eli chimed in. "I'll cover that. We just need enough to bring in a meal's worth at a time."

"How do you suggest we do that?" Hank bellowed.

Seamus ripped at his fingernails and the pieces to his feet. "I'm not going to lie, it'll be hard… We're gonna have to take a few from each station. We'll be using the same methods the ancient Chinese used to harvest fine strands… But only for a couple of weeks," Seamus tried as a small mob formed around the table.

"How could you assume our stations don't need us?" A shrill woman shrieked. "You don't know what we do! We have the most important job. *We* need a break."

"I would argue against that, ma'am. Why should you have more of a break than the people growing our vegetables, or the two lovely women caring for your children?" Eli shot back.

"*Preach!*" Nina shouted.

"Oh, shut up!" The grasshopper of a woman cried.

"Teach your snot-nosed boy his 5-times tables and I will!"

"Settle down!" Anita commanded, pointing to the two women with just her eyes. "We're here to be civil. So shut up or step out!"

"That's Kathy. She cried her way into patrol. Nina hates her and her kid," Diana whispered to me. I giggled. Someone to the side heard us and nodded.

Eli didn't have to raise his voice to penetrate the silence that followed Anita. "Keep in mind, we'll hold everyone to the same standards. I also think this could give a good insight to how many of us slack throughout the day, and aren't contributing as much to the moving gears of this community."

"I think this says a lot about your views on the former standard forty-hour work week. Wasn't that proven to be less efficient than allowing several breaks and rest times to improve mental wellbeing?" Bryce from the kitchens said. "It's the twenty-first century. Aren't we past this?"

"It shows my unappreciation for *freeloaders*. We cannot afford freeloaders," Seamus pronounced. "I'm sure Shannon would love to have a talk with you about that."

"Finally! We've been trying to get him off his ass for days!"

That was Chrissy.

"Will this mean more work for the butchers and kitchen?" Someone shouted.

Eli answered this one. "Yes, but we'll have more opportunities for meat. Which we all need a lil more of."

A woman raised her hand. "I'm vegan!"

"Then I don't know how you've made it this far, ma'am." Eli cracked a grin. The woman's face blossomed red. The amusement dripped off his face. "I mean, you know, this will leave more plants for you. Cause we're all eating the fish. Right?"

"What about religious restrictions?" Shannon peeped up. Necks craned to find her. She shrank back down.

Seamus nodded slowly. "We're not forcing you to eat fish. If you don't want it, don't take it. Vice versa. Our goal is to provide more potential meat and protein. We are not taking advantage of a reasonable resource. The hunters will continue gathering on land as needed."

"How many people will need to go out fishing at once? How drained will the other branches be of workers?" Misha boomed.

Anita answered this one. "Three people will go out minimum for safety."

"Right. And we ask that anyone who does join has a background in leisure fishing, at least!"

"Why are you being so restrictive if you want people so bad?" Someone close to us jabbed. I stuck my tongue out at them.

Seamus glanced at Eli, who declined to answer. "Well… wouldn't you like the people getting your food to… know what they're doing?" Seamus offered. The person considered this, nodded, and settled back down.

"What if this all fails?" A voice echoed from the back.

"Let's not think that far ahead. We have every reason-"

The uproar resumed. All three of us clamped our hands over our heads. Anthony leaned into my side when people started trampling over us.

"How is it safe?"

"What about bad weather?"

"-heavy and too much-"

"I don't want my kid working on the net!"

"Your kid has never done a lick of work all her life, Lupita!"

"-storms and rocks. I don't-"

"Why don't we-"

"You people are just lazy!"

"-no one ever needed-"

"I'll join them!" A woman announced, leaping to her feet. All other voices cut themselves silent.

Seamus slightly jumped on his heels. "Sylvia! Hi!"

"Hi," the woman named Sylvia pushed to the front. "I fished for sport way back when."

"Where do you work now?" Tveit raised a hand.

"Sanitation." Sylvia took Eli's hand and climbed onto the table. "This seems like a good opportunity. I've always wondered why we live on a beach and ignore the ecosystems in front of us."

"Great. It's gonna be down to just me and Alice," Anthony muttered. I patted his knee.

"Does anyone else wish to join us on the waters?" Seamus called out. A hopeful smile graced his stubble-covered face.

Crickets.

"Why not start in the rivers and lakes?" Misha suggested. "It would be safer to test the general interest in fish. Rather than dedicate weeks of work for nothing."

Eli sighed, shrugged, and raised his arm. "Who here would like larger rations and/or second helpings of meals?"

Almost everyone but the vegan and Shannon raised their hands. Misha grunted.

"So where is the confusion?" Tveit spoke. Anita nodded. "We all agree that we need more food. We can find the resources. Where is the disconnect?"

"They don't want to sacrifice their free time for a full stomach," Eli muttered, loud enough for the audience to hear. Murmurs of guilt ascended. Diana scoffed.

"Do we need a minute to think? Or is it settled?" Anita asked. Most of us nodded.

Tveit gestured to push us down. One by one, each of them meandered helplessly before taking seats on the cold floor.

"Close your eyes. Everyone will vote, and I can see *everyone*," Tveit ordered. We obeyed. Anita called for everyone in favor of the old ways to raise their hands. I couldn't hear much. "*Eyes closed*. Don't vote what your friend says."

"Are we in kindergarten?" Diana asked. I giggled.

Anita then gave us time to vote for Seamus and Eli's plan. My arm slowly rose, pointing my limp fingers to the ceiling.

"Eyes open."

The vote was 22 to 8. In favor of the fishermen. Work started the next day, as ordered by Tveit.

xxiv.

I believe we're now in March. The weather warmed. The sun thawed our frigid skin, thawing our fingers with every counted morning. Life in the gardens was more plentiful when the seeds from last year's batch found their time to shine. The fruiting trees were soon to blossom, soon to drop juicy polyps of the gods.

The effort to find and restore fishing vessels took less time than expected. A depot was found only two or three miles south of our beach that offered a wide variety of boats to choose from. As came with the boats, so did nets and gears. It was a miracle veiled in sails and unusable motors. Seamus and Eli impromptu redirected the plan to use sailboats and canoes. Dmitri led a movement with five other men to haul the supplies back. It took them three trips. They were gone for six days in all.

The boat wasn't too much of a hassle. A small team spent an entire day trying and failing methods to repair the rot damage and reinforce the lines. A little sap and emergency duct tape finally mended the water rot damage. A supply run was made for metal repair supplies, which returned a replenishing stock for sanitation. The canoe was made entirely of plastic and rubber, making it invincible to weather while sure to coat our fish dinners in microplastics.

What was difficult were the nets. Marine carcasses and decay plagued the tendrils. The threads had worn bare over hard weathered months since being abandoned. Many types of mold and fungus grew in the creases and knots. For hours every day, someone worked cleaning and fine-tuning the tools. They cleaned the rusting gears and hooks, too, fixing them to the boats with prayers that usable material still wore proudly on the beams.

Not everyone was happy about the new work. They felt their efforts would be wasted, and the three fishermen would never be able to find good sea life off the rocky New England shore. I will be the first to admit that though I was one to vote for the change, I was among the complainers for a short time. But when the kitchens were left for days to scrape the bottom of the barrel to feed every mouth, we wised up and shut our mouths very quickly.

Eli, Seamus, and Sylvia embarked on the seas on the first possible day. On the first day, all three were on the sailboat. On the second day, two manned the boat while Sylvia paddled alongside in the canoe. The days provided not much different results by safety and bounty.

The first fish dinner was the next day. The trio came back with enough flounder and bass to feed all of us and have leftovers. The kitchen staff had to cook it fast before it went sour in the rising March temperature. Food preservation was solved for us in the winter months. In all of our preparations, no one had thought to construct a functioning ice box. Because where would we find ice in March?

Fishing proved to be an instant success. With Tveit's instructions not to come back with more than needed every day, the trio went back out. And out again. And out again.

Those who voted against the new plan never spoke on the matter again.

Some days were more successful than others. Some days they didn't come back until late at night, and they kept the meat in traps in the cold night water. But it worked. Combined with the regular forest creatures by the hunting teams and more plant variety in the gardens, we had enough to fill each and every belly in the Community. Any leftovers were thrown to Barbosa and Fox.

No more sleeping with tantalizing stomach growls. No more complaints about which demographic got more than others.

We were fed. We were healthy.

It was at the end of March when we had to construct a new garden bed to accommodate the supply and demand. Hank explained how when the Community first began, they didn't have half as many people. Everyone else filtered in as time passed. Now, we needed more space. More seeds. More nutrient soil. *More, more, more!*

My favorite seasonal fruit to harvest was honeydew melons. They took up most of our space but returned a lovely hydration to our mouths. As well, it does good to wash out the dirt that gathers in our mouths.

My favorite task in the gardens was harvesting seeds. Slicing the fruit, letting the juice cover my fingers and drip to my toes. Cutting into the casing and revealing the bearer of a plant's life; the beginning of filled stomachs and energy for countless people. From that one seed would come another plant. Another ten filled stomachs. Another day of joy and sorrow and laughter and tears.

Shannon went into labor at the end of February. Cillian kept her in his tent for five days. Everyone could hear her screams and the medics' voices guiding her through childbirth on the second day. She gave birth to a boy who she named Nicholas, after the diner that she had an impulsive fling in the back of after escaping home. I met Nick when he was four days old. The Community's firstborn child.

Nature understood the change of the good tides too — pun intended. The field of flowers bloomed with a wider variety of colors and diverse petals. Flower crowns galore! After an intolerable day of net's work, I taught Leta, Tveit's little girl, how to make them. They became a statement piece of her caramel head.

But not everyone was happy. Not everyone was satisfied with the cards they were dealt. This was such an obscure idea for me, given that as an adult you could choose where you worked. You choose how to spend your days. I never before considered that a younger teenager may despise their job until Chrissy approached Diana and me one night as we changed for bed.

"I hate work." Chrissy threw herself towards us. We sat at Diana's bed early in the evening when not five others shared the room with us.

"Welcome to the world," I remarked, slipping my socks off and tucking them into my new boots. Peter brought them for me days ago.

Chrissy motioned for us to cover her as she began rifling through Diana's things for clothes. "No, like, I *hate* it. There are only two of us now and I hate cooking. No one cares about us."

I held up the blanket I was sitting on in front of her body. "I promise, people care about who feeds them. It's a rule of people as old as time."

"Not when they're preoccupied with complaining. Everyone *complains!* That's all they do. Ever!"

I wasn't going to mention how ironic her words were. "Trust me, girl, that's what people do when they don't have control of the situation."

She yanked her sweater over her head. "You do have control of the situation. Just shut up. Boom, problem solved."

"You liked it in the kitchen last week." Diana blocked her into the wall.

"Now I want something more."

I covered her other side from the pervish glances of one older man. "You have a valuable job right now. I don't think Shannon wants to go back until Nick can be away from her."

Chrissy played with the hem of the blanket. "I don't know. I feel stagnant in life. I want to do something more." She threw herself onto Diana's bed without bothering to put her shirt on. I chucked the blanket over her. Chrissy buried her face in Diana's pillow and groaned into it. "I fee- -o use-ess," the words muffled through the feathers.

Diana and I sat on either side. "You're not useless. You're young," I mumbled.

"Those are synonymous."

"That's a big word."

Chrissy flipped me off.

I made many mistakes in my years of living. Some greater than others. But I have not and will never forgive myself for this.

Anthony, Diana, and I enjoyed the bonfire someday afterward. I remember joking with them about Hank. Or maybe it was Tveit's accent. Or maybe we were complaining about baby Nick waking everyone in the night from the other end of the building.

Peter approached us a little after dusk. We didn't acknowledge him quickly enough. He crossed his arms and stared at us hard enough to burn a laser hole in the side of my head.

I finally glanced up at him. "May I help you?"

"Yes."

Anthony smiled toothily at the other man. "Pull up a chair. Get comfy," he held out a welcoming hand. I pictured Peter's gaze could freeze Anthony in an instant. He would if he could.

"Can I have a minute with my sister?" Peter spoke to Anthony slowly and deliberately. As if Anthony were dumb.

"Sure thing, dude." Anthony pushed himself to his feet with Diana, swerving slightly into Peter's personal space. Peter pushed him aside with a flippant stare.

"What the heck, man!" Diana cried, tossing a hand up. I launched up, fell with wiplash, and landed back on my butt. Anthony pulled Diana away before she hit Peter. My brother disregarded them both as he sat by my side. I scooted inches away.

The party continued in front of us despite the growing pressure above that was ready to swallow me whole. This was the first time all month he volunteered to spend time with me.

I wasn't going to be the first to speak. I was tired of making an effort when he cared so little.

"Is he your friend?" Peter finally spoke up.

"Yes," I responded icily. "You would know that if you bothered to sit with us at meals, or check up now and then."

"*Us?*" Peter dared.

"Us. The people you lived with for two months." I watched Anthony and Diana join Eugene in the wake. Eugene was teaching Elliott how to skip rocks. "We've been doing fine, if you must know."

"Hey, *you* haven't tried to stay in touch either."

I stared. "There are forty other people. How out of touch can you get?"

"That's not the point."

"No, it's not." I forced my gaze back on the waves.

We were quiet for another several minutes. This had become the routine for us.

"The weather is getting warmer," Peter eventually stated.

"Indeed."

"It's a fine travelin' time."

"Good." I popped my knuckles absently.

I didn't miss the scoff that left Peter's mouth. "D'you really wanna stay?" He demanded.

I squinted at him. "Yes? Why would I not?"

"You want to *stay here?*" Peter motioned wildly at the people around us. He lowered his voice even more. "No respect. No privacy. Nothing for yourself. You *want* this?"

"Maybe they don't give you any respect because you don't give it first," I snapped back. "I have friends. I like it here."

Peter shook his head ruefully. "Why are you being so damn defensive?"

"Why are you being an asshole?"

"I'm trying to protect you! I don't trust these people," he seethed through his teeth — a rabid pack animal.

I buried my bare feet in the sand, wiggling my toes deeper and deeper. If even a small part of her could hide from him it would be enough. "Why not? They've been nothing but good to us. They have food, shelter, clothes, medicine. They care about public opinion, which is worth more than we've ever known. I see nothing to be protected from. What possible red flags are you seeing?"

Peter watched Tveit play with his little girl by the Flame. "You're not looking careful enough."

"Peter, you're paranoid after Cal. But he's in the past. He's gone. We got you away from him and he's gone. You're far from him and anything he could do to either of us," I said.

"*Don't talk so loudly.*"

"I'll talk at whatever volume I damn well want to!" I stood up, kicking scratchy sand up my pants in the process. "We're happy and are safer than we've been in… since… a year! We like it here. If you don't, leave."

Peter scoffed, staring at the sand grains that had fallen into his socks. "You want me gone? Out of your life?"

"If you're gonna keep acting like this. You aren't happy. Why stay somewhere if you're gonna be miserable about it?"

Peter's cheeks and neck bloomed with red. "*Fine,*" he rose, gave the others of the Community one last sour gaze, and trudged his way up the grassy dune. I watched his back grow smaller in the distance. The shadows overtook him.

It was done. He was leaving us.

At the moment, I was too upset to worry about what may happen.

There were several times while we were quarantined on Carmel Road when I suspected he would walk out at any second. Peter was unreliable. He was flaky. He was a narcissist. I told myself I was glad to see him go. There wasn't anything positive left to miss.

"Is everything okay?" Diana's voice arrived before me. I peered up between my fingers, hoping the angry tears wouldn't break the dam. She brought an entourage.

"Peter's leaving." I plopped myself back on the sand.

"What?"

"He's leaving the Community. He hates it here."

Eugene scoffed. "Ouch."

I nodded, pulling my legs to my chest. "If I wanted to talk about it, I would've come to you first."

Never take for granted the friends who know you well enough to see through you.

"He'll be okay," Diana said. She reached one hand out but retracted it before I could reject her. The movement was so miniscule, she probably thought I didn't notice. I did.

Then Eugene opened his mouth.

"He'll be able to take care of himself, Vivienne. Mark my words. I'm not worried. It's only as hard as you make it out there-"

"I want to swim!"

The Storm

April

XXV.

Peter wasn't in the dorms the next morning. No one heard him sneak out in the night. It was very plausible that he slipped out last night while we swam, shamelessly leaving us behind in the shadows of the night.

I told Tveit that Peter wouldn't be working that day. Or the next day. Or the day after that.

No one outside of the butcher's room noticed his absence. Tate and I would ask if someone had seen him and they frowned with confusion. If Peter knew this, I would never hear the end of it.

So be it. I forced myself to believe that there was no way he could've been happy, therefore it saved all of us grief. If Peter set himself out for something, there was no way to shake him off the idea. That was one thing that remained from the past. He was a stubborn bastard.

But can't we all be? No one wants to admit when they could be wrong. That often feels better than being right.

One thing I discovered about the New and Improved Peter was that he needed you to approach him. He never made the first move. He required you to do all the work in the relationship, and the moment you asked him to reciprocate he called you selfish. If someone didn't work hard enough for him, it wasn't good. It wasn't enough to keep the relationship afloat. There were several other instances that I will not write because they're personal. They stung too much to recall in permanence.

When I realized the world retreated a century and I would forever lose my precious smartphone, I never anticipated dealing with such a manchild.

(I still have my smartphone. It hasn't turned on in years. But I have it tucked away deep in my best bag. Just in case. Old habits die screaming.)

To anyone who knew him before, the work his "boss" did for him was obvious. Cal degraded him, chipped away deeper and deeper until all that was left of Peter Hammond was an instinct to do the same. Unfortunately, no one else knew him. No one knew the man he was supposed to be. No one cared enough to try.

I did try. And he left.

Peter was kind. He was compassionate. This was a boy who hated killing ants when they snuck into the kitchen in summer. This was a boy who lied about eating his packed lunch because he gave it to the less fortunate kid who carried his mom's food stamp card.

This Peter was a different person with the same face. And one less arm.

But he wasn't my business anymore. My business was in the Community garden. The garden was a distraction. The garden was a way to focus on something tangible; something that couldn't run away and leave me as a lone child again.

Eden wasn't there when I stepped through the archway. Odd. Eden was never tardy in the morning.

"Do we know where Eden is?" I flipped the garden fork in the air, barely catching the abused handle by the tips of my fingers. Hank snatched it from me.

Elliott threw himself to sit on the edge of the new garden bed. "Grace saw Cillian help her to the infirmary last night," he reported, picking brown from his fingernails. The boy was only working for five minutes, and already he was covered head to toe in soil and mud. I don't know where the mud came from. It hadn't rained in three days.

"The infirmary? And no one bothered to check up on her?" I stared at Hank.

Lily began picking at the bush beans. "She's really old."

"Exactly. She's *really old!*" I grabbed the fork from Hank. "Is no one concerned?"

"It's a miracle she made it this far," the man regarded me with a discarded glance.

"That's morbid of you to say."

"Don't pretend you haven't thought it," Lily whispered.

I did think about it. All the time. Shame filled my gut at what could happen. It was inevitable. No point in denying it.

Still, she was human. She was a better human than my brother.

I made it my next mission to visit her in Cillian's tent. I ran off the instant Hank let us go. I knocked down a small child somewhere between the childcare and the butcher shop.

Eugene answered my shout at the tied canvas flap. He didn't leave anything for me to see but his pimply face.

"Hi." I smiled.

He coughed up a lung of phlegm. "You having trouble?"

"Is Eden in there?"

"Yeah…" Eugene looked over his shoulder, shouting my name to someone in the dark depths of the neverending tent. He gave them a thumbs-up and turned back to me. "Yeah, come in."

I slipped through the crack. The tent was dimly lit as always, this time offering a strange aroma of sanitizers. Eden lay on a far cot. She was resting, but not asleep. Eyes closed, but not unconscious. She didn't hold the calm of someone unconscious, oblivious to the outside world.

Cillian slammed a drawer shut when he saw me. "Um, Eugene- can you check on Kathy?"

"Blood pressure or diabetes?"

"Pick one."

I watched Eugene snatch a pressure gauge and speed out of the tent as if it were ablaze.

Eden's eyes ripped open. "*Who? What?*"

Cillian stepped to her bedside, gently pushing her shoulders back to lay back down. "Mom, Mom… stop. Don't move. It's Vivienne… stop moving, Mom," his whisper hit me like a feather in the roaring outside wind. Cillian nodded to me. "Take as long as you want."

Before I could thank him, Cillian disappeared behind the plastic curtain.

"How are you?" I crouched by her cot. Eden waved my words away, rolling her eyes at the prospect that she could be anything less than marvelous.

Cillian materialized back at her side and offered me a wet cloth. "Her heart is declining. She's at a high risk of heatstroke, which will likely kill her," he announced.

Eden and I stared at him. He stared right back, oblivious, and turned away.

"There it is." Her voice matched the newfound frailness of her body. I rubbed a thumb over the thin skin of her hand. Delicate skin tends to happen to the elderly. But this was new. This was a state similar to that of a glass window with a machine gun pointed at it.

Seeing her reminded me of the brutality of old age. You could survive the third world war and death could still find a way to capture you. You could live the healthiest, happiest life of all, and still, your heart gives out. Death chipped away at your bodily systems one by one until there was nothing left. Like torture. Death was infuriated at you for beating his design.

Eden wasn't wearing her beloved hairpins. Her short, white curls ungraciously cascaded — more like *flopped* — down the side of her head in frizzy clumps. It served as a reminder that even the most glamorous people we know are just that — *people*. People do not ooze a natural deity glow or have the pristine softness of an actress from the glory days of Hollywood. People die.

"Have you replaced me yet?"

I must have zoned out. Eden's voice was a jumper cable pulling me back to reality.

"Not really."

Eden clicked her tongue; tried to, at least. "Find someone, then. Quit dilly-dallying. Lord knows I won't be much longer."

"Don't say that."

"Ain't no point beating around the bush. I'm old and on the edge of cardiac arrest under the care of a doctor with leaves and year-old IV bags," she exclaimed before dramatically lowering her voice. Cillian wasn't anywhere near, but sound traveled well in the tents. "I love my boy. I know he does good work. But there's nothing he can do for me. And I think he knows that."

I nodded at the treatments spread out, decreasing day by day. "It's different being asked to treat a random nobody, but then being asked to treat your own mom…"

"I know. If I ever seem bitter, know that it's not towards anyone. And certainly not towards Cill." Eden leaned her head back. I was tempted to hold it up for her. It looked like it would roll right off her neck at any second.

"I'm so tired of being old. I'm tired of being in pain. Tired of not being able to move. Miss my old face, my old body. There are fewer things in this world worse than a vain woman forced to watch herself deteriorate."

"You're not vain."

Eden cracked the tiniest of grins. "Don't you know not to lie to an elderly on their deathbed? It's in poor taste."

Eden had a special way of speaking that you never knew if she intended the words to be sweet or short. I spent the next long while contemplating what next to say; whether it was the right time for humor or anger or fear.

She lightly brushed a hand across my thigh. "I have a trunk in the married dormitory. It's wooden and a century old." We watched the doctor run out of the tent when someone fell outside. "It's under the bed. The lock is broken. I want you to bring it back to me, please."

I pushed myself to my feet, marching out of the tent without another word. The sprint to the dormitories sent a frightening pain down my calf. No one noticed as I limped into the second building, hauling the doors open around me.

No one was home. I found Eden's bed instantly. It was the only one that hadn't been touched in days. From the noises of objects rolling and falling around inside the trunk, it seemed only half full. The urge to investigate almost overwhelmed me. I beat the urges down like the black widow spider last night and hauled the trunk out of the building.

When I returned with the trunk, Eden was asleep in her cot. I set the trunk down with a thud, wincing at the reverberation up my spine. Eden's eyes peeled open before she slowly found me again.

"I'm sorry. I meant to be quiet," I began to apologize.

She waved me away once more. "I need to be awake. I have something to give you," she scooted up in her bed. I stared at her dumbly. "Open it. There's a dress in there."

Her trunk was filled halfway with various nicknacks of her former life, all of which were thrown around — I'm sure that was my own doing. Palm-sized jewel boxes, aged hardback books, faded photographs of her, baby Cillian, and who I assumed to be her husband. But peeking from underneath a collection of well-weathered papers was dyed cloth.

I pulled the dress out, brushing the dust from the soft yellow fabric. It was light and sleek between my fingers, embodying perfect morning sunlight. Tiny pink and orange flowers dotted the bottom of the skirt, fading in concentration upwards. Off the shoulder the sleeves were hemmed a few inches long, making the impression of a built-in shawl. The skirt was wrinkled from years of living, but nothing that couldn't be fixed with a little water and heat.

"It's beautiful!" I breathed out. I held the dress up to my body. It fell just below my knees. "Was it yours?"

Eden gravely shook her head. "My sister made it for any daughter I may have. We used to fantasize about raising little girls. Neither of us ever had one." She noticed my tiny smile and shrugged nonchalantly. "I was going to give it to someone. You're the first to visit."

That was a polite roundabout way to say I was the only one who cared to be concerned, which was cruel but I embraced it.

I peered around the tent for a private space. "Can I try it on?" My excitement about wearing nice clothes threatened to bubble over. It had been so, so long since I wore a proper dress.

Eden gestured at the curtain. "Be my guest."

I launched myself toward the curtain before she closed her mouth. The curtain was thrown over me with one deft movement. My surroundings were blocked from most light, settling everything in an opaque, white-gray aura.

"Did your sister ever make a living off her skills?" I slipped my clothes off, yanking the dress up and over my head as quickly as possible.

"She had a guidance counselor who advised her not to pursue a career of art when she could get married." I could hear the smile in her voice. "So she opened a textile business with our parents. This was the age when women couldn't take a bank loan themselves, mind you. She didn't marry until forty-three."

I felt the fabric under my hands, smoothing it over my torso. Nothing could be smoother under my touch. "What was her name?"

"Charlemagne."

The curtain flew open. I kicked my other clothes across the floor and spun with glee. The skirt floated around me, fluttering magnificently. "How do I look?"

"Magnificent." Eden rested her head back on the pillow. "You'll find someone who loves to see it. And you'll love to wear it around them."

"Are you sure it's for me?"

"Of course. I have no one else to give it to," Eden sighed. "It does fit, right? You like how it feels?"

The dress was slim, but not too slim to unflatter me or cut off my lung capacity. The sleeves landed perfectly just off my shoulders, exposing the bony collarbones that had managed to fill back with increments of fat.

I wore the dress for the rest of the day. Things were turning for the better. I could feel it. Life was settling back into a pace of normalcy. Then something happened that night in the darkest hour.

"The fishermen are in trouble!" Someone shouted through the darkness. "Get up! They need help!"

My eyes ripped open. The room was so dark that before my eyes adjusted the only signs that other people moved were the sounds of blankets being thrown off and footsteps on the floor. The window was uncovered, but the clouds and rain did nothing to let in the moonlight. It wasn't until lightning struck that the dormitory was fully illuminated. I saw the terrified faces, the wet hair from the rain blown in by the monstrous wind.

Eugene struggled to light one of the mounted candles as everyone poured out the single door. People trampled over one another with no regard for whose toes got squashed or who lost their glasses.

Everyone left barefoot. No one bothered to cover up or protect themselves from the storm. A few boys jumped out the window.

I tried to stay at the back with the Dawsons. Diana was the first ripped away. Chrissy followed when a man forcibly pulled her out. It was finally Tate and I left standing on someone's mattress.

I caught sight of a moppy head as he was caught between four others. He was pushed and pulled left and right, up and down. I jumped off the bed despite Tate's objections. Anthony was forced through the door and into the larger hall, where everyone from both rooms rushed to get out the grand double doors first.

We were like bats; echolocating off each other to find our end goal. I found Anthony and grabbed his arm. He clammed frigid, head whipping like a spasmatic eel. It broke my heart to see the pure terror on his face.

"I'm here," I whispered, rubbing his back. "Let's wait for them to pass."

"We have to get out there!" Tate shouted when he finally caught up to us.

I tried — and failed — to push Tate towards the door with the rest of the mob. "Then you go! Find your sisters. I'm staying with him."

"I'm not leaving-"

"Vivienne, I'll be fine," Anthony urged before grabbing my hand tighter when someone tripped into him.

I walked him into a corner, far from any crazed lunatics that may harm him. "We're going together," I promised. He didn't give a verbal thank you. I could feel it in the muscles relaxing under my palm.

We made it outside on our own. Wind and rain instantly battered our bodies. Lightning illuminated the path by milliseconds. Hand in hand, we ran to join the mob on the beach. It didn't take a moment to see the horror.

Still floating atop the ocean, flames engulfed the sailboat. The horrid sound of the masts breaking and the vessel surrendering hit us on the shore, blending with the thunder. Parents shielded their children from the sight. Screams and pleas to help deafened the beach.

"What's happening?" Anthony shouted over the wind. Water dripped down his curls, turning his head smooth and flat and pathetic.

"The ship is on fire!"

"And we can't *do anything about it?*"

"What do you suggest?" Hank shouted in. I pulled us far from his materialized form. "We have no more seamen. We can't get out there fast enough in that damn canoe!"

Demanding Tveit to do something about it was worthless; we all knew. Flames engulfed the entire boat. The battering rain and sea did nothing to temper it. Eli and Seamus built no lifeboats for the vessel. The fishermen were dead in the water.

A shrill voice pierced the air.

"Stop! Stop- *Chrissy!*" Diana screamed.

The girl was sprinting toward the water. Hair flying in the wind, legs pumping against the wet sand. Lightning illuminated her journey to the sea. The cacophony of voices grew for her. Diana and Tate ran after her with everything in their power.

Before they could reach the tidal zone, Chrissy dived into the waves.

Her body disappeared under the surface. Diana stood at the edge of the water, screaming into the foam. Tate stood petrified, letting the fresh wave slosh his knees.

The rolling waves would've been tossing her underneath. They would've smacked her back down with every effort to surface for air.

I clenched the circulation out of Anthony's hand when Chrissy's head emerged from the surf. She'd swam almost a quarterway to the boat in one breath.

"No one else goes in!" Tveit ordered.

Tate yanked off his shirt. "Absolutely not. I'm getting her."

"No one is going in!" Tveit shouted, pointing one stubby finger at him. In a lower voice, he added, "We can only lose so many tonight."

Chrissy's small body paddled to a floating object in the wake. A wave would overtake her, she resurfaced, and continued. In one swift movement, she threw her arm over the thing and began the long haul back to the shore. It wasn't until they made it to standing depth did I realize it was a human.

Eli. She was pulling Eli.

Misha, Dmitri, and Tveit met her at the edge of the water. Chrissy vomited seawater over Tveit's legs. Misha grabbed the man in her arms before she collapsed into Dmitri.

Another bout of electricity charged the air.

"*Get out of the water!*" Nina screamed at the last few in the tides. "Get out! Lightning!"

Surely, a bolt of white-hot power struck the ocean. Anyone remaining in it was fried. Who couldn't make it dry in time fell to the sand, convulsing before the retreating wave.

I held Anthony as they did chest compressions on Eli's body. The People silenced for Misha to announce Eli dead. Drowned.

Dmitri carried Chrissy back to us. Tate collected her, laying her by our feet. Diana covered her head from rain pellets with her own body.

She wasn't dead. Not even unconscious. But she was crying. I held her hand as the tears rolled down her red face and sobs hiccupped from deep in her throat.

"Did I save him?"

I couldn't tell her the truth. She figured it out when they pulled out Sylvia's electrocuted body the next morning. They never could find Seamus.

XXVI.

The People By The Sea have a funeral tradition. Just as the sun sets the next day, the Community gathers around the Flame and they hold a service to honor those who passed. It's not required, but no one skips out. Everyone understands respect for the dead.

Someone in the top five of succession makes a speech celebrating whoever passed. How light-hearted, funny, or gut-wrenching the speech will be is determined by who makes it. Tveit had the responsibility that night.

Chrissy walked away from the service ten minutes in.

No one mentioned the fishermen the next day. No one mentioned Eli's absent snide remarks, Seamus' intelligent chiming into every conversation, and Sylvia's intense excitement to find a solution to any problem.

Every mouth lost food. We went through the last of the dear fish rations, slowly preparing ourselves for the reality that we would be right back where we started.

Tveit, Anita, and Dmitri scrambled to regain order among their people. Eugene was left to care for Eden, Chrissy, and the electrocuted patient while Cillian ran around tending to grieving bouts of depression.

We were all infuriated with Chrissy for jumping in. For sacrificing herself to save someone who probably didn't even know her name. But it's hard to be too mad at someone who swallowed enough seawater to dehydrate her for a week.

Between vomiting and diarrhea, Chrissy always found time to grumble. That's how we knew she was okay.

I don't remember spending much time with Anthony. He was

working overtime to destroy the remnants of the fishing expeditions, as per Misha's order. Sanitation had to recruit another child.

Who I did spend most of my time with was Tate. Since joining the Community, the two of us drifted apart. He was on patrol on six-hour shifts twice a day. But with the People slowing down to find a new pace, Tate allowed himself time off. He allowed himself to rest.

We sat on one of the two docks the majority of the time. The edge of the smaller dock was lifted two feet above the surface of high tide. Perfect height to dip your ankles and let all the troubles of the world melt away.

We talked about the water. The sky. Breakfast, lunch, dinner. Our annoying coworkers. Knives. Guns. Food.

It was on the third day after the fishermen's funeral when I finally gained the courage to ask the one question that I'd shoved down for so long it was nearly ready to erupt, spewing angry lava like a long-dormant volcano.

"Peter told me I had to kill someone to rescue him. Is that true?"

Tate's head snapped up. His spine instantly froze rigid. "When did he tell you that?"

"It's true?" My head whipped to him. Tate's hard gaze couldn't meet my eyes. I nudged his leg with my foot. "Can you tell me the truth for once?"

Tate rubbed the bridge of his nose. I know I didn't mistake the scorn in his sigh. "I haven't been lying to you," he swore.

"You haven't been *truthin'*."

"Oh, you *really* lost a few brain cells," he muttered, shaking his head with a pitiful chuckle.

I couldn't help but smile. Then nudged him again. "Come on. You know I don't remember a thing from that concussion."

Tate scratched his head. "You still don't remember anything? Zero? Squat?" He spread his hands as if he offered all the truths of the world, but I was too stupid to decipher them.

I paused, staring off into the waves. "A little's come back, but not enough to form a story... or dislodge anything stuck in the concussion amnesia brain sector thing..."

He nodded slowly. "How far back did you forget?"

"I dunno. Last thing I solidly remember is you crashing my house and passing out in my yard. You told me you found Peter. And we talked about saving him."

"And then?"

"I woke up in the master bedroom with a headache." Everything in my bones felt sad and weak to be confessing this to him. "I drifted in and out of consciousness when you were carrying me back, but nothing meaningful."

Tate didn't seem convinced. I kicked a splash of rainbow into the sky. "I mean... I've picked up a few pictures now and then that I can't put a name on... so I assume they're correlated. Watching you check my gun. Breaking open a rotten door. Men I don't recognize. Yellow store labels. But I can't connect them so I never told anyone."

Tate picked at the peeling primer on the dock wood. "Speaking of, where is your gun?"

"In the bottom of my backpack. Along with the bullets."

"Good. Just checking."

"Why? Think I may need to use it?"

"Just checking." Tate ripped at the paint scraps. He was a ruthless paint torturer. "So you have about a week of memory missing. But you're not missing out on much. It was a lot of waiting, a lot of planning. Nothing you need to remember."

"Because I killed someone."

Tate didn't look at me. "Yeah. You did. He was threatening me," his words leaked like an oil spill; flowing out greasy and ready to stain the world.

I stared at him, watching his face turn a sickly shade of beige. "If it was just a threat, that seems like an overreaction on my part."

"You saved me," he whispered.

I finally tore my eyes away from Tate. "Peter told me I killed the man to get to him. He made it seem like I just... ruthlessly did it. Is that true?"

"No. Peter is a fucking liar. You can't trust anything that son of a bitch said." I never heard Tate swear with such vindictiveness before.

"Hey, that's my mom you're talking about…" I threw out. Just for the sake of eliciting a smile from him. A chuckle. Eyes rolling.

Nothing.

"But he's right about me murdering someone?"

Tate pushed the paint scraps into the blue depths below. I watched them sink to the unseen bottom, forever to remain, as he answered. "Yes. That much is the truth."

There it was.

I suppose it didn't have to change anything about me. I did it whether I knew the truth or not. Whether I remembered one detail or not. This was not how I ever imagined discovering that I was capable of that.

I saved Tate.

"Why would you keep this from me for so long?" I whispered, swallowing back the thick tension gathering in my soul.

"You never asked."

xxvii.

It was on the same dock that Anthony and I sat on one late afternoon, not one week after the storm. I was wearing my new dress, sitting in a precarious position not to let it get too dirty on the rocks.

This was the first time we talked in a week. I didn't talk to anyone beyond the gardens after the revelation with Tate. I didn't care to bother anyone else with my thoughts. The Community had bigger fish to fry than my opinions and concerns. They were the same as anyone else.

I talked with Anthony so often because he never shamed what came from your mouth. He had comments, he had jokes. But he never shamed you. He stayed in his business. It's refreshing to have someone who lets you work through your mental messes when you can't tell right from wrong, can't tell survival from hate.

Anthony was the only one who didn't talk me out of blaming myself for Peter leaving. He let me hate myself. It wasn't after I hated myself that I began to realize his actions were not my fault. Now I was free to accept that Peter was gone. Just as before; nothing changed. And that could be okay.

We had a deep discussion about which kids we were trying to recruit when their years came. I was eyeing Bobby, one of the butcher's kids who was eleven and liked to get in the dirt. Anthony had his sights set on Hope: one of Hank's girls.

This was the first time I discovered that Hank had kids. They were each independent; I never connected the faces. Hank had four children: Hope, Faith, Miracle, and Jonah. They ranged from ages fourteen to seven. Hank was very religious and let his wife take charge of the names, which tops the long list of the last things I ever expected from the man. Hope was the oldest of them and was training with Nina, but Anthony was convinced he could change her mind.

According to Anthony, there was also a fifth one. But they died with Hank's wife in birth.

Just as we launched into a lively debate about whether Misha was a widower, divorcee, a 50-year-old virgin, or a womanizer, a single finger tapped my shoulder. I turned to face a very bored Dmitri.

"Can you come with me?" He jabbed his head to the side. His bangs flopped like a beaver tail.

"Oooh… you're in trouble…" Anthony teased. I kicked him.

"Does Tveit want to see me?" I asked innocently. I didn't think anyone saw when I smuggled a slice of venison from the dining hall to Eden.

"Just come with me, please."

As I stood and followed him away from the safety of the sea, a cold sensation settled over my spine. It was one piece of meat for the sick old lady!

…But what about the small fire in the sanitation closet?

I'd never been scolded by Tveit. I didn't know how harsh he was or how long his lectures lasted.

It's fine. He's a sweet man. He has a daughter; he knows how girls can be. It's fine. It's fine.

…But what if Anita does the scolding?

I'm a grown adult, I reminded myself. *They can't ground me.*

But what if they can?

I let Dmitri lead me towards the buildings and tents… and on. The last thing we passed was the childcare tents. Soon the entire town was left in our dust and he made no sign of a mistake.

Dmitri steadied on without another word as we reached the trees. He led me into the woods to dip just inside. Just along the inside of the tree line, we paced horizontally to the beach through blooming trees.

We walked. And walked. And walked. It had to have been for miles. The sun retreated lower in the sky, and we still walked.

This is it. This is where he takes me to die.

"Where are we going?" I shouted. Dmitri remained stone silent. "Okay. Good to know."

We continued for a day. A day where the sun never moved across the sky and the shadows never grew.

Dmitri didn't speak for so long. He made no acknowledgment of me or the noises of me tripping over the foreign terrain. But then again, if he wanted me off his back it would be no hard feat. He could disappear in a cloud of smoke and leave me stranded in the middle of the forest.

"We're coming up," Dmitri finally said when I considered giving up. I never realized how out of shape I became during the last two months of gardening and sitting in the sand.

Peeking between the trees, seated just on the edge of the grass, was a house. A simple rectangle wooden shack with only two windows. A mold species grew on the nearest corner. An instant vision swiped my mind of the entire structure succumbing and falling to rot the next week. The roof was hanging on by a miracle of God and nature's mercy.

Dmitri left me in the dust. His body floated to the house as if by magnetism.

"What is this place?" I crept up.

"My house." Dmitri wiped the dirt from one of the windows. "I was evicted from my apartment a few years back. Lived in a city where the minimum wage could afford you one meal a week and a few loads at the laundry. An uncle had this place for sale — as if anyone was gonna buy this hunk of shit. He gave it to me for free after a while. I was homeless for three months and floating from one food bank to another, but still. A shitty roof over my head is still a roof."

I sidestepped a discarded metal scrap poking from the sand. "You *lived here?*"

He flung the door open. A bird flew out and hit his face with one brown wing. "Whoops- don't know how he got in there. Technically, I still do live here."

"You sleep with us."

"Where do you think I go all day?" Dmitri ushered me inside. "After you."

Dmitri's house suited him. His bed was tucked in the furthestmost corner; with two thin blankets and one uncovered pillow. Grouped with the bed were two small bookshelves that only housed fishing bait boxes that were not filled with bait. At the other end of the back wall was a curtain rack, pulled back to expose the toilet and an overhead shower that drained into a small drain cut into the floorboard.

What was most odd was the purpose of the free space. Stationed along the right wall and jutted out in odd angles were several round motors. Mismatched limbs of wires and coils extended from each machine. Above our heads were multiple lines of bulb string lights, hung with care from hooks in the ceiling.

My fingers gently grazed over the cool outside of the motors. "I guess I didn't expect anyone to be living in the area when the Community started…"

"Mhm. They discovered me when Anita came snooping for resources." Dmitri threw one hand towards the shotgun propped on the wall. "Neither of us liked that."

Why was I surprised? "When did you join?"

"Not long after. I figured they had food. I needed food."

I watched him kneel by one of the machines, unscrewing somethings and twisting wires inside. I peeked into the tackle boxes on his shelves. Bullets and blades. He was holding bullets and blades in his tackle boxes.

"Your uncle was a… creative house builder," I threw out.

"Polite way to imply this place is a shitter."

"I didn't say it."

A puzzling grin spread across Dmitri's cheeks. Of all strange things to see in my life, that topped the charts. "I still come back sometimes to keep these guys working. You never know when you'll need a refuge."

He began fiddling with the second motor. Something shocked him, zapping his hand back and hitting a bar. His lips emerged from the ferocious bite pink and indented. Any harder and he could have drawn blood.

"What are they?"

Dmitri whipped around, whacking his hand again on the way out.

"You don't recognize these?" He was flabbergasted.

I stared at him. "*Honey*, I like to plant my pretty flowers and was never taught how to change the oil in a car. No, I do not recognize them."

"Your dad failed you." He returned to work with a disappointed head shake.

"It would've been wasted knowledge anyway." I pointed to the coils he now held. "Whatcha doing?"

"Making this damn thing work." Dmitri tightened a bolt in the machine and pushed himself back up. "This is why I wanted to bring you out here. I need to show someone who won't go blabbing while I make my last fixes."

He held up one finger and flipped a single switch on the wall. One by one, the string lights illuminated as the motors worked themselves up. A semi-steady thrum filled the room as the generators blossomed to their full power. The entire room filled with yellow light, casting our faces in the glow I'd missed so dearly.

Electricity.

I could kiss him.

"I went to school for energy engineering. Primarily solar and hydro; we were developing better ways to replace nonrenewable sources. Turns out there isn't much for us when a state lobbyist can manipulate university funding for the chance to stop research," Dmitri explained. The weather had warmed so much I couldn't see his sigh.

"They really did that? And got away with it?"

"They had better lawyers than us." He shrugged, inspecting another humming gadget. "I'm not mad about it anymore. I have these little guys to cheer me up."

"How were you unable to support yourself with an engineering degree?"

Dmitri's cheeks sucked in. "I never finished that degree. They cut funding to our research and so many had to be laid off. I stopped caring. Dropped out four months later. *And* I had a short stint of probation during my last year of high school. I was lucky to even get into that program." Dmitri stood on his mattress to inspect one string.

"It's hard to care about saving the world when someone would rather see a few more zeros added to their net worth."

I didn't have time to feel too sympathetic when *electricity buzzed before me!* "How did you get these going? Where did you find them?"

"Stole them a while ago. Had to drag them each in a wagon all the way out here. And that's not to mention finding the wires and crap. No one noticed when people were burning front lawns over a parking ticket. True story; happened to an ex. Served them right."

"Don't these things still need an external source to turn mechanical energy into electricity? Or kinetic to electric- or potential to mechanical and whatever?" My high school physical science class taught me little, but that I retained.

Dmitri pointed one finger at the floor directly beneath the machines. "Magnets. The current is harnessed in here-" he gestured to another foreign gadget "-where it's then converted to mechanical energy after pushing and pulling electrons, which is then converted to electrical. You were on the right path."

"How do you keep the magnets so… placed right?"

"Math. And guesswork."

"You had no power before?" I reached on my toes to reach a glass bulb. The warm, almost hot, glass against my fingertips transported me to the better times. Euphoria.

"EH. My cell phone was a piece of junk and candles serve you just fine." He sat back on the floor.

I sat with him. His talent was incredible. His skill to maintain a working source of electricity in this ramshackle little house… I had forgotten someone could possess technological knowledge. How he could have changed with world…

Then the realization hit me. It crashed on my skull like a thousand dumbbells.

"You have motors. You have wires. You know how to maintain it. Why are you keeping it to yourself?" I demanded. Shouted.

"I know what you-"

"*We could use this!*" I couldn't hold back. Dmitri flinched. Genuinely flinched. "We could have *power* again! Why keep it hidden?"

"It's not ready!" Dmitri threw his hands up. "I just had to fix the damn coil on that one for the fifth time this month! Do you know how much of a hassle it would be to keep them running 24/7 across town? And we'll need to get more parts should one break. It's just too much. They're not ready."

I leaned away from him. "But tell people. I think they deserve to know. It's wrong."

"You think? How would you feel if someone told you there was a chance for something so intangible, so *fantastical.* And then how would you feel if something broke beyond repair? It's a mess, Vivienne. The less everyone knows until it's ready, the better."

"Then why show me? Are you not worried about me?"

"I figured you would be the only one who could keep their mouth shut," he grumbled. I watched his dark eyes fall downcast at the face of his misleadings. "I needed to tell *someone.*"

I pulled my legs to my chest, pulling the dress's skirt as far down my knees as possible. What he was telling me should have shocked me. It should have infuriated me. Made me want to hit him. Kill him for being so selfish. But I would be selfish with my talents, too. If gardening and swimming were forbidden secrets of a past age, I would keep them to myself, too. It's less dangerous that way. People expect less from you.

It's also dangerous to risk losing the trust of your entire society, but that was his prerogative.

"I understand," I whispered.

We didn't say another thing for so long. The waves crashed in the distance. As the sun met the horizon, the light bulbs were all that illuminated us. The evening bugs came out of hiding, forming an orchestra of mating calls and shared complaints of *"What the hell are these two freaks doing?"*

"You're not afraid of a hunting party coming along and seeing this?" I finally asked.

Dmitri shrugged. He laid back on the disgusting wooden floor. "If they do, I'll tell them the same story I told you. Only one of them is above me. What are they gonna do about it?"

"I never took you as one to take advantage of authority like that." I lay next to him, my hair sprawling over him in the process. He made no effort to push it away.

Dmitri chuckled, throwing one pebble at the ceiling. It hit my knee. "Politicians did it all the time and people still loved them."

"I thought you were a Libertarian."

"I'm an Anarchist. There's a difference. But I know what power can do for me when I need it. If that makes me a hypocrite, so be it."

"No, I get it." I stared out the dark window. "I don't suppose we can make it back in time for dinner."

"I can catch you something if you're hungry."

I scoffed. "So sweet."

"I'm serious." His head cocked sideways at me. "It's my fault you'll miss dinner."

So there was a kind bone in that body.

"I'll just pick something up from the garden. Thank you, though."

"Won't you get in trouble for that?"

I whipped my head around, narrowing my eyes. My hair hit him again. "I grow the damn plants! They can suck it up." I giggled.

He laughed too.

I made it for dinner the next evening.

Work was work. Hank was Hank. Eden didn't recover, but she wasn't getting any worse.

For a few hours, I forgot about the secret I held with Dmitri. I forgot about the weight of what I knew, what could change the People By The Sea forever. But I made a promise to him. I'm not a woman often in the business of breaking promises.

Shannon approached me shortly before dinner. Her hair stuck in five different directions and sweat dripped from every conceivable pore. "Have you seen Chrissy today?"

I glanced into the small sliver of the kitchen that the open door allowed. "No? She's not in there?"

"Bryce hasn't seen her all day. I had to chip in… and…" Shannon hunched over with her hands on her knees. Her postpartum belly stuck out of the bottom of her shirt. As well, her milk was draining through the flannel breast pockets. "I can't keep doing this. I've been running all over for the last hour."

"Okay, okay, I'm sure she's hiding somewhere." I rubbed the woman's arm. Chrissy was very outspoken about her dislike for the kitchen work, but she would never walk out with no warning. Never. She was better than that.

Shannon composed herself, straightening her hair when Misha passed. "Can you find her? Or one of your… posse?"

"Of course. Where's Nick?"

"With Nina. I'm trying to balance feeding him and this crap and… I just… I can't." She shook her head, letting it hang like a sorrowful puppy. It was then she noticed her breasts and wailed. "And they *hurt!*"

I hugged her; one which she melted into. "No one is expecting you to be Hercules."

"But I have to be." Shannon smiled; I saw that smile forced by my own mom far too many times.

With a community so large, and in a work field so simple, it shouldn't have to be that way. Someone new should be able to sacrifice a few hours a day to help stir pots and chop vegetables. We should not be making a postpartum breastfeeding first-time mother do the work to feed fifty ungrateful people.

"Is there anything I can do to help?" I rubbed her shoulder.

Shannon sighed, answering Bryce's call to come back to work. "Find that girl."

I sat with Tate and Diana for dinner. None of us spoke much during the meal. The day was exhausting for everyone. A missing girl, one of Anita's boys being stung by a wasp, allergy season, and the hunters coming back with less than satisfactory results.

The tension would unwind itself. The search party would come back. We would lecture Chrissy and send her to bed without her metaphorical dinner. Cillian would cure any pain Teddy had. We would suck up all our snot and be okay. The hunters would compensate tomorrow for all the animals they missed today.

Everything would be alright. We would be okay.

I'll never forget the following seconds. The following minutes.

I was the first to see her. Anita appeared at the head of the table. Her sons bombarded her; she ignored them to beeline for us. Her face missed all semblance of confidence and power. The three of us stood, acting as one through the hive mind.

I stepped back to allow them privacy. Anita's news was drowned by the oblivious crowd of happy diners.

Dmitri burst through the door. We made eye contact across the wide hall. Slowly, burdened, his head shook.

Tate froze. Diana buried her face in his shoulder. I stepped forward as Tate pushed Diana off and ran out the door. Anita shouted for him to wait. Strangers who couldn't mind their own business followed him outside.

"Mom! Mom!" Liam shouted. Anita begged them to quiet and urged us to follow.

Diana stayed, paralyzed. Two tears slipped down her cheek as I almost had to pull her outside.

Silence met us outside. An impenetrable semicircle formed that cost all of my strength to break through. Diana and I joined Anita and Tate at the very edge of the dirt roads.

It wasn't until I moved to block the golden-hour sunlight that I recognized Tveit's shape. His hair, his clothes… and two extra limbs. One dangling to the side.

A body.

Everyone's gravity bore me down. Boxed me in.

Tveit moved in slow motion. Cillian ran to the leader. Tveit gave him one solemn look confirming that there was nothing he could do to save her.

I felt Dmitri approach me from the right. "I wanted to warn you first. We found her by a lake," he whispered. I wanted to slap him.

Tveit stopped before us with Chrissy's body.

His eyes were rimmed red. Hers were wide open. As was her mouth, contracted and frozen to form a poisoned smile.

Clutched in both her hands were bouquets of white-flowered stems. Bunches of deadly buds, toxic spiked tubers. They hadn't been able to pry the water hemlock from her lifeless fingers.

xxviii.

Everyone went to her funeral. Not many stayed to watch her be surrendered to the Flame and returned to dust.

Dmitri had to do most of the service. There was no mistaking the grief from Cillian, Anita, and Tveit. They believed they failed her. It was their duty to protect the People By The Sea. Once again in a single week, they failed.

The three of us were asked to say a few words. I spoke more like a drone than a human being. Tate addressed his sister wrapped in old cloth and twine bindings as if she could still hear. Diana clutched a stick in her two hands so hard I was convinced it would snap. The stick was worn free of bark; she did that through mere friction when waiting for her turn.

The heat of the fire never comforted me less. Anthony never left my side.

No one spoke of her, but the effects of her death rippled through the Community.

With Shannon on maternity leave, Bryce was the only one left in the kitchen. All four butchers had to be moved to the kitchen. None of them were happy about this. Anita told them to "suck it up or starve."

Parents kept their children closer. Kids were no longer allowed to play in large groups at bonfires, no more night swimming. One of the hunting women stepped down from her position to help Nina and Diana. She said it was because the two were completely understaffed for the daycare and elementary school. We all knew — by the lingering glances and tighter clutch to her daughter — she didn't trust Nina anymore. As if Chrissy was a toddler let loose at recess.

Hank brought Jonah and Faith, his two youngest, into the garden. They played well with Elliott and Lily, but it was clear they could see their father's worries. During this time, Hank laid off the hallucinogens. I caught him slipping one dried mushroom into his pocket before lunch on the third day, though.

They demanded Anita add more security. She and Tveit created a new protocol for people even walking between buildings — a rudimentary buddy system. This was an annoying new rule in a community that held such basic laws: don't murder; don't steal; if you lie, don't make it obvious. But I wasn't the one complaining. It was wandering away alone that led to Chrissy's demise.

Patrols added three more stations every shift. Some like Dmitri or Tate were strung three shifts in a row. By protocol, patrolmen were not allowed to sleep or eat during a shift. They are our guards, our first and only line of defense. They could not risk sleeping or being distracted by a meal when lives were in danger.

When I did see Tate, the dark patches under his eyes stretched to his cheekbones, which sharpened over the weeks. Fewer words left his mouth. Any food I begged him to eat would retch upon the grass an hour later.

Any action Anita tried to fix these circumstances was shot down. They claimed starving and working our security to unconsciousness was better than letting them eat on the job. They said this because they were not targeted by the rules.

The Community was angry. They were afraid and losing trust in their superiors. Within days people were underhanding Tveit and Anita. Some deliberately ignored Dmitri's orders for peace and attention; others turned to more popular liaisons for order.

Diana spent any time that wasn't with the kids in bed. It was hard to get more than five words out of her unless she initiated, which was rare. Her mattress was soon imprinted with the shape of her body; always turned to the wall and curled partially fetal. I brought her meals wrapped in the hem of my shirt. She accepted them in silence.

Nina asked me if Diana was suicidal. I couldn't give her a solid answer.

Tate took his responsibility more seriously than anyone. Dmitri confessed he wished he had the power to move people up in succession. He would make Tate as high as #6 if he could. Unfortunately, that power only lay with Tveit, and there were five others I can name who would be outraged to the point of rebellion by such a dramatic shift in rank. Tveit would never be so daring.

My walking partners revolved between Anthony, Lily, Hank (plus children), and Anita's older boy, Liam. Lily talked my ears off about the bugs she found in the soil that day. Hank was a toss-up whether he would be curt or smiling with his kids. Anthony was the only constant I could rely on.

Liam was thirteen years old when the first missile fell. They watched as a family two days after his birthday party. That was in Manitoba, Canada. His parents, Anita and her husband who disappeared in the airport, hitched a ride on the next plane out of the territory. They landed on the edge of Quebec and hitchhiked across the national border.

Now Liam was fourteen and not heeding my advice to stay a kid as long as possible. You don't grasp how young and immature you are until you look back and wonder why you didn't take advantage of those years when you had them.

There were no whispers of restarting the fishing expeditions. We would need a new boat, new nets, and new fishermen. That glorious fire died before we were able to feed the flame.

I think that's what upset Diana so much. Everyone moved on so fast.

One week passed after Chrissy's death, and I couldn't handle ignorance of what happened to Peter. I pulled Dmitri aside after breakfast before he left with the first patrol shift.

"I need you to find Peter."

I don't know what was going through my head. I don't know what I expected to happen. But I did. And he listened.

Dmitri slung his arms through the sleeves of his jacket. "Peter left on his own accord."

"So did Chrissy. I need you to find him."

"Why should I?" Dmitri held the door open for anyone leaving the dining hall, which was plenty. "Not that I won't, but why should I?"

I held out my hands. "Because it's nice. What else are you going to do?"

Dmitri let the door slam back shut. Someone in the back yelped at the echo. "I'm going to need a party. You're asking us to surrender three patrolmen to find your brother because… you want us to?"

"I'm scared!" I'm still embarrassed today by how whiney I sounded. "I don't know what to do! He left angry, and he's so paranoid and… I just…" I took a deep breath. "I don't think he's safe. I have a gut feeling."

"I understand. But he's been gone for *weeks*. He could be the next state over. Imagine how long we would have to be gone. I'm not in the business of losing my job because someone complained to Anita."

Tate waved at us. When I bared a smile for him, my eyes didn't miss the single-shot bottle of bourbon tucked in his palm.

"You could lose your job?" I murmured back to Dmitri.

"You don't know what anyone'll say these days. Anita can't risk the public's anger anymore."

"But you're her right hand! They can't boss you around."

Dmitri's head darted to Kathy, who had been eying us from her seat like a rabid vulture. "Keep your voice down. Angry people can do whatever they want in the right circumstances."

"Then get *permission*!"

"That doesn't happen among the leaders." I had a feeling he bit back a remark along the lines of *"You wouldn't know."*

"So you can't get permission, or you won't?"

Dmitri pulled us back to the corner. The dark, bug-infested corner that convinced me my friend would try to kill me. "You're asking a lot of me, Vivienne. I can try-"

"I'll take the fall," I grabbed his hands. The pads of his fingers gritted against mine like sand. "If you get in trouble. I'll take the fall. Please."

"That would be a cowardly move on my part."

I glanced over my shoulder. It was time to pull a low card. "It would be a real shame if Tveit knew about your... house," I whispered between us. My effort to exude confidence was no good. He could smell the fear.

Dmitri gave me one sharp look before barking out a laugh. "You wouldn't."

"You don't know."

"No, I don't know. But you care too much about my loyalty, or you wouldn't have come to *me*." He was an infuriating man. An infuriating man who did have me figured out. "What's really in it for me?"

"*Bragging rights!* I don't know!" I cried.

Dmitri ignored me to order his men to their stations in their sign language, but didn't leave with them.

"Please. I'll owe you a favor," I pleaded. He crossed his arms. "Anything you need in the future, I'll do it. I just need this one thing right now."

Dmitri nodded slowly, biting his cheek. "Okay. Tomorrow," he muttered. I jumped. *Literally* jumped with joy and threw my arms over him. He waved me away lazily. "Yeah, yeah. Whatever."

I couldn't believe the words that were tumbling out of my mouth. "Do you need a buddy out there?" I offered. I was asking for me. My only choices left in the dining hall were Crying Kathy, Shannon and her crying baby Nick, and Cillian, who was smuggling out food for Eden. Cillian was a fine choice but looked emotional; I didn't want to mess with that.

"That's not going to be your favor." He threw open the door.

"That's not what I meant." I threw on a smile that probably would have me sent to a mental asylum in the 1960s. Dmitri grunted, motioning for me to follow.

The sun hit me like a bomb. I threw my jacket off and tied it around my waist. I gestured to his faithful wool jacket that never parted from his torso. "How can you exist in that thing? It's getting warm."

"I'm cold-blooded."

Dmitri was a fast walker through town. I was practically jogging alongside. I didn't notice it when he led me to his house because I was too afraid of being viciously executed or sacrificed.

"Do you believe in God, Vivienne? Or anything like that?" Dmitri asked out of the blue as we passed the medical tent.

I stared up at him, almost tripping on a pothole. "Where did that come from?"

"Just a question."

"I believe there's something out there. I pray when I'm scared."

"But you don't know who you're praying to." He grinned and waved at Misha. Ever the two-track-minded showman.

"Sure."

"It's a yes or no question."

I stopped to pick a rock out of my shoe. "Why do you care? Do you believe in God?"

Dmitri nodded.

"Good for you."

"I'm not trying to witness to you. I'm curious." He smiled at me.

"Well, um, I guess it just makes me feel better," I mumbled. Dmitri was the last person I wanted to have a theological talk with. "My thing is, I guess, it would be really sad if we're the highest power in the universe and we did what we did."

"And you have no problem with the idea that God let all that happen?" He offered. "That's my biggest struggle."

"I don't think I care enough to think about that. The guy probably had a lot on his plate."

"Probably. Or it's something like Noah's flood." He grabbed a tig from the grass and chucked it into oblivion. I was beginning to think who I was talking to was an alien who abducted and took Dmitri's place. "We'll never know. I could be wrong. But I don't think I am."

"You should be talking to Hank about this." I scoffed.

He shook his head. His hair flopping back and forth reminded me of a yappy dog. "I know what Hank thinks. I'm talking to you."

I slowly down, examining him like a lab specimen. "You're so odd," I marveled.

"Thank you."

We made it to the furthest reaches of the Community. The trees held darkness and cover now that life was plentiful and the trees had fully bloomed. Anything beyond this point was patrol and hunting territory. After Chrissy, no one was allowed in the trees.

"Do you actually have a personality, or is everything you do crafted around other people?" I asked, half as an insult, half as a genuine question.

Dmitri shrugged, backing away. "We all do it."

Before I knew what was happening, Dmitri slipped away into the lively trees, leaving me helpless and alone on the far reaches of the Community. Not another soul could be found. It hadn't even occurred to me when we embarked across town that we were going in two separate directions.

"Dmitri!" I shouted into the space he disappeared from. No response. "I need to get back!"

Nothing. The guy was a fart in the wind.

(Dmitri, if you're reading this now I want you to know that's said with utmost offense.)

I checked left and right, up and down, back and forth for Anita. When I was confident I couldn't feel her gray eyes ready to smite me from behind a birch, I booked it for the gardens.

The bonfire wasn't fun anymore. Most people skipped out to get extra sleep. What once united the People By The Sea now served as a reminder about everything missing in the world.

The Flame wasn't lively. It lost its enchantment. That New England beach was dead.

It was there I sat with Anthony and Alice that evening. Grace, too, but she was passed out on the sand with a dragonfly flitting on her.

The most interesting thing of the night was a big wave. I watched the waters retract farther than usual. I alerted the other two that it could be a tsunami. But what was the point of running? There are no high grounds in the Community. Better to accept your inevitable fate. No one else paid attention, but then again, people can be clueless.

The wave crested and rolled down, surging lazily towards the coast. It extended as far as the bonfire pit. The Flame was extinguished. Someone's kid screamed. Another wave came. Then another one. Several feet got wet with the reach. Then it was done. The tides returned to their normal rhythm.

Well. That was dramatic for no reason.

The excitement settled back down. More returned to the safety of their beds. The familiar dread settled back over the beach.

Alice and Grace left after Grace woke when something inside her pants bit her thigh. The two girls ran off to Cillian — Grace inconsolable and Alice laughing behind her.

Anthony and I didn't leave. With my head resting on his legs and his fingers drawing on my shoulder, we could fall asleep right there on the sand. No one would notice. No one would miss us. I was almost ready to doze off when Anthony's hand froze.

"Hey… tell me if this is stupid, but I have an idea."

I gestured for him to continue and was reminded of the language barrier when he poked my head to see if I was still awake. "Shoot."

"Okay. Hear me out. What if you hold classes to show people how to distinguish poisonous plants?" He scooted forward on the sand, pushing some on my bare feet. "Think about it. You could get someone else in the garden to help you. Or a hunter! And anyone who wants could learn how to differentiate between elderberry or… or baneberry! That's a thing, right?"

I sat up and smiled at my lap. "I don't know if this was your point, but elderberries are poisonous too."

Anthony threw up both hands. "I did not know that! Exactly my point!"

I knew his intentions were good. The gears turned in his brain like a perfectly crafted machine, ready to change the world. And as per usual, my brain was concocting every possible way his plan could go wrong.

And to be truthful, I wasn't sure I could handle much more of the townspeople than necessary.

"I can't just *make* that happen. Tveit would have to say yes."

"He's not gonna say no."

"You never know…" I exhaled slowly. "I just… It's a lot. It's a lot to consider."

"I know, but Viv, you could save so many lives." Anthony grabbed my hands, which hung limp in his. "If Chrissy knew what hemlock was, don't you think she would be alive?"

"Yes."

He smiled, shaking my arms gently. "So let's help people not make the same mistake."

XXIX.

Dmitri was gone the next morning. He took two patrol members with him. The young adult dormitory was lonelier than usual.

Tate begged for my help. Hank didn't put up too strong a fight. I took a break from the gardens to help in childcare. It was an excuse to be with Diana outside of her bed; curled up in her single blanket, eyes fixated on the blank wall. Watching her reminded me of my mother, who in the worst of her trials was never satisfied with the life she settled for.

Diana was sick. Sick of the mind, sick of the body. We were lucky if we got her to stomach a full bowl each day. Water was even harder to get down unless fashioned into lemon-leaf tea. I held her hand endlessly as she struggled to poop, tears racing tracks on her cheeks at the angry convulsions in her organs. We tried getting her to exercise by playing with the dogs or racing across the beach. Nothing succeeded for longer than twenty minutes, and she returned to her place as before.

Cillian and Eugene had nothing to cure her, save for the tea and pain pills. But there were only fifteen of those left. Diana begged them not to use them up on her.

Nina gave up trying to educate the kids when all Diana could do was show up. It's not that she *wouldn't* put the effort in. The energy was entirely drained from her malnourished body.

Have you ever heard of Pompeii? It was an ancient Roman city that was buried under volcanic ash in less than a day. After millennia, what was left of the innocent citizens of Pompeii was nothing more than cavities in the hardened ash where their bodies decomposed; their shapes forever preserved in their final fearful positions. Diana was a Pompeii cavity, one which I desperately craved to mold and give new life.

This is a fact that hasn't changed. People love to be sympathetic towards the depressed until it causes genuine consequences. We love to express how serious of a condition it is until you interact face-to-face with someone truly battling their mind and body. Then said depressed person is lazy. A waste of space.

Diana blamed herself for what happened to Chrissy. The root of the problem came to light when we sat at the back of the classroom after all the children had left, watching Nina struggle to clean despite her insistence that she needed no help.

"She told me she was going out there," Diana muttered out of the blue.

"Hmm?"

"Chrissy told me she was going out the day before," Diana spoke again. She scuffed the dirt under our feet with the toe of her shoe. One tear prickled at her eyes, which turned into two, which became three. "She *told me* she wanted to be useful. I didn't take her seriously. I thought it was just another rant."

I threw one arm around her. "There was no way you could've known."

The few tears turned into a waterfall within a minute. "I didn't tell anyone! I didn't listen to her!" Diana descended into a mad fit of hiccups. Nina minded her business, but I could feel the trained ear on us. "She s-aid there was a lake. It- wasn't too far from the border, but… I don't- know how s-he described it. She was ta-lking about f-fish or something. I w-wasn't paying atten-tion!"

"*It wasn't your fault.* I wouldn't have taken her seriously, either."

This was not the right thing to say. The girl started to bawl, whimpering and shedding tears enough to water the garden's seeds. I didn't know what to do other than rub her back in slow circles and shut my mouth.

"W-what did she h-have in her hand?" Diana finally asked.

I stopped rubbing her back. I clarified if she truly wanted to know. She nodded. "It's called water hemlock. It's a plant that grows around water sources. It suffocates and causes muscle spasms. You die with a smile from the contractions."

"How do you know this?"

"Mr. York's botany class. We had a unit on identifying poisonous plants." Mr. York died of pancreatic cancer four months after the end of that year.

Diana's head hit my shoulder in one loose movement. "Someone could've found her if I told them she was leaving."

I leaned my head on top of hers. It was glass under my weight. "I'm going to say this one more time. *It is not your fault.* We never knew when to take her seriously."

"But it was."

"Okay. Then it was. Regardless, blaming yourself now won't do anything productive," I finalized. Maybe it was rude, but beating yourself up about the unfortunate truth never helps your grieving. The final step of the process is acceptance.

Diana said nothing. Nina bid us goodbye and ran out.

"Do you think she committed suicide?" I whispered only after Nina left the tent.

Diana shook her head and wiped her face. "I think she was trying to help. She didn't know."

"She could have come to us in the garden. She could've asked the hunters." We would've been happy to take her in as a gardener. The hunters always needed new arms. If it was a problem of not feeling useful to the Community, she had options. She had so many opportunities.

I cleared my throat. "So you think she was foraging for new plants to feed us?" I offered. Diana shrugged. "She didn't know how to identify between poisonous and safe... tried one herself, and..."

"It doesn't matter now."

That was all it took for me to approach Tveit about teaching classes against poison.

Tveit wanted to sit in on our first class. He called our proposal brilliant, magnificent, *world-changing*. Why hadn't someone come up with it sooner? It had to start immediately!

Without another word, he sent me away to collect samples with Lily and Elliott. That was the most dangerous thing I could imagine, but I wasn't about to argue with the thunderous man. I made sure to stop by Cillian's for bags and medical gloves.

Hank agreed to teach the classes with me. Lily and Elliott managed the gardens themselves, harvesting cabbages and sprouts dutifully in the distance. By the garden gates, we stood in front of five people the following day. I could tell two of them were just there to be traveling buddies. Tveit was the largest of them, standing out like a hangnail against Leta on his lap.

"Hi." I sent them a small wave. Leta was the only response; a wave higher than her head.

"Y'all listen up now," Hank spoke up abruptly. I snapped my mouth shut. At my side, he took a quick swig of the rancid-smelling moonshine. "Chrissy Dawson's death was preventable. Our goal here is to educate ya so ya don't make the same stupid mistake an' get yourself dead in a hole."

I faced the audience tentatively. Ever the wordsman he was. "That is… yes. That's why we're here."

"What're those?" One of the attentive ones asked. His hand, which was missing one finger, pointed to the mound of red, spiked bulbs.

I handed it to him, and they began passing the stem around. "I wouldn't touch the bulbs. Buried in those shells are castor beans. You've heard of castor oil? Just a smidgen of this stuff will cause organ failure within a day."

We scoped out at least two miles past the border with one patrolman. Back with us, we brought five species that looked the most like regular flowers and edible fauna. Castor bean, ivy, belladonna, foxglove. Why do poisonous plants all have poisonous-sounding names?

And of course, we had hemlock. Hemlock with its white budded clusters.

Everyone paid attention once we brought out the berries. It's so easy to mistake lethal berries for edible. Distinguishing between them can come down to factors as simple as three triangle leaves instead of four, or the length of tuber spikes.

I don't think we were too boring. We engaged with them and popped a few jokes. Still, their eyes strayed to stare blankly at the ocean. Grass jewelry was crafted. Tveit had to physically lift their chins to face us multiple times. You would think when people are telling you how *not to die*, you would want to listen. I was almost convinced to pack it all up and give up trying to make lives better.

When it was all done, Hank bid me ado and crept off, no doubt to harvest his latest batch of "ailments". For once, I wanted to join in.

Word spread across the Community like molasses from a bottle. The second afternoon yielded four people — two of them were repeats who I'm sure would rather listen to me drone on about chemical compounds than do their regularly scheduled work.

Hank couldn't be found the second time. I wanted to crawl deep into the garden soil and wait for a beautiful bulb to sprout from my buried head. That may feel better than facing their faces alone.

To spice the lecture up, I tried to come up with gruesome poison stories from my old days of dark Internet addiction. When all I could procure was Socrates' cause of death, I made things up. It's not like they could fact-check me. Grins and disgusted laughter flurried through the four of them. More questions were asked; more wary gazes were incited toward the plants. Mission successful.

We weren't too far deep when my eyes caught a man watching from the edge of the gate. Anthony leaned against the ironwork, that cheeky grin cracked against his face. He stayed there for the rest of the lecture, offering a few questions and encouragement when someone decided to drawl into boredom again.

When the class dispersed, one was left: Leta. She fiddled with the hem of her white dress over hot pink leggings. How that thing wasn't dirt brown by now, I will never have a clue.

"Can I help you?"

"I like it here," she said, smiling at me crookedly.

My eyes strayed back to Anthony, who flashed an encouraging thumbs-up before retreating back to town.

I stepped over to the tomato section of the first garden bed. "You're Tveit's daughter, right?" I knew the answer but had nothing to talk about.

She made a bowl of air with the bottom of her dress, which was riddled with bug holes. Her hair was the color of honey, skin was tanned as a real-life goddess; one that chose to perpetually look like a prepubescent child.

I ushered her closer to the tomatoes. "You guys are Greek? I've always wondered."

"Daddy says we're Americans, and he tells me to not listen to anyone who calls me illegal." The little girl slowly approached the raised bed, watching me study the stems. "What are you doing?"

"I'm checking how long these have to ripen." We were on day 62 and the fruits were still a sickly green color.

Leta stuck her face in the stems. "How do you know?"

"They'll be red and semi-firm. We're in the right time that they should be turning red. But they're just not. So I'm a little concerned." I let the fruit fall from my hand to ungraciously hang, pulling her back before she climbed into the dirt. "How old are you?"

A wide smile cracked her delicate face. "Nine and a half. I'm ten in June!"

My heart sank to think that she may never know when June passed. I estimated it to be early April. It very well could've been late May and I would be none the wiser.

"You said you like it here? What do you mean?"

Leta shrugged simply, fidgeting with a tomato leaf. "I don't wanna go back to school."

"You have to go to school," I said.

"Nu-uh! We're not doing anything!" Leta clenched her baby fist at her side.

Oh, how I miss being a stubborn child begging my parents to miss a day of elementary school. The number of times I attempted to fake a fever by pressing my tongue harder over the thermometer to heat it more. I opened my mouth to correct her when a monster in the background interrupted.

A looming crescendo approached from behind. It was the type of sound that could trample you. The type that could roll over and turn you into nothing more but a speck on the sidewalk. It was in the sky.

We turned as one body, one mind. Racing overhead was a controlled machine; a sleek metal creature whose solid wings glided on the atmosphere like a perfectly crafted bird. The exhaust leaked from each side, permeating the clear sky in two gray streaks.

The white commercial airplane passed the Community in less than a second, flying low enough to send waves of force across the coastal waters.

XXX.

Clothes flew off the drying line. Logs went rolling. Our tall plants jerked back and forth; some broke in the middle. A child cried from the dirt street.

"What the *FUCK* was that?" Lily screamed. My soul jumped from my skin. My eardrums were still popping from the dramatic air pressure change.

"Can you find your dad?" I grabbed Leta's shoulders. I knew he would be hunting or supply gathering, but it was worth seeming like I knew what to do. Leta ran away.

"Does this mean the machines is back?" Elliott piped up.

"Maybe." I grabbed the kids' shoulders and steered them to the garden gates. "I don't know what to do now."

One by one, the patrol emerged from the tree line, charging down the slope like buffalo. Two hunters came through, guns almost flying from their hands.

Compared to this, the fishing meeting was a peaceful Sunday gathering. Parents shouted at their kids as they ran around in a panicked little-limbed fury. I watched someone shove Bryce to the ground to get to his partner. Anyone inside was out now. Every single body in the Community milled around aimlessly, shouting back and forth like silence would mean their end.

Undergarments were strewn on the grass meters from their drying lines. Garbage littered the street under every foot. A childcare tent was thrown up and away; the metal poles crooked in the soil, the strings knotted among themselves.

Eden emerged from her prison. Cillian took five seconds to notice before sending her right back to her cot.

"Have you seen Anthony or Diana?" I asked someone in passing. They walked away with no word.

The muddled dissent craved to suffocate me. The torches and

pitchforks were itching to be brought out. Who are the leaders if they can't protest us from commercial airplanes?

Tveit arrived at the head of town. His voice echoed for his daughter, scanning every inch of trampling mosh. Misha was flagged down and demanded for her. Before that moment, I had yet to see the weathered military man look so afraid.

"I sent her to find you!" I chimed in, jogging up to them.

"Why was she with you?"

"She was in my class ag-" a bag came hurling at me from behind. Tveit pushed me down. Misha's voice rocketed at whoever threw it. I was too focused on Tveit's hands pulling me further from the road.

Tveit brushed his pepper beard with two bandaged fingers. "Where did she run?"

"I don't know- I was too focused on the *plane*!" I threw my free hand out to the horizon.

"*Daddy!*" A little girl's scream rang from the other side of the street. Leta zoomed across the road, cutting off people and tripping others, causing a cascade of adults. Tveit knelt and swooped her up. She smiled as he nearly squeezed the breath out of her.

"What happened?" Someone asked Tveit, carelessly shoving me away. The leader shook his head, motioning for them to apologize to me. The person sent me a discarded grunt and moved on.

"Community meeting! Everyone in the mess hall pronto. Sit down and *shut up!*" Anita's alto poured out from the unknown. Immediately, like drones, the crowd turned and flocked into the double doors.

Tveit set Leta down and turned to me. "Take her. I'll be soon," he ordered. I grabbed Leta's hand. Together, we braved the crowd and inched our way into the building.

The math didn't check out, but the hall seemed filled with triple the amount from before. Heads melted into heads. Limbs tangled into one horrible knot of arms and battered jeans. Anita and Cillian were taking a scrambled headcount, urging everyone to stay in one place and be quiet.

I couldn't breathe in there. Every other lung was sucking up all the oxygen, leaving me to suffocate among sweat particles and body odor.

"Stay with me until your dad gets back," I whispered to Leta. From how the girl clutched my hand like a life buoy, I knew she wasn't going anywhere. "Can you help me find my family? Do you know what they look like?"

Answering the search for me, a firm hand grabbed my shoulder. Tate.

"How close did it get to you guys?" He asked without greeting.

"Um- pretty close. Could feel the jets." I pushed Leta after him. We slid to the outskirts of the crowd.

Diana stood against the wall with Anthony and Eugene. Eugene hit Anthony's arm. My friend parted from the wall and searched for me, angling his head to the right as best as possible. When he finally found me, his eyes relaxed and jaw unclenched. I tore my hand from Leta's and jogged for him. I feel bad for colliding into him, but sometimes that's what it takes to achieve a good hug.

At the front, Tveit's boots thundered onto the stage table. Anita whistled for attention. For once, her whistle was ineffective.

"We're all worried about-" Tveit couldn't get out an entire sentence before the mob bombarded him.

"Is someone coming to rescue us?"

"Is there a new government?"

"How long has there been power?"

"Do hunters know anything?"

"The world is ending!"

"I know we are all confused!" Tveit boomed over the mania. Several settled down. From his side, Anita sat on the edge of the table and grabbed Liam and Teddy. "No, we do not know what's happening. If we did-"

"How could this happen?" Shannon yelled.

"The government people pulled their strings and brought back nuclear power!" A voice that I regrettably had not visited in weeks chimed in from the center of the crowd. "I told you they would!"

"Mom!" Cillian jumped down. "I told you to stay in bed!"

"I heard a bomb! They're killing us!" Senility did not look good on Eden.

Cillian gently guided her back to the door. Eden murmured something to herself. Her hair was thinned. Her clothes hung off her body like a potato sack. "It wasn't a bomb, Mom. It was an airplane," he said.

"Probably carrying bombs!"

The two of them weren't yet outside before the People erupted again. I had to clamp my hands over my ears to protect them from permanent deafness.

"Who do you think it was?" Diana whispered to me.

"Hmm?"

"Did you see a logo on the side?"

My head slowly turned back to the leaders. "No. I was distracted by fear and impending doom."

"If anyone knew we were here, they would've found us by now!" Misha bellowed at the front.

"I don't believe you!" Someone shouted.

Anita jumped up. "Then you can get out! We don't have time for this. We either need solutions, or we move forward." She jabbed one finger at the double doors. "If anyone else doesn't want to take this meeting seriously, leave now. I don't have the patience to dance around children who refuse to come together like one People."

Crickets. Serendipity.

I slid down the cool wall, soaking up the precious silence. The drum beat in my head subsided. One by one, I could feel my muscles relax and my joints settle back in place. I imagine this is what a high feels like. This is what the addicts chase so desperately.

Tveit was the first one to speak again when Cillian returned. "I don't think there is anything we can do," he admitted. A cloud of murmurs filled the space. "I think the best we can do now is move on. Live our lives normal."

"But how could this happen? We would know if the power was back on!" A butcher chimed.

"Not necessarily," Cillian perked up. His glasses slid almost off the tip of his nose. "We are miles from the nearest town. This area was privately owned and operated independently. Gauging how fast the U.S. government can get everything back 'online', so to say, there is no guarantee they would even consider our area."

"That's funny to suggest we still have a government," Diana commented. I couldn't help the morbid grin that spread on my face.

"Whoever is left is gonna care about where all of their own families live. That's what I would do. Unfortunately, that means expending all the resources to places that suck it all up: Chicago, Los Angeles, New York, St. Louis, Seattle. If that works, they'll think about others. Maybe. It's going to take a lot of people to get the entire country powered again."

"You're saying we would be a second thought." Anita hung her head.

"Not even that. A third thought. A fourth thought."

"There's no reason to think they even know anyone is still alive up here." Tveit shook his head solemnly. "Are we on our own?"

Cillian wrung his hands. "Likely, yes."

"And this is all speculation?"

"Well, yes. But I can't think of anything else-"

A hand shot up. "Someone had to be in that plane! They passed right over us. Someone has to know now!"

"Yeah! Maybe that was a reconnaissance mission."

Misha shot down their theories. "They've had remote-piloted aircraft for ages. That doesn't mean anything."

"But we can hope," they jabbed back.

"And *what if* someone saw us?" Anita sighed. "No one will consider us if it's not convenient, is that right?" Cillian confirmed.

Tveit held a hand up, settling the protest festering in the audience. "We've managed on our own for a year. I see no reason to stop."

"What about the day we run out of supplies to take from neighboring towns?" Tate whispered to us. Our eyes collectively widened. "I've seen the stores they're ransacking. They're getting bare."

"I am *not* going back to newspapers and scarves for my period!" Diana exclaimed, a little louder than our conversation.

My head jerked. "You still get yours?"

"Sometimes. You don't?"

"I haven't had one since October."

"Thanks for the info," Eugene grumbled.

My head whipped back around to him. "Just because you've never felt the touch of a woman doesn't mean the rest of us have to be prudes."

At the back of the room, Dmitri and his traveling party joined the mob. I heard the large doors open and shut with as quiet a slam as they could manage. He sat down, glancing around the crowd. His shoulders sat rigid, his eyes not holding their usual icy stare. Unsettled. Unnerved.

We made eye contact through the mess of bodies. He made a subtle gesture for me. I whispered to Anthony where I was going and slipped away, only narrowly avoiding my fingers getting trampled by a butcher.

"When did you get back?" I whispered.

"Two minutes ago." Dmitri ushered his men to the front. Tveit's voice faded away, if the statement could ever be true. "Vivienne, it's not pretty," he muttered.

"What do you mean?"

He breathed deeply. "We found Peter-"

"*Really?* You really did?" I exclaimed, grabbing his arm. His arm froze under my fingers. "But where is he? Surely you forced him to come back-"

"Vivienne."

"Where was he? Did you just leave him there?"

"Vivienne."

I threw a hand up, my harsh whisper raising in tone. "I'm sorry. This is all a mess. You saw the plane, right? Why am I worrying about a stupid-"

Dmitri's hand clamped around my mouth. It tasted like dirt. "Stop. We found Peter dead. He was somewhere three miles out," he stated. My mouth closed. He lowered his hand. "There were two bullet wounds in his chest and one in his lower abdomen. He looked dead for days. A week, maybe."

I didn't say anything. I don't remember saying anything. Tate called back to me. Was it Tate? I couldn't hear what he said, much less process enough words to respond coherently.

Anita called Dmitri to the front. Dmitri held a hand up to acknowledge, but stayed still. He turned his back to the audience. "There's one more thing. He- uh… well, he was branded."

My eyes bulged out of my skull. "Like a *cow*?"

"Like a cow. A big **C** burnt into his left cheek. Someone knew what they were doing."

"But Peter doesn't know anyone." Didn't know anyone.

"Someone knows him. Can you think of anyone?"

My head shook. I could feel it shake harder and harder until it was about to rip from my shoulders. My head would rip off my shoulders and fly into Dmitri's arms.

Did I stop? I couldn't feel my own body. I was a phantom watching myself from above, and it was no pretty sight.

There was one name. One I only heard on a single occasion, but held enough weight to burden my mind for six months.

"Dmitri! We need you up here!"

"Wait! What did you do with him?" I grabbed his elbow. "You didn't leave him there!"

Dmitri was pulled to his feet by the angry mob. "We burned him on site. He was already decomposing," Dmitri urgently explained. I gagged at the floor. My eyes and throat and mouth and ears and nose burned.

"I have to go," he whispered. And he was absorbed by the bodies.

xxxi.

It was now May. I know this for certain because the songbirds were hatching. Every morning we woke up to the sounds of robins and bluejays singing from the rooftops, swooping in front of the windows and flapping among the tent creases. A nest appeared on the top of the garden archway,

Barely anyone outside of the butchers missed Peter. I only told those who asked, which was almost nil. I think people got bored of the tragedy and mysteries of March month. The excitement of the plane died down and was ignored. There hasn't been another like it. No hum of turbines, no roar of supersized engines. People moved on, as they always do.

I found myself settling into the same condition from years of repetitive and non-stimulating high school. I thought less, talked less. What was there to talk about? The birds were singing again! Why would you drown them out with your meaningless human chatter?

Spirits rose with the weather. People were more patient in the meal lines. No one yelled at the hunters to bring in more game. No more mild rebellions against Tveit and Anita. Working efficiency remained mild, which served as a better indicator of positive mental health than anything. People danced and played around the fire again. Some went to bed with wet and sand-covered feet from splash wars in the wake.

My life melted into a series of fine days — not good, not bad, fine. Incessantly fine.

One afternoon, I sat with Diana and Nina for dinner, both of which were venting to me about Lupita's son who refused to learn basic math or how to read. But he did like making potions in the buckets with mud and saliva.

Just as they were getting into the juicy stories, a finger tapped my shoulder. Behind me stood Anthony. "Wanna slip away for a minute?" He offered, nodding at the doors. He held up a stuffed backpack.

"What do you have in mind?" I scrambled over the bench.

Anthony's gorgeous coffee eyes lit. "Picnic. But did you eat enough already?"

I glanced down at my three slices of cooked radish and a single thin strip of turkey. "I don't think I did." I waved the girls goodbye and led the journey outside. "Let's blow this taco stand."

"It's been a while since I've heard that one."

He walked me out to the beach. The sun was on the edge of the horizon, painting the sky in a lovely scene of pink, orange, and purple. The first stars and planets peaked from the clouds.

We approached the Flame pit. It was there he grabbed my hand and led me farther south than I'd ever wandered. It was rockier down there. The meager sand was dotted with sharper rocks. The evening surf was calmer. The tides were lower. We only walked half a mile, but the new beach was another world. Another dimension.

Anthony felt around on the sand with his bare foot until he found a concave spot in the eroded surface. He smiled with pride and set the backpack down. "Bingo!"

"What if the tide washed away your marker?" I helped him pull out a blanket and spread it on the ground. It was buffalo flannel print and frayed around the edges.

"Well, that would've sucked. I spent a long time scoping this area with Alice." Anthony gestured for me to sit first, his head following me carefully before claiming his spot. "I hope we made a good choice." He pulled over the backpack and felt around for cloth-covered packages. I watched him hesitate before handing me one small wrapping. "They may be dry."

Delicately wrapped in the thin fabric of an old shirt was a sandwich. Two pieces of sliced wheat held together one slice of tomato and two slabs of mystery meat. I hadn't had a sandwich since we last had deli meat in the house, back before the refrigerator broke and there was no one to fix it.

The smile stretching my cheeks almost ached. "Where did you get the bread?"

"Hard bargaining with a forager. No one brings back wheat and yeast because it takes so long to make a good loaf. And for so many people? It's 'a worthless waste of time and water', as he put it. But I got it out of him. Made it with Bryce the other day."

"Every time they come back, I'm more and more surprised there's still anything left." I relished the weight of the sandwich in my hands. "Isn't there anyone else out there? They need supplies too." There were shopping mall pirates in my hometown from the beginning and to the end.

The supply foragers were special hunters who volunteered a few days out of their months to venture further out to the nearest town and bring back modern treasures. They brought everything in the wheelbarrows and red wagons that could fit. Cleaning supplies, first aid assortments, new clothes, good liquor for celebrations (not the crap made by our amateur Moonshiners).

"That's something to ask them. I guess any competitors in the area have dropped off by now or given up." Anthony scoffed. "More for us."

I brought the sandwich to my face and smelled it. Savored it. Let the mere truth of it settle in my nose and my breath. It took everything in my will not to devour it whole, but when I finally let my teeth sink in… it was nothing short of Heaven.

The stiff and tasteless crust did nothing to quench the mouth-watering savor it drew from me. The bird, which I discovered was goose, was a little overdone and desperately needed a dollop of honey mustard. The tomatoes weren't entirely ripe — we had to harvest them early to appease the growling stomachs. It was glorious.

The meal in my hand was nothing more than godly ambrosia. It was a miracle. A gift. I must have moaned at the mixture of flavors and textures because Anthony immediately hid his face.

"You like it?" He asked. His voice was muffled by his knees.

"YES!" I didn't mean to yell. That was the only way to express how delicious that stale, bland sandwich was.

Anthony smiled and bit into his own. It moved in his cheeks for a minute, his chews slowing distastefully. "Sorry. It tastes like crap," he confessed through a full mouth.

I giggled, setting the second half of my sandwich on the cloth. I couldn't possibly let it be swallowed into oblivion so quickly. "Yes, but it's good crap."

"You don't have to eat it all if you don't want to."

"That's like telling a kid they don't have to finish their ice cream." I rubbed his knee. "It's perfect. Did you make them?"

Anthony scoffed and began disassembling his food. "Yeah. Probably why it sucks."

"It doesn't suck, love."

I watched the Flame's light in the distance. The bonfire just started. I couldn't hear anyone, of course, but I imagined Nina breaking out her prized ukulele and busting out a soothing tune.

"Is there any particular reason we're out here? Or you just wanted to spice things up?" I asked.

Anthony shrugged, picking at his goose meat. His grip tightened on the meat at the louder, nearer surge of a wave before us. The tide reached only mere meters from the blanket. "I like it out here."

"You come out here often?"

"Nope. Just discovered it three days ago." He smiled cheekily.

The conversation dropped off. For just a minute, I let everything shut down. Let my senses take over. Let the world blend into one indiscernible artistry.

The waves crashing into the shore. Seagulls. Wind over your ears. Sand insects maintaining their mighty underground kingdoms.

Letting everything seep into the background is a relief no self-help pamphlet will ever provide. It was so sweet to melt away and float amongst the water forever; like Ariel in her last moments before turning into seafoam. I swear I saw a marine mammal out there… but it could've been a trick of the waves.

"Can I be honest with you?" Anthony offered when the tide retracted.

The art of the world separated itself again. I hummed, watching a single crab scurry across the sand.

"I don't think I want to live here anymore," he picked at his bread.

My response to his statement was a long time coming. I loved the

Community. Without them, the Dawsons and we would have made it to Massachusetts, but where would we go from there? What was there to do, to settle into? We had no goal for reaching Massachusetts.

In the Community, I met friends. I found food and water. I found a way to work at what I do best for the rest of my foreseeable days. I found new things to care about.

But edging at the corners of my mind, I knew I couldn't stay there forever. My life wasn't meant for the lifestyle the People By The Sea had constructed. Even in an age of deconstructed governments, they found a way to reinstate a workforce that guilted you for wanting a day to yourself. I doubted it was intentional on Tveit and Anita's part. It was an unintended product of relying on what you know to keep each other alive.

I got used to the space of the trailer. I could never go back to that level of solitude, but there had to be a happy medium. An in-between space. There had to be a way to live your own life and rely on the security of someone else.

"Same."

Anthony perked up. "Really? It's not just me?"

"I don't think so."

Was I giving that answer because I genuinely felt it? Or because it was the selfish answer and I wanted a moment to be selfish? A moment to think only of myself? I would be lying if I said I missed moments like those. I missed only having to consider my own needs.

What about Tate and Diana, who have stuck by my side through thick and thin when all I craved was to give up? What if Diana declined again, and Tate could do nothing to help from his stations in the woods? What about Leta, who had grown fond of me in the few weeks since she attached herself to my hip? What about my family in the gardens?

Despite the polar directions my mind was splitting, it would be egotistical to think the Community would crumble without me. They stayed alive before me. They could do the same after.

But would I be able to stay alive after them?

Anthony ignored the roar in his stomach. "So much has changed.

I don't know what you're feeling, but I've been here long enough to know that things are just different. The dynamics shifted somewhere between December and now. People don't seem to care as much as they used to. They're ruder to each other. I heard someone insult Anita in the dining hall. And when she overheard it and asked them to repeat it, *they did!* And then I think they just walked off!" He shook his head in disbelief. "Those four are doing their best to keep everything together. People don't care anymore."

"Surely that's not your only reason for wanting to leave."

"It's one of them." Anthony took one more bite of his bread before surrendering it to the pestering seagulls piece by piece. They swarmed in to attack his crumb offerings. "What do you think?"

I doodled in the sand with my pointer finger. "I think people are going to be self-absorbed no matter what."

My nose was running. When I threw my sandwich off its cloth to use it as a handkerchief, the birds attacked my food. The five of them seemed to multiply tenfold. I shooed them away with my feet and shoved the sandwich between my legs. I felt one seagull beak scrape at the top of my foot. Its tongue swept across one toe. I squealed and kicked wildly.

"*Stop feeding them!* They think we're free range!" I screamed. Anthony laughed and shoved the rest of his meal into his mouth. One bird squawked at him. "You teased him. He didn't get anything." I giggled.

"I can' do a'yth'n' righ'!" He exclaimed through an overflowing mouth. My squeals bubbled into giggles as the seagulls conceded to my thrashing feet and retreated to the waters.

Sunset was over now. The constellations took over the night sky, basking the sky in the mesmerizing display of the cosmos. The Milky Way shining all around. Orion, Cetus, the Great Bear, Cygnus, and Cassiopeia watching from the Heavens.

You take for granted how beautiful our universe is when you live in such an age of light pollution. When nature is returned to its original state… you're gifted with all the forgotten wonders of what's been right beyond our fingertips for centuries.

"Why did the Gatwes leave? That was their name, right?" I finally asked after he finished chewing.

Anthony watched the surf roll out before deliberately nodding. "Nadia and Rami with their eight kids. there were originally eight. A few died before they made it to us. One more was found with a cracked skull on the beach just a few days before you guys showed up. I think that had something to do with them leaving."

"How long were they here?"

"Seven months, I think. Rami was the leader of sanitation for a long time. But on the day their fourth kid was found dead — her name was Marjorie… her parents kind of gave up. They saw that the Community couldn't protect them."

"Do *you* think the Community can't protect us?"

"I think we're just a bunch of people. People make mistakes," he hesitated. "I think we need to have a suspension of faith in others for this operation to work. In a way. If that makes sense."

I don't know how my mind processed that, but now I know it was the wrong way.

"Chrissy and Peter both died under their watch. Are you saying I should blame Tveit and Anita for their deaths? I should blame Cillian for not finding Chrissy and pumping her stomach? I should blame Dmitri for not entertaining Peter?"

Anthony frowned. "Vivienne, that's the opposite of what I'm saying."

I had the sudden urge to throw my shoe into the ocean. "Then what am I misunderstanding?" I raised my voice against my better judgment.

"I don't know! I don't know what I'm saying!" Anthony exclaimed.

"Neither do I!" I threw both hands up.

"Then we should stop!" He kept shouting for the sake of shouting.

"*Agreed!*" As did I.

We didn't talk for a while. I tried to let it all melt off and return to my safe space between the sand below and the ocean ahead and the universe above. That failed. I was left sitting on that blanket in the middle of the rocky beach with half a sandwich squished between my knees. Just one girl who overreacted about death and seagulls.

"Can I ask you a weird question?" Anthony finally broke the silence.

I turned my head. He seemed genuinely uncomfortable for the first time since I'd known him. "Anything," I whisper. Anthony cleared his throat. The gears turning in his head flashed through those stunning eyes.

"What do you look like?"

I chuckled, leaning my chin on my hand. "Where is this coming from?"

"I've been wondering for a long time."

I stared at the Flame's light in the distance. I knew I could go many ways with this response. All of which risked coming off as insensitive. It was also so, so easy for me to lie. I spun the wheel.

"What do you think I look like?" I prompted. "You can see a little bit, right? So what little bit of me do you see?"

"Yeah, only a *little bit!* Not enough to form a solid picture when everything is so blotchy." Anthony shook his head. "Nevermind. I can't… it's probably wrong," he mumbled.

I could see him retracting. I instantly regretted prompting the game. "No, no. Humor me. Genuinely, what do you think I look like?" I touched his arm to reassure him of my sincerity.

He sighed, conceding. "Well, I picture you with reddish hair." His hand slowly found the edge of my locks just beyond my shoulder blade. "Down to here. And horrible split ends." He smiled.

I smacked his arm. "Shush."

He held a hand up, laughing. "Okay. Then I know your medium-ish build? Yeah? And I picture an oval-shaped sort of face?"

"Eh… I lost a chunk of weight in the last year," I confessed. "Forty or so pounds, if I had to guess. I gained a bit back, but I still don't… never mind. It's not important. Close enough." I pat his knee. "And I have a narrow face. You could wedge it between a door and not be able to tell it's open."

"I'm sure it's a gorgeous face," he stated. That was one of the many times I was *glad* he could not see my heated cheeks.

"Any other questions?" I offered.

Anthony didn't take nearly as much time deliberating about this one. "I would ask you how to describe your lips, but I have my own way of judging that."

I shoved him away. "*No!* That was so bad!" I squealed.

He burst out laughing. I struggled to contain my own amusement. A snort escaped me somewhere in the mess. We soon were rolling around on our backs, filling the night air with giggles and shrieks.

"I despise you," I muttered once we both settled down.

"I'm sure." He gave me a tight side hug. It took everything in my conscience not to lean into his touch before he moved away.

I was the first to lie down. We watched the stars for so long that I swear they changed in the sky above. I don't know who fell asleep first. Whoever it was, the other didn't wake them up.

We didn't make it back to the dorms until sunrise. Tate got onto us when we finally showed up at the doors. I'm very sure he thought we stayed out doing things too mature for the general reading audience. We didn't, but that I wouldn't have objected to.

Hank dug away at the garden soil with a hoe. He ignored me when I approached. Usually, he would grunt or tell me to go away. "Cat got your tongue?" I posed, sitting by the patch of carrots.

I watched Lily lead Leta through the archway. Neither said anything as they marched to the other bed where Elliott sat drawing in the dusty dirt with a stick. Quiet, slow, low.

"What's up with everyone today?" I murmured.

It wasn't until I nudged his leg with my foot did Hank set the hoe down and barely looked up. "Eden died this morning."

I don't know why I was surprised. I don't know why the news sent such a chill down my spine, curling every nerve in my body. She was an old woman in a world without the amenities that afforded humans long lives. It was a miracle all in itself that Cillian was able to keep her alive as long as he did.

"We saw them carrying out her body after breakfast." Hank cleared his throat. I could see the tremble in his bottom lip. "I'm as surprised as anyone that she lasted so long."

"Yeah, no kidding…"

So many opportunities to visit her that I passed up in favor of swimming or an extra hour of sleep. So little… and she gave me her dress. She let me glimpse into her glory years with Cillian and her husband.

There was so much I'd been meaning to ask her. So much I wanted her opinion on. Experiences, stories. Now she joined the other millions and billions dead, and I had not one more opportunity.

I was a horrible friend.

"Her pyre is tonight. Don't miss it, or she'll probably come back and haunt the cabbages." Hank sniffled through one congested nostril before throwing down the hoe and marching to the others.

The dull pain that had been tormenting my lower abdomen for the last several days heightened. I was left clutching my organs through stabbing courses, massaging my hips to naught effect.

I ran away from Eden's funeral milliseconds after Cillian's speech. A clot gushed from me with the quick motion. The first hideaway available was a bush, just barely wide enough to cover. Not bothering to check for company, I ripped down my shorts.

Blotched in the base of my underwear was fresh crimson.

The Stranger

May

XXXII.

Nothing that I would call "out of the ordinary" happened until three days later when a strange man showed up at our metaphorical front gates.

Cillian was the first to see him. He was coming back from harvesting the ginseng that grew by the pond, the same pond that grew water hemlock, and noticed the man standing at the front of the town. Just standing, staring. Cillian asked if he could help him. The man said nothing, only watched Nina and Diana corral the children back into the school.

It wasn't long after that a crowd formed. The man hadn't moved, hadn't spoken a word to anyone but the kids. When I approached the wide blob of an audience, he was sitting on the grass with Jonah. The boy was playing with a twig. All the man did was watch and smile.

"How did he make it past the patrol?" I heard Anita whisper to Tveit.

"Oh my goodness, Jonah, come to me!" Miracle stepped out of the mob. Her brother laughed at the stranger and his sister. Miracle held her arms out. "Jonah! Don't make me tell Dad."

"He has candy!" Jonah argued. The stranger did, in fact, have small rainbow hard candies wrapped in wax paper poking from the side of his hoodie pocket.

"Jonah, please come back here right now!" Miracle shouted. Many others joined in on the pleading. Jonah found the entire situation hilarious. The man did not remark to acknowledge anyone. One of the butchers finally stepped out of line to grab him.

"Who are you?" Tveit demanded, donning the rough intimidation tactic he first used with us.

The man said nothing. He only smiled back at us like he knew. What exactly did he know?

He knew.

The man couldn't have been older than forty, and I expected that a year of roughing had dramatically decreased his physical state. Touseled and greasy white hair decorated his wide head, showing that he hadn't had a good bath in months. The color could not be a natural white, but one that was a product of bleach and an alcohol wash. One navy blue hoodie accompanied white and green athletic shorts, making him look like a character out of some cheesy coming-of-age 80's film. A pathetic excuse for a peppered beard was growing on his double chin, but it reminded me of if someone took a black paintbrush and let it drip aimlessly on a rough canvas.

He was uncanny. It was impossible to believe a child could approach him with anything less than tears, much less *giggles*.

"What is your name?" Anita snapped.

The man breathed deeply, clasping his hands over one knee. "Silas."

"What are your intentions on our border?"

"This is your border? I thought all borders were dissolved." The man named Silas tilted his head. He loved the attention.

"We have our space. When you come too close, we get curious." Anita's gray gaze shot lasers to slice the man's soul. It's true. I watched it from the far end of the audience.

"I'm just sitting." Silas smiled.

Tveit ushered the rest of us to leave. "Go back to work. Nothing interesting here," he ordered in a distracted voice. Barely anyone moved.

I suppose there was no reason to feel threatened by this man. He was not doing anything. He only seemed to be interacting with the kids if they talked to him first. And I never saw a piece of candy in Jonah's hand, so maybe the stranger was hogging it for himself. If I had access to sweets of my own I would've stashed it, too.

Tveit wasn't so kind and open-arms to this stranger as he was to us. Sometimes, I wondered what would have happened if Anita or Dmitri alone found us that fateful day in the woods. I doubt either of them had the charm Tveit held for strangers. The charm he used to have.

Too many things happened to the Community between then and now for Tveit to be so warm to strange men who talked to little kids.

"We can't keep waiting. We have to go," I watched Tveit flag Dmitri down and whisper to him. I could only hear because everyone else was listening, too. "Do you think you could deal with him?"

Dmitri patted Tveit's shoulder. He and Anita broke from the mess of bodies and made for the treeline, passing Silas on either side. No one went with them. To this day I don't know where they went, but their weapons were visible and ready with the jerk of a wrist.

With one snap, Dmitri urged Silas to his feet. "Come on. We can get you cleaned up," he called to the stranger.

"I'm not harming anyone by sitting right here." Silas wiped his greasy hands on the edge of his shorts.

"You're saying you don't want a warm meal and a sponge bath?" Dmitri deadpanned.

"He's not coming anywhere near my kids!"

"Why are we wasting our food on him?"

Dmitri held up one hand for the protestors in the crowd. "We will discuss this in the mess hall. Anyone who has a problem can spend a month scrubbing our shit," he ordered. Everyone shut their mouths.

Jutting out his chin, Silas scrambled to his feet. One hard candy fell out of his hoodie pocket. "I wouldn't mind. Thank you."

"Mhm."

A path was cleared by Dmitri as the man approached. Dmitri guided him into the town with one hand gripped firmly on a shoulder. Naturally, every member of the audience followed.

The Community was divided on how to receive the man. Who didn't see him as a rodent creeping on the kids saw him as a pitiful shelterless man seeking refuge. People fawned over him or spat on the ground he walked.

Dmitri and Cillian discussed the visitor right in front of him. Several times they made comments about where he came from, and

Silas corrected them. Dmitri ignored him every time. Cillian respectfully nodded but never acknowledged his corrections.

Silas offered many variations of the same story. He came from Dover; he came from a town just north of Dover. He had a family; his family walked out. His spouse committed suicide during the winter; he left his partner behind.

Translation: a bunch of bullcrap.

No matter what you thought of him, no one believed the Dover and dead spouse story. That was his downfall in the meeting.

Silas sat in the middle of a fan circle at the front of the mess hall. Diana and I stood at the back, eavesdropping on his interrogations from a safe distance. Every few minutes one of his fanclub would shift on their feet and a line of sight would clear. I saw him kiss a woman's hand tenderly. Diana swears she saw someone bless his feet.

Nothing more occurred until the early morning patrol party returned. They filtered through the double doors one by one. No one paid attention.

A finger tapped my arm. My soul briefly left my body before Tate smiled and rubbed Diana's and my shoulders.

"We just got back," Tate said, wiping the dirt and sweat beads on his head with the inside of his tan shirt. "They said someone showed up at the border? What's that all about?"

Diana grabbed her brother's arm. "He wants to be a member."

"He hasn't made any sign of wanting to stay," I remind her. I hoped to God he wouldn't.

"Who?"

Diana nodded toward the front of the room, where the man named Silas was talking with Hank's son again. Tate's eyes settled on the man. His entire body seized to my side.

"What's wrong?" I squeaked.

Tate grabbed Diana and me and viciously threw us behind him. "He needs to get out of here," he whispered. I didn't mistake the tremor in his voice.

"What are you *doing?*" I hit his arm away.

"Hey! That man is dangerous! We need to get him out of here!"

Tate shouted, pushing through the crowd. People cried as his brute force shoved them aside. Dmitri pushed him back, fairly fighting to defend Silas. "You need to get him away from your kids!" Tate pleaded with those around him. "He's a goddamn killer!"

"Calm down!" Dmitri ordered, shoving Tate back one last time. "Take a breath."

Tate's eyes never tore away from the man — whoever he was. "I need to talk to Tveit."

Dmitri blocked Tate from one last effort to surge forward. "He's not around right now. You get me," he stated.

"You need to get that man away from everyone!" Tate urged. His face contorted with an unknown grimace.

"What does he mean?" A mother cried. A wide berth burst around Silas.

"How do you know him?"

"Where did he come from?"

"Tate," I grabbed his arm. He was seething; the forehead vein bulged more than his enlarged pupils. I wouldn't be surprised if he started foaming at the mouth. "Who is he?"

He pointed one shaking finger at the visitor. "*Cal.* The son of a bitch dyed his hair and thought I wouldn't notice."

Dmitri glanced over his shoulder. "Who?"

"He's a cult leader. There are plenty of them out there, but this guy is the worst of it." Tate threw out his arms, shaking me off with violent passion. A few nodded. "He's one of those rat bastards that like to play God."

"Are you sure? It doesn't look like him," Diana whispered. Tate nodded gravely at her.

He turned to the rest of the mess hall. "Cal followed us from New York up to Maine. He was the one who trafficked Peter for months. Anything this man tries to tell you is a lie! You have to believe me."

"I knew nothing about this," Dmitri muttered.

"You have to believe me," Tate pleaded, bearing the familiar sting of trauma rather than anger. "That man is a psycho."

"I have no idea who you're talking about," Silas insisted, spreading his hands wide like a priest addressing a congregation. "I've lived in Dover all my life. I traveled south with my spouse-"

Tate rolled his eyes. "Oh, *shut up!*"

"I believe you," I heard Dmitri whisper to Tate. It was so soft I could be mistaken, but I don't think so. Dmitri was growing the same horrified look as Diana.

"What happened to accepting anyone with open arms?" Lupita scoffed.

Eugene straightened. "This is why you aren't top five in succession."

"Shouldn't you be in the medical tent?"

"Shouldn't you be six feet below with all the STDs you're carrying around?" He shot back. Lupita gasped (as if we didn't all know).

"Where are Tveit and Anita?" Kathy whined.

"Not here. Tveit put me in charge. So you guys are gonna have to shut up and listen to me," Dmitri ordered. He took one deep breath and turned back to Silas. Cal. Whoever he was. "Who are you?"

"Silas. I come from Dover. I seek refuge and a hot meal."

"Ask him how he got past us!" Tate jabbed a finger at his own chest. "*No one* on patrol or hunting saw anything before he showed up. We don't miss anything."

Misha chimed in. "Maybe you did."

"We didn't." Tate backed down. "He's a goddamn *ghost*," he whispered.

Dmitri stared at the ground, drumming his foot on the dull wooden planks. "Keep him in one place and don't leave him alone until Tveit is back," he ordered, gesturing to the stranger. He pointed at Silas. "*You* don't go anywhere. There's a room in the married dorm that we can use as a cell until Tveit can make a further judgment."

Silas shrugged, the words rolling right off his shoulders. Misha grabbed him and threw him towards the door.

xxxiii.

Whispers filled every space in the Community the next day. He was a local celebrity.

Tveit kept a guard stationed in front of Silas' room on five-hour shifts. They finally cut back on patrol and hunting shifts to compensate for people watching him. He was good-mannered but didn't speak much. He didn't eat when he was brought food. He didn't grovel and relieve himself when they replaced his bedpan.

Silas made a spectacle of himself. Theories ran rampant along the edges of the Community. Someone spun it out that he was a CIA operative who was undercover to gather intel on the new societies.

Some believed he was our salvation. They believed he was here to pluck us out of harm and bring us back to the reconstructed modern age. Others believed him to be the enemy. They saw their imaginative versions through the greasy exterior as he tried to fit in with the younger crowd. It depended on whether you believed Tate and Diana. If you believed their recollections of New York.

The Community divided itself. No one knew what to accept. Accomplices turned on each other. Meals grew quiet and awkward. Tate and Diana weren't making it any better. Their friends were torn between supporting them and feeding into the mob mentality that was so willfully manipulated by the enigmatic stranger.

I believed them. I believed he was the "business" leader who brought Peter back to Maine. The one who trafficked and manipulated "employees" until they didn't recognize themselves.

I made a list of everything I knew for sure. It was the only way to keep straight. The only way to not fist fight the next person who called Tate crazy or Diana overemotional.

I work in the gardens. I like my work. It calms me. I like swimming. I like picnics on the beach. Flower crowns make me happy. I wear Eden's dress every full moon, and it brings me comfort. It's a treat when the hunters bring back a few turkeys for dinner. I have friends in the Community. I like my leaders and I trust them more than any former president.

But I couldn't stay forever. If the People By The Sea continued down this slope, I wouldn't be able to stay sane. I had someone to leave with. And if we wanted to leave safely, I had help.

This is how it all started. Just like before. Coming full circle.

"I have a favor to cash in," I whispered to him before breakfast the next morning. People were beginning to filter out of the dorm building and trudge their way to the double doors in the zombie coma that never outgrew us.

Dmitri nodded, slinking us to the back of the great hall. "I have the right to reject, let's make that clear right now," he clarified through a shallow breath.

I wrenched free from the death grip he had on my bicep. "I have the right to stand on a table and shout your secret to the entire breakfast audience," I shot back.

"I never took you as one to blackmail." He bit his cheek and glanced over his shoulder. "What do you want?"

I wanted to take him seriously. It was impossible. His hair had grown out so much it now fell carelessly over his eyes. Soon enough he would pass as a fantastical ebony Sasquatch. "I don't suppose we would be able to sneak out and go… *shopping* in the woods, would we?"

Dmitri got onto another young man for acting a fool with little Elliott. He scurried up, cursing all the way out of the building. "Who's *we*?" He absently demanded, his chin barely turned my way.

"Anthony and I."

"Absolutely not."

I watched him answer Misha's question from the opposite end of the hall. I wanted to hit him for it. "Okay. Sure. So then we need your help. You're the only one who won't make a big deal about it." I raised my voice to get his attention.

Dmitri patted the air as if pushing down an obnoxious dog. "Keep your voice down. Not make a big deal about what?"

I wanted to throw him into a chair and gag him. Sexual context or not. Maybe that would make him pay attention.

"We're thinking about leaving," I threw out.

Dmitri finally looked at me. His head snapped so quickly that I expected it to break and for him to drop dead at my feet. A universe of things happened within his gaze in a millisecond. Hard, soft, disturbed, amused, confused. I didn't think he was capable of experiencing so many emotions.

"Oh." He brushed the bangs from his face. It accomplished nothing. "And where do you plan on living?"

"That's where you need to come in. We need a proper house. Please." My hands clasped together. "You're the only one who can leave for so long and not raise questions."

The door slammed closed for the final time. The silence of the concrete building drowned us out. "I'm not the person to ask about this. Go to Tveit or Anita. Hell, *Cillian* even!" He muttered.

"I don't... that's..." I struggled to say I didn't trust them. I trusted them in a way a pet trusts its owner to feed them every day. I just didn't trust them as I trusted the man before me.

"Please. I'm asking you as a friend. Or as a humble subordinate. I need you. Just this once."

Dmitri sucked in a sharp inhale before pinching the bridge of his nose. "*Okay!* Fine. You two meet me at my place after lunch. We'll talk there," he grumbled, rubbing the base of his neck the way one does when an unavoidable headache forms.

"Both of us? Even Anthony?"

"Pff. Yeah. That kid's not gonna peep. I told *you*, right?" Dmitri winked.

My eyes flicked down. "I could if I wanted to."

"But you won't."

"You don't know that." I planted my feet like a cranky toddler.

Dmitri nodded slowly. "Mhm. You won't. Come on."

"You have to swear on whatever you believe in," I restated for the fifth time as we walked down the treeline.

"I'm astounded you still don't know I'm Jewish." Anthony shook his head.

"You've never mentioned it- That's not the point! I'm serious." I grabbed his arm. His torso shook dramatically. "We cannot tell anyone. Dmitri is risking a lot just by letting us meet him here. He has something that made me want to boil him alive when I first saw it, but I understand why he's keeping it under wraps for now. *For now.* You just have to trust him."

Anthony tripped on a twig. He jammed his walking stick into the sand and clutched it for dear life. "You're scaring me," he confessed.

I rubbed his shoulder. "I'm sorry, love. Trust *me*, then. Screw him. Trust me. Have I let you down yet?" He shook his head slowly. "Right. Let's keep going."

"How far is it?"

The first time I'd made the journey, I was too afraid to pay attention. "Um… you'll see when we get there."

"Rude." A small grin cracked on his cheeks. I gently shoved him.

We neared the cabin over the symphony of high tide. A fox scurried into the trees, not before taking a detour behind my legs. I squealed, and Anthony grabbed me.

I held his hand down the sand towards the building, kicking away the hundreds of birds in our path. The door was cracked open just enough to be intentional. He was already home.

"Hello?" I propped the door with my hip and guided him through the opening. Anthony drifted away, scanning his head wildly to observe everything.

Dmitri was lying on the bed with the pillow discarded on the floor. His ankles hung off the long end, his shoes thrown haphazardly below. He slept like a mummy. I slowly approached the edge of the bed and tickled his feet.

Dmitri snapped awake, groaning and cursing at the air. "What is *wrong* with you?" He kicked wildly, scooting up and falling off the bed. Laughter bubbled from the pits of my chest until he rose to stand, glaring at me as if I threw his grandmother down the stairs.

"What are these things?" Anthony called out from the other side of the room. He was trying to observe the generators with his fractured left side of sight.

"Electric generators. My little toys," Dmitri answered, pulling his shoes on reluctantly. He groaned like an elderly man, pushed himself to his feet, and looked at me. "You know how to turn them on?"

I slowly walked the five steps to the first motor. I searched for the switch on the side with the dash and the circle, something silly I always missed from modern technology. The motors hummed to life, and slowly so did the bulb strings above.

I watched Anthony's head tilt back and his jaw drop. "*Woah.*"

"What do you think?" I asked, turning on the second one. One more strand lit up.

"Did I *die?*" Anthony crouched in front of them, studying the outer bars with tender palms. "How long have you had these?"

Dmitri picked at a spot on his scalp. "Years. I used to live here."

Anthony's head whipped one hundred eighty degrees. The curls flopped like a black Sheepdog. "*Excuse me?*"

"I told you…" I mumbled helplessly.

"You've had this the whole time and never thought 'Hey, other people may like this! This may be useful?'" Anthony shouted.

"It's not ready."

"What the hell?"

"This is what I was talking about." I planted my hands on Anthony's shoulders. He stared blankly over my shoulder. "We can trust him. I don't think he has ulterior motives."

Anthony hesitated to touch my hands, fingerprints faltering over the delicate hair, before throwing them off of himself.

Dmitri couldn't look at either of us. "It's unstable. We need to shut them back off in a few minutes."

"And *you* knew about this?" Anthony demanded, jabbing his hand my way.

"I wasn't happy at first, either. But I promised." I went to hold his hand, which he backed away from.

"It's too much of a risk to tell people right now. Someday I will.

But not when they may… violently explode… or something…" Dmitri painstakingly explained for a second time. He shook his head sadly. "I have to fix them."

Anthony looked back and forth at both of us, focusing to see beyond fragmented shapes. "I guess that's a fine excuse," he finally conceded.

This time, he accepted my affection. "This is a good place to talk. It holds enough secrets for all of us." I watched the waves outside the dusty window. They rumbled against the shore, collecting the miseries and pains of the land and carrying it all out to the sea.

He shrugged and turned back to the motors. "You ever worry about carbon monoxide poisoning?" Anthony asked, running his fingers over the outer rim.

"Not until today."

Anthony returned to his curiosities. He knelt, switched the second one off, and let his fingers explore the inner workings of the motor. The very next engine was live. Watching him play with the machinery so carelessly sent fearful shivers down my back.

"This is beside the point." I tapped him on the shoulder. "We need to stay focused." Anthony hopped to his feet and fell right back down. Vertigo. I pulled him to his feet, letting him rest most of his body weight against me until the crystals and clouds settled throughout his skull.

"You need a house?" Dmitri prompted, jamming his hands in his back pockets. "And you can't go out yourself because…?"

"Because Anita's been monitoring who goes in and out like a hawk," I said.

"Misha stopped us on the way this morning! Anita hasn't been enforcing the three-person rule, you know, but Misha insisted we were up to no good," Anthony explained. The memory made me bark a bare chuckle. "He was itching to tell me to grab a broom."

A cockroach scurried across the floorboards. My shoe stomped it with one fell stomp to oblivion. "They're doing everything in their power to stop another Chrissy or Peter incident. And now Silas. They know they're losing control."

Dmitri paused. His tongue bloated his cheek. "They don't know about Peter," he slowly confessed.

I slowly blinked. "Pardon?"

"I never told them."

My fists clenched at my sides. "You never... *Why?*" I inhaled deeply, staring at his tiny bed and tiny pillow. "Nope. I actually can't. I can't deal with two things at once. Will you help us?"

"They never asked! So I never told," Dmitri threw out.

"I don't care. Will you help?"

My bitterness curdled sour in the absence of a response. Our heads were drowned in a thick fog of the reality that only one of the top five leaders knew the truth about a rogue Community member, and none of the other four seemed to care. He told them his intentions with that expedition — he had to have. They knew why Dmitri left, and they knew that he wouldn't return with anything less than results.

They never asked.

Realities like that made you think. Made you question things you didn't want the answer to.

Anthony slid in when Dmitri didn't answer. "We don't have to leave immediately. So you don't have to do all this immediately. We just want to stay proactive, right? We can wait a little bit if things are too busy for you, or if it may cause suspicion or something-"

"No, no... it's fine." Dmitri waved him away. "I have nothing better to do. We really don't need as many on patrol as we have."

"Are you sure?" I muttered. I didn't think it would be so easy to convince him.

"Yeah. It's no big deal. I'll draw up a map soon."

"Thank you!" Anthony stepped forward, to which Dmitri scooted just as far back.

Dmitri held up a dismissive hand. "Yeah, yeah. You're welcome. But what do I get in return?"

Before I could throw out the first favor my mind could conjure, the same hand pointed one crooked finger directly at me. "I refuse to be properly blackmailed. This secret is your exchange for my mere willingness for favors. All sharing this would do is speed up my project to stabilize these motors. And I know you wouldn't do that."

"How could you know that? Maybe I want to."

Dmitri hummed. "Because you're smart. You wouldn't do anything for no other means than getting back at me. But then what leverage would you have? Who else would cash in your favors?"

"I know other people who can get things done."

"No, you don't. Or you never would've come to me in the first place." Dmitri cocked his head to the side.

He was right, and he knew it.

I looked at Anthony. "You have any ideas?"

"What do you want, man?" He whined.

"I want scrambled eggs and a good bourbon whiskey."

"We can't do that."

The right generator started to make a funny noise. Dmitri nonchalantly walked over and smacked it off. "Well, that's a shame."

"Be serious. What do you want in return?" I demanded.

Dmitri threw himself on the bed, leaning his head on the barely stable wall. "I want to be left alone. I want to age in peace," he mumbled.

I couldn't believe the mind games. The parables he seemed to whip out of his butt. "You're number four. How on Earth do you expect us to do that?"

"Tell Anita I'm tired."

"But you won't retire your position?" I jammed my hands into my hip bones. I knew he wouldn't. He was too proud to let anyone else take his place. "Hypocrite."

"You must be new to politics."

"If you won't actually help, you could've just said so," Anthony cursed.

"No, I *am* going to help. But I want peace. Just for a bit."

I swung my arms in a wide, lazy circle. "So tell us to leave."

"You can stay if you want. Just be quiet." He stared off into the space by his feet. "It's Silas. He's a little parasite on my mind." Dmitri closed his eyes. "We should meet like this more often. It's fun."

"You want friends, is what you're saying." I bit down a grin.

"I want a nap."

This was his fun way of admitting he needed a mental health day. No wonder no one understood him. It was willful on his part to not be understood. If this were a fantasy story, he would be the troll under the bridge that asked people riddles as they tried to cross.

He would have been a good politician.

"Alice and I can be your friends," Anthony offered after a moment. I chuckled and leaned my head on his shoulder.

Dmitri's eyes opened in slits and peered suspiciously at the younger man. "Thanks."

I smiled and rubbed Dmitri's arm. "We'll tell Anita you'll be back tomorrow-"

"Two days," he threw out. His eyes closed again.

"You'll be back in two days," I corrected. "Don't miss us too much."

"Mhm…"

We left him to sleep. He was out cold again by the time our feet crossed the threshold. Anthony and I made the long walk back home with him chattering away about the generators, electrical engineering, and fantasizing about everything we could fix up in town. Now that the reality was set, nothing could stop his excitement. It was adorable.

"Think of everything we could fix up!" He was practically jumping. We could have lights, functional plumbing, and tasers. He was especially enthusiastic about the tasers.

Strangely enough, that was what sparked my mind of another person I'd been meaning to meet with. Someone who made my skin crawl, but deserved a listening ear. Just on a small chance that he was innocent.

A single guard stood watch over his cell. They obstructed the door from the outside with a wooden plank and one small boulder.

"Can he have visitors?" I whispered to the unknown guard.

"I dunno why you would wanna, but yeah." He lifted the plank and let the door swing free. I could feel the lifeless pull of the cell from the hall. The guard gestured for me to move after there was no motion inside. "I'll leave this up for you. He's in no rush to get out. Have fun."

Slowly, I crept into the room. The door slammed behind me. Dust settled in the air, clogging my sinuses and eyelids. Only the sunlight streaming through the double windows lit the space. It was decorated with gray paint and minimal furniture. Just enough to not drive a man insane — that is, if he wasn't already.

On the cot lay Silas. Cal. He stared at me across the room. Studied me. Admired me.

I was in Eden's dress. Suddenly the skirt felt too short. The modest collar felt too low and scandalous. My thighs felt too far apart. I wanted to peel my skin off. Rid my body of anything his eyes traced.

"Good afternoon," was all he said.

I leaned against the farthest wall and watched him sit up. The cool stone sent shockwaves of fear through me. "Is this a housewarming gift?" A grin spread his wormy lips.

"You're disgusting."

Cal leaned forward. I averted my eyes. "Is it disgusting to appreciate something nice?"

"I'm half your age." A physical shiver trickled down my spine. Coming here was a mistake, I could see that now. "I want to talk."

"I'm all ears."

I forced my eyes to meet him again. He now stood, staring across at me like a game hunter and his lonely rabbit.

"You killed my brother." The bile in my words forced themselves out.

"I have no idea what you're talking about."

I stepped away from the wall, nearing the demon. "Don't shit me. You murdered him."

"If you're a little more specific… it may spark my memory." His gaze slithered down my body.

"*Stop!*" I covered my chest with both arms. "His name was Peter!

He said you saved him on the interstate after a pile-up. He was one of the only survivors. You amputated his arm and made him work for you in exchange. He told me everything."

"Anyone I knew died of natural causes before I left Dover. You're mistaken."

"Cut the crap. Please. It's just you and I," I barked.

His tongue clicked as if I were a toddler. "I sincerely don't know what you're talking about."

"Fuck you."

Cal held a hand up. I remember the exact smile painted on his face from old Bond movie villains. "We started on the wrong foot. I'm Silas Amspoker. What's your name?" He held one dirty hand out to me.

"You made that up." I scoffed.

"Maybe I did. It's not safe to use your birth name in this day and age."

Touche, Silas. "My name is Adelaide Graves." She was a girl in my class who moved to Germany in eighth grade.

"Hello, Adelaide. How are you enjoying your time with the People By The Sea?"

"I wouldn't have stuck around so long if I didn't like it," I stated, glancing out the window. If I made the SOS sign at the window, what were the chances of someone seeing and saving me?

Cal nodded slowly and crossed his caveman arms. "Amazing! I'm thinking of staying." He grinned with large yellow teeth. I could feel him welcoming me into his cold, grimy embrace.

"I actually hate it here. I dread waking up every morning and slaving away at this Rockefeller-ian capital machine."

"If we can't cooperate, I'm afraid I don't see a point in continuing this conversation," his huff of breath reverberated through my skull like a booming bass from the other side of the room.

I sat on the dank, dirty floor. "Yes, I agree. So how about *you* start." My eyes narrowed at him.

"I am. You are the only one not being truthful."

"I don't believe you."

"I'm sorry."

I pushed myself up. "I can't! I can't keep doing this." I walked up to the door. "Last chance to cooperate."

Cal took one step my way. "Then I'm afraid we're at a standstill."

"Please. I just want to know the truth of what happened to my brother."

"I don't know who you're talking about. I don't know what happened to him. I have nothing for you."

"Fuck you."

But maybe he was telling the truth. Maybe. Tate was constantly so stressed… it was entirely possible he mistook Silas for the man who attacked them in New York. That, or Cal was a perfect actor. He managed to convince half of the People.

Regardless, I was wasting time.

"Florence kept a nice house," the man spoke up as my hand fell on the cool doorknob. Cold enveloped my body. "Riley kept a good lawn. I wonder what they would think of their only daughter being so ungracious to an injured, sickly man."

The air seeped from the room. I stood there; suffocating, dying.

My grip on the knob tightened. No one had uttered my parents' names in a year.

"Get their names out of your mouth."

"And what about Michael?" Cal continued. I turned, and he had halved the space between us. As he inched closer, I willed myself to meld deeper into the wooden door. "Or didn't you call him Mikey? He wouldn't be so proud of you now. You know it."

"Shut up."

Cal stepped closer. "What tree did you keep in your backyard? Was it mulberry?" I forced my neck to hold firm and let his words trample me. His two fingers snapped beside my face. The sharpness reverberated through my skull. "No, that's right! It was Dogwood!"

"You don't know what you're talking about." I choked on my words. Peter wouldn't tell him these things. He wouldn't. There was no tactical advantage.

Cal's face was so close that the stench of his breath tainted my air.

Vampire. "It's convenient how you were able to fit everything needed in just three bags, wouldn't you say? Most weren't so lucky."

The air pressure dropped.

He was in my neighborhood. He watched my house.

One hand reached to my face and tucked a single lock of red hair behind my ear. His lips almost touched my earlobe. "I would've taken more from my bedroom. All the books… all the pictures… And how could you leave Ruby behind?"

The whisper smacked me like a tidal wave.

Ruby.

My stuffed white rabbit I won from a claw machine when I was barely four. I called her Ruby after the cartoon kids' show. She was stuffed deep in my closet after I started the fifth grade. I never saw her since, but I refused to let my mom donate her. It'd been so long, Peter would've forgotten about Ruby.

The blood drained from my body. "*What?*"

"Ruby. What would baby Vivienne think about you leaving Ruby?" He kissed the edge of my cheek just by my ear. I ducked away, willing my hand to work. Forcing myself to hit him. Punch him. Slap him.

"Were you in my house? Were you in my room?"

Stupid questions. Stupid questions from a stupid girl who let herself get trapped with a maniac.

He moved between me and the door. With each passing millisecond, he pressed me further into the other side of the room. "You and your brother were so different. It's funny, almost," he muttered.

"*Shut up!*"

He caged me beside the window. My muscles turned to stone. Nerves turned to water and weeds.

"I am sorry about your brother. But it had to happen. He wasn't a good person when it mattered…" His hand grazed up my side, gripping my waist. "But I know you're a good person. Good people keep good beds."

My free arm flew up. My fist hit his chin with a disgusting smack. He stumbled away, holding his bruised face and swearing.

The room was ten times bigger than I imagined. My chest, face, limbs, knees collided with the door and wrenched it open. The guard threw the plank down with a wild shout.

My fists' pain didn't register until I cried in front of the guard. He shouted for help from the adults' rooms. Anita appeared not a minute later in a yellow nightgown. My tears fell harder.

I cried on her bed for what seemed to be a week. A month. A Plutonian year. Anita sat with me through it all. One other man I didn't know sat at the far end of the dormitory, trying to pretend he wasn't paying attention. After a while, Anita sent him to find Anthony or Tate because I asked her to.

Tate let me hug him and melt into a puddle of useless girl goo. No matter how hard I forced, the bad thoughts wouldn't seep out of my ears and eyes and nose and mouth. Around and around they went. Pestering and bickering and sending me back down the waterfall.

My red eyes puffed and stung. My mouth dried up after so long of swallowing down spit and mucus.

As my attack simmered to a close, my thoughts began to change. They warped. Evolved. Bent and molded to find a new purpose.

When my body ran out of tears, I stood. I let go of Tate's hand lest I break it. We thanked Anita. I tried to ignore the tremor when I had to pass his cell one last time.

I never told Tate what was running rampant through my mind. As he walked me back to our dormitory, one thing above all else was clear as glass.

I wanted Cal dead.

xxxiv.

Two days passed. I slept on my thoughts. Ate to combat hanger. Hit things. Threw things. Screamed into the trees. Nothing could shake the unending plague on my mind. The urge to see the light leave Cal's eyes.

I never told anyone. They wouldn't understand. They would try to talk me out of it. But I knew I couldn't do it myself. Your moral compass often trumps what you know needs to happen. People assume it's the opposite. The key is your willingness to carry it out another way. Bend a few rules to convince the angel on your shoulder to sit down and shut up.

Fortunately, Dmitri was back from his house-hunting trip. It's funny how life can work out to be so convenient.

Dmitri didn't tell me anything when he passed by my breakfast seat that morning. He mumbled something about "yours" and "after lunch". I told Anthony it was to talk about the house he may or may not have found. Truthfully, I had no idea if Dmitri followed through. I didn't care.

He wasn't there when we arrived. It was a little past noon. We climbed in through the back window when the door was irrevocably jammed shut. I guided Anthony from the shattered glass spread under the entire front.

A creature blabbered outside. I don't know what creature it was, but it belonged in the early Cambrian period.

We stood and waited. No footsteps outside the windows, no sand crunching under boots. Dmitri was many things, but one thing he wasn't was unpunctual.

"Can we turn these on?" Anthony asked. He knelt before the closest generator to the door, feeling the sides for the switch. The temptations took not ten minutes to overtake him.

I began to worry that I'd gotten the time wrong. Or he meant a different meeting place. Or perhaps he was a secret mind reader and detected my brilliant plan and was stopping it before it started.

The door slammed open minutes later. A bird squawked outside. In the dirty hole that opened the house to the world stood Dmitri. A well-worn backpack with one missing strap hung off one shoulder.

"How long have you guys been here?" He demanded, fitting the hinges back.

"Just a minute-"

"Did you find anything?" I cut Anthony off. Dmitri held his hands up when I leaped to my feet. "Is it good out there? Any people?"

"Let me sit down." Dmitri yanked a roll of perforated copier paper from the ratty bag. "I only slept three hours for this shit. Be grateful." He spread it over the bed. His thumb made an ink smear on the side. "Enjoy."

The map provided a detailed bird's eye view of the coast, the Community, the woods far beyond, and a house. He left a key at the foot of the page labeling one mile as one inch.

"Did anyone give you a hard time about leaving?" I asked, studying the bags under his eyes.

He scoffed. "No. Who do you think I am?"

"My bad for being concerned." I turned my shoulder to him. I think I heard Dmitri mutter an apology.

"It's not too far. I started after dinner and found it before the sun dipped below the treetops. Only about eight miles." He traced his pointer finger from the triangles and rectangles that symbolized the Community to the larger house shape. "I think there was a garden bed that you can try to work with. And it had a walkable yard and a cement path to the front door." He rubbed Anthony's shoulder.

"Any sign of habitance?" Anthony angled his head to observe the map. I pointed to each significant piece, which one by one made him more excited.

Dmitri cleared his throat. "I'm pretty sure the last tenant was face down in the front yard," Dmitri threw out like it was nothing. I gagged. Anthony laughed. Dmitri waved his hands nonchalantly. "*Don't worry.* I moved them out of the way."

My tongue ran over my front teeth. I could taste what the property must have smelled of in my throat. "Thank you for being so gracious."

Dmitri cocked an eyebrow. "Really? You don't want it? Okay…" He slid the parchment away from under their hands.

"Wait, no! Please!" Anthony reached to grab Dmitri's arm and smacked me instead. "She's just tired. She's cranky."

My jaw dropped. "Excuse you-"

It didn't matter that he was right. It didn't matter that I was ready to collapse right on Dmitri's musty bed and pass into a permanent coma.

Anthony stared down at me. "Vivienne. We need this."

"He's bullshitting us!"

"Yes, I am. Calm yourselves." Dmitri smoothed the map back out on the mattress. "When are you leaving?"

I sat on the bed next to the map. It fell into my thigh. "Good question. We haven't really crossed that bridge yet," I admitted. Anthony slowly nodded. "We didn't expect you to come back with results."

"Why wouldn't I? There are like fifty houses immediately out there." Dmitri distracted himself to play with his generators.

Anthony pushed the hair on his forehead back. "Let me rephrase: we didn't think you would actually agree to help us."

"Harsh."

I had to admit, Dmitri was reliable. He made a promise and knew how to keep it. Now all we had to do was trust him to the X on the map.

"*What did I just touch?!*" Anthony screamed, jumping out of his skin onto the bed. He nearly squashed the map between us. I kicked my feet up and scurried back, probably screaming with him.

Dmitri inspected the floor by the bed. "Pff, just a dead bird. They get in here," he mumbled, kicking the animal behind the table. "All gone. Keep your britches on."

I shoved Anthony off the creased map. "Careful! This is precious cargo."

"I have it memorized," Dmitri threw out. My glare shot at him, boring a hole into his forehead. He whipped out his flask and winked. I never was told where he and others supplied their alcohol. Not the Moonshiners; genuine good liquor. If I were in on the secret, I too would value it more than clean water.

There was no more avoiding the elephant in the room. We were wasting time at this point, and I could feel Dmitri getting bored with us. He was itching to get back into the woods.

"I have something else for you. If it's not too much," I stated.

Dmitri sat on a generator. "Share with the class."

"What are you talking about?" Anthony whispered. I gently rubbed his leg before standing up.

"I need you to kill Silas."

Dmitri took a swig. "That's bold. What do I get out of it?"

I shrugged. "One less person eating your food."

"Vivienne!" Anthony grabbed my arm. "You can't be serious."

I crossed my arms to contain myself. It made me small and feeble. No better representation of how I felt. "You weren't in that cell yesterday. He threatened me. He *stalked* me! He was in my house, in my room! He knows everything about me… and my family- and *he* was the one who killed Peter. I know it. And he's gonna kill me too if he gets out of that cell!"

"Do you know all of this for sure?" Dmitri asked.

"He told me."

"He *told you* he's going to kill you if he gets out?"

"No. But what else would a stalker do? Or he'll kill someone else!" My hands reached to the universe, stepping toward him. "Please. I wouldn't ask if I didn't see an absolute reason."

Dmitri held a palm up. "I believe you. I just don't think that's the way to fix it," he muttered.

"That's the biggest bullcrap I've ever heard!"

"He's right." Anthony found my hand. His familiar soul comfort was absent. "This isn't what we stand for and you know that."

I could feel that lump forming in my throat and behind my eyes. "Someone has to do it. He's too dangerous!" I shouted. It was more of a pathetic plea to be affirmed.

Dmitri offered me the flask. I accepted it and gratefully let the liquor burn away at my senses. I went back for round two when he snatched it from my hand. "Hey, slow down. This is all I got for a while."

"Viv." Anthony shook his head. I didn't think he saw that.

"Can you kids find the way back on your own?" Dmitri called out as he switched off all the generators. The magnificent lights flickered to sleep.

"We made it here just fine without you holding our hands," I shot. Anthony sent me a short glance, a more concerned point to his eyebrows than agitation.

I don't know what was coming over me. After so long reminiscing and recounting this string of days, I've never discovered where the dark cloud originated. Unshakable.

This was something new. Something more painful. More tiring.

Is this what Peter felt before running off? I was resisting the urge to march out of the little cabin and slam the door behind me, leaving bad blood behind with every step. No wonder he left.

Silas... Peter... I wanted to punch a wall. I wanted to punch a person.

To everyone reading, take this as a poor example of how to grieve. People get hurt and there's no way to reconcile it with yourself.

Luckily, Dmitri ignored me. "I have another errand to run. If anyone asks where I am, say I'm on patrol." Dmitri pulled his jacket over his shoulders, "You know what I think? I think you need to get that stick out your butt. Chill out. Anita is a teddy bear."

"And Tveit?"

Dmitri clamped one hand on my shoulder. "Have you seen the guy? All bark and no bite. Calm down," he assured me, which made me worry more. "They're too focused on Silas to give two craps about where anyone else goes. Trust me." Dmitri propped the door open on his knee before turning back to us. "You coming?"

"We'll be along. Thank you," Anthony piped up. Dmitri regarded us with one last thumbs up before letting the door slam behind him.

We were left alone with the dust and bird carcasses. We stood there for a minute; three; five. My eyelids itched from the hanging must and despair Dmitri enjoyed so much. Anthony reached down and held my hand. I pulled it away and rolled the map up with both hands. Anthony gaped at my attitude — which I didn't process myself having — and threw both hands up.

"What? What did I say? What did I do?" He asked cluelessly. I ignored him.

Dmitri had long disappeared when we stepped onto the outside sand. "You didn't have to speak against me," I muttered.

Anthony spat on the ground. His saliva was filled with dirt. "What are you talking about?"

"*She's tired? She's cranky?*" I shot. I threw the plank over the door and marched off without him. "It was rude. I don't have to be cranky to talk back to someone acting like a total idjit."

"Idjit?" He cocked an eyebrow.

"Don't change the subject, idjit."

Anthony scuffed his shoes on the coarse grass desperately peeking through the rock particles. "I'm sorry about that. But I really thought he was gonna take it away from us."

"You still didn't have to disregard me like that," I tried hard not to lower my voice from a sudden tsunami of self-consciousness.

"I didn't mean to say it like that." His thumbs pushed down every other finger, none of which popped because he'd done it so much that day. "I wanted to get that map. You know how he's, like, up and down and hot and cold."

"He's messing with us." I dug a trench in the sand with the side of my foot as we trudged along. "Let's not make a big deal of it. I just wanted to tell you."

We didn't talk for a long stretch of the walk back. I think he was annoyed with me. The feeling was mutual. This was our first mildly heated conversation. I didn't appreciate the tense feeling between us like a stretched rope struggling to stay together. I could feel it pulling on my ribcage every few steps I took ahead of him. I would pause to let him catch up, and the itching stretch would ebb.

We weren't walking much longer before a plume of dark gray rose in the distance. It started as a low haze before I watched it ascend into the atmosphere, blending dark into the white clouds above.

"I see smoke." I grabbed Anthony's arm.

"Hmm? Did they start the bonfire early?" He piqued.

"No. It's darker." I steered his chin in the direction of the plume rising from the far side of the Community. "Can you see it?"

"Kinda…. No… wait! *Yeah!*" Anthony shouted, aggressively pulling me forward. "Something's on fire!"

"No shit!"

I'd never run so fast in my life. Never when chasing my dog on a leash down the neighborhood sidewalk. Not in the seventh grade when I took a shot at the middle school track team. Never when running from bullets in the movie theater. Never when I missed the bus leaving the carbon monoxide-infested church.

With every step, the pounding in my skull magnified. Breathing became heavier. Gravity pulled me further into the core of the Earth.

I pulled and directed Anthony along until we reached the sanitation shed. The lot was vacant. Everyone was running rampant through the dirt streets and between billowing tent flaps. Most flocked towards the farthest side: medical and childcare.

Through the gray haze of ash-permeated air and bodies, I could barely make out two figures pulling bags and carts out of the medical tent while more smoke billowed behind them. The screams of children and mothers blended with the cacophony of vultures overhead.

"Wait! We need to hide that!" I grabbed the map from Anthony's hands. I shoved it somewhere behind the dwindling supply of bleach and the microfibre cloths.

We joined the audience at the fire. The smoke was bearable only for a minute before we had to mirror the rest with our shirts protecting our noses and eyes squinting from the sting. The flames lapped at the crisped side of the medical tent.

"Are you guys okay?" Diana grabbed our arms and spun us around so fast my head almost flew off my neck. She engulfed us in a group hug, kissing the side of my head and squeezing Anthony's shoulders tight.

"*Where is Cillian?*" Eugene shouted, breaking out from the mess of bodies. As no one answered, he inched closer to the mouth of the tent.

"Stop!" Tveit ordered from the back. No one was letting the leader through.

As Eugene bent over from coughs, a scream erupted from the inferno. I clamped my hands over my ears. It pierced, jarred, grated on my eardrums.

Something fell and crashed inside. Eugene ran into the tent when the last of Cillian's cries hit our ears. His head disappeared in the mess of smoke before I could grab Anthony's arm, keeping him, one person, grounded.

"Did he just go in there?" Anita shoved her way through the mess of us.

"Silas did it!" A man screamed from the crowd.

Tate shook his head from the very edge of the flames. He viciously hacked the black from his lungs. "His name is Cal. Call the bastard by his name," he sighed, finally defeated by the man plaguing his life since New York.

Tveit shoved himself to the front. The light of the flames turned his face to a morbid flickering orange. "*Where is he?*"

"Anyone who finds him, turn him in immediately!" Anita roared. I would never compare the woman to an animal, but in that moment she was a dragon. Not human. "We'll have his head!"

Several men ran off. I heard them shout back and forth at each other, planning to weed the murderer out and trap him. Everyone else was stuck in a pathetic paralysis of fear and heartbreak as we watched the flames rage on before us.

Eugene dragged his mentor out by the legs not a minute later, beating out all the lapping flames from Cillian's clothes as they moved.

Most of the caramel hair was singed off his head. His clothes had been scorched to specks off his body. His skin was burned straight through.

Who used to be our jittery and kind doctor was now a charred, leathery scrap of a person.

Eugene began chest compressions to restart Cillian's heart. He was beginning to convulse, his skin red and raw beyond repair. I could hear his wheeze from the edge of the circle.

There was nothing anyone could do about the burning medical tent. Even if ocean water could cure it, there was no way to efficiently transport the surf — not enough to quench the flames in time.

Eugene was okay. The ash in his lungs and the red tint of his skin would flush itself out in time. Nothing like the man he watched leak away, perfectly incapable of saving him.

He propped Cillian on his knee as Anita approached. She whispered kind words to her old friend, soon helping to support most of his weight. After a minute they gave us a thumbs up: *he was safe*.

Cillian trembled, melting into Eugene's leg. Tears paved tracks down his inflamed cheeks as Eugene lost the fight to keep him conscious.

Tears stung my eyes trying to see the wreckage of the tent. My sinuses burned with the spreading smokey haze.

"I saw Silas do it!" Kathy cried out. Another woman screamed.

"Me too!"

"What about a trial?" Misha offered.

Kathy hit him with all the fury her aging body could handle. "I saw him do it! He snuck into the tent and ran out when it caught fire!"

"That could mean anything-" another man chimed in.

A competition was forming among the People. "He's right. It could be a freak accident," one of the butchers interjected.

"Are you defending a murderer?" A woman accused Misha.

"Attempted murder."

"You're a horrible person! Cillian is dead!"

"No, he's not!" Eugene shot back. His words escaped in desperate sobs.

"How did he get out of jail?" Dmitri appeared behind us. The brewing fight settled. "How did he get past the guard?"

This silenced the protestors. A cloud of shame settled over us.

"Killed 'im!" Elliott finally chirped up. I whipped my head to find him cowering behind Lily. "I-, I think so. I seed 'im dead outside the cell."

"Why didn't you tell anyone?" Misha marched over to tower above the small boy.

Lily shielded him with her body. "He was scared! We were going to tell someone when the fire started," she radiated more courage than I've ever seen from those kids.

Just writing this now shocks me. They were little kids. No older than fourteen at the time, which doesn't seem very young to a fourteen-year-old, but no child who didn't get the opportunity to earn a driver's permit should have to address fifty people and explain why they were too afraid to turn in a dead body.

I wasn't much older. Here I stood in the moment judging Elliott for not speaking up… and I wasn't much older. Not really.

We were children.

"Did you think no one would believe you?" I elbowed Misha out of the way to kneel by Elliott. He slowly nodded. I rubbed his back. "I know. It's scary. No one blames you."

"Yes, we do-"

"Can you kindly shut the fuck up?" I nearly smacked Misha; self-preservation instincts be damned. Tate slipped me a thumbs-up.

Anita finally stood before the boy, her eyes glazed in a practiced softness. "Is there anything else you remember, honey?" She gently urged.

"There was a weird mark on his face…" Elliott recalled slowly. Lily winced. "It was a weird mark thingy."

My hand moved on its own to cover my cheek. I made eye contact with Dmitri. He nodded. "Was it a burn? Really red and dark? Kinda deep in the skin?" I whispered, urgently waving the boy along. "Was it a *C* shape?"

Elliott confirmed. The six of us who understood hung our heads. "The guy loves his fire…" Tate muttered.

Dmitri threw both arms up. "Where the hell did he get a brand?"

The talking made my mouth taste more of ash. Covering my nose and mouth accomplished nothing.

"Boss! Boss!" One of the men jogged back to the mob. "Jackson is dead!"

"We know!" Tveit boomed.

"He has this ugly brand on his face-"

"*We know!*" Anita shot, sucking in a sharp breath. She pulled a weapon from her vest and violently gestured for him to move.

Dmitri helped Eugene pick up Cillian, one limb at a time. "What do we do when we find-"

Bang!

A single gunshot rang out. Tveit fell, convulsing with two short coughs of blood.

In his wake revealed Cal, who pointed Tveit's own rifle in the space he stood. Cal aimed the weapon at each of us while slowly backing away, daring anyone to step out of line. Anita raised her pistol. Cal booked it, taking Tveit's rifle with him.

XXXV.

Something in the tent exploded. The smoke cloud grew. Wind carried everything into town. Several people tried fanning the flame with ash-coated shirts before others smacked them away. They were making it worse.

I stayed motionless, sounds playing lifelessly around my ears. The haze covered every innocent thing in its path. Lungs stung. Eyes watered. Mind numb, teetering as I watched someone fall to their knees.

A single voice shouted at me. A hand gripped my arms, shaking me awake.

Tate half-dragged me from the dying flames as my lungs began to seize up. Wheezes, convulsions, gasps for clean oxygen. He held me as coughs racked my body, adrenaline fighting to keep me from the edge of that glorious, unknown cliff. Someone else pushed my head to the ground when a burn surged up my throat.

I fell next to my own vomit. Two birds in the gray sky were the last I saw as unconsciousness won its tug on me.

The fog lifted for just a moment when I felt a tug on my socks and my pants. They shushed me when a low grunt escaped my throat. I couldn't hear what they said before their touch drifted away once more.

I awoke in my bed that evening. The last few inches of the orange and pink sunset layered on the horizon. Remnants of the haze filtered out among the evening atmosphere, tainting the world with gloom. It was a ghost town through the dirty windows.

A cool cloth flopped off my forehead when I lifted myself. It plopped on my lap in a sad blob. A new pair of joggers were on my legs when I kicked the blanket off. A series of coughs racked through my body, shaking my shoulders with every forceful contraction.

On the three beds to my left were Faith, the older toddler Bobby, and one unknown man. To my right was Liam.

Faith and Bobby were still asleep. The grimy ash was poorly wiped from their chubby faces. The other man tossed a rock at the ceiling. Two dents had been made in the poor plaster above him.

"Where is everyone?" My voice scratched at my esophagus. Every dry swallow made tears prickle. A wheeze tickled at my upper lungs with every inhale.

Liam stood up, quickly rushing to my bedside. "In the mess hall."

He handed me a black metal water bottle. I unscrewed the top and threw it back. The stagnant water poured down my mouth, moisturizing every crevice of my tongue and throat. I couldn't swallow fast enough. I hardly choke on water, but the gurgle was enough to make me lose my breath.

"Slow down!" The boy yanked it from me. Water spilled down my front.

I let myself fall back on my sad excuse of a mattress. I wanted nothing more than to sink deeper and deeper and deeper until all that was left of the me-shaped canyon was never-ending darkness. I wanted to become a speck of dust on the surface of the planet, blending in with the ash that now coated the Community.

We stayed in silence until Liam spoke again. The sun had completely disappeared from the late sky. "They found Cal. He's on trial right now," he said.

"They didn't kill him on the spot?"

Liam swirled his water around before taking a sip. "Too many people care about fair trials."

I giggled hysterically. "What is there to trial? He killed three people!"

"There's only proof of one."

My eyes widened. "...Isn't that enough?" I demanded.

Liam held his hands up. "I know. It's stupid. I walked in for one minute and they were just arguing and yelling and fighting. They don't even know what the charges would be."

I could not believe what I was hearing. Two were dead and one gravely injured, and they still couldn't agree. "I have a suggestion... Maybe it could... be for *murder and arson!*" I fought back another dry cough.

"We can't know he intentionally set that fire," Liam muttered. I didn't bother tearing my eyes from the stars to look at him. "Just saying. I don't believe he's innocent. But they need evidence. No one else was in the tent to see it."

"Cillian was there."

"He's barely responsive."

Bobby tossed and turned in bed. A faint whine escaped his lips with every minuscule movement. Faith hacked up half a lung in her sleep.

I forced myself to sit back up. "Can I leave?"

"No."

So I laid right back down and went to sleep.

The trial was a waste of time, to put it most kindly.

Anita, now as judge and first in command, ordered Cal to be executed on two charges of murder, one of attempted murder, and arson. A consensus agreed on execution by hanging in the outer rim of the forest line. That much was solved quickly. It was how they got to that conclusion that so many had a problem with.

But Anita and her supporters won in the end. Cal — who had been captured and wrestled back to jail before the flames could die — was held under maximum security until they could arrange a proper time for the hanging.

I would've put a bullet in his brain and be done with it in a minute. I'm not as classy as others.

The five of us were secluded inside until our lungs could clear the smoke. I got all my reports from Tate and Diana, who returned to the dorms with dinner. The People were left to forage for the night, held to the honor system to not overeat. No one felt like cooking. No one felt like doing much of anything.

For the several days following the fire, I doubled on a regular schedule with vicious, obnoxious coughs. Eugene told me the cough would dissipate in time as my respiratory system healed. I didn't believe him.

The next day ticked by like a broken clock. Every time I thought it was noon, I looked up and the sun was still inching over the horizon. Every time I thought only several minutes had passed, the sun and shadows had moved in the sky and ground tenfold.

The universe was a cosmic Jenga puzzle and someone had removed a block on the bottom. Here we were — wobbling precariously on what remained of our foundations.

Eugene, Anita, and the new medical apprentice, Hope, never left Cillian's side. He was alive, but on a thin string. Third-degree burns riddled his frame from top to bottom. His nervous system was a ruin. What was left of their supplies, *very little*, were used on him despite his garbled protests.

Cillian wanted to die. He was in so much pain, yet couldn't feel his body. Fully awake, yet mostly unresponsive. Any effort to open his mouth that wasn't spent being spoon-fed was a plea to let it all end.

The days following the fire gave me an insight into how succession worked in the Community. The fishermen's deaths didn't make so much of an impact because they were so low on the pole.

Your rank was determined by how much time you spent with the Community and how much the first five could trust you. Only adults were allowed a place in the rank, making Eugene and I the youngest. But because Eugene had been with them since the very beginning and Cillian trusted him more than anything, Eugene surpassed Tate, Peter, and Diana.

Anyone could be withdrawn if the situation necessitated. This was rare. If you had a problem with your position, that was an issue only solvable by shutting up or leaving.

They did the calculations, and everyone was booted up a spot or two. Not that it made much of a difference, but to mongrels like Misha or Kathy, those two spots counted. Anita made the executive decision to withdraw Cillian from the succession. Dmitri surpassed him to become number two.

By the third day, the People by the Sea began to adjust. They started to realize no amount of whining and waiting would do anything to repair the Community. We started the long and tumultuous journey of letting the past stay in the past.

It only took a two-minute conversation for Anthony and I to agree on a time to leave: as soon as possible. We owed our loved ones the respect of telling them. Anything more would be too much. Anything more would be classified as stalling. Too much had happened in a month to risk stalling.

Life is worth so much more than sitting around and waiting for something to happen. It was time to take responsibility. Time to be active in the underappreciated gift we call life.

The Community was doing fine. Things slowed down. Anita and Dmitri adjusted to their new roles. We were on our way to heal and move on with life with a new leader.

Then Cal was discovered missing from his cell after dinner. How that little shit managed to do it a second time still baffles me after all these years.

Naturally, there was outrage among the People. Some were stupefied by how careless his guards could be. Some were more impressed by how he pulled the stunt off again. The Community meeting lasted only ten minutes.

Regardless, Cal was out. He was free. He wanted to be free, and if one thing was true about the man, it's that Cal got what he wanted.

I think Cal thought he wanted to find Peter. When he did, it wasn't satisfying. I think Cal remembered one Alabama family he met in New York City. The boy who gave him a scar. Or perhaps Cal was tracking us from the very beginning. Ever since our attack on his hideout. Perhaps every little mishap, every little misfortune since breaking Peter out of the cult was Cal's doing.

That's just what I think. We haven't found him to this day and I don't want him to be found. These days, I'm not so upset about his escape as I am upset that I couldn't watch him swing.

Anita had nothing to say when Anthony and I announced our decision. We picked a poor time; that being not half an hour after the prisoner made his escape. She was massively preoccupied but peeled a listening ear just as always.

"I wish you would stay. Especially him." She gestured to Anthony with a deep sigh.

"I already arranged for two more to train with Alice when I'm gone," he reported. I chuckled at the recollection. "They're a little young, but Nina almost kissed me after hearing they were leaving."

Anita shouted something to one of her forming search parties. "I don't know what we're going to do about this," she confessed, nodding loosely to her inferiors. "It's my time to step up… and I have no clue what I'm doing."

"No one else does," Anthony chimed. He grabbed my arm when I started to hack the dirty phlegm out of my lungs.

She threw a hand up. "I know! I shouldn't be doing this. Tveit made all these decisions. I'm not made for it." I could feel the terror forming in her throat as if it were my own. For the first time, our dragon woman was nervous. *Scared.* "It shouldn't be happening this quickly. Three days in and I already need a break."

She shook her head with defeat. I would've hugged her if I didn't worry she would burst into flames. "I miss him. He was my closest friend. They both were. I hope you aren't leaving because of all this."

"Of course not! It's just poor timing," I assured her. I paused to cough up my other lung. "No one blames you for any of it. I hope you know that." I reached for her hand. It was cold and squishy, two things I had never yet encountered in a hand.

She clutched it gingerly. "Thank you, Vivienne." Anita took a swig of what I smelled to be the Moonshine. The liquid was almost spat from her mouth when she leaped up. "*Wait!* You can't leave until tomorrow. We need to get a care package for you!"

I glanced at Anthony. "We really don't need it, thank you tho-"

"Please! It's my gift. Call it a thank you for being friends with my boys." Anita stood and kissed me on both cheeks. The liquor reeked against my face. Anthony gave her a full hug. "You two are good kids. Stay safe out there."

I waved one of Tate's patrol friends goodbye. "We will. We'll visit," I promised.

Anita turned to Anthony, who was leaving so much more with the Community than I. "If you see Nadia and Rami out there, say hi for me." Anita smiled, quickly rubbing his arm.

He nodded. The curls had grown so far over his face that his bouncing head finally revealed his eyes. "Will do, ma'am."

"Will do what?" Tate materialized on my other side.

"*Nothing,*" I shot too quickly to avoid suspicion. He was the last person I planned on telling.

Anthony rubbed my shoulder. "I'll be around," he whispered.

"Don't leave!" I begged through clenched teeth.

Anthony was already halfway down the pavement. "I'm sorry. He scares me."

"You better not have a reason to be scared of me!" Tate yelled after him. Anthony shook his head obediently before tripping over his own foot. Anita slipped away to join the last of her patrolmen. My eyes were fixed on the ground when Tate finally looked back at me.

"What were you talking to her about?" He asked, softer for me.

I stared at the crashing waves. "Why aren't you going with them?" I threw a hand out at the patrol team.

"Anita told me to take the day off. She said the dark circles under my eyes are darker than the butt of my gun, and that is unacceptable." He propped his hands on his hips. "What were you talking about just now?"

"I'll tell you tomorrow."

"What's special about tomorrow?" He gently nudged my arm. "Come on. I won't be mad."

I chuckled sadly. "Yes, you will."

"Are you pregnant? On drugs? Sold your soul to the Devil?"

"No."

"Then try me." Tate tilted his head. "Tell me things in your life."

I watched a seagull fly over the beach and swoop into the fire pit. His family followed shortly behind. I watched them dance in the wind, far more carefree than any human could ever be.

The pop of a bullet echoed through the beach. My heart hitched in the split second before one of the gulls fell to the sand. One of the hunters raced to retrieve it. The rest of the birds evacuated, squawking all the way home. I wished that hunter could do that to me.

"We're leaving the Community soon," I finally let the words spill.

Tate looked onward, sucking in a deep breath. "Who is *we?*"

I threw my head back. "You said you wouldn't be mad!" I whined.

"I'm not mad. I'm concerned. Who is we?" He remained poker-faced. I hate how he can still do that amid the highest turmoil.

"Anthony and I. There's nothing for us here anymore."

"No offense taken."

"That's not what I meant." I grabbed his hand. Two of his fingers were bandaged with a scratchy excuse for gauze. "I'm *tired.* I need something new. Dmitri found us a place not far from here. He drew a whole map and said it's close enough that if we ever need anything, we can walk right back in. And Anita is okay with it."

Tate squeezed my hand before dropping it. "Do you love him?"

"I don't know what to think about that."

"Are you leaving with him for the sake of not being alone again, or because you want to spend the rest of your life with him?"

Anxiety clawed at the back of my brain; fearful possibilities of my future. "We can separate. Just 'cause we move out together doesn't mean we're eternally bound. Right?"

"Yes. But there aren't many other options if you really want to get out of here. You can't do everything yourself," Tate pointed out. He held the same exasperated shoulder hunch as a dad who worked one too many hours that day so his kid could have a new pair of shoes.

I miss my dad.

I watched the hunting parties leave, with either fresh meat or a white-haired arsonist on their minds. What I would give to be among them...

"I don't feel better around anyone else. We'll be happy," I finally confessed. It wasn't anything Tate didn't already know, but it was a burden weighing on my soul. "I don't want to be alone again. *I can't.* I'll kill myself if I have to be alone again."

"You don't have to be. You can stay."

"Sometimes I feel more alone here than ever."

The blond hair hung limply over Tate's brows, unlike the meticulous state I first met him. "I don't think it's a good idea. Not yet. You just inhaled a butt load of smoke. You need to recover," he felt the burn in his chest. As if we shared the same pain.

"I feel fine. Eugene said the cough would come down in a few days. I may develop asthma, but... whatever. You have it!" I assured him, actively holding back another tickled throat.

"A few days. But not now."

My lips pressed. "You're not gonna convince me not to leave," I murmured, and secretly wished he was trying harder.

"I'm not trying to. I'm telling you the truth." Tate's voice became ever more so pleading.

An instinctual urge gnawed at me to stay put. A voice was ordering me to unpack my bags and sit down. Just go back to the gardens and become another mindless drone of the Community, following Anita's orders and harvesting radish after cabbage after pumpkin for fifty more ungrateful people.

I didn't listen to that voice. I was tired of listening to things telling me to stay put.

"And I'm telling you that I need to start a new chapter." For the first time, I saw that missing piece in his eyes. That crucial puzzle piece that was stolen by water hemlock. "I need to pave my own path instead of... *all these people* determining my life. It's not right."

Tate shook his head. The missing piece was growing larger. "You have to be careful, Vivienne. I can't lose another sister."

Sister. No one called me that with affection for a long time. "I won't make the same mistakes. I know what I'm doing," I whispered. "I promise."

Tate tore his gaze away, and the puzzle hole sealed itself over. "Okay. I respect it." With that one movement, I could see him become one more person shielding out the world so as not to feel what was truly on their heart.

"I don't want to leave on bad terms."

"We're not on bad terms. I respect your decision."

Whether or not I believed him is unimportant.

I told Diana and everyone in the gardens the next morning. Diana teared up but pulled herself together as soon as I told her I wouldn't be alone. Lily and Elliott said nothing, which was nothing less than expected. Hank offered me a chunk of his latest batch of mushrooms. I pocketed it and promised to share it with Anthony on a rainy day. Leta refused to part from my side. I had to carry her back to Nina once it became an inhibition on my last day of work.

They let Cillian die after four days. Someone smothered him with a thick pillow in his sleep.

He was the first of us who didn't return to the Flame. Dmitri and Anita spent the evening digging a grave, refusing any other help. I watched them lower him into the ground as the sun set over my final night with the Community.

xxxvi.

There wasn't much to pack. I joined the People By The Sea with only two bags and I left with two bags. Anthony came with a suitcase that was now overflowing.

Another Community tradition was donating the belongings of the dead. Anthony inherited two pairs of pants and one pair of Eli's boots by drawing lots with three other same-sized men. It was a fine idea on its own — the deceased victim wasn't going to be using those items anymore. I was more concerned that I had never noticed the twins walking around in Chrissy's leggings. She had one specific pair of teal athletic leggings with pockets. I always assumed the twins had the same pair...

Packing was self-conscious Hell's work. Everyone in the dormitory watched, but could not be bothered to help. About fifteen people watched us scurry back and forth, folding and rolling and smushing and pressing everything to fit efficiently. When the chore was completed, we were congratulated and sent on our way. These people we had known for months, many of which were friends.

Somehow, their audience helped build my confidence that this was the right choice. The average Community member is not selfish, but they're not selfless, either. But that's no different than before. That's what drove people crazy at the start.

I am not built for that lifestyle long-term, and that's okay. The Gatwes weren't. Peter wasn't. The difference between me and my brother is that I tried to understand humankind. I haven't been led to believe all humans are inherently horrible creatures.

I've come to several theories of why hate exists. Why discourse and misfortune at the hands of others happen so much. But I also considered why love exists. Why we make choices over and over to sacrifice for the people and things we care about.

Motivation is the cornerstone of human decision-making, whether the motivation is of monetary value, relationships, food, or pride. People will make the decisions that impact them and their valuables most positively, one roundabout way or another. If they think hate and greed will serve them and their loved ones best, they will do so because the impacts will have no erosion upon themselves. The same, I believe, is true just for the opposite. People will sacrifice their entire worldly livelihood and comfort for the "greater good", which will come back for them. Yet, they forget that their children now can't eat.

Around and around we play mind tricks with ourselves to convince the little voices in our head that this is the right way.

It all depends on perspective. As does everything. Our opinions and values entirely depend on our livelihoods and upbringings. Which is what I've also noticed people refuse to understand. Any circumstance so slightly divergent from your own experiences is "wrong". It's an ignorant mindset that is destined to set everyone as a villain in your life.

No one considers themselves the villains of their actions. There is always someone on the other end who forced your hand or wronged it themselves between points A and B. Despite that the trigger is under your finger, someone else is at fault. No one can be wrong within their own perspective.

I begin to think that mankind is not built to comprehend themselves as being wrong. It's an inherently offensive mindset. We would combust if we thought so.

No one would do such things if they truly thought they were making the wrong choice. If we understood the nuance between "good" and "bad" choices within the edict of our own omnipotent consciousnesses, the world would be much different and I would not be explaining my perspective on this now.

This is what I've observed. So many worlds; so many populations; so many nights spent watching the forest fireflies and wondering what the heck we ever did to ruin it all.

People aren't selfish. They aren't selfless. They survive.

All of my discoveries collapsed when Diana grabbed my hands outside of breakfast. "Are you sure you don't need anything? I can get you something. I can make it. I can help you. I hope you know that," she rattled off. By the simple act of rubbing my knuckles, she shook my self-confidence to the core.

"I love you," she promised, shaking the sense into me.

This was the part I'd been dreading. As I pulled her in, the cloud of reality crashed down. This was it. This was my chance to back out. My chance to ignore everything and relax in ignorant bliss. Unpack everything and settle back down and pretend I would be happy for the rest of my life, as long as I had that family by my side. That little family from Mobile, Alabama.

But if I broke my plans in the face of every sadness, I would've learned nothing from my predecessors. Learned nothing from the billions who wiped each other out in the face of adversity. We wouldn't have anyone left if we did that again.

"I love you guys," I whispered. The one singularity in the twisted cosmos. I left before she could say anything more.

The entire Community lined up along the road out of town just as they did for Nadia and Rami. It was a confessedly odd feeling to be on the receiving end of the gratitude, tears, and various prayers. People touched our backs and shoulders with every step. I had to shake the feeling people were more upset to see Anthony gone than me.

Standing at the end were Anita, Tate, Diana, and Alice. Tate clapped us both on the back, nodding modestly the way men do. The kind that says they would be more emotional if societal expectations wouldn't crush their egos for it. Alice knuckled Anthony's head. Diana engulfed me in a rib-crushing hug. She didn't let go until Tate forced her to.

We pretended not to notice the wagon of supplies. Bandages, several vials of ointments, three pairs of shoes, one fuel lighter, and two canteens of water filled the bed of the red wagon. It was hard for me to imagine that any more medical supplies lasted the fire.

A small hand tugged on my wrist. Leta stood at my side, staring up at Anthony and me with miles of expectations. She snuck up on us like a little ghost. I crouched and properly hugged her. Her arms just barely reached around my torso.

"You'll visit?" Alice squeaked.

"Of course! We promise to visit sometime!" Anthony swallowed thickly. If I knew him any less I wouldn't be able to sift the anxiety layered within his voice.

I squeezed Leta's shoulder and bounced to my feet. "Okay. It's time." I breathed deeper than ever, facing the other Community members. Hank stuck out like an ingrown toenail, and I was flattered to see such displays of emotion from the man. Dmitri found me from the back of the audience. He flashed a thumbs up and a nod. I smiled before biting my cheeks back.

Anthony held the wagon's metal handle white-knuckled. Anita kissed us on both cheeks finally. I blew everyone kisses before breaking past the edge of the farewell line.

The wagon wheels squeaked behind us. We were several meters from the crowd before we noticed a little tagalong. I glanced down to be met with those brown cow eyes.

"Leta, we have to say goodbye now," I insisted gently. She said nothing.

"What's happening?" Anthony whispered.

"Oh… Leta, come on." Anita reached out her hand.

The girl shook her head. "I wanna go with them!" Leta whined back at Anita, pouting her cracked bottom lip. I shook my head sadly, ushering her back to the crowd. She was only a second away from throwing a clumsy fit. "My daddy told me to stay with you!"

I knelt, urging her to look at me. "You have to stay here. It's safer here." I held her shoulders. She lowered her eyes, murmuring incoherent nothings. "No, you can't. You have to stay. I'm sorry."

"*I don't want to!*" Leta squealed.

"I'm sorry. I wish you could. But it's not safe. You just can't-"

"You said we were best friends!" Leta cried. Those young, strong eyes overflowed. "And my daddy told you to stay with me, and he told me to stay with you!"

I wiped her tears, rubbing her arm with my other hand. "I know, honey. He was scared when he said that. Now you need to stay with Anita. She can take better care of you. Your daddy would want you to be taken care of."

"My daddy's *shot!* And we are best friends."

"Yes, we are! *We are.* Just because I leave doesn't mean we have to stop being best friends. I promise." I now understood the impossible duty of a mother holding herself together for her child. It's impossible. Anthony's hand on my back was the tip of the tidal wave for tears to grow in my own eyes.

Anita now joined us. "Sweetheart, we talked about this," she whispered to the girl, who only cried into her shirt.

"You promised you wouldn't leave me. You told me over there!" Leta threw her hand out towards the gardens. "Best friends don't break promises. You're a *bad* friend!"

"I know…" I hung my head. Anthony was muttering things in my ear that I couldn't grasp. "I have to leave, Leta. I can't take you with me."

Anita's head snapped up. The older woman smiled, slowly exchanging a silent conversation with someone in the audience. We watched her head turn back to us, a tiny grin inching at her cheeks.

"But do you *want* to?" She offered.

My eyebrows furrowed. I tried (and failed) to subside my hiccups. "What?"

"It's your choice, the two of you. Don't make any decision you'll regret just for right now." Anita wiped the last of Leta's tears and kissed her forehead. "I'm asking you now, do you want to take her under your wing? Do you think you have enough supplies or food?"

Anthony held up a hand. "What are we talking about?"

"I don't know-"

Anita laid a hand on Leta's shoulders. "I'm asking if you want to adopt her."

Everyone heard. Diana slapped her mouth. Behind her, Nina threw her head up and down enough to knock it off the spine.

"You can't be serious!" Anthony laughed, blinking like a madman.

Anita stood. "I am very serious. Do you want to adopt her?"

Leta's bottom lip stopped quivering. "What does that mean?" Her head tilted back to see the leader.

"It means you would come with us." I scrambled for hold of Anthony. "And we would take care of you."

This wasn't part of the plan.

"*Parents?* Does that mean *parents?*" He urgently whispered just to me. Someone in the crowd cheered. "I'm not ready to be a parent. I can't even take care of myself, Vivy!"

Anita prevented Leta from physically combusting from joy. "It means adoption. Take it however you want."

The beads of sweat started bubbling from my neck. "She's smart. We just need to feed her. Right? *Right?*" My lungs were on their own terms, speeding on their own accord. "Cause… um… cause she's potty trained. She doesn't need that much more parenting now, right? And it's not like- they're like pets at this age, right? Just feed and bathe them!"

Anita shook her head, chuckling to herself. "You're overthinking it. If it's too much, she can stay. It's your choice. Don't do something you'll regret," she warned, before throwing out a small smile, "but I don't think you'll regret it. Not if you're so bent out about a goodbye. Just my two-sense."

Leta turned back to me. "I want to go with you."

"I know, sweety. And I want you to."

"Don't think of it as parenting. She's just living with you." Anita winked.

I touched Anthony. He was cannibalizing his fingers before us. "I don't know what else to do. Are you okay?"

Anthony huffed long out his mouth. "I just- we didn't… it's *sudden*. How old are you again?"

"Nine!"

His jaw dislocated itself in five different ways. "Oh God. I'm too young for this. We're too young for this. We don't know what we're doing. I can count our age difference on my hands!"

"Excuse us…" I marched away and left the wagon. I regarded the remaining audience with a cold glare over my shoulder. "Can you tell them to leave? This isn't a stage play."

Anita excused the Community members, keeping Leta firm on her side. As I pulled Anthony away for a private discussion, I could see her little legs itching to run after us.

"If you don't want to, that's okay!" I insisted. I planted a kiss on his cheek for good measure. "I don't want to force you into anything that'll make you unhappy and hate both of us forever. But I'm afraid she- well- I don't know, but I'm afraid for her!"

Anthony fiddled with the jacket tied around my waist. "I wanted to be twenty-one. I wanted to have all those stereotypical stupid twenties experiences. Aren't you worried about missing all that?"

"I don't think those were ever achievable," I confessed. He pinched his lips. "I don't think anyone can have their stupid years anymore."

"Just wild to think about."

I chuckled like a wimp. "I'm just gonna point out, we skipped all the baby/toddler stages. I think we won there."

Anthony shuffled his feet in the grass. "I more can't believe Anita trusts us to take her."

I scoffed sadly. "No kidding. We're messes."

"Well, if anything, it probably comes with a return policy," Anthony wise-cracked. I shot him a terse side glare. He cleared his throat and dismissed himself. "Sorry. Wrong time."

"We need to work on your comedic timing. You're gonna tick off the wrong person and start World War 4," I muttered.

When I turned my back to him, his arms slithered around my waist. "I'm sorry. I phrased that wrong. I wouldn't return her."

I turned back to face him. The twinkle in his eye lit the spark in my soul.

"You're serious? *Serious?* You're not fucking with me? I swear, if you're fucking with me-"

"I'm not!" A crooked grin grew on his face.

The End

Four Years Later

xxxvii.

The unpaved road to our new home was simple. We walked for three hours, only stopping for a lunch of beef jerky and mulberries. Leta insisted on dragging the wagon the entire way. She did better walking than I expected. I suspect the adrenaline was pushing her through, as it certainly was for me.

The weather was perfect. We stayed hydrated. It was like the world was telling us this was the right choice.

The lodge was there, just as promised. Sunlight streamed through the luscious treetops, bathing the entire property in an otherworldly light of gold.

Leta collapsed on the jean-colored couch immediately. We dropped our belongings on the floor, taking a moment to breathe in the dusty atmosphere.

For the last time, I cried.

And now, here we are.

Four years have passed, to be nearly exact.

Twenty-two feels weird. Uneven. I feel that my experiences put me higher in age than my body.

Life in the lodge is treating us well. The three of us found a way to make the best. We made it work.

The lodge was a fixer-upper. It took the entire summer to clean it all up, and most of the furniture couldn't be used after being surrendered to the happy diet of household insects. Anthony did the majority of the furniture moving so he could keep track of everything. We covered the broken windows with cloth and fixed the jammed doors with hours of handiwork.

The lodge was built to house only one person. There is only one bed and the couch, which had a butt-sized indent right in front of the television set. When she was little, Leta would crawl in the bed with us every night. She'll hate me so much for sharing this, but she still does it during the winter months for the shared body heat. It's sweet.

We're doing okay. Over the years, we've decorated the house with as many random things as we can find. When one of us grows out of clothes or wears it beyond use, we don't throw it away. We pin it to the wall as a trophy of living life to the fullest. Leta has her own collection of cool rocks, leaves, and long dead wildflowers. When Tate goes into town, he always makes sure to pass by and bring back a few useless nick nacks for us. It's his love language.

Food is going well, too. Anthony and I trade out shifts hunting thrice a week. Our main diet consists of birds and aquatic life. There's a good fish and turtle population in the nearby lake. Anthony is a good trapper.

I keep my garden surrounding the house. I grow flowers, medicinal plants, and vegetables. It keeps me grounded to the People By The Sea and lets me have a slight control over the world. There is also a blackberry bush not a mile from the lodge. When in season, blackberries are a treat.

I've been homeschooling Leta best I can. I teach her various sciences and how to survive in a world without electricity or the Internet. Leta is a good student, but gets distracted by the falling leaves or the butterflies visiting from the open windows. I try to teach her complex math, but unless she wants to become an architect, there's no use of them in today's world. Which is sad, because she seems to be very good at it. She likes the structure of numbers. Anthony does his best to explain the equations and formulas, but he can only do so good between stomach growls.

They're not painful anymore. They're reminders that we live.

Above all, I teach her our histories. I've written down every civilization I can pull from the depths of my brain, every major development, and every major war. I won't let the legacy of us die, and I certainly won't let it start with Leta. I teach her what humanity used to be, and how we ended up.

I also emphasize not to blame those before us for ruining it. That's as good as blaming Cillian for letting Cal set fire to the medical tent.

Leta is fourteen years old. It's hard to comprehend. The moods and constant eye cartwheels are just beginning, but that's nothing we can't handle. She's so insightful about the world. About the birds, the trees, the water, the soil, the sun, the moon. Leta appreciates nature and what she's given much more than I did at her age.

There have been a few pregnancies since we moved out here. All have been accidents. We know we want kids of our own someday, but not this day. We would've kept them, regardless, had any of them survived. There's no safe alternative. My longest carried was five months. Leta only knows about two of them. I can't help but wonder if my body simply isn't meant for carrying a child too long. Anthony asks me not to think that way, but sometimes it's unavoidable. It's a plague on my mind some nights.

Anthony grows to be wiser and stronger every day. He has matured a lot compared to our first meeting. I could not be the same without him. We still find time to be silly twenty-year-olds at the pond and dancing in the rain at midnight. That's become our new "Flame" tradition.

He's growing a beard after I was too busy to help him shave. Between us, I keep making myself "busy" when he thinks about shaving again. I think he's caught on by now. He has yet to complain.

We still visit the People By The Sea quite frequently. They are our family through and through, no matter how many years pass.

The Community has changed since we've been gone. It's nearly unrecognizable from when the five of us were found by the patrol.

Anita stepped down as leader, leaving it in the hands of Dmitri. He was not thrilled at first, but he's taken the position with pride and responsibility. Under his leadership, the population has grown by half. More and more families are finding them and seeking refuge. The People By The Sea have the opportunity to become a new fully fledged city. Dmitri will never admit it, but he's a good leader. He also won't admit that we're still his only friends.

There have been new romances. Diana and Eugene are an item; a pairing I never would have expected. Nina and Shannon married sometime last year. They're raising Nick together, who is now mouthier than Kathy.

Tate isn't romantically involved with anyone, nor do I ever expect him to be. He adopted a young boy whose mother died of pneumonia the winter after we left. His son's name is Gabriel. He's a rat bastard of a toddler. He and Chrissy would get along.

The gardens have tripled in size. Hank is still leading, and he's managed to strangle his addiction. Lily just reached adulthood and is dedicated to the gardens. Elliott disappeared after the second year. No one will tell me anything about him. I suspect he walked out like Peter.

I wrote this memoir for the future generations. I wanted to give the future children, those younger than Leta and Gabriel, a peek into the perspective of someone who could remember the old ways.

I wanted to form a bridge for those who never had the chance to experience a world with an *eight billion* population. It's still crazy for me to think about. I've gotten so used to the fact that you may not see ten people for a month that the idea of eight billion people on this planet is foreign.

There's a boy named Finn who has ways to copy books using recycled paper fibers and ink cartridges; almost like they did with printing presses. I had the idea for this book and ran it by Finn the next time we stopped by for tea. He was overjoyed with the idea.

I had Tate, Diana, and Anthony read over the final manuscript as fact-checkers. I made Diana cry in three instances. That means I did my job well, Tate said.

Machines fly over sometimes. Airplanes and helicopters. It's a bi-monthly occurrence these days. Leta swears she heard a motorbike in the distant woods a few months ago. We don't know if we believe her, but she swears she remembers motorcycles riding down her hometown street.

I can't help but wonder if this means the world is getting back to normal. Maybe enough of those left got together and sorted out all the problems. Anthony tells me not to get my hopes up. The world's remaining billionaires likely found a way to get the machines running. But they won't share it with us little guys. That's out of the question.

So maybe the world is recuperating. One can only hope.

I don't think I would mind if things stayed just the same. Life isn't so bad.

Acknowledgments

First, I want to thank God, for giving me these gifts to share and create.

I next want to acknowledge my first Beta readers. From the very beginning of this journey, I've been supported and advised by my lovely partner, Landon, and my best English teacher, Mrs. Sharlynn Cochran.

Landon, though not in his biggest reading phase of life, always found time to go over the latest chapters and encourage me through the deepest pits of Imposter Syndrome. Mrs. Cochran was dutifully there to print out the new pages and to pester me enthusiastically for new material 0.5 seconds after reading the last words. They were both the most supportive of all, and I likely would not have finished if not for them.

I would love to acknowledge my parents and sister, but I never told them anything about the work until it was completed. The thought of them reading this still sends shivers down my spine. So, hi Mom, Dad, and Liz.

As is the truth for so many authors, a good amount of these characters are named after people in my personal life. Each character of mine is based in some way on someone I know or another fictional character. I feel like many authors don't like to admit that Person Stealing is an integral part of the writing process. Each character you read or write is a magical cacophony of tiny bits dropped off from others — your classmates, family members, the random people in the Kansas City airport.

Whether they are personal friends or happened to be in my line of vision at the wrong time, this book is finally dedicated to those fellow students who earned a place in this world.

9 798999 139 0309